Mystique

KAILA NIKE

Dedicated to Bryson and Hero
You're my world.
Thank you for your unwavering belief in me.

TABLE OF CONTENTS

CHAPTER ONE

"**W**hoa, slow down there buddy." Octavia reaches her hand out to slow her six year old son, Cory.

Octavia's family loves camping during the summer months. Each year, the warm weather becomes a green light for their treasured adventures. For nearly a decade, this has been a return to a cherished spot shared with the same group of her friends. It's their way of celebrating her birthday. And this weekend, she turns twenty-seven. Their site of choice is a private park about an hour from home. Living in Havenwood Ridge, British Columbia fosters a deep appreciation for these summer escapes where winter's grip can be long and unrelenting. So, when the sun finally breaks free and paints the days warm and beautiful, it's a call to action. It's time to dust off the tents, pack the marshmallows, and reunite with loved ones under a canopy of stars. Camping becomes more than just a vacation; it's a celebration of special moments under a sky finally free of winter's chill. Octavia, finally packed up and ready for adventure, is about to enter the house to gather the boys when a little ball of blond sunshine runs out, nearly knocking her over.

"We're going camping!" He shouts with a grin that stretches from cheek to cheek, revealing a gap in his mouth from the two top teeth he'd lost just a week earlier.

"We sure are, my little buckaroo." She picks him up and pulls him in close for a hug. "Where's your brother at?"

"He's just looking for something." A puzzled look forms on his face. "But I don't know what he's looking for." Genuine curiosity glimmers through his big brown eyes.

"Alright, let's go give him a hand," she says, and Cory, already halfway down the path, grins back at her. They climb the stairs, the wooden steps creaking beneath their feet, and step onto the white deck. It's a small space, just big enough for a swinging chair and a few flower holders that are yet to be filled, but it's cozy and inviting.

On their way in they are met with Ryan's confident demeanor.

"We can't forget these." He declares, his binoculars in one hand and Cory's bug catcher in the other.

"Good thinking!" She praises her eldest son, who just so happened to have his 8th birthday just a few weeks ago. She recalls that the binoculars, along with a bird book, were gifts that were at the top of his list. "It will be a great opportunity to use your new binoculars. And we both know how much Cory enjoys bug catching!" She says, simultaneously smiling and winking.

Making their way outside, she inhales the crisp summer air, the anticipation of the scent of pine needles and campfire smoke already clinging to her senses. But a pang of familiar guilt flickers within her. Her friend Maya and Maya's boyfriend, Mateo are likely already there, campsite secured and efficiently organized. Octavia, on the other hand, is the perennial latecomer. Her mornings with Ryan and Cory, her two energetic children, are typically a whirlwind of mismatched socks, forgotten lunches, and last-minute sunscreen applications. She opens the back passenger door and Cory enthusiastically hops in.

Ryan climbs into the other side. His light brown hair catches the sunlight that streams through the window. "Here Cory, you need to move these out of the way." Ryan says as he reaches over to move a couple of toys.

"Thank you, my boy." Octavia grins, always grateful for his help. Despite the morning chaos, Octavia wouldn't trade this annual tradition for the world. They might be late, but she knows they will arrive in time for the most important part: making memories that will last a lifetime. She holds on so dearly to this trip that reunites her with her closest friends. Once a year she gets to see all of her favourite people in one place. Maya, Ben and Ali, her closest friends, and their families.

Six years ago, Octavia, who was only twenty at the time, found herself alone. The father of her children, David, a man who was never truly present, chose to walk away entirely. Their relationship, riddled with inconsistency and toxicity, had offered no real partnership. David was a ghost, flitting in and out of their lives when convenient for him, leaving the weight of raising Ryan and, soon to be born, Cory, solely on Octavia's shoulders. Though the desertion was painful, it wasn't a drastic shift. In many ways, Octavia had always been a single parent. David hasn't attempted to reach out to Octavia or the boys since he left all those years ago. She's built a life for her boys, a life filled with love and laughter, a life their father has no part in. The separation, while difficult, was a confirmation of a reality she had already embraced.

Over the years, Octavia had not only survived as a single mother, but had learned to thrive. She found strength in her own independence, a fierce love for her children, her guiding light. Being a single mom is a challenge, yes, but it's also a badge of honor, a testament to her unwavering spirit. She's grateful for all of the support she receives from her family, such as her mom, Frida. And her friends, like Maya, who is always supportive no matter what. And although Octavia gets lonely at times, she's found peace in single motherhood. She's found it hard to trust another man since her break up with David. She has attempted to date but due to the lack of trust and fear of abandonment, she never lets it get serious. After only a few dates, if things begin to get serious, she cuts it off completely. A protective mechanism that she has only recently learned about herself and become aware of.

However, part of her holds on to hope that one day she will meet *the one*. He will be patient with her, he won't give her any reason to doubt their connection or their relationship. He will be good to her, he will be her protector, he will assure her how ever many times she needs it that she's the one. In her fairytale dream, he exists. He has to. And when the day comes that she does meet him, she'll know. She has the perfect role models for a perfect relationship; her mom and dad. Her dad used to tell her all the time how it was love at first sight, the day he met her mom. They knew. They both just *knew* they were meant for each other and that they would spend their life together. And they did. Up until the day her dad had passed away a couple years ago.

Reaching the park, Maya's car is spotted nestled amongst the trees. Sure enough, everyone else is already there as well. They'd arrived early, as they always do, determined to snag their preferred campsite, the one that comfortably accommodates the whole group. Ali, Josh and Brit have been here for a few days already, they always extend their stay as they come from out of town. Ali has been a friend of Octavia's for the past ten years, ever since they met through Octavia's ex, David. Though they were only really acquaintances, Octavia became close with Ali during her relationship with him. At first she thought that Ali pitied her. And maybe so.

Octavia tried so hard to make her relationship with David work, but it seemed like no matter what she did, he just lost all interest in her after they began having kids. Perhaps David realized he just wasn't fit to be a dad or meant to be a family man. Perhaps he lost interest in her changing body. Maybe he just realized they weren't actually happy together or thought she was better off on her own. Octavia had never given up on David. Ali was there, alongside Maya, to wipe away Octavia's tears after he had left. In any case, Ali is well aware of her dating history, with David and thereafter, and she's always been grateful for her support. They haven't missed the annual get-together since.

The campsite is a serene picture that triggers a sense of peace of belonging. Nestled amidst a verdant forest, towering trees draped in vibrant foliage provide a canopy of shade, while sun draped clearings offer perfect spots for picnics and relaxation. Octavia parks her car next to Maya's. As soon as the car is parked and turned off, Cory, the extroverted social butterfly of the family, whose personality is as expansive as the summer sky itself, opens his door and runs out to meet up with Jonny, Stan, and Adrian. The children of Ali and Josh.

"Alright my love, let's go say hi." Octavia prompts Ryan, who like herself, hosts a much more reserved personality. Casually, they make their way out of the car. But just as Octavia stands up, she loses her balance.

Her vision blurs and her ears deafen. The world goes black.

She hears a woman's voice. It's faint and she can barely make it out over the pounding in her head.

"Octavia–" her name sounds strained, the voice gripped with fear, "–go back."

It's over as soon as it began. Her vision clears and she steadies herself, blinking a few times as the darkness recedes to the periphery. She takes a deep breath as she stands up straight. Was that just a head rush? Did she nearly faint? She skipped breakfast this morning, perhaps her blood sugar is low.

"Mom, are you okay?" Ryan asks. Noticing her leaning against the car, unsteady.

She shakes it off and smiles, "Yeah, of course buddy, I think I just need a bite to eat." She wraps her arm around him as they continue to the site. Ryan reaches up and holds her hand in his, his fingers intertwining with hers. A wave of warmth, potent and comforting, washes over her, starting from their joined hands and spreading through her entire being. She glances down to see him, his small hand nestled in hers, looking up at her with trusting eyes. Her gaze then drifts to Cory, off in the distance, as he finds his way to the other boys. In that moment, a profound realization settles in: she created these two, the most beautiful and loving little humans she knows. An overwhelming sense of pride swells within her, consuming her thoughts and filling her heart to the brim.

She offers a wave and a friendly "hello" as she spots Josh mingling with his kids. No sign of Ali at the moment, perhaps setting up inside the tent. A gentle breeze rustles through the leaves, carrying the sweet scent of pine needles and damp earth. A symphony of nature's sounds can be heard intermingled with distant chatter and laughter of each site dweller. A sense of peace lifts her spirits. She belongs here. She needs this. Being a single parent often feels like a thankless job, a relentless 24/7 marathon. While her boys are good about doing their chores, Octavia still carries the bulk of the household's weight, just as most parents do. The comfort of knowing the cupboards are always stocked with their favourite foods is a testament to her constant effort. She takes immense pride in the quiet rhythm of their mornings: waking before dawn to prepare a warm breakfast and pack nutritious school lunches, ensuring the house is tidy, and that fresh, clean clothes are laid out for the day ahead. These are just a few of the countless tasks she seamlessly weaves into her daily routine while also managing her full-time career as an author. She writes under the pen name Priscilla Zinn, a name lovingly borrowed from a cherished fictional character from her favourite childhood stories.

As she continues to survey the site, she spots Maya right away.

"Hey girlfriend!" Octavia raves as her eyes meet Maya's, offering a friendly hug.

Maya, her best friend since childhood, is a vision of organized chaos. Their connection upon meeting was instant and have been inseparable since. Her long, dark hair, usually a cascade of curls, is tamed into a neat

French braid, a practical choice for the weekend camping adventure. With the chaos that life can sometimes throw, they cherish this traditional trip as an opportunity to connect if they otherwise don't get a chance to.

"Hey girl, I'm glad you made it out." Maya responds, reciprocating the hug. As she pulls away she addresses Ryan, who's still standing close to his mom. "How's one of my favourite little dudes?" Maya asks, reaching out for a fist bump.

"Hey guys!" A man with bronze skin and a youthful looking face appears next to Maya. It's Mateo. For the past two years, Maya's boyfriend had become a fixture in their camping crew, gracing them with his outgoing and carefree personality. This year is no different. "I was just about to cut some kindling for tonight's fire. And I could really use a helper to stack it for me." Mateo's attempt to make Ryan feel comfortable and welcome seems to be working. "You think you want to help me with that, Ryan?"

He looks up at his mom with his big brown eyes searching for a sign of approval.

"That sounds like a really big job and I think you would be a perfect helper for that." Octavia approves.

She ruffles Ryan's hair and off he goes to help Mateo. She watches her boy go off with this man, who she's learned to trust over the last couple of years, to teach her son some important and necessary skills. The logs are piled up, uncut near the treeline, the ground is covered in shavings from past trips, although they are darkened and weathered, it provides a sense of homeliness. The ground is still a little bit wet in some areas. The last of the snow melted only a month ago, but May long always offers the perfect opportunity to get out. By this time, they're usually itching to. It's typically the first weekend that is warm enough to camp. Well, suppose it depends on who you ask. Octavia's mom loves camping and goes whenever she feels like it, despite the weather. Even in the snow!

"Hey Octavia!" Brit, Josh's sister, hollers a greeting.

"Heey." Octavia turns around to see Brit walking towards her. Behind Brit, she can't help but notice her glamorous set up. She's staked her claim next to her brother and Ali's. Her tent, a vibrant red that stands out amongst the muted greens and browns of the surrounding trees, is a far cry from the utilitarian two-person shelters favored by most of the group. Bigger is always better for Brit, who believes in camping with all the comforts of home. Or at least, as close as you could get in the wilderness. Octavia doesn't know too much about Brit, as she typically just tags along with her brother and his family on these trips, but she does know she loves her high maintenance lifestyle, including her make-up. She's probably got her entire vanity set up in there.

"Do you want a tour?" Octavia's obligation to accept is strong.

"Sure." The word slips out, accompanied by a smile that's surprisingly authentic, despite the tremor of insecurity she feels being next to someone who seems so utterly perfect on the outside. This woman, with her undeniable beauty and an aura that suggests a certain high-maintenance lifestyle, is undoubtedly the kind any man would be thrilled to call his partner.

There's no need to duck into the tent as it's large enough just to walk into. Of course Octavia's suspicions are right. This is as glamorous on the inside as it is on the outside and the vanity completes the look.

"There's so much room in here! Where does a person even find a tent like this?" She asks, eyeing up her space.

Brit, ever so ostentatious, glances in her direction revealing a sleek smile.

"This is the perfect amount of space for me and my nephews." She says, a contented sigh escaping her lips.

Despite the odd mud-caked handprint or grass stain left behind by her rambunctious nephews, she adores them, everyone knows that. She talks often about how there's nothing quite like the chaotic joy of having her nephews around, even if it means sacrificing a bit of pristine tidiness in her personal sanctuary.

Just next door, Josh and Ali's campsite buzzes with activity. Their longtime camping companions are already set up, their three rambunctious sons, Jonny (the cautious eldest at seven), Stan (a ball of energy at five), and Adrian (the ever-curious three-year-old) are tearing it up at the playground, oblivious to the newcomers, aside from Cory who has gracefully joined their play. Their tent, expansive enough to house two queen-sized beds on air mattresses, is a testament to their over-prepared nature. Packing for them is an art form. Two overflowing totes brimming with beach toys, enough clothes for a small army crammed into two duffels, and a pair of coolers. One overflowing with food, the other dedicated to keeping drinks icy cold for both adults and children. They are the quintessential over-packers, the friends you turn to when you inevitably forget an essential item. They are, without a doubt, the perfect camping partners, prepared for anything and everything the weekend could throw their way. Octavia can only dream of being that prepared. She just doesn't have *that* kind of energy.

Following the detailed tour of the site, Octavia sets about finding the perfect spot for their tent. Tucked ten feet away from Maya and Mateo, there's space close enough to everyone else to deter any curious wildlife (bears especially), yet far enough to ensure their own privacy. The location boasts the best of both worlds: bordered by trees in the back for seclusion, and open at the front towards the campground road for easy access. And, it's relatively close to one of her favourite friends, she recognizes his tent. Ben, like Maya, has been a constant in Octavia's life since their grade-school days, a friendship spanning two decades.

Making her way back to her car to grab their stuff, a sudden warmth blooms in Octavia's chest at the sight of the familiar honey blond hair and blue eyes that mimic the summer sky. Her gaze meets with his just as she gathers a hair elastic off her wrist to put up her long, blonde hair into a tie.

"Hey Ben," she says with a smile as big as the moon.

Ben reaches in for a hug, lifting her up and twirling her around. When she smiles, it's as if the sun itself shines a little brighter, revealing perfect, pearl-white teeth that add to her enchanting allure.

"Hey gorgeous." He says with a sly grin.

"You're wet," she laughs, her eyes sparkling with amusement. "And freezing!" Ben, shirtless and not quite dried off yet from his swim, throws his towel atop her vehicle. He turns to her, a small smile playing on his lips, and places a flower behind her ear. A wildflower. Just like the ones he would pick for her when they were kids.

"Let me help you unpack." He offers, his voice warm. He picks up the overloaded cooler out of the back, his perfectly sculpted muscles rippling as he lifts the heavy object with ease. Octavia catches a glance, it's hard not to.

CHAPTER TWO

The plan for the day is to head to the beach, which is conveniently close to the campsite. The promise of a fun-filled day awaits, a shared adventure waiting to unfold. There is a nice big clearing between the trees that offer the perfect space, covered in a mix of grass, sand and pebbles. A dock lives to the left of the beach, offering a spot to hook up small boats. The kids love to jump off the edge of the dock, to see who can jump the furthest. There are a few picnic tables that line the beach, creating a haven for a delightful lunch or snacks. Octavia absolutely loves the beach. It's a place steeped in her most cherished memories with her boys. Their summers are typically spent near a lake or any body of water, and these moments are a testament to the beautiful life she's built. Even though David might have left them, it just means she gets to experience all these precious moments with her two main people. And honestly, what could be better than a relaxing day under the warm sun, building sandcastles and making new memories under the sun? She's actually based three of her best selling romance novels near a lake.

Upon their arrival back to the campsite, a convoy of pickup trucks, an unusual sight in this family-oriented campground, rolls through the entrance. Music throbs from their windows, a pulsating difference to the chirping birds and chatter of the campers. Heads turn and curiosity replaces the usual lazy languor of a summer's day.

"Oh wow, this is new." Maya states, intrigued by the new entertainment.

Whispers ripple through the campsite. Who are these newcomers, and what kind of weekend are they planning? Cowboys? Cowboys are never a good sign. They are known to be rowdy and obnoxious, only caring about themselves. *Everybody* knows that. If those cowboys plan to stay the whole weekend, they can pretty much say good-bye to their typical peaceful weekend.

"Ooh, cowboys!" Brit squeals, clapping her hands together with childish glee.

The prospect of meeting a group of rugged cowboys clearly appeals to her adventurous spirit. Octavia, however, does not share Brit's enthusiasm. In fact, a slight frown creases her brow. She's perfectly content with her quiet weekend and the company of her close friends. The thought of loud music and boisterous strangers only a few campsites down isn't exactly her vision of a relaxing weekend.

"Don't get too excited, Brit. They're driving Fords. Real men drive a Chev." Mateo jokingly points out, with a grin on his face.

Josh shakes his head.

"Hey now, you can't go wrong with a Ford." Ben chimes in. "My dad and I fixed up my 1980 F-150 and it's been going strong ever since. Fords are built to be solid, man."

"Have you ever thought about getting a lift kit on your old truck?" Josh asks, genuinely curious.

"Nah, it's not my style. Besides, I'm not nineteen years old anymore." Ben says with a chuckle.

"Touché." Josh shoots back.

"Trucks are more than just a vehicle. They are a statement." Mateo adds. "And my Chevy is a beast. It can tackle any terrain that you can throw at it and would blow any of those Fords out of the water."

"Okay." Josh laughs. "Maybe we will put your truck to the test with the cowboys over there."

"Alright guys, who's hungry?" Ali interrupts, considerate of the time. "We should probably get dinner started." After a long day spent at the beach, rumbles are heard from their stomachs.

"I'm with you on that." Mateo lightly pats his belly. "Who's on grill duty?"

"I'll start the fire," Ben offers.

"I'll join you." Octavia says. "Just let me get changed and get the boys set up with a small snack and a bit of quiet time."

Once her boys are settled, she climbs out of her tent, throws on her slides and makes her way towards the fire pit where Ben sits solo. She feels a small wave of relief wash over her. Ben is alone, and she knows this will likely be her only real chance to catch up with him during what promises to be a busy weekend. They have history, these two. A lifetime of shared moments, stretching back to simpler days. She remembers how they used to ride their bikes together from dusk until dawn, the wind in their hair, the world feeling vast and full of possibilities. Every single time, without fail, Ben would pull over to the side of the road and pick wildflowers for Octavia to take home with her.

As she walks up and greets him by the warmth of the fire, one memory, in particular, blooms vividly in her mind. They were just twelve years old, having spent a lazy summer day by the river with their friends. On the bike ride home, Ben had suddenly pulled over, his face serious for a moment as he suggested they get married. Octavia, caught off guard, had laughed it off, telling him they were far too young for such a thing. Ben, ever quick on his feet, countered with a new proposal: 'Well, how about if we're not both married by the time we're thirty, then we'll just marry each other?' She'd thought he was entirely joking, a silly childhood pact, and had readily agreed to his whimsical plan. A smile graced her lips. He's still the same sweet Ben she's always known.

"Hey beautiful, all good?" he gracefully greets her, the words tumbling over each other as he speaks.

Octavia, radiant as ever, turns towards him, her smile is as vivid and cheerful as a burst of spring flowers.

"Yeah, the boys are just gonna watch a show on my phone for twenty minutes while they warm up in their dry clothes, they are pooped out from all that running around at the beach." Her voice is laced with the comfortable ease of their long friendship. She's grateful to see that he's already got the fire going, a comforting heat to keep her warm after the water's chill.

"Are you cold?" Ben asks, his voice a touch too high-pitched, his breath misting in the frigid air.

She watches as his blue eyes follow her, a lingering warmth from the icy water still coursing through her veins.

"Always," she giggles. "Doesn't help that you kept throwing me into the freezing cold water." Octavia responds. She begins rummaging for a pot so she can boil water for tea, a quiet contentment settling over her despite the cold.

She stops and turns to Ben, her eyes sparkling.

"You know," she says, her voice soft, "fresh air, the kids laughing, my best friends... it doesn't get much better than this. It reminds me of when we were kids."

A blush creeps up Ben's cheeks, and for a fleeting moment, she wonders if he's feeling the same way she is.

"I've already got it," he offers, correctly interpreting Octavia's rummaging.

"Aw, you are just the best," Octavia says with a genuine warmth in her voice. "You know exactly what a girl needs."

She feels Ben's gaze linger. She looks at him with her big blue eyes that resemble the depth of the ocean, she wonders what he could possibly be thinking. Why is he acting all *weird* this morning? Bathed in the warm glow of the fire, she takes a seat next to him.

Ben clears his throat, the sound harsh in the quiet, late-afternoon air.

"Octavia, do you ever think about that night, a couple years ago, when we..." he hesitates, his voice a low rumble. Every muscle in his body looks tensed, as if bracing for the impact of the words about to erupt from his lips.

A mild shriek interrupts him and shatters the peaceful moment.

"No no no no no!" The voice, unmistakably Brit's, echoes across the campsite.

Octavia shoots up, creasing her brow, concerned about what could possibly be going on in Brit's tent. Her frantic panic can be seen wrestling within the confines of her tent.

"Uh oh, now what?" Octavia whispers, quiet enough so only Ben could hear.

She looks at Ben, who looks back at her, his eyes are filled with a mix of frustration and resignation. Octavia's attention is fiercely caught by another.

"Are you alright, Brit?" She calls out as she begins to make her way over to check on her.

A defeated sigh is heard escaping Ben's lips as she walks by. Ben, like the rest of the crew, knows Brit and her penchant for drama. Last year, Brit had the entire campsite looking for her little yorkie, Yip, after she'd 'run away'. The tears were rolling, everyone was looking. Turns out she had forgotten her in the vehicle. Little Yip, and the cute little bow that held her hair up, was okay of course. Octavia knows this about her too, but she won't allow herself to shrug it off, not in the off chance there might be a real emergency.

Quickly following, another blood curdling shriek pierces the peaceful afternoon air.

"A spider! There's a spider on my shirt!" Brit squeals from her tent, clearly oblivious to the rest of the campsite.

Octavia lets out an exasperated sigh as she walks back to her seat and sinks back down into it, giving her head a slight shake, completely forgetting that Ben was just about to say something seemingly important. Disappointment prickles at Octavia as Brit obnoxiously makes her way out of her tent.

"Water's almost ready," Ben informs Octavia, his voice slightly strained.

He glances at Brit, his eyes filled with a mixture of amusement and apprehension.

"Anything I can do to help with the spider situation, Brit?" A flair of playful annoyance seeps through his words.

"Very funny." Brit scoffs as she looks in his direction.

The sound of children's laughter mingles with the crackling of the fire as Ali prompts her freshly changed boys to go to the playground. With Ryan and Cory not far behind.

"Well, I guess that's one way to get the afternoon rolling." Josh looks at his sister with a knowing look as he pulls out the cooler containing the food.

"Sorry, but there was a spider, like actually crawling right on me." Brit attempts to defend herself and looks around as if her charade is just.

Josh and Mateo begin to prepare dinner, the aroma of grilling food soon fills the air. Once again, the campsite is bustling with activity.

Twilight paints the sky in gorgeous colours of orange and pink and the smell of sizzling steak fills the air. Octavia always packs her own veggie burgers as she's the only vegetarian in the group, but they are happy to cook them for her. She's never really liked meat so when she was old enough to make her own decisions she chose to cut meat out of her diet for various reasons. She doesn't judge others, but she can't stomach the thought of eating what was once a living animal. That and as a kid her mom would make her eat whatever was on the table and she would find herself gagging on the meat that was provided. She would often try to find creative ways of discarding the meat when no one was looking. It's just something that has never appealed to her, and her friends respect it.

Dinner is a lively affair, fueled by laughter and playful banter. By nine o'clock, the children are tucked into their tents, and the crackling fire becomes the focal point. Octavia, nestled comfortably in her chair, finds herself mesmerized by the dancing shadows that stretch and morph on the faces of her friends gathered around the warmth.

"It's not very often we see cowboys out this way, is it?" Octavia casually addresses. Curiosity creeps into her mind as she tunes into the eccentric sounds of their not-so-distant music and hearty laughter. The day was so peaceful before the rowdy cowboys showed up, blaring their country music. She has high hopes that they will soon quiet down, concerned it will be disruptive to the sleeping kids.

"There must be something going on in town that brought them out here." Maya observes, gently poking the fire to liven it up a bit.

Taking a deep breath, Octavia tears her gaze away from the flames and meets Ben's eyes across the fire. He offers her a small, tentative smile, and a blush creeps up her cheeks. A contented smile plays on his lips as he watches the firelight dance in her eyes. She loves Ben, she always has, but it's a love rooted deeply in friendship. He's one of her most cherished confidantes, a constant in her life. And while they might have shared a "romantic and sensual night together" in the past, a brief, beautiful deviation from their established dynamic, she simply can't bring herself to move forward with him romantically. The thought of losing him is a cold knot in her stomach. They're perfect as friends, a seamless, supportive duo. Why risk changing that? If they were to become romantically involved and things went south, if he decided to leave, she would be utterly devastated. She'd never be able to live it down, the thought of that heartbreak too much to bear. So, for both their sakes, it's undeniably best they remain just friends. That way, she knows with absolute certainty he'll be by her side forever; she'll never truly lose him.

Next to Ben, Josh and Ali together is the picture of domestic bliss. Snuggled up in their double chair, Josh had draped a blanket over them, ensuring Ali's comfort against the cool night air. Ali and Josh have always welcomed Octavia into their world, like an extra set of parents, they look out for her, despite being only a couple years older.

"Would anyone like a refill while I'm up?" Ben offers as he springs up to grab his own.

He returns with a hoodie hanging on his arm and his gaze settling on Octavia. The vacant seat beside her seems to beckon him, with a smile in her direction, he slides into it.

"I thought you might be cold," and hands her his hoodie.

"Oh wow, you shouldn't have. I could have grabbed one," she hesitantly accepts. "You're so sweet." There's a subtle way he looks at her sometimes, a lingering touch, the way his attention sharpens when she speaks. These aren't the gestures of a man content with just platonic affection. Yet, she also believes he accepts that they are better off as friends. Perhaps it's the way he always respects her boundaries, or how he never pushes, even when the unspoken tension between them is thick enough to cut with a knife. He understands her, and in that understanding, she finds a peculiar kind of peace. Friends, they will stay, an unspoken agreement.

A sudden crackle breaks the peaceful lull, not from the fire, but from Mateo's phone. He glances down at the screen, his eyes widening in surprise. A burst of excitement erupts from him.

"No way!" he exclaims, his voice sharp with disbelief. The others, lulled by the comfortable rhythm of the evening, look up at him in curiosity. Brit, the first to latch onto the excitement, practically vibrates in her seat.

"Okay, what is it?" she demands.

Mateo, barely containing his energy, shoots to his feet and scans the campsite.

"You're kidding me," he mutters, more to himself than anyone else. "I need to go check this out," he blurts out impulsively.

Octavia's grin widens as she playfully prods Mateo, "Seriously, spill the beans! What's all this excitement about?"

Mateo, now the center of attention, puffs out his chest slightly.

"It's Liam, guys," he declares, his voice brimming with blunt eagerness. "Liam's out here somewhere!"

"Liam?" Ali raises an eyebrow.

"His hockey buddy," Maya clarifies, clearly less enthusiastic than Mateo.

"Why don't you go find him and invite him over?" Josh gracefully suggests.

Ali, the practical one, chimes in, placing a hand on his shoulder.

"Just remember the kids are trying to sleep, and we don't want things to get too noisy." She gently reminds him.

Octavia concurs with Ali's suggestion. She always makes an effort to ensure her kids' well-being comes first, whether it means sacrificing time for herself and her friends, or their desires to let loose. Their sleep is also important and she'd rather it not be disrupted by extra visitors. She's a little nervous, because if her boys wake up, it also means it will likely be bedtime for her as well while she tends to them.

Mateo, already buzzing with excitement, doesn't wait for another word.

"Yeah, man," he says, throwing a thumbs-up over his shoulder. "This guy's the bomb diggity. You'll love him!"

With that, he looks at Maya, and is off like a shot, determined to find his friend Liam. Mateo, though typically laid-back, has a knack for igniting excitement and energy in any situation. His outgoing personality and infectious enthusiasm are undoubtedly part of his appeal to Maya.

Octavia watches him go, a flicker of concern crossing her features.

She leans in towards Ben and whispers, "Uh oh, I hope this *Liam* guy isn't a walking party."

Her voice is laced with amusement, but also a hint of apprehension about the potential disruption to the peaceful night and the sleeping children. Being a single mother, Octavia lives with a constant undercurrent of anxiety, always striving to maintain control in every situation.

Ben chuckles, squeezing her shoulder reassuringly.

"It will be fine," he murmurs back, "if it's just one friend, it'll be alright, I don't think he will bring the entire party over here. And besides, it wouldn't hurt for you to allow yourself to let loose once in a while."

Octavia takes a deep breath in. As always, he's entirely convincing. His gaze follows Mateo's retreating form. Ben has a unique ability to quell the anxious storm that sometimes brews within her. He's like her rock, a solid foundation that she can lean on. She glances at Maya who seems to have shifted her attention towards them and offers a warm smile.

Mateo's absence stretches towards the half-hour mark before materializing back into their circle, Liam trailing beside him. However, that isn't all. Two additional figures flank Mateo on either side, their faces slightly obscured by the bouncing fiery light.

"Hey guys," Mateo announces, oblivious to the uncertainty felt by the mothers of the group.

"This is Liam," he gestures towards his companions, "his girlfriend Kel, and..." He pauses for a second, gesturing towards the third person. "What's your name again?"

"Chad." The newcomer replies.

Octavia's heart skips a beat, and a sense of nervous wonder washes over her. It's as if time itself is holding its breath, waiting for this moment to unfold.

CHAPTER THREE

Octavia's gaze collides with Chad's for what seems like way too long. She can't help but notice his statuesque and striking features. It's almost as if he stepped straight out of a modern Western film. The wide-brimmed hat that rests at a rakish angle, completes the look. Standing at least six feet tall, he possesses a confident and captivating presence. In this instant, the flickering light from the fire seems to intensify, bathing him in a golden glow. The world around them fades away, the chatter and rustling leaves replaced by a sudden, intense awareness of just the two of them. This catches her by surprise, she doesn't understand the reaction she's having as she absorbs her new surroundings, this unknown man.

Chad's casual greeting, "Hello, miss," hovers in the air. He seems way out of her league, why is he looking at her?

Octavia's cheeks heat up.

She can only manage a small, breathless, "Hi," in response, she's thrown back by his rugged charm. The words seem to snag on the lump that formed in her throat. An awkward silence stretches between them, thick with a tension that she can't explain.

"Octavia, what a beautiful name." When he speaks, his voice is deep and resonant, carrying the cadence of the countryside and just a hint of a Southern drawl. A nervous warmth blooms in her chest, a spark igniting with a potency that surprises her, it's unexpected and exhilarating, like a shooting star streaking across the vast canvas of the night sky. Chad's gaze remains fixed on her, a slow smile tugging at the corner of his lips.

"Thank you." The words barely roll off her tongue. A warmth creeps its way up her shirt. Why is it that she can't seem to manage a real conversation? This man is way out of her league.

The interaction is broken by the sound of Mateo's voice.

"Alright," he chuckles, bustling around to fetch extra chairs for their new guests.

Octavia forces her gaze away from Chad, accidentally meeting Ben's. Intuitively, she senses that something is amiss. The way he's looking at her. The shift in his energy. She can't quite place it, but she knows. Feeling embarrassed, she just hopes that Chad isn't still looking at her. She can't help but glance back for a second to find out. Of course he is.

Brit, the social butterfly, pipes up from across the fire.

"Wow, you're so handsome!" She says.

Chad finally tears his gaze from Octavia, a flicker of amusement crossing his features. He hosts a side smile that sends a flutter of nerves dancing around in her stomach.

He raises his hand to his cowboy hat in a mock salute, a playful dip of his head accepting Brit's compliment.

"Why thank you, little lady," he drawls, his undeniable charm radiating outwards. Octavia, momentarily forgotten, feels a pang of something that might be jealousy, or maybe just a flicker of disappointment. She quickly squashes the feeling, reminding herself that she doesn't know this man. She literally just met him a moment ago. Still, the intensity of her unexpected connection lingers, a warmth beneath her skin. Someone like Brit seems more like his type anyway, gorgeous and high maintenance (although slightly annoying).

Maya, a few seats down, shoots a knowing glance in Octavia's direction.

"What?" Octavia mouths, a slight lift in her shoulders.

The unexpected arrival of Liam and his friends has slightly changed the trajectory of the evening's chill plans, but perhaps, a welcome one. The camping trip takes a thrilling turn, leaving her heart pounding with a mixture of excitement and uncertainty. As the night wears on, the fire dwindles from a roaring blaze to a bed of glowing embers, its crackle settling into a low, comforting hum. The conversation flows easily, the newcomers seamlessly woven into the circle. A sense of camaraderie fills the air.

"Well, I think I'll turn in for the night." Ben announces, his voice lacks its usual enthusiasm. He stands up and throws his can into the recycling bag.

Octavia feels something heavy drop in her stomach, the ever attentive friend, turns to him.

"Awe, already? Everything alright?" she asks, looking up at him.

"Yeah, just a rough night's sleep last night," Ben answers, a touch of forced cheer in his voice. "Gonna get an early start and hope to catch some Zzz's."

Octavia's smile softens.

"Sorry to hear that. You know, if you need anything at all..." Guilt creeps into the corners of her mind. She can't help but think there's more than he's letting on.

Ben offers a small, detached smile.

"Thanks, I appreciate it." With a final goodnight to the group, he retreats to his tent, leaving a palpable silence in his wake. The spark he had been carrying throughout the day seems to have extinguished.

As she watches Ben return to his tent, she feels a pang of unease settle in her stomach. It isn't just about the abruptness of his departure, but a deeper disquiet, a sense of something unspoken feels almost smothering. She glances around the fire, the flickering light dancing in the eyes of the remaining group. Laughter mingles with conversation, yet a hollowness echoes within her. Had she been so caught up in the unexpected arrival of Chad and the new dynamic that she missed something significant with Ben? The question gnaws at her. There is a definite shift in Ben's demeanor, a sadness that seems to cloud his usual easy smile. Has she misread the situation entirely? Was Ben's sleepless night a result of something more than just physical discomfort? A seed of doubt has been planted, and Octavia can't ignore the disquiet it brings.

Mateo, the self appointed fire-keeper, rises to add another log to the blaze, sending a shower of sparks dancing upwards into the night sky. A distant cry from one of Ali's children pierced the conversation, pulling her attention away.

"Well, that's my cue," Ali announces, already rising from her chair. "Sounds like bedtime for me."

Josh, her ever loyal husband, mirrors her movement.

"I'll join you, love," he murmurs, his voice a soft caress.

Their love for each other, a constant undercurrent in their interactions, is as undeniable as the rising moon. They are the epitome of a perfect love story that began with a highschool spar, it's truly admirable. A comfortable silence settles between them as they walk hand-in-hand towards their tent, a testament to a love story as enduring and familiar as the crackling fire. A love story that reminds her of her parents. Their love for each other is undeniable; a postcard marriage. A love so many could only long for.

The stars glow brighter and conversations lull, and a strange energy fills the air. Chad rises, a purposeful glint in his eye, and moves towards her. Her heart begins to race, a mixture of anticipation and apprehension swirling within her. Her mind races. What's he doing? This man, so unexpectedly handsome and captivating, is now mere inches away. Brit definitely seems more like his type. Why would he choose to leave her company and sit next to *me*, she thinks.

"I hope you don't mind," Chad says, his voice a low rumble in the deepening twilight. He's dressed in well-worn leather boots, faded jeans, and a sturdy, button-down shirt, and sends a confident grin towards her. "This chair was calling my name."

"Oh, was it now?" Octavia laughs softly, her voice a little breathless. "In that case, I guess I don't mind."

"What's this I hear about a birthday?" He asks.

"Who told you that?" She asks, crossing her arms, "It's not something I like to advertise."

"Why is that?" Chad pries.

His question is met with silence. And honestly, it's a pretty simple story, the reason she keeps her birthday under wraps. But it's *her* story, and she's not about to spill it to some random guy, no matter how good-looking and charming he is. She'd much rather just spend her time with her family and friends, on a peaceful outing somewhere quiet, just as they are doing. For her, these are the real moments worth cherishing, far more than any big, showy party and making a spectacle of it. After all, in her eyes, it's just another day.

"Okay, you don't have to share. My big three-oh is coming up in a couple of months."

"Thirty?" She questions. "You don't look thirty." Mid-twenties maybe.

He lets out a snicker. "I'm older than I look." he says, stating the obvious. "But I can say the same for you, too. You don't look a day over 20."

A sudden, fiery blush spreads across her face, pulling her breath short. She scrambles to find words, but they claw at her throat refusing to escape her lips.

"So, are you from around here?" Chad removes his cowboy hat and places it on the arm of his chair. His rugged good looks are complemented by a strong jawline and a clean shaven face that adds to his raw charm. His dark hair gives him a wild, untamed appearance that only enhances his allure.

Octavia, absorbing his presence, vaguely replies, "Yeah, just from in town."

"Really? Me too. Well, I've only been here for a handful of years. But I am surprised we haven't crossed paths." He continues. "I know I would remember a face as pretty as yours."

Once again, her cheeks flare with heat, a blush creeping up her neck as the butterflies in her stomach don't just flutter, they take flight in a chaotic swirl. Is *this* what it feels like? This dizzying, almost breathless sensation, the kind of love her parents have always talked about with misty eyes, the moment they first met? Could this really be happening, just out of nowhere, this sudden, overwhelming giddiness, this utterly unrealistic pull toward someone she barely knows?

Around them, stories flow. Yet, for Octavia, the world is seemingly shrinking to the space between her and Chad. All else is fading into the background, being replaced by a heightened awareness of the man beside her. As midnight approaches, the campsite buzzes with a newfound, yet calmer, energy, and for Octavia, at least, a thrilling uncertainty is nagging at her.

Liam's voice cuts through the laughter, a touch of regret lacing his words.

"Well folks, it's getting late. We've got an early start and a long day ahead tomorrow."

Kel, however, isn't quite ready to end this budding connection.

"Hey," she interjects, a mischievous glint in her eye, "if you guys are interested in seeing some real excitement, come to the rodeo tomorrow. There will be bull riding, barrel racing, and the whole shebang. You should totally come check it out!"

The suggestion is a tempting prospect. Octavia doesn't typically engage in the local rodeo's, it's never been of interest to her. The people there are so... boisterous, an energy she isn't really excited to be around. And everyone knows that they can get pretty rowdy at night. She doesn't know exact details but it's not a scene she's ever cared to submerge herself in. She typically lives a quiet life with her boys, they go to the movies, to the playground, the swimming pool, sometimes even take a road trip out of town. The rodeo isn't something that has ever drawn her in. But for the first time, it sounds kind of interesting.

Chad looks at Octavia, his lips curving into a charming wink. There is no need for words; a silent understanding is created between them. A spark of amusement dancing in her eyes, a silent question lingers. Does she want to go? To see this man again. Could it be the perfect excuse to do just that?

As goodbyes are being exchanged and the group begins to disperse, Octavia finds herself lingering for a moment beside Chad.

"It was nice to meet you," she offers, her voice laced with a hint of something more than casual courtesy.

His gaze mirrors hers, a slow smile spreading across his face.

"The pleasure's all mine."

He leans forward slightly with his breath warm against her ear. Then, in a gesture both unexpected and thrilling, he grabs her hand and brushes his lips against the back of it. A jolt of electricity shoots through her and a spark that travels from her fingertips straight to her heart. In this moment, time is seemingly slowing down, the world narrowing to the single point of contact where his lips are meeting her skin, a fiery touch that sends shivers down her spine leaving a sensational burn searing on the top of her hand; a red contrast against her porcelain white skin.

Pulling her hand away, a blush creeps into her cheeks, the lingering warmth feels like a brand against her cool skin. Chad winks, a hint of amusement in his eyes.

"See you around, beautiful," he utters, his voice husky with unspoken possibility.

With a final tip of his hat, he turns and saunters away, leaving Octavia breathless and flustered in his wake. The sound of his departing footsteps fade into the dark night.

The night air, once crisp and clear, now feels thick with unspoken tension. Octavia's heart pounds with a mixture of excitement and uncertainty. She crawls into her tent, shutting the zipper behind her, and climbs in next to her sleeping boys. Sleep, the solace she craves, feels miles away. Tonight has been a whirlwind of emotions swirling like smoke from the dying fire. A spark has been lit up inside of her. Flabbergasted barely covers it. She's caught between the confusion of what's going on with Ben, and unexpected desires for a new man she just met.

She replays the scene in her mind: the lengthy glances, the shared laughter, and then, the final electrifying touch. Butterflies flutter in her stomach as she remembers the heat of Chad's lips against her hand, a brand seared into her memory. Is this real? Had a genuine connection sparked in a single night, amidst the crackle of the campfire and the company of strangers? Or is this a dream, a fantasy conjured by her imagination? The uncertainty gnaws at her. But she thinks about her parents and the long life they shared together that was based on the love they felt the first time they met. It's possible, and maybe, just maybe, she's one of the lucky ones, too.

One thing is undeniable, though. Chad's different. He's a shudder of excitement in the ordinary rhythm of her life, a melody that sends her heart into a sweet, chaotic rhythm. He's a cowboy, unfamiliar territory. But with the thrill comes a tremor of fear. Stepping outside the familiar, especially with someone who appeared so suddenly, and who is so different, is terrifying. Yet, as Octavia stares at the red imprint on her hand, an area distinctly inflamed and warm, a different kind of fear whispers in the darkness. Questions dance around in her mind as she finally drifts off to sleep.

CHAPTER FOUR

Exhaustion clings to Octavia like a second skin after the meager few hours of sleep she managed. Morning mist drifts lazily through the trees as she joins the others for breakfast, a forced smile plastered on her face. While dishing out pancakes, Ben's gaze snags on the angry red mark marred on her hand. His concern is immediate. Reaching out, he gently grasps her wrist.

"Whoa, Octavia, what happened there?" His voice holds a tremor of worry.

Flustered, Octavia yanks her hand back, the movement abrupt and defensive.

"Oh, it's nothing," she lies, hastily shoving her hand up the sleeve of her hoodie. "Just a bug bite, must've gotten me in the night."

The lie sticks in her throat, a bitter taste against the sweetness of the syrup on her yet to be pancakes. She knows better than to underestimate Ben's perceptiveness. But the memory of Chad's unexpected kiss, the electric thrill that still dances on her skin, is a secret she isn't ready to share. Not yet. Part of it is a need to understand it herself. Why the physical remnant? What does it mean? Until she has some answers, she can't bear the thought of anyone else, especially Ben, scrutinizing it with suspicion.

A heavy silence descends upon them, broken only by the clinking of silverware. Ben's worried frown etches a line between his brows, an invisible question mark hovering over his head. Octavia looks away, the weight of her secret burns in the pit of her stomach. Octavia isn't able to shake the image of Chad, his easy charm and lingering touch is a constant presence in her thoughts. The rodeo and Kel's suggestion gnaws at her, it's a tempting possibility. But loyalty tugs harder. This camping trip is about friends and laughter shared around the fire or down at the water, a respite from the daily grind. They came together for her, to be together for *her* birthday. Can she justify abandoning them, even for a few hours, for a man she just met? The answer's evident. Her friends come first on this trip. How could she even question it?

The day passes by in a daze, and Octavia's mind is a tangled mess of daydreams and new feelings. Conversations with friends feel distant, their jokes landing with a dull thud. The easy camaraderie she's always cherished seems strained, replaced by a disquiet she can't explain. As the sun begins its descent below the horizon on their last night, Octavia finds herself wrestling with a decision. Part of her yearns to follow this unexpected spark, to see where this connection with Chad might lead. The other part, cautious and responsible, urges her to stay put, to cherish the familiar comfort of her friends. The flickering flames of the campfire mirror the battle within her, a war between thrilling uncertainty and the safe harbor of routine. The rodeo crew returns to their campsite for one final night. Octavia tries her best to act casual, to mask her furtive glances towards their area.

"Hey, I see you scoping them out," Maya utters quietly, nudging her with a sly grin.

"What do you mean?" She feigns innocence, a blush creeping up her cheeks.

"Oh, come on, Octavia," Maya gently teases. "I saw you two last night. You were drooling over that new guy, Chad." Nothing gets past Maya.

"I don't know what you're talking about," Octavia scoffs, the heat rising in her face betraying her words.

Maya just smiles knowingly.

"Uh-huh, you keep telling yourself that, I know you better than anyone."

It's true, she does. The question echoes in her mind like a silent mantra. Where is he? His absence is a tangible weight, his energy a presence that lingers even when he isn't there.

"Why don't we go over there and find you a little birthday somethin' somethin'" Maya jokes.

"Come on, you know I don't like making a big deal out of my birthday. All I need is my loyal friends who always show up for me." Octavia explains.

Brit's ears perk up, she must have caught a snippet of the conversation about the cowboys. A spark of jealousy, perhaps mixed with a dash of FOMO, must be igniting within her.

"Maybe after we've cleaned the site," she chimes in, her voice bright and eager, "we should go hang out with them cowboys for a while!"

Her suggestion lingers, a playful challenge aimed at the group. Would anyone bite? The prospect of extending the night, of mingling with the new arrivals, seems to hold a certain allure for Brit. Besides, who knows what kind of fun they could have with this mysterious group of cowboys? Her gaze darts between the entire group, searching for a willing accomplice.

Mateo, the typical life of the party, erupts with a cheer. "Hell yeah! Let's do it!"

Ali, however, throws a wrench into their plans.

"Sorry guys," she announces with a sigh, "but we have to head out early tomorrow. We will need to get the kids settled."

Josh offers a silent agreement, helping Ali tidy up their campsite. Mateo's enthusiasm dims a touch, but he turns hopeful towards Maya.

"Yeah, let's do it!" Maya concedes.

Maya's never able to bring herself to say no to Mateo's pleading eyes, but sounds like she wants to go anyway.

"Octavia, you should come," she adds, turning towards her friend.

"Oh, this is gonna be fun, you guys!" Brit can't resist but to butt in.

Brit's interjection is like a splash of cold water on the simmering tension. Octavia, caught between her desire to see Chad and her responsibility to her children, hasn't quite formulated a response. Now, with Brit's enthusiastic declaration, the pressure shifts. Octavia caught a glimpse of the mischievous look that sparkles in Brit's eyes. Is it simply a love for adventure, or is there a hint of jealousy bubbling beneath the surface? Perhaps the sight of Octavia's lengthy glances towards the rodeo crew ignited a competitive streak within her. For whatever reason, Brit's bold statement is changing the dynamic. The focus is shifting from Octavia's internal struggle to a group decision. Maya shoots Brit a quick glance, then turns back to Octavia, silently urging her with a look. The pressure mounts, the decision is weighing on her.

"I mean, I've got the kids," Octavia mumbles, the excuse sounds hollow even to her own ears. Deep down, she knows she's grasping at straws.

"Bring them!" Maya insists, her voice laced with a knowing cheer. It's clear Maya sees right through her flimsy objection. "It'll be fine. Besides, I'll help you watch them."

Is there a double motive behind Maya's encouragement? Sure, she wouldn't mind joining Mateo at the cowboys' campsite. But more importantly, she senses Octavia's awakening interest in Chad and perhaps, is determined to be her wing woman.

The pressure is on.

Octavia struggles, her internal thoughts swirling around in her mind. Could she justify dragging her children into an impromptu visit, fueled by a desire to see a man she had just met? Or would she let this chance encounter slip away, forever wondering *what if?*

"Alright," she finally concedes, "But only for a bit because I'm gonna have to get the kids to bed at a decent time."

"Works for me," Maya chirps, clearly relieved that they wouldn't be completely outnumbered by the cowboys. She links arms with Octavia, a silent promise of support.

"Do you ladies mind if I join you?" Ben asks hesitantly.

Octavia's smile feels strained as she turns to the source of the question.

"Of course, how is that even a question?" she responds.

Octavia's breath catches in her throat. Ben's unexpected question is throwing a wrench into her carefully crafted plan to seek out Chad. The dynamic is shifting once more. What was supposed to be a carefree visit with a chance encounter now feels like a delicate balancing act. Octavia is finding herself caught between the familiar comfort of Ben's presence and the thrilling spark ignited by Chad.

The minutes stretch into a seemingly endless loop of small talk and faint cheer. They've cleaned up their camp, bid farewell to Josh and Ali, and are finally making their way to Liam's campsite.

Disappointment gnaws at Octavia as she hopelessly scouts the site. Chad remains frustratingly absent. In the meantime, she sets up a seat comfortable enough for her and her kids. Sixty minutes of awkward conversation pass in a blur and her kids are getting restless. Maya, Mateo and Ben are fully engaged with Liam and a few of his friends in a conversation about the rodeo circuit, their voices are a distant hum against the backdrop of Octavia's growing impatience. Every rustle of leaves and every flicker of movement sends a jerk through her, only to be followed by a wave of deflation when it isn't him. Finally, deciding she can't bear the charade of small talk any longer, Octavia stands with a forced smile.

"Well, it's getting late," she announces, her voice brittle. "We should probably head out."

She corrals her children, their sleepy faces mirroring her own exhaustion. After a quick goodbye to Maya and a casual farewell to Ben,

Octavia packs up her chair and heads back to her campsite, her boys following closely behind. Just as she exits the campsite, a voice rings out, sending a thrill of electricity through her.

"Hey there, beautiful," he drawls, his voice a husky caress. "Didn't expect to see you here."

Octavia's breath hitches. Her heart, like a hummingbird trapped in her chest, beats frantically. For a moment, all thoughts flee, being replaced by a rush of pure, exhilarating relief and nervousness.

"You're here," she manages, the words tumbling out in a quiet tone. A near whisper. Chad chuckles, a rich sound that creates a warmth in her chest.

"Of course I am. I couldn't just let you leave without saying goodbye." He says. "I was just at the other site and I caught a glimpse of you, I didn't know you were over here."

Relief washes over her, sweet and cleansing. The slight embarrassment of Ben's protective presence, the disappointment of a fruitless visit, it's all melting away. Here, bathed in the chilled air of the approaching dark night, stands the man who has awakened a spark within her, one she hasn't felt in a long time. And at this moment, nothing else matters. A yearning tugs at her, a desire to bridge the physical distance that separates them. The warmth radiating from his presence, the easy confidence in his posture, it all whispers a silent invitation. Yet, a sliver of reason holds her back. They are practically strangers, bound only by a fleeting encounter and a stolen kiss on the back of her hand. Octavia's voice, though filled with a genuine need to leave, holds a tremor of regret.

"I was just leaving." She admits, gesturing towards her children. "I need to get these guys back."

"Let me walk you." Chad insists.

"Sure," She says, a soft smile blooms. "Then I have to get them to bed."

Entering her campsite, she looks at her boys, "I need you two troopers to head into the tent to settle in and I will be right there, okay?" She instructs.

Chad's smile softens, his gaze shifting to the sleepy-eyed youngsters clinging to Octavia's side. There's a flicker of understanding in his eyes, perhaps a respect for the responsibility she carries.

"Of course," he replies smoothly, his voice warm and reassuring. "I understand. Family always comes first."

Without hesitation Ryan and Cory make their way, running towards the tent as if it's a race who gets there first.

Chad looks over at Octavia, pauses for a beat, then leans in a touch closer, his voice dropping to a conspiratorial whisper. "Let me take you out sometime," he murmurs, his breath sending a delicious tingle down Octavia's spine.

The invitation persists, a tempting promise laced with unspoken possibility. Octavia's heart skips a beat. The idea of spending time alone with Chad, of exploring this newfound connection beyond the fleeting encounters of the campsite, fills her with exhilaration. A slow smile blooms on her face, mirroring the one on Chad's.

"Maybe," she teases, her voice light and playful. "What did you have in mind?" The question is an invitation, a hesitant step towards something more.

Chad's eyes gleam with a mischief that matches hers.

"Well," he lingers, "there's this little bar downtown that's great for hosting events. They have these incredible live music nights…"

The image of a dimly lit environment, filled with the smoky haze of conversation and the sounds of an acoustic guitar, dances in Octavia's mind. It's a world away from the dusty campsite and lullabies she sings to her children, a world that whispers of possible mischievous and unspoken desire.

She struggles internally whether she should skip the night out, or take Ben's advice and let loose. Maybe he's right, she's probably interpreting his advice out of context, but maybe she does need to let loose once in a while. So, her mind is made.

"That sounds nice," she admits, a slow smile tugging at her lips.

The idea of a night out, of dressing up and losing herself in the music, was a forgotten fantasy given a sudden shock of life. The thrill of possibility courses through her.

"I would love that," she says, reentering the conversation with Chad, her voice betrays the excitement bubbling beneath the surface. This is exactly what she's been craving since their first encounter, a chance to explore this spark that flickers between them. With trembling fingers, she opens up her phone, once again, the screen illuminating her face in its cool glow. "Here, put your number in," she offers, extending the phone towards Chad.

"Yes, ma'am." He readily agrees as he taps in his digits.

She decides on a little playful action of her own when he hands the phone back.

"This might be bright for a sec."

She tries to snap a quick picture of him with her phone's camera, to associate it with the new contact. However, just as she raises the phone, Chad's hand shoots up, tilting his stetson down to shield his eyes in a quick display of mock surprise. A strange flicker of unease shoots across Octavia's mind, a fleeting dissonance in the symphony of their newfound connection. Why is he covering his face? But she quickly dismisses it, attributing it to nothing more than a playful cowboy pose.

"Just capturing the moment," she chirps.

The playful gesture masks something deeper in Chad's eyes. A hint of an emotion flickers there, an emotion she can't quite place, but one that sends a shiver down her spine nonetheless. With the contact saved, Octavia buzzes with nervous anticipation. She texts him her number, the simple act imbued with a significance that sends her heart into a happy gallop.

"I'll give you a call," she declares, pushing the phone into her pocket with a playful glint in her eyes.

Chad's response is immediate, his hand reaches out to capture hers. This time, the movement is swift, his fingers brush against the sensitive skin on her wrist before gently pulling her hand closer. He's so warm. Octavia's breath catches in her throat. A memory flickers in her mind – the heat of his lips on her hand the night before, the brand that still slightly lingers on her skin. A flicker of apprehension plays on her face, a silent question in her eyes. Before any further questions could cloud her mind, Chad surprises her. He leans closer, his warm breath whispering against her ear. His voice, a low rumble that sends shivers cascading on her skin, speaks words that are both a promise and a challenge.

"I look forward to seeing you again, miss…" He trails off, leaving the space intentionally blank. Octavia's cheeks burn with a mixture of shyness and excitement. A slow smile curves her lips. She meets his gaze, a silent answer sparkling in her eyes. "Octavia," speaking softly, his voice barely a whisper.

The sound of her name on his very kissable lips transforms a question into a promise, sending a surprise nervousness through her. The weekend, once a chance for relaxation, has become a catalyst for change. An unexpected connection has sparked, leaving Octavia with a heart full of nervous anticipation and a head full of questions.

As Chad leans back, a satisfied smile plays on his lips, Octavia knows one thing for certain, the camping trip isn't quite over yet. The embers of desire have been fanned, and she's eager to see where this unexpected spark will lead.

"Oh, before you go," Chad says, "I know that you're not like the others. And that's what I like about you."

CHAPTER FIVE

Back home, days after the camping trip, the silence from Chad becomes unbearable.

Fueled by nervous excitement, Octavia finishes cleaning the dishes, dries her hands and takes the plunge with a simple text message:

Hey stranger, how's the cowboy life treating you?

The response is immediate, a warm welcome followed by a promise to meet.

Hey, I was just thinking about you! I am having some people over tonight. Care to join? This isn't quite what she had imagined for their first 'date'. It definitely isn't the bar that they had originally discussed. However, she can't wait to unfold the mystery of this new man. She has an undeniable urge to meet up and doesn't really care what they do.

A get-together at your place? Sure, sounds like fun.

While the invitation warms her heart, she also feels a perturbation of nervous energy through her. Meeting his friends and getting a glimpse into his regular life is a whole new challenge. Will they accept her? Will she fit in with his established group? The initial excitement of the invitation is becoming entangled with a sudden wave of self-doubt. Taking a deep breath, Octavia steadies her mind. Meeting Chad's friends is simply a chance to get to know the people who are important to him, a way to see him in another light. Pushing aside the self-doubt, she rushes upstairs and delves into her closet, determined to find the perfect outfit. It needs to be stylish yet comfortable, something that reflects her personality without trying too hard. She puts on a black dress that accentuates her curves, and heads back down to the living room.

"Hey, boys!" She calls out "How does this look?" Twirling in her outfit.

"You look beautiful, mommy." Cory's adorable, big brown eyes looking up at her.

"I like it." Ryan concurs. "Where are you going?"

"I'm meeting up with a friend tonight," Octavia replies, opening her arms for a hug. "And you guys get to have fun with Grandma!" She gives Ryan a quick kiss, her hand resting gently on his cheek. "How does a sleepover sound?"

"Okay." Ryan accepts. They do love their time that they get to spend with their grandma.

"I love you boys more than anything," Octavia says, her voice filled with unconditional love.

"I love you, more." Cory says, reaching his little arms out for a hug.

"I love you, most." Her love for her sons is a force stronger than anything she's ever known.

The time for her to meet up with Chad is fast approaching. The hours feel like quick minutes. As she pulls up to his charming farmhouse, she gasps. It's idyllic, a picture right out of a storybook, lit up by the golden hues of the setting sun. The arrival at Chad's farmhouse is a symphony of joyous greetings. An ever-enthusiastic border collie materializes in the driveway the moment she pulls up. His tail wags a friendly welcome, a blur of black and white fur.

Settled on a small hobby farm, Chad's house is a grand two-story home clad in rich brown siding. The warm shade conveys a sense of timeless elegance and stability. A spacious white wrap-around-deck creates a warm embrace around the house, beginning with a beautiful set of stairs. Each step is crafted from rich inviting wood that gradually and gracefully sweeps upwards. Its railings complement the stairs, flowing with elegant curves.

With each step, Octavia feels a sliver of her anxiety melt away. Instead of focusing on fitting in, she tunes in to the music emanating from inside the house and decides to embrace the unknown. Perhaps, she thinks, her unique perspective will be a welcome addition to their group. A smile tugs at her lips as she envisions the evening with laughter shared, stories exchanged and newly formed connections. A wave of nervous energy washes over her as she knocks on the door. Can he even hear the knock? She waits before letting herself in, slowly peeking through the door.

"Hello?" The quiet of her voice is a failed attempt to announce her arrival. Behind her, the dog pushes his way through the door, finally clinging on to Chad's attention.

"Hey!" Chad greets her with a grin on his face and a drink in his hand.

This isn't the quiet intimacy she'd envisioned for their first meeting. One thing is certain, Octavia's carefully crafted image of a casual gathering has gone out the window. This is a full-fledged party, and she's the lone outsider, unsure of the social etiquette or the unspoken rules.

Self-consciousness lances through her. She instinctively perches on the edge of the couch, feeling a bit like a lone feather on a boisterous bird. Chad, seemingly oblivious to her initial trepidation, skips any introductions and turns the volume up a notch, a playful glint dancing in his eyes. Perhaps it's to energize the room, or perhaps it's a test, a dare to see if she can keep up with the lively atmosphere. Yet, amidst the swirling emotions, a spark of determination ignites within her. She won't let her nerves get the better of her. Taking a deep breath, she forces a smile onto her face, ready to face this new challenge head-on. After all, what is a little music compared to the melody that plays in her heart?

"Dance with me," Chad declares, his voice a husky caress against the backdrop of the lively chaos.

Chad seems as if he's already a couple drinks in. He extends his hand, palm open, the simple gesture radiating both a challenge and a promise. Octavia, a vision in her carefully chosen outfit, is a paradox. Nervous energy crackles around her like static, yet it only serves to heighten her allure. Hesitation lingers for a beat, a delicate dance between fear and excitement. With a playful glint mirroring Chad's, a silent answer forming in her eyes, she slips her cold hand into his. His touch, warm and confident, shoots a thrill through her. Taking a deep breath, Octavia allows him to guide her towards the makeshift dance floor. Self-consciousness threatens to engulf her again, but Chad's reassuring grin holds her steady.

Their bodies sway to the rhythm and a sense of liberation washes over her. The blaring music, once a source of anxiety, becomes the soundtrack to their own private world. In Chad's arms, amidst the swirling chaos, she finds a pocket of peace, a connection that transcends the noise and the stares. Lost in the melody that only their entwined bodies can hear, a soft laugh escapes her lips when she stumbles slightly. With a swift, playful motion, he spins her around, catching her in his arms and bringing them closer. Their eyes meet, a universe of unspoken emotions swirling within them. For a heartbeat, the music fades, replaced by the quiet symphony of their beating hearts. Then, just as quickly, they melt back into the rhythm, their bodies now moving in perfect harmony. The distant chatter of his friends and the melody of a sentimental song fills the air, a natural orchestra serenading their impromptu waltz. A slow smile blooms on her face, genuine and radiant. In Chad's arms, surrounded by his friends, she feels a sense of belonging she hadn't anticipated. This is a glimpse into a future she desperately craves, and the feeling blooming in her chest is undeniable.

The idea that he captivates her echoes in her mind, a melody far more invigorating than the music thrumming through the room. She feels as if she's a teenager again and needs to share this, to express the joy that bubbles over like champagne. With a quick excuse about needing some fresh air, Octavia slips away from the makeshift dance floor, her phone a lifeline in her hand. She finds refuge in the quiet bathroom, the pounding music a distant echo.

Her fingers fly across the screen, composing a simple yet powerful message: *I am in love!!!* The recipient? Maya, of course. *Obviously not actually.. That would be ridiculous LOL but you've seen him.. He's soooo handsome, and just as charming!* Their bond transcends words; any major life update, good or bad, finds its way to her best friend's phone in a flurry of texts.

The reply is immediate, a burst of virtual confetti exploding on the screen: *I am so happy for you!! As long as you're happy. I'm happy! And he better treat you like the queen you are!* Maya's joy resonates through the words, a testament to their deep connection.

Octavia knows Maya understands, understands that Octavia deserves a love story with a happy ending, a love that cherishes and respects her.

I know it is only the first time we are actually hanging out but I don't care! I can't wait to see where this goes! Octavia replies impulsively, the emotions overflowing. This isn't just about fitting into Chad's life; it's about building something new, something beautiful, together. Her parents are perfect examples of how strangers can fall in love and build a beautiful life together. If this is her chance, she's not going to let it slip, despite what others might think.

You go girl! I am so happy for you. You will have to tell me all about it tomorrow! Maya's response is a warm embrace across the miles. She has always been Octavia's cheerleader, her rock, and tonight is no different. Octavia tucks her phone back into her purse. The night is far from over, and she, with a heart brimming with love and a best friend by her side (even if virtually), is ready to face whatever comes next. A wave of warmth washes over her. Maya is always her number one supporter, going all the way back to grade school, and her excitement only amplifies her own.

With a renewed sense of confidence, she slips back out to join Chad, a secret smile playing on her lips. Chad is the embodiment of Octavia's deepest desires. Tall, dusky, and undeniably handsome, he possesses a physical magnetism that draws her in like a moth to a flame. His eyes, the color of deep emerald pools, hold a hidden mystery that both captivates and terrifies her. They are windows to an unseen world, promising adventure and whispered secrets. And the fact that *he* wants *her* only enhances his allure. They're basically still strangers and he already makes her feel like she's *the one.*

When Octavia emerges out of the washroom, Chad is nowhere in sight. Scanning the room a sudden wave of nervousness envelopes her. She doesn't know these people. There is not one recognizable face in the room. There are a few men dressed in jeans and button up shirts. More cowboys probably. The women are dressed nice, but casual. Their make up looks like it was thrown on in a rush, but they still look nice. Except for this one woman. She's not wearing make-up and she looks a little bit older. She seems out of place. However, she's the first person that looks the most welcoming.

"Hey, have you seen Chad?" Competing with the music, Octavia raises her voice to ask. Forget small talk or introductions, this music is too loud to make anything out without yelling.

"Yeah, I think he slipped out the back." She yells, generously pointing in the direction of a sliding door.

"Thank you!" With a smile Octavia turns to follow her direction.

"You don't belong here." A dismissive voice echoes behind her as she makes her way through the room. She pauses, a flicker of doubt crosses her face. She turns around, no one is looking into her direction, it's as if it came from nowhere. Could she have misheard? There's no way that's what she heard. She shakes her head, dismissing the thought, although she can feel the burn at the back of her head, as if someone is watching her. She slips out onto the deck.

"Hey, cowboy." Octavia greets him, her gaze drawn to his Stetson. The rugged cowboy look is a potent combination. It transforms him.

"I'm glad you found me." Chad says, his half-grin sets her heart racing.

"Are you looking for an escape from your own party?" She asks, a hint of challenge in her voice.

He shakes his head. "I am just as happy being out here with you. I knew you'd find me." Chad, sitting on a wooden bench, welcomes Octavia to do the same. "You're different, you know." He continues, his tone mysterious and serious.

"What do you mean?" She asks, recalling he said that the other night as well. She's unsure whether to accept it as a complement or brush it off as an insult.

"Well," he pauses. "I like it."

Okay, so not a bad thing.

"You know, there's something really different about you, too." Octavia adds as she reaches her hand out to meet his. "You're so warm, unlike anything I've ever felt." Chad slowly pulls his hand away, but before he could do so, she pulls it back in. "And I'm drawn to it. It feels so nice against my skin."

His gaze is filled with a mix of intrigue and assurance. "How is someone as pretty as you single anyway?" Chad asks. "Um, excuse me, assuming you're single."

Octavia laughs. "Yeah, I am." She pauses, attempting to find the words. "Uhh, I don't really talk about it."

"And you don't have to." Chad interjects.

"No, I want to," she pauses. "There's something so familiar about you, and about your energy. Kind of like someone else I know. Or like someone I've known for a long time. But your touch, it's magnetizing. I think it's one of the reasons why I feel so attracted to you."

"Oh really?" He smirks.

"Heh, yeah." She looks down at her lap as she fidgets with her fingers. "The boy's dad left a long time ago. We were so young and it all happened so fast. At first, it felt like he really loved me. We were right on track, you know, to creating that perfect, *ideal* family." She emphasizes with air quotes.

"Well, he's an idiot." He says. Her eyes shoot up in his direction. "I know that because an idiot is the only person stupid enough to leave you." Chad assures her. "And what about the kids? Does he see them?"

"I don't think I will ever understand why he left." She says. "He hasn't tried reaching out for me or the boys since. They get curious, mostly Ryan, he's older. But I just tell them that they have me, and that I will always be here, no matter what."

"You sound like a great mom." He tells her. "I'm sure they know that."

"When we met the other night, I felt a spark that I haven't since... well, him." She looks into his eyes. "It's probably not what you want to hear." He gives his head a little shake, indifferent to the idea. "I've been scared to date since then, scared of a broken heart, not only for me but the boys, too. I try, but I just haven't felt a spark with anyone, not like I do with you. And I know that sounds stupid because we just met."

"It's not stupid." Chad interrupts.

She offers a soft smile.

"Plus, I try so hard to create the idea of a perfect life for my boys. Basically everything I do revolves around them. I haven't given myself much chance to really explore anything else. Not seriously, anyway. And well, I think I'm ready to. Especially since I met you. I'd really like to see where we can take this, you and me."

"Well, I have an idea," he shoots back at her. "Why don't we take this upstairs and see where it leads us."

"What?" She giggles and drops her jaw in mild shock, his playful remark broke the seriousness of the conversation. "That's not what I meant."

"I know. I'm just teasing." He says. "I wouldn't do that to you. Why don't we take this back inside and I can introduce you around. There's two people I want you to meet."

She hesitates, "I'm not so sure I'm welcome in there."

Chad stops, "What do you mean?" Unsure of how to explain the rude remark that was thrown into her direction earlier, she puts it aside.

"Ah," Octavia hisses, a sharp gasp escaping her lips as consciousness suddenly snaps away like a tripped wire. For a fractured split second, everything dissolves into an absolute, suffocating blackness. The woman's voice, the one she'd heard before, echoes from an impossible distance, like a whisper through a vast canyon. "Get out," is all that registers, a single, urgent demand that barely pierces the void before her vision slams back into place, the room rushing back into focus with dizzying speed.

"You alright?" Chad asks, his voice cutting through the ringing in her ears. A spark of genuine, worried concern ignites in his eyes, fixed directly on her.

"Uh, yeah." She manages, the word a dry, flimsy shield. She's utterly unwilling to explain that this isn't the first time it's happened, that these unsettling flickers into darkness are becoming a terrifying pattern. There's *got* to be a logical explanation, she tells herself. It happened so fast, she's surprised Chad even caught on.

"Okay, well don't pay no mind to them." He grabs her hand and guides her into the house. "The couple I want you to meet, James and Baily, they will love you. Don't worry about anyone else."

CHAPTER SIX

Dawn paints the horizon and the music finally fades. Octavia, back in the familiar comfort of her own bed, feels a wave of exhaustion wash over her. Yet, beneath the tiredness, a current of nervous excitement hums through her veins. The night was a whirlwind, a sensory overload of music, conversation, and passionate glances with Chad. Her initial doubts about meeting Chad's friends faded as the night progressed. He was right about James and Baily, they were welcoming and kind. James is a typical cowboy just like Chad. His dark brown hair, short stubble, and blue button up complete the look. Baily is something else, she looks like a *real* cowgirl with fiery red hair. There aren't many women who dress the part around this town, but she pulls it off with ease. Her blue jeans, accompanied by a classic belt buckle, stood out the most. Well, that and her smell. Her perfume had a hint of earthly elegance, almost like a mix of floral and cedarwood. Neither of them carry the same hint of southern drawl like Chad does, but when they speak, it's almost as if they're from another world. A world Octavia is unfamiliar with.

Now, nestled amongst the familiar softness of her sheets, the events replay in her mind like a cherished movie. Every smile and touch resonates with a deeper meaning. She can't shake the feeling of being utterly enchanted, as if Chad had woven a spell around her with his easy charm and genuine warmth. A single text from Maya, waiting on her phone screen, is a reminder of the life she'd left behind for the evening.

How was your night, girlie?

Octavia rereads the message and a smile blooms on her face. This wasn't just a night out; it's the first chapter in a story she is eager to write, a story where love, laughter, and a touch of the unknown promise of an exciting future with Chad. The swift pace of their new relationship, exhilarating and filled with butterflies, somehow feels frustratingly slow. Maybe she *should* have followed him upstairs to his bedroom. She longs for his touch that warms her natural coolness. Each striking glance and the playful banter only intensifies the burning desire to be closer to him. Octavia finds herself daydreaming of a fast-forward button, skipping past the awkward first meetings and navigating straight to a future where their lives are intertwined. The rational part of her understands the need for patience, for their bond to grow organically. Yet, the emotional tide threatens to pull her under, a relentless current urging her to confess her feelings, to bridge the gap that still separates them.

With a new sense of ease and confidence, a yearning tugs at her heart. She sends one last quick text before moving on with her day. It isn't just a text. It's a link to a song. 'Are you gonna kiss me or not.' It may not be a perfect fit, but she's pretty sure it gets the message across. She might not have followed him to his room last night, and part of her might even regret it a little bit. She hopes that this will nudge him to make another move on her, now that she's a little more comfortable.

* * *

Saturday morning's ever-rising sun casts a glow across the vibrant flowers in Octavia's backyard. She's deep in thought as she kneels amongst the petunias, her fingers gently loosen the soil. Planting flowers in her raised beds brings her peace each year. She absolutely loves the look of the flowers that surround her house just as much as she loves sitting in the sun planting them. When she gets caught up in her thoughts, her flower bed is her go-to place to calm her mind.

It's been several days since she's sent that link. Their phone conversations and text messages carry on as usual, but there is no acknowledgement of the song. Octavia questions whether it even went through at all and she's too embarrassed to ask. What if he did read it but thinks she's just kinda pathetic?

A shadow suddenly falls over her. She looks up, expecting the clouds to be a blanket over the sun, but instead she is met with the sound of a familiar voice.

"Hey beautiful."

Chad stands behind her, a mischievous look in his eyes. Before she can react, he leans down, his hand reaching out presenting a bouquet of flowers in front of her. They aren't just any flowers, the velvety purple petals mimic the color of twilight and, more importantly, Octavia's favorite colour. Surprise melts into delight as she stands up.

"Oh wow! For me?" she exclaims, her voice tinged with disbelief as she brushes a strand of hair from her face.

Instinctually, she reaches out with her dirt-smudged hands, then hesitates, realizing the state they are in. Chad chuckles, his gaze lingering on her with a warmth that makes her feel safe and loved.

"Don't worry about it," he says, gently taking the bouquet and placing it in her clean arms.

A "thank you" slips past her lips. These flowers, this simple gesture, holds a deeper meaning. It feels like a tiny declaration, a promise of more to come. Looking up at Chad, her eyes shining with a mixture of gratitude and affection, she says, "This is so sweet. How did you know purple is my favorite color?"

Chad's smile widens. "Good guess, I suppose," he replies, a touch of playfulness dancing in his voice. But the way his eyes hold hers, it hints at something more. Perhaps, like Octavia, he senses the potential for something deeper, a connection that goes beyond a lucky guess about a favorite color.

A wave of warmth washes over Octavia as he wraps his arm around her. The yearning to see him has been almost unbearable.

"Awe," she sighs, leaning into his touch, "I missed you."

Chad chuckles, the sound a familiar melody to her ears.

"Me too, baby girl," he murmurs, his voice a husky caress.

He seems to have an uncanny ability to understand her, to speak the language of her heart with effortless ease. This simple phrase, 'baby girl' gives her goosebumps, a term of endearment that feels both intimate and possessive. It's a stark contrast to the playful banter they'd shared only days ago at his house, a testament to the rapid pace at which their relationship is progressing. They met in May, it's now the beginning of June. Nearly two weeks. It seems like such a short time, yet in that span, Chad has woven himself into the fabric of her days. They've had some high's and low's, no doubt, but now, his texts are a lifeline throughout the workday, with the anticipation of seeing him on evenings and weekends. Perhaps it's a touch naive, this whirlwind romance, but right now, nestled in his embrace, all she feels is a giddy happiness, a thrilling sense of possibility.

Octavia's pulse races as Chad's arm tightens around her. She reaches up, seeking closer comfort, and that's when it happened. He leans in, his face brushing hers before his lips land on her cheek. A gasp, involuntary and surprised, escapes her lips. The touch is brief, a fleeting brush of warmth. Yet, something unexplainable is happening between them. For Chad, it's a faint echo of the burning heat that courses through his veins, a secret he holds close. But for Octavia, even through the innocuousness of a cheek kiss, she feels a spark of something new.

She pulls back slightly, a flicker of confusion in her eyes. Is it the heat of the sun? The intensity of their reunion? Whatever it is, it throws her off guard, leaving a tingling sensation on her skin and a delicious flutter in her stomach. What is the burning sensation that Chad's lips leave on her skin? It's unlike anything she's ever known.

"You okay?" Chad, slightly concerned, instantly backs away unsure of how Octavia will react to the sensation on her cheek.

She reaches out to him and takes hold of his hand. Her touch is a cool counterpoint to his infernal heat. It makes no sense to her but she doesn't care. Not that much. This man shows interest in her. The heat has to come from a place of desire.

"Chad?" She whispers. A sensual burn, could it be an echo of love that defies the very laws of existence? Her fingers tingle as the memory of the bittersweet aches from his touch lie shallow in her mind. She reaches up to softly brush her fingers along where he'd just kissed her. But the agony that she feels being apart from Chad inflicts more pain on her than his sensitive touch. "I feel the fire. It burns within me too." Her voice thick with emotion.

He pulls Octavia in for a hug, with one arm around her back, the other he slowly places on the side of her face. Their newfound love is a twisted tapestry woven with forbidden threads that she doesn't quite understand. He holds her for a brief minute before releasing his arms from the grasp he has on her. Freed from his warm embrace, Octavia instinctively gazes up at him. A silent invitation hangs between them, a promise of their first kiss intensifies the energy around them. Their lips meet with a spark, a tentative touch, turning into a slow burn. Pulling apart, they lock eyes, a silent question evidently present. Octavia, who was unsure just a couple days before about the song that she had sent to Chad, is now reassured by his act of irresistible charm. It's evident now that he didn't ignore her advance.

"Octavia, there's something that you need to kno–..."

The back door swings open, revealing Ryan and Cory, Octavia's sons, bursting with boundless energy. They have just arrived home from playing with the neighbour's kids. A blur of energy, eight-year-old Ryan, skids to a halt, his eyes wide.

"Mom! We finished the fort! Can we..." He trails off, his gaze landing on Chad, who stands awkwardly beside Octavia. Ryan approaches him cautiously. "Hi," he mumbles quietly.

Chad, with his initial surprise melting away, crouches down to meet Ryan's gaze.

"Hey there, buddy." He offers a friendly smile, hoping to ease the boy's evident shyness.

Cory, a whirlwind of blond fury barely reaching Octavia's waist, barrels past Ryan, oblivious to the unanticipated presence.

"Look, Mommy! I found a whole bunch of shiny worms!" He holds up a handful of earthworms with a triumphant grin.

Octavia winces, mentally bracing for the chaos.

"Whoa how cool, buddy! Let's find them a home in the garden." She kneels down, checking out the worms in Cory's grasp.

He finally registers the new person as well and tilts his head.

"Are you Mommy's friend?" He asks, A spark of amusement in his eyes.

"Yes honey, you got it, I don't know if you remember, but we met on our camping trip with Maya at the beginning of summer." Octavia informs him.

"Oh." Cory shrugs his shoulders, suddenly a smile appears on his face, a cheerful glint in his eyes.

"He was actually just dropping something off for me." Octavia tells them. But before she could finish, Cory bolts towards the house with his arms in the air. He's a tornado of youthful energy. Turning to Ryan she finishes her sentence, "why don't you say bye to Chad and I'll meet you boys inside, okay? Oh, can you please take these flowers in for me, hun?"

With that, Ryan heads inside. His energy, a lot more tame than Cory's.

"Sorry," Octavia says as she turns to Chad. "I'm just not quite ready to *really* introduce them yet."

He waves his hand in a forgiving gesture.

"No apologies needed. I get it." He assures her. "Still gonna come over?"

"Yeah," she says with confidence. "You cookin'?" She asks with a smile.

"You bet."

Chad gives a quick look around before moving in on Octavia for what she thinks is a hug. But instead he reaches around her backside, pulls her in and lowers his hands and gives her butt a good tight squeeze before letting go.

"I'll see you tonight," he whispers in her ear before backing away.

The interaction was short but it was powerful. Octavia hasn't been touched like this in a long time. She's experiencing a longing for a physical sensation she didn't know she was missing. The butterflies in her stomach, the warmth in her chest, the tingling in her fingers, these sensations collide all at once leaving her in a whirlwind of romantic lust for this man, more so now than ever before. He's mysterious, dominant, and utterly irresistible.

Octavia, attempts to pull herself together and watches Chad drive away in his heavy duty pick-up truck. She takes some deep breaths as she grounds herself in preparation to head back inside to her boys. On her way back in, she can only hope they didn't see anything. Perfect, they are playing in the living room, there is no way they could have seen Chad's possessive embrace around her. An embrace that has awakened another dormant part of her, the longing for a man's touch. More specifically, a man's dominant touch.

"Hey boys, what do you think?" She asks Ryan and Cory as she sits next to them on the floor with their toys.

"About what, mom?" Ryan asks.

The living room is a big open space. A space where they spend most of their time as a family. There are two toy bins, black with beige bins, that match the decor of the room. The curtains, picked out with care, match the art on the walls. Octavia finds elegance in the black, white and gold colour scheme, which also compliments the beige carpet. The living room is carefully constructed to be appealing as well as convenient, so that she can keep an eye on her boys as she works through the daily grind. Her desk is set up in the corner, although she typically only writes when her boys are away, with friends, family, school or daycare.

"Well, I suppose it's about me hanging out with a man." She explains.

"You mean Chad?" Ryan asks.

"Chad, Chad, Chad," Cory chants, his input isn't overly helpful to the conversation, but he's only six. And besides, Cory likes pretty much everyone.

Ryan has a look on his face as if he has questions he'd like to ask but isn't quite sure how to find the words. Octavia places her hand along the side of his face, a gesture of comfort.

"You know, I will always love you guys more than anything in this world. Nothing can ever change that. You will always be my number one." She looks towards the floor and picks up a dinosaur toy as if she's going to play with it. "I know it might be a little hard to understand right now, but sometimes adults need the company of other adults."

"Is he gonna be our new dad?" Cory pipes up. Sometimes the things he says come as a shock, he's much more in tune and aware than Octavia gives him credit for.

"Oh hun, we haven't decided anything yet. It's much too soon to tell." She assures them.

Ryan, seemingly lost in thought, asks another question.

"But what about dad?"

David. Ryan's question triggers a flashback. How could a man up and leave his family, his wife, baby and unborn child? There is no way

Octavia can explain this to them in a way that they could understand, especially when she struggles to understand it herself. It took her a long time to overcome the fact that he's just up and left without warning and never came back. She can't imagine how the boys could possibly process it. She struggles to find a way to explain to them in a way they could understand. They were so young when they brought Ryan into this world. Whatever his reason for leaving, is inexcusable. Who leaves their family with no explanation? The boys deserve better. Octavia longs for the boys to have a father figure. She just hasn't been able to let anyone in. Not until Chad, that is. There's something about him that is just so alluring. She finds herself wishing for that nuclear family she didn't know she craved.

"Mom?" Ryan, the more serious one of the two boys, asks. Octavia is thrown back by his question. He hasn't really asked a lot about him before. Holding back tears, he looks up at his mom. He was too young to remember his father before he left, but old enough now to know that he isn't around.

"Come here," she opens her arms welcoming Ryan in for a hug. Cory joins too, he wouldn't miss an opportunity for a snuggle. Octavia's heart aches for them. A familiar pang settles in her chest as she honestly just hopes David made the right choice, that he left because staying would have done more harm than good, slowly eroding their peace. She can only hope that one day the boys will understand they aren't the reason he left, that it wasn't their fault, that it won't be a burden they carry at all. She wishes she could just fix everything, make it right again, but she knows she can't. There's only so much she can do, her efforts often feeling inadequate. She's here for them, loving them more than anything. Beyond that, what else can she really do? The question hangs heavy, a quiet burden.

"I can't speak on behalf of someone else, and I can't control that he isn't here. But know that you will always have me. I will always be here and I will always love you, no matter what." She tells them with gentle emotion in her tone.

"I think that if you like Chad then you should date." Ryan says, his voice thick with emotion. Ryan astounds Octavia, he is wise beyond his years. Although her guilt as a mother is strong, this is a burden they shouldn't carry. But she also believes that it is important to teach them about dating, and that dating, relationships, and even separation, is a natural part of growing up.

She gives them each a kiss on their forehead.

"Alright, well I'm gonna go out tonight and you guys will get to hang out with grandma, okay." She motions towards the toys that are already lined up on the floor ready for their dino battle. "But for now, let's play."

CHAPTER SEVEN

Chad's house seems to get more gorgeous every time she sees it. Picture a sprawling green canvas of lawn wrapped around from the front all around to the back, complimenting the rustic beauty of his ranch house. With dessert in hand, she makes her way up the stairs to the front door. She knocks, anxious feelings begin to arise, she hasn't made herself available for another man in years. Her entire motherhood has been dedicated to her kids. This is a big step. No answer. She knocks a little louder, maybe he didn't hear it the first time, it's a pretty big house. After a few minutes with no answer, she decides to open the door, after-all, she was invited here so he knows to expect her arrival.

"Hello," Octavia calls out, stepping foot into the house.

It's silent. The lights are on, it looks as though someone has to be here. The enticing aroma of a freshly cooked meal lingers in the air. But where is he? She's definitely in the right place, his truck is outside. Yet, Chad is nowhere to be seen.

A whimper drifts down the stairs as she enters. What is that?

"Hello?" She calls out once more, her voice echoes through the house. Footsteps pound down the stairs and a dark figure bursts into view. Octavia jumps. "Oh hey, buddy. You startled me." She says, petting the enthusiastic border collie, Zipper. "What are you doing up there pup? Is Chad with you?" She says as she pets him. Balancing the dessert in one hand, she makes her way into the dimly lit kitchen, her eyes scanning for Chad and a safe spot for the treat. She sets the dish down, gives her hands a quick wash, then turns around, taking in the view.

"Oh, wow," she mutters, a look of surprise crossing her face.

"What do you think?" Chad's voice startles her, appearing behind her.

"Oh, there you are. I was beginning to think you weren't here." She turns to face him, her eyes wide with wonder. "This is so romantic." She looks up at him with a sparkle in her eye, "how do you go from not dating to a romantic?" She asks, looking around at the candlelit table and the food that's been prepared ahead of time.

"I suppose I've had a change of heart." He explains, "I've met someone pretty special and I think we could make this work. So, I'd like to try."

She raises an eyebrow. "Are you sure you're not just trying to get into my pants?" She asks, teasingly.

"Well, there's that, too." He grins as he pulls out her chair. At least he's being honest. "But for you, m'lady, I can be a gentleman."

For me? What exactly is that supposed to mean? Is he typically not a gentleman? Is it all for show? Or is he being authentic? Just as fast as the questions come, they vanish. This man who just sat across from her at the table has snatched her undivided attention, how is it that his hair can still look perfect, even after taking off a cowboy hat. One of the extra added bonuses about him not wearing his hat that he looks so sexy in, is the clear view of his captivating green eyes. All throughout dinner, she can't help but find herself drawn into his features, his dark skin, his deep voice, his charm. Chad makes her yearn for a love that she had no idea she truly longed for.

After dinner, Chad stands up and reaches out for Octavia's hand.

"Care to join me for a dance?" He insists, and it doesn't look like he's going to take no for an answer.

With a snap of his finger, the music turns on like magic. One slow song is all it took for her to fall into his warm embrace. Chad looks down, his gaze fixed on her eyes and leans in until his lips meet hers. His lips feel like a warm buzz, kind of like a cinnamon heart, it's got heat but it's sweet. Addictive, even. Octavia reaches her hands up grasping the back of his neck. Chad's hands slowly climb down her back until they reach her thighs, he picks her up. Like an invitation, she wraps her legs around his waist. Their lips break apart but he continues to kiss softly along her neck.

"Can I have you?" Chad whispers into her ear causing the hair on her neck to spike. Octavia's breath hitches, she knows what he means. Is she ready, is this what she wants?

"Yes." A shaky whisper escapes her lips. It seems like too easy of an answer.

With little effort, Chad carries Octavia up the stairs to his bedroom. In one swift motion, he lays her on his bed, her sundress creeping up her legs, his hands follow. He leans in to kiss her, she reaches her arms up and wraps them around his neck pulling him closer.

"Why do I feel a burn when you kiss me?" She asks with a heavy breath.

"Does it bother you?" He whispers back.

"No, I just–"

He cuts her off and stops to look her straight in the eye.

"Then don't ask questions you don't want the answer to."

Nerves dance around in her stomach. There's something so sexy about his mysteriousness, though it makes no sense, she isn't about to break up this moment of intimacy. She wants it too badly. Chad's hands slide down Octavia's hips, he reaches up her dress, grips on to her panties, and gently pulls them down, admiring her body every inch of the way. Simultaneously he unbuckles his jeans and brings his attention back to her face and whispers in her ear as he presses his body into hers.

"Octavia," he says.

"Yeah?"

"Don't forget to breathe."

* * *

"Wow, are you even human?" Octavia accuses, rolling over to meet his gaze.

"What makes you say that?" He asks and mirrors her position.

"Well aside from the fact that I'm allergic to your spit or something? Even though it's not nearly as bad as it was the first time you kissed my hand" She trails off...

"Octavia..." He interrupts.

"Huh? Right, umm because that was some amazing sex." With a gloss in her eyes, she looks up at him. "How do you even know how to do some of those things, I mean..."

"Octavia," he interrupts once more. "There's something that I've been meaning to tell you." She silences him with a gentle touch, her fingertip pressed against his lips.

"Let's just enjoy this," she murmurs, her head finding comfort on his bare chiseled chest. He pulls her closer, his arms wrapping around her.

"Stay with me tonight?" He asks, gently sweeping away a strand of hair from her face.

"You said you have to work, though." she replies, her voice soft.

"Yeah, but not until one," he says. His hand slides down her side and rests on her hip. "I've got to move some equipment tonight. Besides, it will only be a couple of hours. I'll be back before you wake up."

"I don't think I could ever get used to your weird work hours. How do you even get enough rest between work, the animals, and everything else you do?"

"Let's worry about one thing at a time." He says.

"Well, the boys are at a sleepover," she muses, a smile playing on her lips. "So, yeah I can stay."

* * *

Music has always been Octavia's sanctuary. At home the next day, while she's supposed to be working, she finds herself drawn to her phone, and in particular an app that plays her favourite music. The melody that swirls within her demands release. Her phone is a portal to a universe of emotions captured in song. She presses play, a familiar comfort settling over her as she scrolls through her carefully curated playlists. Searching for a melody that reflects the emotions swirling inside her, she finds a song that resonates perfectly. As the music washes over her, it becomes a reflection of their new life, the nervous excitement of a new beginning, the tentative steps towards an unknown future, and the blossoming hope that blooms in her chest. The lyrics seem to speak directly to her heart, capturing the whirlwind of emotions she can't quite articulate herself.

As the last note fades into the twilight, a sigh of contentment escapes her lips. Perhaps she could share this song with Chad. 'Heaven.' The melody became Octavia's secret sanctuary. It plays on repeat in her headphones, a constant echo of the emotions the song unlocks. It's a language only her heart understands, a map leading to the tangled web of feelings Chad evokes within her. Unable to contain her desire to share this newfound voice, Octavia burns a CD for Chad. The song, their unspoken anthem, blazes as a beacon of the swirling emotions it ignites within her.

As soon as they finish up work for the day, they meet back up at his house. She has an hour before she will pick the boys up from daycare.

"I've got something for you." Bashfully approaching Chad, she's so excited to gift this CD to him.

"What's this?" A shimmer of playfulness on his face. "Wait here. I'll be right back." He doesn't hesitate for a second to play the CD. He pulls the truck up to the back of the house and blares it on the speakers.

He gets out of his truck and walks towards Octavia, his boots cutting a rhythmic path across the deck. She admires his nice teal coloured button up and of course, his stetson that casts a cool shade over his face. The space between them charges as Octavia awaits for him to walk up to her. She slowly walks towards him, her sundress glimmering in the light. The tension of the passionate moment is quickly broken.

"Turn that shit down!" The neighbour yells from across the yard prompting Octavia to chuckle.

Chad looks at her, looks at the neighbours, who are well over a hundred feet away, and walks back towards his truck. He gets in and cranks the music up louder, loud enough that it would drown out the sound of anything or anyone nearby. Octavia's heart pounds, a core memory is in creation. Then with a slow deliberate turn, he retraces his steps. Octavia watches, her heart hammering against her ribs, as he closes the distance once more. His steps unfaltering, he tips his Stetson up to reveal his charming smile. He stops in front of her, 'Heaven' playing loudly in the background, the world shrinking to the space between their eyes. Gentle as a summer breeze, he then dips his head, his lips brushing hers in a kiss that tastes of sun-warmed earth and possibility.

Their hands intertwine as if by muscle memory, swaying to the rhythm, a silent testament to a love story as unfiltered and authentic as the song itself. Despite the fact that they have only known each other for a few weeks, they have surprisingly fast-tracked their relationship. They can't seem to keep away from each other. The last few weeks have been filled with highs and lows, mostly highs. Each day paints a vivid picture of the bond that's been growing between them.

CHAPTER EIGHT

Several more weeks fly by in a whirlwind of blossoming love and connection. Each day that goes by, she falls for him even more. Morning texts become routine, weekend get togethers are woven seamlessly into their schedules. Octavia is a mom first, always. But her spare moments are mainly shared with Chad. Octavia, basking in the glow of newfound 'love', has let down her guard completely. Chad feels like a dream come true, an unexpected romance that has swept her off her feet. But even in this blissful state, a tiny seed of doubt begins to sprout. In the back of her mind, she still questions if this is real, if it's too good to be true. With a determined glint in her eyes, she reaches for her phone.

Hey Chad, I've been having such a great time with you! Maybe we could get together this weekend?

Pausing, she rereads the message. It feels tame, almost impersonal. Taking a deep breath, she adds a single, daring sentence. A sentence that sent a jolt of nervous excitement through her.

Just the two of us. I've been thinking about you and could really use some Chad time, if you know what I mean.

Her thumb hovers over the send button. Is this too forward? The question lingers, a tiny seed of doubt threatening to blossom. But she pushes it aside. This is how she feels, and Chad deserves her honesty. With a final surge of courage, she hits send.

The message speeds through the digital ether, carrying with it the weight of her unspoken emotions. Now, all she can do is wait, the silence stretching into an eternity as she stares at the blinking cursor on her phone screen. A single thought echoes in her mind; the weekend can't come soon enough. Finally, it buzzes. A message from Chad, as expected. Her heart hammers in her chest as she opens it, eager to see his response.

I've got dinner plans this weekend. I haven't asked yet but I am hoping you will join me.

It doesn't address the intimacy she's hoping for but relief comforts her as she reads his message. His desire to connect matches her own. The week passes in a blur, their connection deepening with each shared message. Octavia's writing, typically a constant, now takes a backseat, with Chad a new priority. A small sacrifice, perhaps, but one made willingly, for the chance to write a new chapter in her life. A chance to grow her family, a man to lean on, and a male role model for her boys.

Actually, I have a better idea. Come over tonight? Have some of that one on one time before the dinner tomorrow.. Chad's message stares at her as she glances down at her phone. It's tempting. It's exactly what she wants. Can she make it work, though? A little heads up would have gone a long way but she also loves the spontaneity of their relationship. With a quick text to Maya the plan is set. She can always count on Maya, who's agreed to babysit for the night.

* * *

Chad is in the shower when Octavia arrives. Her nerves prickle with a mixture of excitement and apprehension. The thought of surprising him, of walking in on him in the steamy confines of the bathroom, both thrills and terrifies her. But the image of water cascading down his sculpted muscles, the sight of him glistening with droplets, a chance to see him naked... she can't resist. She slowly pushes open the bathroom door, the humid air and the sound of the rushing water hitting her like a wave. She slowly and quietly creeps into the bathroom, closing the door behind her with a soft click.

She pulls back the shower curtain ever so slightly, catching a glimpse of Chad's nude body. His man part is something to brag about. But she wouldn't, she's a lady. Butterflies erupt in her stomach, fluttering wildly. He's rinsing his hair out, with his eyes closed. A mischievous smile tugs at her lips as she closes the curtain with a soft sigh. She reaches up the back of her dress and unzips it. The dress slides down her slender, sunkissed body, pooling at her feet, followed by the whisper of her panties hitting the floor.

The room is steamy and warm. Octavia quietly opens up the curtain once again, this time from the other end. Chad stands with his back to her, seemingly oblivious to her presence. With a silent grace, she lifts her feet, gliding into the shower beside him. Her hands, cool against his warm skin, slowly reach out, wrapping around his waist. Chad, startled, whips his head around, his eyes widening in surprise. Water droplets fly from his hair as he spins, his gaze locking onto Octavia standing inches from him. A slow smile spreads across his face, a playful glint in his eyes. Octavia looks up, their gazes locking. A slow, predatory smile spreads across her lips. She reaches down, her hand trailing along his front side, grabbing onto what feels like an oversized banana, marking the beginning of an intimate and passionate night.

* * *

Octavia lies in bed, she always struggles to sleep soundly in new settings. Especially with Chad, it doesn't take much to get her adrenaline going when they are intimate, and it takes a while to come down. She drifts off but is awoken by every little sound. It doesn't help that her adrenaline is on high alert after being intimate with Chad, who's sound asleep by the way. His brawny arm is sprawled across her waist, a comforting weight against her. She rolls over, eyes landing on the glowing numbers of the alarm clock: 11:30. Octavia grabs her phone and settles in, jotting down any ideas that spring into her mind. It's become a ritual, this late-night writing, as a way to quiet the restless thoughts that always seem to surface when sleep eludes her.

She's always been great with words and wants to share, in her own way, how amazing she feels and how deeply she feels about Chad. With a surge of inspiration, her fingers fly across the keyboard, the words flowing freely onto the screen, a romantic gesture for him when he awakes.

> *Divine delight. As I lay here in the warmth of my comfortably tucked blanket, I look up only to see the clear skies; peace calms my soul.*
> *The moon, shines down on the tips of the luscious green trees; joy vibrates through every cell of my being.*
> *The brisk breeze, flows softly through the slightly open window, ever so gently caressing my skin with a refreshing wave of gratitude.*
> *The birds sing a graceful song of harmony while thoughts of my love fill my mind, body, and soul with contentment.*
> *Divine delight. Warmth. A taste of heaven.*

"Moonlight Serenade" she titles it, a love note flying on the wings of the night. She hits send.

It speaks of the joy that paints her world with Chad, the way his presence fills her with a sense of peaceful contentment. It hints at dreams of a future intertwined, a future brimming with anticipation for all that awaits them. Sending the poem with a loving tap, Octavia can't help but smile, she peaks over at him with a grin and love in her eyes. The intense romance between Octavia and Chad is still in its fiery first act. Their hands seem permanently magnetized, a constant hum of desire. She's grown accustomed to the heat that blooms on her skin after their encounters, a tingling brand she secretly cherishes. It fuels the fantasy that she's special, the only one who could ignite such passion in Chad. In her mind, it mirrors the inferno he feels for her; a possessive love that echoes her own. They are two souls intertwined, a blissful dream she clings to fiercely.

The peaceful silence is broken by the buzz of Chad's phone vibrating vigorously against the wooden nightstand. The vibrating device is a jarring intrusion in the otherwise tranquil night. It startles her. Chad reaches out blindly for the phone, his fingers fumbling on the nightstand.

"You have got to be kidding me." He groans, his eyes fluttering open. He squints at the phone, a look of annoyance crossing his face.

"Who's calling at this hour?" Octavia asks, concern laced in her voice.

Chad sighs, rubbing a hand over his face. "Sorry, babygirl, it's work. They need an extra hand."

What kind of job calls in the middle of the night for an extra hand? She's aware that he moves heavy machinery as a part time gig, but how demanding is it, really? Is it actually *work* that he's going to? Or could it be something else entirely? She really has no reason to doubt him so she accepts the explanation.

Chad crawls out of bed and heads downstairs to get ready for work. Before he leaves, he makes his way back up the stairs to give Octavia a gentle kiss on the forehead. She feels the tingle of his lips against her skin before it fades, leaving behind a lingering warmth. She gets up to use the washroom before heading back to bed. On her way out she catches a glance of herself in the mirror. She leans in closer, her breath misting the cool glass. Faint red marks, like faint love bites, circle her neck. Octavia suddenly feels lightheaded, a dizzying sensation washing over her. The world tilts slightly, and a high-pitched ringing fills her ears, like tinnitus, drowning out the gentle sounds of the night. Fear, cold and clammy, grips her. This isn't normal. She takes a deep breath, trying to steady herself. The dizziness passes as quickly as it came, leaving her feeling shaken and confused. What had just happened? Was it just a momentary lapse, or was something else at play? The ringing in her ears subsides, leaving her feeling drained and exhausted. She feels a powerful urge to retreat, to escape back into the warmth and safety of the bed. Perhaps after a good rest she will feel much better.

Back in bed, she glances at the alarm clock; 12:55. She lays there for what feels like an eternity, trying to fall asleep. She feels fine. Whatever that was, was short lived. Not enough to dwell on for too long. Moments after she finally dozes off, the sound of thunder claps through her dream, BANG... her eyes are rapidly moving, BANG, BANG. With a racing heart she shoots up right out of her sleep. It's dark, she gives her eyes a minute to adjust and attempts to steady her breath. It's silent, the night is silent.

It's not raining, there is no storm.

It had to be another one of those vivid dreams she regularly gets. Although she doesn't always hear noise in her sleep, she is used to vivid night terrors. She's had them for as long as she can remember. That must have been what it was. Or could it have been Zipper? No, Chad takes him to work with him. In any case, she decides to get up and look around, anyway.

Her feet touch the cold hardwood floor, a shiver is sent up her back. Her first move is to turn on the light in each room she enters. She checks upstairs, and downstairs, the doors are locked, there's no way anyone could get in. There is absolutely nothing, as far as she can tell, that is out of the ordinary. It's likely all in her head, or possibly even the sounds of this old house shifting. Whatever it was, it probably isn't as dramatic as her mind made it out to be.

With the lights out, she crawls back into bed. If she doesn't get back to sleep, she's going to have a rough day with the boys tomorrow. A nap will definitely be in order. She lies in bed, listening to the sounds of the house, still a little spooked, unsure if she will even be able to fall back to sleep. She drifts in and out of consciousness, wondering if she's getting any kind of real sleep at all.

Around five a.m. she jumps awake by yet another startling sound. Footsteps. Footsteps in the room, footsteps beside the bed, footsteps beside her.

CHAPTER NINE

Spooked, she shoots up in the bed looking around for the source of the noise, her nerves jittering and her breath fast. A figure stands at the foot of the bed, a shadow, a person? Fear haunts every cell in Octavia's body, she's frozen, unable to move. The figure remains motionless, an eerie stillness in the room. It's dark, almost shadow like. Her eyes, wide and terrified, strain in the darkness. Fear holds her captive, unable to blink, as if the slightest movement would shatter the fragile silence and unleash whatever horror lurks within the shadows. After what feels like a full minute, the figure begins to fade, as if it's dissolving into thin air, the edges blur and soften until it's gone, vanishing without a trace. Octavia lies there, her body trembling, the scent of dust and fear clinging to her like a shroud. Every creak of the house sends a fresh wave of terror crashing over her. The silence, now deafening, presses down on her, heavy and suffocating.

With trembling hands, Octavia finds her phone and activates the flashlight. The sudden beam of light cuts through the darkness, illuminating the room. Her heart racing in her chest, each beat a deafening explosion in the sudden silence. Her skin prickles, and a shiver, cold and clammy, runs down her spine. She scans the room frantically, her eyes wide with fear. Nothing seems out of place. A drawer in the tall dresser gapes open, a reminder of Chad's hurried departure. The floor is surprisingly tidy. The closet door remains firmly shut. Despite the sudden illumination, an eerie stillness pervades the room. Octavia feels a sense of unease, a tingling sensation on the back of her neck that tells her she's not alone, even though logic dictates otherwise.

The first rays of dawn begin to creep through the window. Octavia, still shaken, dials 911, her finger hovering over the send button, ready to press in an instant. With trembling hands, she throws on some clothes, the phone clutched tightly in her grasp, a silent guardian against the unseen threat.

Once dressed, she stands beside the bed, fearful that something might be under the bed, ready to pounce at any second. She takes the risk, taking another frantic look around the room. She peeks into the hallway, her eyes straining in the dim light, but sees nothing. The feeling of being watched intensifies. It could all be her imagination, another night terror plaguing her sleep, but the fear that crutches onto her is too real, too visceral to ignore. With a surge of adrenaline, she bolts for the front door, the icy grip of fear urging her to flee. Feeling as if someone is breathing down her neck, she scrambles into her car, slamming the door shut behind her.

In the car, a slight sense of calm begins to wash over her. With a quick peak into the back seat, she makes sure no one or no thing is occupying the rear. As she drives away, she stares at the house. It looks... peaceful, almost idyllic, bathed in the soft morning light.

"Ridiculous," she mutters to herself, shaking her head. Just a bad dream, a product of an overactive imagination. These dreams could be the source of really enticing thrillers, but she prefers to write romance and more of the 'light' stuff instead. These kinds of experiences or thoughts are just a little too real and scary for her.

She longs for her own bed, for the familiar scent of her sheets, for the promise of a few hours of undisturbed sleep before her boys come home. If she's able to.

* * *

"Mom!" Cory shouts as he and Ryan burst through the front door, backpacks tumbling to the floor.

"Hey guys," Octavia manages a smile, always excited to see her boys, though a little tired this morning. She'd decided to relax on the couch while she waited for them. She sits up and opens her arms for a welcoming hug.

"Did you have a sleepover in the living room last night?" Ryan asks, his eyes gleaming with curiosity.

"Well, I didn't sleep very well last night and am kind of tired, so I was thinking that maybe we can have a lazy day today, watch some movies, and have some treats. What do you guys think?" She asks, quickly trying to divert their attention. "How about you guys put your bags away and go grab your blankets and stuffies."

She kisses them both on the cheek, watching them disappear down the hallway with a mixture of relief and a pang of guilt. Lazy days are rare luxuries, and she knew they'd want to make the most of it. Their laughter echoes through the house.

"Chad keep you up all night?" Maya asks with a grin on her face as she steps in and closes the door behind her.

"I think my dreams are getting worse," Octavia admits, a hint of unease in her voice.

Maya, who knows Octavia has always been a vivid dreamer, doesn't seem too surprised.

"Worse how, exactly?" she asks, settling onto the couch beside Octavia.

"Do you remember the time I told you about the conversation I had with the doctor about sleep paralysis?" She asks Maya. "I think that happened last night while I was at Chad's. It was so real and I was really scared. I thought that there was actually someone in the house."

"Could it have been Chad?" Maya asks, completely captivated by her story, her eyes filled with a mixture of curiosity and concern.

"It couldn't have been. He got called into work," she explains, her voice dropping to a whisper.

"Work? Who gets called into work in the middle of the night?" Maya questions. "What would he even be doing?"

"Something to do with moving equipment, maybe farm stuff, I don't know, he never really goes into detail," Octavia explains, shrugging her shoulders. "But I did some research this morning when I got home and there is this thing called hypno-something hallucinations. And–"

"Got it, Mommy!" Cory exclaims, as he makes his way into the living room arms full of 'lazy-day' items. Nearly tripping over his own blanket, he scatters toys and pillows across the living room floor.

"Good job, buddy!" Octavia praises him with a smile before turning her attention back to Maya.

"Needless to say, this is why I am so tired today, so we're just going to relax before I go to dinner with him tonight."

"I think that we should definitely continue this conversation later." Maya suggests, standing up.

"Thanks so much for watching the boys." Octavia says, "You really are a lifesaver."

CHAPTER TEN

The anticipation of the dinner grows. Octavia tries to prepare herself mentally, but the anxiety she feels is too real. Chad's social life is so much more active than hers. As much as she enjoys being involved in Chad's world, it can be overwhelming. Parties, dinners, continuous social gatherings, it's out of her norm. Despite her lazy day activities and short nap, she's still feeling the exhaustion from that lack of sleep from the night before.

Waiting for Chad's truck to pull up in front of her house, Octavia adjusts her lipstick in the hallway mirror. She's tired but she's also nervous to meet one of Chad's friends, Lilah. He's mentioned her a few times over text, referring to her as a *good friend*, and apparently since Chad 'doesn't date', he needs her approval. Apparently, that's not just a girl thing, who would have guessed? Unease begins to settle.

What if Lilah doesn't approve of her? And approve of what? How much weight does her approval really have? She and Chad have already established their connection, so what does it matter what Lilah thinks? Now, more so than ever she's curious to learn who this Lilah is and what she really means to Chad. The house is quiet, a stillness that amplifies the drumbeat of Octavia's heart. She glances at her reflection one last time, her eyes wide with a mix of fear and determination. She takes a deep breath and turns away. As she slips into her heels, she feels a pang of self-doubt. This is a world so far removed from her usual routine. But she's going to embrace the unknown and cherish the memories it will bring. For Chad, she's willing to step outside of her comfort zone.

Chad appears at her door, looking handsome and relaxed, as usual.

"You look amazing." He says and hands her a single red rose with bright white specs.

His confidence is infectious and Octavia tries to absorb it. She figures if she's going to be the woman on his arm, she can play the part and do her best to be as confident and charming as he is. With a forced smile, she meets his gaze.

"Are you ready m'lady?" he asks, his hand outstretched. She nods, her hand trembling slightly as she places it in his.

The drive to the restaurant is filled with a tense silence. Octavia tries to focus on the passing scenery, as her mind processes her anxious thoughts. She fidgets with her hair – as she typically does when she's nervous. She glances at Chad, who seems oblivious to her turmoil. He's humming along to the music, his expression carefree. Now is the time to ask questions, any one of the hundreds that are popping into her head. But her voice is stuck, it's as if there's an invisible wall the words are unable to pass. As they pull up to the restaurant, her stomach churns. It's the fanciest restaurant in town.

"You're so quiet tonight," Chad puts the truck in park and asks. "There's no reason to be nervous, ya know."

A brush of heat creeps into Octavia's cheeks.

"Oh, I know. I'm just really tired. I–"

"I'm so sorry for leaving you last night." Chad interrupts. His voice filled with genuine remorse.

"Oh, no. It's okay, I..." Octavia hesitates, unsure whether to risk telling him and risk the embarrassment of being scared of her own dreams. Perhaps it will add a layer of understanding. Maybe if she tells him, he will understand why she left before he got home. "I just had a bad dream and wanted to be in my own bed, is all."

"You had a dream so bad that caused you to leave?" Chad asks as he furrows his brow in concern. "Octavia, you know you can talk to me about anything, right?"

She looks up at him, her eyes searching for his understanding.

"I thought I saw something, I just got a little spooked. But it was just a dream. It's really no big deal," she pauses. "But I'm ready to go in, now." she says in an attempt to change the subject.

Chad's glance lingers uncomfortably long, as if he's deep in thought.

"I'm sorry I wasn't there for you." Chad says, finally breaking the silence.

She offers him a soft, forgiving smile. And taking a deep breath, she steps out of the truck.

Chad's arm encircles her shoulders, offering a comforting warmth. His touch and attention dissipate her worries like unfamiliar magic. They open the front door revealing a bustling crowd of people. Laughter and clinking glasses fill the air, igniting a new surge of panic within her. This is much busier than she had anticipated. She clings to Chad's arm, her grip tightening as they step inside, but it does little to quell her rising anxiety.

The noise level escalates as they enter the main room. The hum of conversation and mixture of sounds a busy restaurant makes creates a dizzying cacophony. Seems like everyone who's meant to be here, already is. Octavia looks around, searching for anything that gives her comfort. Familiarity, anything. People turn to look at them, their eyes scanning Octavia from head to toe. A comforting warmth settles over her hand, drawing her gaze downward. Chad's hand, large and steady, covers hers. Their eyes meet and a sense of calm washes over her. The frantic pounding of her heart slows, her mind clears. In this moment, the world fades away, leaving only the two of them. He must have sensed her distress. She graciously welcomes this strange allure that he has on her. A soft smile graces her lips, a silent thank you for his calming presence.

They're ushered to their table, a lively group already engaged in animated conversation. Chad guides her towards the commotion, introductions flying thick and fast. Names and faces blur together in a dizzying whirlwind. She will never remember any of these names. None of them are Lilah though. They find their seat next to another couple, she doesn't know them, but Chad seems to. Somehow, he seems to know a lot of these people. An unwelcome look is shot towards Octavia from across the table. She manages a weak smile and a polite nod, her mind racing with questions as to why she is even here. A glass of champagne is pressed into her hand. She takes a sip, the bubbly liquid doing little to soothe her frayed nerves. A wave of self-doubt washes over her. She doesn't belong here, she's a fish out of water, struggling to breathe in this unfamiliar world.

Octavia's grip on Chad's arm tightens as the intensity of the scrutiny grows. She feels a lump forming in her throat, her smile faltering. The noise of the party seems to amplify, each conversation a distant, echoing blur. Her gaze darts around the room, seeking an escape, or something familiar to cling on to. But there is none. Overwhelmed by the sensation of drowning, she turns to Chad. His face is inches from hers, and in his eyes, she sees a flicker of concern. His grip on her hand tightens, offering a silent anchor in the storm of her anxiety. That's right, she's here for him. She wants to be a part of his world, and if this is what it entails, she will get through it. Just as her mouth opens to speak to him, the front door swings open, dragging his attention away. An utterly stunning woman enters the room. Chad's face lights up as he releases Octavia's hand and strides towards the newcomer.

"Lilah!" he exclaims, his voice filled with nervous excitement.

Octavia feels a pang of disappointment as she watches him embrace this woman. This is the woman he's been eager to impress, the reason for this uncomfortable gathering. A wave of obligation washes over her, she's agreed to come, and she must see it through. Chad turns back to Octavia, a proud smile plastered on his face.

"Octavia, this is Lilah. Lilah, this is my girlfriend, Octavia."

His girlfriend? A wave of realization washes over her. He really *does* like her. A strange mix of emotions swirl within her; a hint of jealousy, a flicker of hope, and a pang of guilt for her initial reluctance to join the lively gathering in the first place. He really does want her here.

Lilah, with long, straight black hair that cascades down her back, extends a perfectly manicured hand. She can't be much older than Chad, if at all. Her eyes are a striking emerald, oddly, just like Chad's. Except her skin colour is pale white. His sister maybe? He hasn't mentioned anything about her being a sister. Come to think of it, he hasn't mentioned any siblings at all. Octavia manages a weak smile and reaches out for a gentle hand shake.

"It's a pleasure to meet you," Lilah says, her voice barely audible over the din.

As the two women exchange pleasantries, Octavia feels a surge of inadequacy. It isn't because she thinks this woman is stunning, but because she knows how much Chad values her. The contrast between their worlds is staggering, and she worries that Lilah might not understand the depth of her connection with Chad. Lilah, with her effortless charm and sophisticated demeanor, seems to glide through the room like a seasoned socialite making her rounds before settling in. Lilah takes a seat next to Chad after making her round of greetings. Octavia, on the other hand, feels like a deer caught in headlights, struggling to keep up with the conversation. She forces a smile, hoping it doesn't look as strained as she feels.

Chad, clearly sensing her discomfort, steps in.

"Octavia's a brilliant author," he says, his voice filled with pride. "She's got a few best sellers out. And a book that is about to be published as well."

Octavia's heart warms at his support. She manages a grateful smile, grateful for the change of subject. Perhaps she can salvage the evening after all.

Lilah's eyes light up with interest.

"An author? How fascinating."

Octavia manages a small smile. "It's not as glamorous as it sounds," she replies modestly. "But I'm passionate about it."

"Anything that I would know?" Lilah asks.

"I'm not sure. I use a pen name." She says, tucking a piece of hair behind her ear. "I don't share it with others."

Chad squeezes her hand reassuringly, turns to her and offers a wink.

A comfortable silence settles over the group as they sip their drinks. Octavia focuses on keeping her breathing steady. She's starting to feel a little more at ease. With Chad by her side, maybe this isn't going to be as bad as she thought.

Nearing the end of the evening, about half of the people have already left. Octavia turns towards Chad after a long evening of catching up with his friends. Maybe it's the time, or the tired look on her face, but he already knows what she's about to say,

"Alright, I'll get the check. Be right back."

She smiles graciously. "Okay, I'm just gonna use the washroom before we go."

On her way out of the washroom, she notices Chad and Lilah in the lobby talking. Lilah looks upset. She's too far to make out any words, but Octavia feels compelled to watch. She walks towards their table to grab her jacket. Taking her time gathering her items, she continues to glance over at them. It looks as though Lilah is giving him heck for something. What could she possibly have to give him heck for? The nervous pit in Octavia's stomach evolves into anger. Who does this woman think she is?

Octavia furrows her brow and slings her purse over her shoulder.

Before she gets the chance to stride over, she watches Lilah's demeanor change, her eyes flashing from emerald to crimson just before she storms out of the restaurant. Octavia freezes, stunned, trying to process what she just saw.

She turns back to the table, feigning nonchalance, as she pretends to tidy up the napkins, careful not to let Chad see the shock etched on her face.

"Hey, are you ready?" Chad asks as he approaches her.

She turns to him, forcing a smile that feels stiff and unnatural. "Yep."

They make their way out of the restaurant, the tension feels strained between them. Chad stops abruptly, his gaze fixed on Octavia. He lets out a sigh, the sound heavy with unspoken emotions.

"Will you stay with me again tonight?" Chad asks, his voice is low and uncertain, and a wave of concern washes over her.

"Is everything okay?" she asks, her voice soft, her eyes search his face for any sign of distress. A wave of unease runs through her. Did she say something wrong? Had her presence somehow caused a rift between them? Was she the reason for his and Lilah's tension?

"What was Lilah upset about?" She questions, her voice laced with concern.

Chad's eyes widen. Clearly he thought they were more discreet.

"Um, yeah. Lilah?" He asks, with a kittling brow.

"She looked upset," she says, her voice carefully neutral, trying to suppress the urge to ask him about the strange, seemingly supernatural, shift in Lilah's eyes.

"Yeah, don't worry about that, it's just a misunderstanding." His voice is gentle. "Let's focus on what's important."

Octavia shifts her head back, unsure what he's referring to.

Chad leans in closer, his eyes gleaming with a mischievous glint.

"You and me, of course," he says, his voice a low rumble. He reaches down, his hand brushing against her hip. A shiver, involuntary and thrilling, runs down her spine. His gaze holds hers, a playful glint in his eyes. She finds herself inexplicably drawn to him. He leans in, his lips hovering just inches from hers, and whispers, "just us. Alone. In my big empty bed."

Octavia feels a sudden rush of heat, her breath hitches in her throat.

"That... sounds... amazing." She manages to whisper back as his lips meet with hers, her voice barely audible.

"Well then, what are we waiting for?" He says, his voice laced with a playful challenge. "We could go for round two."

A voice of reason takes over her.

"No, I have to get home, the boys are expecting me." She says, her voice firm, though a pang of regret shoots through her.

CHAPTER ELEVEN

Last night was something else. What Octavia witnessed was something she's never seen before. She's unsure of how to process it. Does she continue to question Chad about Lilah? He introduced her as his *girlfriend*. She has all the feels for him and clearly he does, too. And in a strange way, the enigma holds a bit of an exciting allure, like a mystery that's begging to be solved. Lilah's eye's, like a trick of the mind, had changed colour. It was surreal. It didn't seem to faze Chad at all, so he must already be aware of what it is, or what *she* is. But what could she be if anything other than human? Because humans obviously can't do that. So what can? She rubs her temples, a frown creasing her brow. Perhaps she's dramatizing the situation due to her lack of sleep and intense dreams. It happens, right? It's possible to get a little freaked out and see things that aren't there.

The buzz of her phone interrupts her train of thought.

Hey gorgeous, whatcha wearin? Okay, so Chad isn't shy, like at all.

She looks past her phone, eyes her body up and down. Well she's not going to tell him that she's in shorts and a baggy t-shirt. She doesn't know how she's going to answer that text at all. Rather, she ties a knot into her shirt to highlight her form, fixes her hair, and snaps a selfie. Okay, so she snaps about ten selfie's, then sends him the best one.

You're so beautiful. He replies.

The warmth of Chad's word, and his touch, she recalls, the calm that pervades her when he does, reminds her that she isn't alone in this. What happened last night isn't enough to scare her off. There are answers to explain it, and over time, she will find them. But for now, she's going to focus on Chad and the potential of their new relationship. After-all, she's now his girlfriend. A sense of giddiness runs through her.

Thank-you for being there for me last night while I was nervous. Big outings usually aren't my thing. But I appreciate your calm energy and staying by my side all through it. I can't wait to hang out again. Maybe this week? Just the two of us? She looks it over one more time before sending it to Chad.

His reply is not immediate. The minutes stretch into hours and based on their previous conversations, this is unusual. She's aware that cowboy life is demanding tending to animals and what not. Rather than allow her doubt get the best of her, she decides to focus on her boys, inviting them to play a board game with her, 'Guess Who', one of their favourites. The sounds of her boy's voices and laughter is always enough to distract her from anything else in the world.

It's nearly the afternoon when his reply comes through. The boys play in the yard under Octavia's watchful eye. But instead of the enthusiastic reply she craves, a single, cryptic message fills the screen:

Sounds great, Octavia. But this week might not be possible. Something just came up. Let's talk soon?

What 'something' could come up so suddenly? They've been texting continuously for weeks straight and he hadn't mentioned anything, not outside the usual day to day life. Is it a legitimate issue, or a veiled rejection? Could it have anything to do with last night, with Lilah? Could Octavia be the reason she was so upset last night? What could Lilah possibly have against her that would cause Chad to distance himself? A thousand questions swirl in her mind, unanswered and unsettling. As Octavia stares at the message, a single thought stands out amongst the rest, is this the start of a beautiful love story, or the beginning of a heartbreaking goodbye?

Determined to get some answers, Octavia types a reply, her fingers slightly trembling.

Hey Chad, that's a bummer! Is everything alright? Maybe we can reschedule for another night?

Hitting send, she sighs and sets her phone down beside her. The wait stretches on, each passing minute amplifying her unease.

Finally, another text prompts her phone to buzz.

Things are a bit crazy right now. Let's talk about it later this week, okay?

Feeling defeated, she tosses onto the couch her phone and carries on with her day. What kind of weight does the word *girlfriend* carry anyway if he isn't even going to explain himself to her?

* * *

The silence stretches between Octavia and Chad, a growing distance that mirrors the space now forming in their connection. Days turn into a week, with no further messages or calls. She swings between anger and despair. Is this really how it ends? Discarded after only a few weeks together, left with unanswered questions and a heart full of doubt?

She replays their conversations and their lingering glances, searching for any clue that might explain his sudden withdrawal. Has she misread the signs entirely? Is the spark she felt just a figment of her imagination? Maybe he's simply looking only for a short fling. Maybe all he's really after is getting laid. Well, he's got that so he's just going to ghost her now? She's positive their spark is something more, yet is now questioning if she's misread the situation entirely. Surely, this all couldn't be because of Lilah, or... maybe there's more to Lilah and their 'relationship' than he's let on.

She deserves some answers. Introducing someone as your girlfriend, then ghosting them is just plain wrong. It brings up so much of what David had put her through. She's not sure if she can bear a repeat. She focuses her energy into her work, a feeble attempt at a distraction.

Knock, knock.

The sudden abrupt knocking this late afternoon startles Octavia, interrupting her chance to send the text. Probably for the best, as she's spiraling a little bit. Maybe the unknown guest will be a welcome distraction.

"Ben, hey." She greets him with a hint of surprise.

"Hey," he smiles, then just as quickly shoots a confused look in her direction. "You're... not ready."

An obvious statement. She looks at him like a deer in the headlights, unsure of what he's referring to.

"My buddy's dinner party. You're my plus one, remember? We confirmed it just a couple of days ago."

"Oh right," her hand flies up to her forehead. "I'm so sorry! I got so caught up in writing that it completely slipped my mind. Just give me a few minutes and I'll freshen up." She explains, not sure she even believes her half truth. "Come in, it won't take long."

Irritation spikes. Although Ben has nothing to do with Chad ignoring her for the past week, she can't help but wish she were alone. But he's not the reason she feels stuck in this whirlwind of emotions. Guilt churns in her stomach.

"How are you anyway? Are you still working on that same novel?" He asks as she hands him the glass. Same novel? What does that even mean? I mean it's been a year already and it's still not perfect. This novel has been a bitch to write but she's not going to tell him that.

"Yeah, it's coming along," she explains. "I'll be right back, just gonna get dressed."

"Will we be picking up the boys?" Ben asks.

"No, my mom will be picking them up today. It was already planned but for some reason I didn't put two and two together. I'm sorry, I completely forgot about tonight."

The drive to dinner is awkward. Octavia finds solace in staring out the window, watching the buildings and the trees pass by. It's not necessarily unusual to sit in silence, considering Octavia and Ben have a long history, but somehow Ben can always sense when she's off.

"Is everything alright?" He asks, breaking the silence. "You're pretty quiet tonight."

"Yeah, I'm just tired." She tells him. Tired, or preoccupied? Probably a little of both. The restaurant is in sight.

"Octavia," Ben begins, followed by a pause. "We've known each other for a long time. It isn't a coincidence that I invited you to hang out with me. You must know that, right?"

"What do you mean?" She questions. The evening is quiet. All that can be heard outside of their own voices is the sound of Ben's old truck as they sit idle in the parking lot.

"We've been friends for a long time. I enjoy going out with you." He hesitates, searching for the right words. "I... We have so much fun together, don't we?"

"Of course we do." Her answer is immediate. "How is that even a question?"

Ben takes his seatbelt off and shifts his body to face her direction. "What's got your attention?" He asks abruptly. "I know you better than anyone and you're not here with me."

They sit in silence a little longer. Octavia's words echo in her mind: Do I tell him? Will he understand? Of course he will, he's always been supportive.

"You know that guy we met camping? Chad? We've been texting and hanging out... Well, we were." She finally blurts out.

"*Chad*?" Ben asks abruptly. "Cowboy Chad?"

"Yeah? Why."

"Is he the reason you haven't been texting me much lately?" He asks.

"That's not fair, Ben."

"I saw you the night we met them. The way you looked at him." He accuses. "So I guess I can't say I'm surprised." Ben turns back toward the steering wheel and rests his arm on top.

"Well, I'm not even sure he wants to see me again. He hasn't messaged me all week." She continues to tell him. "It sucks because I liked the way he made me feel."

"What do you mean, *feel*?" He challenges. "You just met the guy. What's it been, like a week?" He asks with judgement laced in his eyes.

"Actually, it's been more like five." She iterates, her voice a shade too tight, her gaze darting away from his. "And he makes me feel a certain way." She continues, attempting to force a path through the sudden, suffocating awkwardness that's enveloped them. "I'm sorry but I don't feel comfortable talking about it anymore."

"Talking about it, or talking to *me*?" Ben asks, his eyebrows drawing together in a bewildered furrow, his tone carrying a distinct edge of hurt.

He's got a point. A hot flush prickles Octavia's cheeks as she's beginning to realize that she doesn't want to tell Ben about her burgeoning feelings for another man, especially since she holds so much respect for him. He clearly isn't taking it well.

"I... I can't really explain it." She admits, her voice dropping to a barely audible murmur, the words feeling too fragile to speak aloud.

"I can't tell you what to do, Octavia, but just be careful." He says, his voice a low, gravelly rumble, a heavy undertone of concern now unmistakable beneath the casual phrasing.

"Be careful? What is that supposed to mean? I know how to take care of myself." She shoots back, her own voice sharper than intended, a defensive wall slamming up.

He shrugs, his gaze deliberately sweeping over her shoulder, avoiding her eyes. "Just... be cautious. There was just something kinda weird about him, the way he stared at you that night... And I don't want to see you getting hurt."

Octavia lets out a frustrated groan, the sound caught somewhere between annoyance and despair.

"Well, don't worry," she assumes, the words tinged with a brittle, self-deprecating edge, "because he might be done with me."

"Octavia–" Ben starts, a plea in his tone.

"Ben, can we just go in and get through dinner please?" She cuts him off abruptly, her voice firm and final, shutting down the conversation before it can unravel further.

CHAPTER TWELVE

O ctavia is unable to bear the silence any longer. She refuses to go another day without some kind of explanation. One man has vanished from her life before, she won't let the same thing happen again. At the very least, she deserves an answer. Deciding to take matters into her own hands, she dials Chad's number, her heart racing. After a few rings, his voicemail picks up. It's been five weeks since they've met, there's an obvious connection, an obvious yearning for each other. The texting, the phone calls, the playful banter, the lingering glances, it's all there. Well, it was there.

What's his angle now? Could it have anything to do with the dinner with his friends last week? Did she embarrass him? Taking a deep breath, she forces her voice to remain steady as she calls him up.

"Hey Chad, it's Octavia. I just wanted to see how you're doing and maybe get some clarification on what happened with our plans. No pressure to reply if you're busy, but I would appreciate hearing from you."

With a shaky finger, she ends the call, the silence on the other end heavier than any words could express. Now, all she can do is wait, a fragile hope flickers amidst the growing storm of uncertainty.

It isn't long before a notification buzzes on Octavia's phone. A single text message from Chad breaks the silence that has stretched on for what feels like an eternity. Her fingers tremble slightly as she unlocks the screen, a mixture of apprehension and cautious hope blooms in her chest. *Hey Octavia,* the message begins, the informality is hardly a relief.

Listen, things have been a mess on my end lately. I owe you an explanation for bailing on our plans, and for the radio silence. Work has been crazy and I've been working long hours. Look, I really enjoyed our time together last week. Would you be up for grabbing coffee sometime this week?

Octavia rereads the message several times, dissecting each word, searching for the hidden meaning. A part of her longs to believe him, to accept his explanation and rekindle the spark they shared. But another part, a more cautious voice, whispers warnings. Is this just another excuse, another delay tactic? Taking a deep breath, she decides honesty is the best course of action. Her fingers fly across the screen, composing a reply that reflects both her desire for clarity and her lingering feelings for him.

Hey, thanks for getting back to me. I appreciate you explaining things, even if it doesn't quite answer all my questions. Coffee sounds good, but on one condition... honesty. I deserve to know where we stand, and if you're not ready for something real, it's better to be upfront about it.

Hitting send, she takes another deep breath, the weight of her message settling in her stomach. This isn't just about another date; it's about defining the future of their connection. Would Chad be willing to be transparent, or would he retreat back into the shadows of his unsaid reasons?

Moments tick by and Octavia finds herself caught in a tug-of-war between hope and skepticism, a piece of her heart on the verge of a break as each day passes by. A part of her yearns for a reply, a chance to explore where things could lead. But another part braces itself for disappointment, for the possibility that their connection, however intense, isn't meant to be. One thing is certain though, the silence is finally broken, replaced by a fragile hope and a shared vulnerability.

The reply came through quicker than Octavia expected. It's short, but it holds a universe of unspoken emotions:

Okay. Grandvilla's on Friday @5pm?

A flicker of a smile touches Octavia's lips. It isn't much, but it's a start. It's a chance to see Chad face-to-face, to gauge his sincerity through his body language and the sentiment in his eyes. Her response:

I'll see you there.

The days slide by and a nervous excitement bubbles beneath the surface. She replays their potential conversation in her head a thousand times, crafting witty retorts and heartfelt confessions, only to discard them all. The truth is, she doesn't know what to expect.

* * *

The day of their coffee date has arrived, the evening air is crisp and clear, unlike the uncertainty swirling within Octavia. This coffee shop is small, kind of crowded actually. It's busy. Typical of this small establishment as it is one of this town's favourite hubs.

The building is lined with a forest green trim. The windows are so big you can see inside, along with the people who sit along the high raised tables that face the window. Octavia knows this place is busy, which is precisely why she wasn't hesitant about meeting here. She arrives at the cafe early, as soon as she walks in her senses are overloaded with the smell that you can only experience at this homely coffee shop, it's a mix of homemade bread, coffee, and community. She takes the only open table, midway through the shop. She's got a clear view of the door and a steaming cup of tea warming her hands. A glass of water sits there for Chad, if he shows up.

Every chime of the cafe door sends a jolt through her, she scans the room for a potential glimpse of Chad. While she waits she can't help but take in the lively atmosphere. James Dean, Marilyn Monroe, Elvis Presley. The walls are covered with legends from another time, adding to the allure of the environment.

Finally, he walks in, a hesitant smile gracing his lips. A knot of nervousness suddenly forms in her stomach. He looks different somehow, a weariness lurking in his eyes that wasn't there before. He spots her and his smile widens, a genuine warmth radiating from him.

"Hey," he says casually, his voice a touch raspy, as he slides into the seat across from her.

The simple greeting lies heavy with unspoken apologies and lingering questions. Octavia takes a deep breath, steeling her nerves.

"Hey," she replies, meeting his gaze as he sits across from her. She's relieved he showed up. "So, what's going on with us... or with you?" She doesn't hesitate to dive right in. These questions have been weighing heavy on her mind for too long and she needs some answers.

"Right down to business, eh." He jokes.

She shoots him a serious look, waiting for an answer. He's ignored her for a week after introducing her as his girlfriend, a treasured milestone. She isn't concerned about bedside manner.

"Alright, the truth is," he says as he takes a seat, "I just don't think I am ready for any kind of commitment, 'dating' isn't really my style. You... you're just so beautiful. I am magnetized to you, but, my world, the people in it–"

He stops and reveals a glimpse of something deeper. A world that keeps him on edge? A world she won't understand?

"Well, what do you want?" She demands. "Do you want me or not? Because if you don't then I can leave, and you will never have to see me again."

It's not what she wants, she doesn't know why she said that, it just slipped out. The anger beneath her skin boils as she keeps her composure. However, on the same token, she doesn't want to play games either.

A flicker of pain crosses Chad's face, a silent acknowledgment of her words. He reaches out, his hand hovering over hers for a fleeting moment before retracting.

"I understand," he says, his voice low. "I won't argue. But know this, Octavia, you were right about one thing. This isn't just about a fling. I..." He falters, the words seemingly caught in his throat.

"You what, Chad?" She prompts.

He looks at her, his eyes filled with a mixture of regret and longing.

"I care about you," he finally admits, the weight of the confession hanging heavy between them.

A bittersweet smile plays on her lips. Butterflies sit near the bottom of her stomach. She's caught between anger and relief. He does care about her. However, care, she realizes, isn't enough to build a future on, not when commitment is the missing foundation.

"So then what's the problem?" She spits back. "If you can't be committed to me then we are wasting our time. Maybe give me a call when you want to take this seriously." She stops and looks at him in his gorgeous green eyes. "Or don't." She adds as and grabs her jacket from the back of her chair and storms out the door. She gathers all the strength she has to prevent herself from him seeing her vulnerability as her chin quivers while walking away. She was so sure he was *the one.* This isn't what she wants but she won't wait around for another man to walk out on her. She deserves better and so do her kids. She needs her man to be all in and be sure of it. She can't put herself through that kind of heartbreak again.

He follows.

"Octavia, stop."

She pauses, her foot hovering on the curb as Chad's voice cuts through the crisp evening air. She turns slowly, the weight of their conversation settling in her stomach like a stone. He looks serious, a raw desperation that mirrors the turmoil within her. He crosses the street in a few quick strides, stopping right in front of her. Their eyes meet, his filled with a plea that is both heartbreaking and infuriating.

"Stay," he pleads, his voice husky. "I want to be with you. Our connection is undeniable. I know this and you know this. I'm sorry. We can't throw it all away over a moment of uncertainty."

Octavia could feel her heart, a frantic counterpoint to the quiet hum of the city around them. Part of her yearns to believe him, to surrender to the intensity that blossomed between them like static electricity. She yearns for him more than anyone she ever has. Inside of her is a battle between her mind and her heart. Octavia's breath catches in her throat. Denial tugs at her, whispering about the undeniable spark, the stolen glances, the way his touch sends shivers down her spine. Here he is, practically begging her to stay, promising honesty.

But logic, her seemingly loyal companion, counters with a sharp retort. Is a thrilling connection enough? Could a relationship survive on a foundation of secrets, built on the shaky ground of 'uncertainty'? What is it he was hinting at about his world and the people in it that could possibly make him want to just ghost her all the sudden? It has to have something to do with Lilah because that's when he began pulling back. It has to.

"Undeniable," she echoes, her voice laced with a newfound strength. "Is that what you call it, Chad? Because it feels like you're unsure about us. And it hurts because I was so sure and I was all in. Then you just up and ghosted me out of nowhere and you know what I've been through before." She takes in a deep breath as she controls a tear from falling down her cheek. "Is it Lilah?" she manages.

"Lilah?" A look of shock spreads across his face. "What? No. Of course not."

"Really, because it wasn't long after I met her that you stopped talking to me."

His jaw clenches, a flicker of anger crossing his features before being replaced by a pained sigh.

"It's not that simple, Octavia," he tries to explain, his voice low. "There are things...forces at play that I can't control. Things that could put you in danger."

His words spark a shimmer of fear within her.

"Danger?" she repeats, her voice barely audible. "What kind of danger, Chad? Are you involved in something illegal?"

He shakes his head, his eyes pleading.

"No, not illegal. Just...complicated. The kind of world I live in, it's not for the faint of heart. It can change you, Octavia. It can change everything."

Octavia's blood is pumping. Danger? It's a terrifying word, but somehow, in the context of Chad's world, it also holds a strange allure. The thrill that has simmered beneath their connection since their first encounter now roared to life, a wildfire fueled by his whispered secrets. So this isn't about him not wanting her after all. It's so much deeper than that. What is it that he could possibly be keeping from her? His world doesn't seem so bad. Well, they are cowboys and they are obnoxious and rowdy, but what's so bad about that?

"What do you mean change me?" she questions, a dangerous glint replacing the fear in her eyes. "Maybe that's not such a bad thing. The life I have now feels... Safe, predictable. I mean, look at me, I'm a mom and my life revolves around my kids." Her tone gradually slows. "I wouldn't change that for the world, but I could use some excitement. Make me feel alive, like there's more out there to experience. I know there has to be more. Besides, I was told that I need to let loose and have a little fun, anyway." She stops and looks him in the eye. "Deep down, I know I am meant for more, and for whatever reason, I'm attracted to you. That has to mean something. Maybe the path with you is my path." She pleads.

His eyes widen, surprise battles with a flare of something that looks suspiciously like admiration.

"You're not afraid?" he asks, his voice is hushed.

A hearty laugh escapes her lips, a sound both playful and laced with a hint of defiance.

"Maybe I should be," she admits, stepping closer to him, the space between them crackling with unspoken desire. "But honestly, right now, the only thing I'm afraid of is missing out on this. On you." She's more relieved than anything that it has nothing to do with a lack of connection. He wants her and she wants him. And by the feel of things, it doesn't seem like he wanted to leave her, he was just worried. Trying to protect her from his world. But she doesn't need protection. That's not really his call to make. She will be the judge of that.

Her hand reaches out, brushing against the coarse fabric of his jacket.

"Don't you get it, Chad?" she continues, her voice trembling with emotion. "I want you, and I want you to want me. This connection, it's not about sunshine and rainbows. It's about the raw, untamed electricity that sparks between us. It's about the way you make me feel alive, even if it means living on the edge. All I need, though, is for you to be committed to me. Don't shut me out."

He stares at her, nearly speechless.

"I want nothing more than to be with you. I–"

The vulnerability in her eyes reflects the storm raging within him. This woman, this incredible woman, is willing to embrace the darkness, to face the unknown hand-in-hand. A slow smile spreads across Chad's face, a glimmer of relief chasing away the worry lines etched around his eyes. He reaches out, his fingers brushing against hers, a spark ignites where their skin meets.

"I just want to protect you." He says, his voice hoarse with emotion.

"You need to let me make that decision, though." She says, reaching out for his hand.

"That's fair. You're completely right." He says, intertwining his fingers with hers.

She looks him in the eye, gaging his level of sincerity.

"Wanna start over, maybe go for a walk?" He suggests, a hesitant smile gracing his lips. "I don't want to leave here having this be our last interaction."

"Sure, I have some questions for you anyway." Octavia agrees with a small smile mirroring his.

CHAPTER THIRTEEN

They leave the cute coffee shop behind with a more appropriate setting in sight. A walk through the park, a chance to, once again, get to know one another a little better, but now on another level. The nearest park is a mere ten minute walk across the bridge that leads out of town. The beauty of this particular park is a haven for tranquility. The trees are the first point of interest, so vibrant and green with new spring leaves. A 'beware of bear' sign is made obvious at the main trail entrance. The trees break up the rays of the descending sun casting shadows throughout the trails. Ducks are in the pond, and birds' song in the sky. The sound of children's laughter is heard in the distance. The playground which is the main attraction for families was just rebuilt last year, and also happens to be one of Ryan and Cory's favourite places to play.

"How is it that you're so warm?" She hesitates before spitting out her unfiltered words. "It's so... unnatural."

"Well, if I told you that, then I'd have to kill ya." He says with a wink and a grin.

The look on Octavia's face is a comedic mix of surprise and dismissiveness.

"Just foolin' ya, sweetheart."

It doesn't answer her question, but she lets it go, for now. Besides, she's getting exactly what she wants - time with this mysterious and ridiculously handsome cowboy that has vowed to commit to her. It's almost a surreal feeling. *He* wants *her*. Octavia's self esteem has really taken a hit since the father of her boys left her. She's questioned many times over the years if she's even loveable. To her children, and to her family, of course she is. But to a man? If the man of her children can up and leave so seemingly easily, then why would anyone else want to stay? She questions this often. She's had two children and is somewhat self conscious about her body. Her clothes hide the stretch marks that motherhood has privileged her with. Despite how pretty she is, it's crazy to her to think that someone as physically fit as Chad could even be attracted to her. No matter the reason, she's grateful that he is. Despite her doubts, she's going to embrace it.

"I don't think that's a very fair answer?" Octavia says.

"You're right. I guess I misjudged the mood." He says.

Or he's just trying to avoid the question altogether.

"I just run warm, I always have." Chad looks at her. "Maybe I just feel so warm to you because you're so cold." He grabs on to her hand. It's true, she is chilly. She's never really questioned it, people get cold hands and feet all the time.

They continue their walk, Octavia deep in thought. She has questions but isn't quite sure how to articulate them.

"Is there...something else you wanted to ask?" He cautiously prods.

Octavia takes a deep breath.

"Last week," she begins, hesitantly. "Lilah?"

"Uh uh," Chad prompts.

"What's her deal, anyway?" She finally asks.

"What do you mean?" A look of confusion spreads across his face. He has to suspect Octavia saw something. Then again, maybe he was too caught up in their argument to realize.

Octavia hesitates, trying to find the right words. "She was clearly upset. I mean, I didn't see much but she stormed out of the restaurant after what looked like an argument with you."

"Honestly Octavia, I wouldn't even worry about her. It's just a misunderstanding. We've talked about this already."

"Right, I remember asking, and getting the same vague answer. But what was she upset about? Was it me?" She interrupts.

Chad clears his throat. His eyes look as if he's deep in thought, carefully constructing his next words. Can it be that difficult of a question? Or is there a complexity to this whole situation that she's missing all together?

"She's always been there for me. I look up to her, she's like family. Pretty much the only family I've got besides James, who's been my best bud since we were young."

"I'm sorry, I–"

"No, It's okay. She's just looking out for me." He finishes.

She wants to ask about the eyes so badly it's a physical ache in her throat. She *knows* he had to have seen them—that unnatural glow, the impossible depth she glimpsed in the darkness. Or was it just a deceptive reflection of the passing streetlights, playing tricks in her periphery? Would she look like a complete and utter fool even mentioning it out loud? The thought of him staring at her, a strange mix of pity and concern in his gaze, makes her stomach clench. She certainly doesn't want him to think she's crazy or seeing things.

She decides against it, firmly waving away the possibility that it could have been anything more than a simple trick of the eye. It's absurd to think otherwise. Nothing supernatural exists in this world, not really. Only what's in the fairytales and the comforting, fantastical stories they were fed as children. But they are just those. Stories. Nothing more.

Silence stretches, feeling like minutes, as they both process the unexpected depth of their conversation. A quiet shock ripples through Octavia as it sinks in: he has no family. After so many weeks, how could she not have known this about him? The revelation sparks a flurry of unasked questions in her mind. But a warmth blooms in her heart, a gentle, blossoming recognition that he's just shared a profound vulnerability with her, a piece of himself he absolutely didn't have to expose.

Octavia, sensing the shift, gently picks up the conversation, steering it into lighthearted small talk about the most mundane things. From there, their words flow easily, the earlier tension dissolving. They move from discussions about mutual friends and the daily grind of work to shared goals, personal dreams, and surprising common interests. As their conversation nears its end, they settle into a peaceful, comfortable pause, the easy quiet between them now a welcome companion.

"Thank you." Octavia says, lacking context.

Chad looks her in the eyes, "For?" He replies. Well, for showing up, for giving this a shot, for being kind and understanding. For answering the questions, well most of them. And for not giving up on this. Isn't it obvious?

"Well, I don't know." Is all she could allow to slip off her tongue.

He lets out a chuckle as he wraps his arm around her. "It's me who should be thanking you."

His heat is enough to combat the chill air around her, wrapping her in a steady warmth. If he's willing to go out of his way like this—to come see her, to quell her lingering doubts, to genuinely give *this* a shot despite claiming he doesn't "date"—then she must be worthy. In this moment, she feels a profound, blossoming type of love, a deep warmth spreading through her chest. She reaches up, her fingers finding and gently lacing with his hand that's draped so comfortably over her shoulder.

"Where are those boys of yours tonight?" He asks as the evening winds down, his voice soft, his attention pulled down towards her, a visible contentment softening his features.

"They're with my mom," her initial answer is short and sweet, a simple fact.

"Gotcha." They're nearing the end of the trail now, the last rays of sun descending behind the mountains making the path harder to see, blurring the edges of the familiar landscape.

"I should probably go get them actually," she muses, a slight shift in her tone as reality begins to creep back in. "I didn't realize how late it was getting already and it's getting dark."

"Yeah, I gotta get going before it gets too dark anyway and check on the animals," Chad says, his words carrying a hint of reluctance to break the peaceful quiet.

Right, he's a cowboy. Of course he has animals to tend to; as they'd discussed before, they eat up most of his time. Octavia doesn't have a lot of direct, hands-on experience with cowboy life, but plenty of people in this area run farms and ranches, so she has a decent idea of their basic operations. The long, grueling hours under the open sky, the constant outdoor living, the strong work ethic, the tight-knit community, and the camaraderie among fellow ranchers—all of this rushes to mind when she thinks about what Chad's lifestyle truly entails. And she considers these experiences not as daunting chores, but as moments she could actually look forward to sharing.

The walk back to their vehicles takes another ten minutes. It's growing increasingly harder to see the trail now, the fading light a clear signal of the late hour. Eight-thirty p.m. is usually her boys' bedtime, though on Fridays, she lets them stay up a bit later. There's still enough light to make out some of the distant scenery, blurring into soft purples and grays. The trail itself has become quiet, the earlier families long gone. They'd seen one person walking their dog a while back, but even they've likely disappeared back home by now.

It's definitely time for Octavia to start making her way home to her kids; she hadn't realized how quickly time had vanished while hanging out with Chad. As they walk along the large, gravel parking lot to get back to the bridge, a distinct shuffled sound breaks the growing silence from behind them, rustling vigorously in the thick bush line. A bear is the first, instinctive thought that flashes through Octavia's mind, tightening a knot in her stomach. She whips her head around, eyes frantically scanning the dense, shadowy area the best she could in the fading light. Nothing in sight, as far as she can tell, but the rustling persists.

"You okay?" Chad asks, his voice calm, clearly oblivious to the eerie sounds surrounding them or unbothered by them. He may not be scared of wild animals, but Octavia sure is, every nerve ending on high alert. The air is thick with the familiar, comforting scent of pine needles and damp earth, but something else lingers now, a strange, musky odor that makes Octavia's skin crawl with an unsettling intuition.

"I think I heard something, maybe there's a bear out here," she says, her voice a low, nervous tremor as her fingers instinctively tighten their grip on Chad's arm.

"Ah, bears are more scared of us than we are of them," he assures, his voice a calm, steady rumble that instantly grounds her. "You're safe with me, I can promise you that."

A simple smile softly tugs at the corners of her lips, and an unexpected warmth blooms in her chest, pushing back against the lingering chill of the evening air. His words, though simple, carry a surprising, comforting weight that settles deep within her. A wave of profound relief washes over her, effectively chasing away the last tendrils of fear. She knows he's probably right. She's always been a bit of a scaredy-cat, even as a child, never truly comfortable with the deep, enveloping darkness that fell after sunset.

Just as they begin to cross the road, a low growl, guttural and menacing, rumbles through the undergrowth, confirming Octavia's absolute worst fears. The hairs on the back of her neck prickle, standing on end. This isn't the sound of a harmless deer or a sly fox. This is something else entirely. She whips her head around, eyes desperately trying to adjust to the deepening darkness that surrounds them. A sharp snap of a branch startles her, and then a large, indistinct figure forces its way out of the bush towards them.

Pure panic sets in, a cold, gripping fear that steals her breath. The air thickens, no longer just pine and damp earth, but with the sickening scent of something rancid and utterly unfamiliar. A predator. Its form is indistinct in the shadows, a blurry mass, yet its raw, untamed energy vibrates through the air, palpable and terrifying. It's too dark to tell what it is, but it doesn't look like any wild animal Octavia's ever seen before. She can't quite make it out, but its movements seem fluid and unnatural, almost as if it's hovering, gliding across the ground. It can't be more than thirty feet away.

"Chad?" she whimpers, her voice a thin, reedy thread in the sudden, heavy silence of the night. Raw terror seizes her, a cold hand squeezing her chest. Her legs tremble violently, threatening to buckle as she instinctively starts to sprint across the road, her heart hammering against her chest. But her knee scrapes hard against the cold asphalt as she hits the ground, momentum failing her. Almost immediately, the sound of a grunt, loud and guttural, steals her attention. Then, Chad's sudden weight pins her to the ground, and for a terrifying moment, she can't breathe, the air forced from her lungs.

"You're okay, Octavia," he whispers, his voice low and urgent next to her ear. "Don't move. It can't see us here."

Her eyes are wide with fright, dilated in the near-total darkness. Chad scans the surrounding area, his gaze steady and unwavering, a stark contrast to her own panic. He takes a deep, controlled breath. His voice is low and reassuring, meant to soothe, but when his eyes finally meet hers, they look as though they're desperately trying to conceal something – a flicker of something she can't quite decipher. Her heart pounds in her chest, a frantic drum against her ribs, as she stares up at him. She catches her breath and tries to look back, to see whatever he sees, but she can't move. She's paralyzed, her muscles locked in fear. Chad's weight presses down on her, trapping her beneath him, a suffocating anchor. She tries to wriggle free, a futile squirm, but his grip is too strong, holding her impossibly still.

"What is it?" she hollers, the word ripped from her in a raw burst of shock.

"Shhh," Chad hushes, his voice a low, urgent rumble as he continues to scan the surrounding area, his body taut.

A wave of nausea washes over her, cold and dizzying. She tries to wriggle free, her breath catching in her throat, a choked sound. Her eyes widen in terror, fixed on Chad, she trembles. *Why is he holding her here? Is he hurt? Is he... scared?* A thousand terrifying possibilities race through her mind, each one more chilling than the last.

The screech of tires on asphalt rips through the night. It's followed almost immediately by a deafening blast of a car horn. The headlights of the approaching vehicle slice through the darkness, blinding her momentarily, painting the world in a painful white. Time seems to slow down, each agonizing second stretching into an eternity. She struggles violently against Chad's unyielding grip, her mind screaming for him to move, to get off of her, to get them both off the road and out of the way of the vehicle that's heading straight for them.

CHAPTER FOURTEEN

"Chad!" she yells, her voice raw with fear, still pinned to the road.

He jolts, as if awakened from a trance. He scrambles to his feet, pulling Octavia up with him in a sudden burst of strength. He pulls her out of the way of the speeding vehicle, and onto the opposite side of the road from the creature. Octavia stares at the disappearing tail lights, her breath ragged. Adrenaline surges through her. She looks around, her heart still pounding, her eyes dart frantically in every direction, searching for any sign of the creature. The creature, whatever it was, seems to have disappeared.

"What the hell?" she demands, shoving him back. "What was that?"

"Octavia!" he roars, his voice crackling with fear, his eyes wide and wild. "It wasn't after you, it was after me! I just don't know how it knew I was here." He raises his hands, placing them on his head as if the words had accidentally slipped off his tongue.

"What? What are you talking about?" she screams, her voice echoing through the night.

Chad looks around, scanning the area. "They can't see very well in the light. I wasn't trying to hurt you. I would never hurt you."

"Who's they?" she demands, her voice trembling. "What are you talking about? What was that thing?"

Questions bombard her: What was that *thing*? What did it want? Why was it after Chad? Is it going to come back? Octavia's mind races, a whirlwind of terrifying thoughts. Chad's energy seems to calm as he realizes the fear and confusion in Octavia's eyes.

A chilling rain begins to drizzle down, fast and cold.

"Look at me! What the hell Chad? What's going on?" She questions. Could this be the danger he was speaking of at the coffee shop? It's unlike anything she could have ever imagined when he warned her of danger. "Is this the *danger* you were talking about? Because–"

"Octavia!" He shouts, slowing his body, giving her his full attention. "I would never let anything happen to you!" He takes a step closer. "I love you!"

She gasps for air, her chest heaving, her heart hammering against her ribs. Chad walks up to her, his hand gently brushing against her cheek.

"Hey," he whispers, his voice rough with emotion. "Hey, you're okay. That's all that matters right now." He assures her.

"You... you love me?" She asks, the rain drenching her hair and running down her cheeks. "Then why–"

"I was protecting you. I will always protect you." He explains, gently cupping her face in his hands, his eyes searching hers. "Now that I know you, I will do anything to keep you safe."

Protecting you. These are more than just words. Her breath begins to slow, the frantic pounding of her heart gradually subsides. His touch, warm and reassuring, sends a surge of warmth through her, chasing away the lingering fear, just as it did the night of their dinner party. She remembers the way David's words had always felt... empty, hollow, devoid of meaning; a distinct difference to the sincerity that radiates from Chad. A strange mixture of fear and exhilaration courses through her veins.

"Will you trust me?" He asks, gazing into her eyes.

She gives a slight nod, not willing to take her eyes off of him.

"Now, can you please let me get you out of this rai–"

Before he could finish, Octavia cuts him off. Her arms wrap around his neck in a fierce embrace and their lips meet in a passionate kiss, silencing his words.

CHAPTER FIFTEEN

The events of the last few weeks replay in Octavia's mind like a fast-forwarded action movie as she sips on her afternoon lemonade. Danger, adrenaline, whatever that creature was, Chad assures her it's nothing to worry about but she's seeing more and more now that just seems so out of the ordinary. It's a glimpse into a world that she doesn't know or understand. If Chad says it's nothing to worry about, and that he will protect her, she believes him, although curiosity still pricks at her. All that along with the chilling revelation about how he feels about her. It's a lot to process. But one thing cuts through the chaos with laser focus. Chad.

The memory of that night, of his unwavering gaze, the feel of his hand steadying her, the scent of pine needles and fear still lingering in the air, sends a sliver of warmth through her. She remembers the way his eyes held hers with a quiet intensity that banished the fear that had threatened to consume her. What if she had allowed fear to dictate her actions? What if she had let this incredible connection slip away? The thought brings a sharp pang of regret. Gratitude blooms within her, a beautiful flower pushing through the cracks of doubt. Chad's quick actions, like a superhero saving her from the dangers of the night, fill her with a sense of awe and wonder.

Chad had initially intended to keep her at a distance, to shield her from the dangerous secrets of his world, to protect her from the pain and fear he knew it could inevitably bring. He made that clear. But in the face of the unknown, he'd also fought for her, for them. The realization hit her with the force of a tidal wave, washing away the lingering fear and uncertainty. No one had ever chosen her like that before, and since that night, they've been inseparable.

The hot July sun warms Octavia's skin as she basks on her lawn while the kids play. She longs to see Chad again, to feel the thrill, the warmth and excitement he brings her. With the previous night's conversation replaying in her mind, Octavia plans her evening. Chad had mentioned a barbecue. A casual get-together and a twenty-ninth birthday celebration for his friend, James. A nervous flutter dances in her stomach. She's met James and Baily a few times, they're great. She looks forward to seeing them again, to get to know them better. But who else is going to be there? Will they be just as welcoming? A flashback crosses her mind like a bolt of lightning, illuminating a forgotten memory of the woman's voice she heard the night of Chad's party, *you don't belong here.* Chances are, she didn't hear it correctly, who would even say something like that, and why... yet, the suspicion lingers. The invite to Maya and Mateo wasn't ignored. It's a gathering to bring all their friends together, and the presence of her own friends will add a layer of familiar comfort. A chance for her closest friend to get to know the man of her dreams manifests with anticipation.

The afternoon unfolds in chaos and preparation. She settles on a dish she thinks Chad will love, picturing his smile as he tastes it. She stands before her mirror, a splash of color adds a confident touch to her outfit. Taking a deep breath, she grabs the dish of food and heads out. Tonight, the boys will stay with their grandma, her main support and really her only family that's left after her dad died, so they are really close.

With each step closer to Chad's place, anticipation bubbles within her. This is it. Her chance to truly connect with Chad's friends, to become a genuine part of his life, and for him to become a part of hers. Her heart pounds a thrilling rhythm against her ribs as she and her friends approach Chad's backyard, ready to embrace the unknown and see where the night will take them.

"You guys remember Chad?" Octavia acknowledges.

"Yeah, for sure, Liam's friend." Mateo says, reaching out for a handshake. "We didn't really get a chance to hang out much, but I remember." A flicker of apprehension flickers across Mateo's face as he lets go of Chad's hand.

Maya's eyes widen as she gazes at the fire pit.

"Wow," she exclaims, "It's beautiful!" She carefully places a bottle of wine on the sturdy picnic table nestled beneath the grand gazebo. "I've never seen anything like it."

"Thank you." Chad responds, gesturing at the pit with a warm smile. "A friend made it for me when I moved here a couple years ago."

"That's so cool, it even has your last name." A puzzled look crosses her face. "What do these strange markings mean?"

The fire pit is engraved with unfamiliar markings, like an ancient language whispering secrets only the owner would understand.

"Oh, those? They don't mean anything," Chad says, rubbing the back of his neck, a slight hesitation in his voice. "They are just a design, I guess."

"Ah, well they look cool." She says, a seed of curiosity planted in her mind.

"You guys are a bit early and I haven't had the chance to start the fire yet." Chad says. "The others should be here soon though."

"Why don't I give you a hand?" Matteo suggests, looking around for the wood. He grabs a few pieces and places them into the pit. "It's kind of damp, not sure it's gonna light very easily, do you have any paper or anything?"

"There's some dry kindling near the back." Chad says, gesturing towards the pile. "I need to go check the oven, I'll be right back."

Chad returns back to the pit, Mateo is still working at getting the fire going.

"Can I help with that?" Chad asks, closing in on him.

Mateo backs away, eyeing Chad up and down. "Go ahead, man. Unless you have some kind of gas or something I don't think it's gonna light."

Chad kneels down, reaching into the pit. He cups his hands into the pit and lightly blows into them, sending the tiny orange spark dancing to life. A look of surprise and bewilderment flashes across Mateo's face. Mateo must have gotten the base warm enough for Chad to be able to light it up like that.

"Why do you look so surprised? You did most of the leg work." Octavia says.

"The pit was damp, it... nevermind."

With unease, Mateo continues to add dry kindling to the fire, with a close eye he progressively adds larger sticks and pieces of wood. Octavia watches with satisfaction as the flames grow larger. The fire is bursting with life, but the fire craves more. Chad adds a larger split log, its seasoned heart hissing as it hits the flames. The fire roars in response, tongues of orange licking greedily at the offering. The heat radiating outwards becomes a tangible force, pushing back the encroaching night chill.

Octavia realizes the fire is growing much larger than she expected and feels a sense of adrenaline shoot through her.

"Is this fire safe?" She questions. She and Maya scramble their chairs back a little bit.

"Oh yeah, definitely." Chad assures her. "It's under control. I wouldn't grow it bigger than anything I can't handle."

The roaring fire dies down after only minutes, providing relief for the group.

"So, what was it like growing up with Octavia?" Chad asks Maya, as he takes a sip from his drink.

"Honestly, I couldn't have asked for a better friend." Maya responds.

"How'd you guys meet?" He asks, curiosity tinged in his voice.

Maya chuckles. "Funny story, On the very first day of kindergarten, Octavia walks into the classroom and..." She pauses.

"And what?" Chad asks, his face lights up, eager to hear the rest of the story.

"She trips over her own feet and lands right on top of me, knocking us both over!" Maya exclaims.

Octavia blushes. "Oh it wasn't that bad. I just landed on your arm."

"Yeah, nearly breaking it." Maya laughs.

"There's no way, you were laughing your head off." Octavia adds.

"And we've been best friends ever since."

Chad places his hand on Octavia's.

"Sounds like a cute way to meet." He turns to Mateo, "and how about you Mateo? How long have you guys known each other?"

Mateo, who had been quietly listening, smiles. "Not as long as these two. I met Maya a few years ago at a local festival." Maya wraps her arm around his and snuggles close. "We ended up talking for a while and hit it off, the rest is history.."

Turning the attention away from him Mateo asks Octavia, "didn't you say before that you grew up on a farm?" Changing the subject.

"Yeah, it wasn't a real farm, just a hobby farm with a few different animals, goats and chickens, we even had pigs at one time. My parents loved animals, and since I was an only child, wanted to make sure I had plenty of company. Oh, we also had bunny rabbits that lived on the property and me and my friends would go out and try to catch them." She smiles and gestures towards Maya as she reminisces. "So yeah, I spent a lot of time outdoors. I loved hanging out with my friends, like Maya and Ben, and playing down by the river." She explains.

"Sounds idyllic. I've always wanted to live someplace like that." Mateo says.

"Yeah, it seems like you had a great childhood." Chad points out. Octavia lets out a soft smile and stares at the ground.

"I guess I did. But it was a lot of work and my parents were always busy with their jobs, on top of taking care of the farm. I had to learn to become independent at a young age." Octavia says, emotion creeping into her voice. The memories of her late dad flash through her mind. She cherishes the life that they had built for her, and all the sacrifices that they had made.

"That's why you're so resourceful now, though." Maya assures her.

"And also must be why she's such a great cook, too." Chad adds, causing Octavia to blush. The conversation continued, filled with laughter, stories, and a growing sense of camaraderie.

"What is it that you do, Chad?" Mateo asks with a hint of suspicion.

"I drive rigs and compete in rodeos in my spare time," Chad responds, his answer leaving a bit of ambiguity. "And of course I've got this farm here."

The sound of a distant vehicle pulling into the driveway breaks the banter.

"Sounds like James and Bailey are here!" Octavia exclaims, a nervous smile gracing her lips. Sure enough, moments later, they stroll into the backyard, carrying a cooler. Not far behind them, Chad's neighbors, Colleen and Eddie, amble over, their easy laughter echoing through the backyard.

Octavia looks at Colleen for longer than a second, a thoughtful expression crossing her face. She recognizes her. "You were there the night of the party a while back, weren't you?"

Colleen looks at her with a squint in her eye, "yeah, that's right, I remember you."

Colleen and Eddie, a middle-aged couple a decade or so older than Chad, have become something of a surrogate family to him since he moved in as a bachelor a couple years ago. Colleen is like a mother hen around here apparently. Though slightly plump, she takes pride in her appearance and exudes a certain charm with her carefully styled hair and tasteful makeup, a testament to her career as a hairstylist, as Octavia vaguely recalls. Eddie, on the other hand, seems indifferent to fashion or upholding his appearance, like many of the blue-collar men in this area. His stained sweatpants and oversized hoodie smell faintly of oil and dirt, suggesting he might be a mechanic or works with his hands. She's never thought to actually ask.

The group spends the evening mingling over the sizzling sound of the steaks. Octavia, close to Chad's side, revels in the wave of pure contentment that washes over her. The evening is filled with joyful chaos. The easy laughter of adults getting to know one another, the lively chatter punctuated by the sizzling of the steaks on the grill.

Once everyone is finished eating, Octavia takes initiative, offering to help clean up. Stepping inside the house, she scans the room, searching for Chad, who's been inside for several long moments, now. Just then, a snippet of conversation drifts from the kitchen. A voice, definitely Colleen's, his nosy neighbour (his words), is laced with surprise.

"So this is actually the same girl you had over that night of the party? Since when do you have the same girl over more than once?" She asks. "Is there something about her that you haven't told me?"

Octavia's stomach lurches. Her steps falter, the cheerful chatter from outside fades into a dull roar. She freezes, her heart sinks into her stomach. Did she just hear Colleen question Chad about her presence? A wave of humiliation washes over her. What does she mean he never has the same girl over more than once. Is he a player? Does he often have different girls around? Is it a personal jab?

Taking a steadying breath, she forces her feet forward. Denial flickers across her mind. Maybe she misunderstood? But the echo of Colleen's words linger, sharp and clear. Swallowing the lump in her throat, Octavia plasters on a smile and enters the kitchen.

"Where can I put these?" She asks nervously, stepping into the kitchen.

"Oh, you didn't have to do that," Chad says as he takes the dishes from her.

"It's nothing," Octavia assures him. "Excuse me, I just need to use the washroom." Reaching the hallway, she sneaks a glance back towards the kitchen.

Colleen's gaze darts towards her before flicking away into Chad's direction, a sheepish grin replacing her earlier amusement. "Oops," Octavia can almost hear her mutter under her breath.

The bathroom door clicks shut behind Octavia, a barrier against the sudden tension. Leaning against the cool tile, she lets out a shaky breath. Her carefully constructed confidence crumbles, replaced by a gnawing insecurity.

What did Chad say? Did he explain their connection? Or worse, had he kept their encounters a secret? The invitation, a symbol of inclusion, now feels laced with suspicion. Octavia's image of fitting into Chad's world momentarily shatters, leaving behind a tangle of doubt and a burning desire to understand what she'd just overheard. She emerges from the bathroom, the encounter with Colleen's words leaving a cold residue in her stomach. She puts on a smile, hoping it doesn't appear strained.

Chad suddenly materializes beside her.

"Hey," he greets her warmly. "How're you doing?" His concern seems genuine, almost as if he can sense her unease, his eyes search hers.

Octavia hesitates, the weight of Colleen's comment heavy on her tongue. Should she confront him? Or is it better to let it go, to trust that there was a simple explanation? Taking a deep breath, she decides on a measured approach.

"I'm alright," she replies, her voice a touch quieter than usual. "Just a little overwhelmed. I usually am around new people."

Chad's brows arch in understanding.

"Yeah, I know, hanging out with new people can be a bit much." His hands trace the curve of her neck, brushing her hair away.

"Do you often have a lot of different women around?" The question slips eagerly off her tongue. It feels accusatory though, and she doesn't want to jump to conclusions. Instead, she opts for a more measured approach. She can't help but to look down at the floor.

Chad leans in. "Is this about what Colleen said?"

She looks up at him, relief washes over her for a brief moment at his understanding.

"Honestly, don't worry about her. She tends to put her foot in her mouth. It's all a big misunderstanding, I promise."

The charm in Chad's eyes is palpable. "Look," he says, his voice dropping to a reassuring murmur. "It's nothing important. Let's just enjoy the party, alright?"

He offers her a warm smile, one that seems genuine. Octavia, despite the lingering unease, decides to take him at his word for now. The overheard snippet still gnaws at her, but causing a scene won't help. Taking a deep breath, she forces a smile back at Chad.

"Alright," she agrees, her voice a touch shaky. "I'll be out in a minute."

A small seed of doubt has been planted. One that she may never bring up for discussion again. She's grown very fond of Chad, and it's clear he feels the same way, too. She wishes to continue to explore and strengthen their bond and she isn't going to let someone's comment get in the way of that. She looks around, catching Colleen's eye across the way. The neighbor offers a light smile.

On her way back outside, she's met at the door by Colleen. It's just the two of them. Octavia looks out the window, the rest of the group gathered by the fire, their laughter mingling with the crackling flames. She looks at Colleen in wonder. What could she possibly want? To apologize? To further criticize her presence? To warn her about the other women? A shiver creeps up her neck.

"I get it now," Colleen says, her hand on her hip and a knowing glint in her eye.

"Get what?" Octavia asks, her voice sharp with confusion.

"The reason Chad is with you." Colleen says, her voice dropping to a conspiratorial whisper.

Octavia takes a step back, her brows furrow.

"What's that supposed to mean?" She demands, her heart pounding.

"You know he doesn't date right." Colleen states as if she's privy to information Octavia isn't.

"What does that have to do with anything?" Octavia questions, her voice firm but not unkind. "I don't know what it is that you're trying to do here, but it's not going to work." She pauses, taking a deep breath.

"No, I... I don't think you understand. You don't actually think he's with you because he *loves* you... do you?" Colleen looks her up and down. "You don't belong here."

There it is. That chilling realization hits her with the force of a physical blow. It's her, that very woman, who spoke those words that night. She isn't going crazy after all; the voice, the strange pronouncements, they are real. What is this woman's problem? She presents such a convincing facade, so nice and bubbly on the outside, always smiling, always engaging, but beneath that polished veneer, she's nothing but mean on the inside, a cold, calculating cruelty lurking just beneath the surface.

"I don't know what it is that you have against me, but I'd like to go back out and enjoy the rest of the evening... with my boyfriend." With a polite but firm smile, she steps back outside, leaving Colleen standing alone in the doorway.

CHAPTER SIXTEEN

Back out at the pit, crackling flames dance merrily. The air is thick with the aroma of grilled food and woodsmoke, a symphony of scents that speak of summer evenings.

"Did Chad ever tell you the story about how he nearly died at the rodeo?" James directs his question to Octavia.

Baily shoots James a sharp look.

"Okay, well obviously he didn't almost die, he's basically indestructible, this guy."

Baily shoots him another look, one sharp enough to put anyone in their place. "We don't have to bore her with those stories," she says.

Colleen reenters the group at the pit.

"Hey Eddie, I think it's time we make our way back home." Colleen says. "It's starting to get late."

Octavia glares at Colleen. "Oh, it's alright, it's a welcome distraction." She says before bringing her attention back to the group.

Eddie accepts his wife's suggestions and with a quick goodbye, they're off.

"Besides, I never hear anyone talk about the rodeos. It's kind of like this mysterious event that comes and goes." Octavia continues, a look of curiosity on her face as she glances at Chad.

Maya leans in, "A distraction from what?" She whispers.

"I'll fill you in later," she says, catching a glimpse at Colleen as she stops to pet a horse on her way back home. Curiosity pricks at her. She can't help but think that she's just trying to stir things up, and she can't figure out why. She takes a deep breath in as she attempts to settle her nerves.

"Yeah, we really don't need to share this story. It's nothing, really." Chad's clearly not too fond of this memory.

Octavia challenges him.

"It doesn't sound like nothing." She says, gently placing her hand on his leg.

"Oh, it's a miracle he even survived it." James continues, "he was competing a couple of summers ago, in bull riding, that's what he does. And we're watching right, I'd just finished my round. He's up there on that big bull, well on his way to winning the competition." James hands wave around, telling the story. "Then suddenly you see him start to slide off the side. Just as he slides down about to fall off, the bull brushes up against the gate. Clunk! That's all you could hear. It was so loud. He's hit his head on the metal gate."

"Oh no!" Octavia's jaw drops and raises her hands over her mouth, a look of shock streaming across her face. "Then all you could hear afterwards was the entire crowd gasping. It was insane!"

"That's terrible!" She takes her gaze off of James and shoots it straight to Chad. "It makes my head hurt just hearing that story. Are these things that I am going to have to worry about when you go off to rodeos?"

"No no. Nothing like that will happen again, baby girl." Chad assures her, although she isn't too convinced. How can he promise that if he continues to go to the rodeos? Is this something she will need to worry about each time he competes? She reaches out for Chad's hand. "I hope not. That's intense. I'm glad you're okay."

"Oh hey, James, if you're gonna be telling this story, don't be leaving out the most important detail." Chad pokes. "Right, right. Of course not." James goes on. "Against all odds, he took home the win that night. It was a night to remember, for sure."

"Awe, that's awesome. A nice way to end an intense story." Octavia leans her head on Chad's shoulder. Time ticks by and the amber glow of the fire pit intensifies, Octavia notices a subtle shift in the atmosphere. The warm camaraderie of the evening was shattered by an unexpected silence, punctuated only by the distant whinny of a horse in the night.

Chad, ever the charmer, regales them with tales of his latest rodeo exploits, while Octavia chimes in with playful anecdotes about their short life together. Maya, an attentive listener, offers witty commentary and insightful questions, keeping the conversation flowing effortlessly. As the night wears on, Octavia feels a deep sense of gratitude for the friends she's found. Mateo, on the other hand, seems to have his own ideas about Chad. He eyes Chad up wearily, his gaze lingering a beat too long. Octavia can't help but notice his typical outgoing energy has been replaced with what seems like slight annoyance and has been fairly quiet.

"Ya know, my boys would really love this place." A pang of guilt settles in her stomach as Chad consumes so much of her time. A bit of a sacrifice she reasons with herself as she attempts to build a relationship with this man who she would like to one day be woven into their family structure.

"Well why don't you bring them out?" Chad offers, "I mean, we've been dating what, a couple months now? And we haven't actually hung out together as a family."

Hearing Chad speak about her sons warms her heart. But is it too soon? After all, he's right, they have been dating a while now, maybe she can start bringing them around, show them what their ma's been up to. A tug-of-war pulls at Octavia, she wants nothing more than to have her boys around with her all the time. But she's also weary about introducing them around a new man, a man that could potentially act as a father figure. But also a man who warns of danger. What kind of a mother would she be, getting them involved in potential danger. Will he protect them, like he does her? They haven't had a father figure before, how would that affect them? She'd love that for them. It could be a really good thing if this all works out, or it could be a mess if it doesn't.

This is what Octavia wants, but hearing the words out loud send a nervous trickle into her stomach. Yet, she remains cautiously optimistic.

"Yeah, I'll bring them out soon, I'll be picking them up tomorrow morning, maybe we can make a day of it." Chad nods his head.

"Sure, bring them here, show them the animals," he says. "They'd love it, I'm sure. I mean, I'm gonna have to meet them eventually, right?"

Octavia hesitates before sharing her thoughts, "Well, tomorrow is Sunday, so we would have the whole day. Maybe we can make something work."

There is a lengthy pause before Octavia speaks again.

"Hey, umm, I just need to run to the washroom. I'll be right back." Octavia says, she doesn't waste a second, and she's already in the house. She doesn't actually need to use the washroom, she just needed some space. She needs to breathe. What is she doing?

Chad follows her into the house, meeting her in the kitchen. "Hey, what's going on? Are you alright?"

"Sorry, I don't know, this just came out of nowhere." She says, leaning over a chair, breathing shallow. "I've never introduced a man to my kids before."

"Hey, it's alright." Chad says, walking up to her, he places his hand on her back. "It's me, We've been getting to know each other for a couple months now and I think that it's important that if we're going to move forward, we do so as a family."

"Yeah," she nods her head. "But what about the weird things that have been happening?"

"What? What do you mean, weird things?" He asks, acting oblivious.

They haven't really talked about these things in depth, if at all;

Liliah's eyes, the creature in the night, the sounds from the house.

"Umm, that creature, I guess?" She's grasping at straws.

"That's not something that you need to worry about. We've been over this." He pauses. "That *animal* will never cause any harm to you or your boys." He says in a convincing tone.

Animal? She's sure it wasn't just an animal, then again, it was pretty dark. She didn't really see it, so if he says it's an animal then maybe it was. Lilah's eyes were likely just a reflection in the night. The warmth of his skin, he runs hot and she's cold. The heat of his kisses, allergic to his saliva? That could be a thing, right? And maybe, the sounds in the house were just in her dreams. Night terrors have been a common thing for her since she was a child. There seems to be a logical explanation for all of it.

"Hey, I'd never do anything to hurt you, or them. Let me show you the good in me." He says, sincerity in his voice.

"Yeah, you're right." She says, taking a deep breath. "My anxiety is getting the best of me."

"Come here," he pulls her in for a hug. "As long as you're with me, you don't need to worry." She wraps her arms around him, finding comfort in his overly warm embrace. "Let's head back out to the fire, k?" As always, his touch sends a calming wave through her, easing her thoughts and nerves.

A shuffle takes place in the group upon their return, creating a change in the dynamics. Baily makes a trip to the washroom, Chad gets up for a drink. And Mateo grabs a seat next to Octavia, using this opportunity to whisper in her direction.

"Octavia," he begins. "How well do you really know this guy?" Unable to pinpoint anything specific, a disquiet hums beneath the surface. It's a feeling that can't be ignored.

"What do you mean?" She asks in a hushed voice, she quickly glances over at Chad, who's in conversation with James.

"I can't really put my finger on it but Chad's easy smile seems a touch too practiced, doesn't it? Every friendly interaction he has with any of us feels like there's a hidden motive behind it."

"Um, we've been hanging out for a while and we talk all the time. I feel like we're getting to know each other pretty well, I mean, we've gotten really close in the last couple months." She says, unsure of what it is Mateo is trying to get at.

"You know a couple of months isn't really that long. Haven't you noticed anything really odd?" Mateo questions.

"Our relationship isn't like yours, you guys knew each other as friends before you started dating. But it's perfectly normal to date someone as you're getting to know them too... I'm not sure what you're getting at."

Mateo looks at Chad, "he does."

"Is everything alright over there?" Chad chimes in.

"You know what? I've been sitting here all night, listening to you go on about the rodeo and what you do for work and there are some things that just aren't adding up." Mateo accuses.

"Like what?" Octavia asks.

"For starters, how about lighting the fire out of nothing?"

"What do you mean? You started it first." She says.

He shakes his head, "No Octavia, it wasn't starting."

Chad stands up, "Hey, look, I don't know what you think you saw but..."

Mateo mirrors his movement.

"I wasn't talking to you," his voice raised, "you might have fooled everyone else, but that charm doesn't work on me!"

With the tension in the air, Octavia's blood runs cold. There's been enough confrontation for one night. What was supposed to be a casual gathering bringing both worlds together, has turned into a drama fest. Disappointment pricks at her.

"Guys, please." She says, her voice firm.

"I think it's time for us to go," Maya intervenes.

Mateo marches up to Octavia and whispers, "You need to be careful around him! Humans can't do those kinds of things."

Maya reaches for Mateo, gesturing for him to leave. "I'm so sorry, O." She mouths as she exits, leaving Octavia alone with Chad and his friends.

Octavia's confused about what Mateo is talking about, but she respects his perspective as he is someone she's learned to trust. A seed of unease has been planted. First Colleen and now Mateo, a nagging feeling gnaws at her that something isn't quite right. What does he mean, *'humans' can't do those kinds of things.* That's just absurd. What else could possibly exist aside from humans.

CHAPTER SEVENTEEN

Octavia paces the living room floor, a nervous energy buzzing beneath her skin. Her gaze keeps drifting towards the clock, each tick marking the passage of time. After much deliberation, she's finally made the decision. It's time. Time to introduce Chad to her boys. The thought had initially filled her with a flutter of excitement, but now, as the moment draws near, a wave of apprehension washes over her. Her motherly instinct wants to protect her children from everything, but the rational part of her wants to include them in this new chapter they have created together. If she's going to continue to see Chad, it's something that needs to be considered.

The echo of Colleen's voice rummages through her mind. What could possibly be her angle? Jealousy perhaps? And Mateo... She can't figure out what he was so upset about. What did he see that she didn't? Maya didn't want to get into it over the phone. Maybe she doesn't really know either.

She glances at the boys, who are sprawled on the floor, engrossed in a video game. Their laughter and playful banter fill the room, a comforting sound that momentarily eases her anxiety. She'd had a long conversation with them earlier, explaining that they were going to officially meet Chad. They already knew about him, but needed to hear their thoughts moving forward. To her relief, they are surprisingly enthusiastic, eager to meet the man who made their mom smile again. With a deep breath, she pulls out her phone. It's time. A quick text to Chad, a simple invitation to come over. She figures the familiar surroundings of their home will offer a sense of comfort and ease the initial introductions. Now, all she can do is wait, her heart pounds a frantic rhythm in her chest. This is what she wants, to create a family. And Chad, he makes her feel like home.

* * *

The addition of Chad shifts the dynamic of the household. The early afternoon unfolds with a game of croquet on the lawn. Something simple to break the ice. Although Cory, who is the social butterfly, doesn't typically need an ice breaker. Ryan on the other hand, who is more reserved, takes time to warm up to new people. Chad, surprisingly adept with the mallet, playfully dominates the first round, much to the boys' (and Octavia's) chagrin.

"No fair, you cheated!" Ryan declares, cheeks puffed out in mock indignation.

Chad raises his eyebrows and feigns innocence. "Cheated? In this game of skill and strategy? Never!" He winks at Octavia, a mischievous glint in his eye.

Cory, oblivious to the playful jabs exchanged between the adults, toddles over to Chad, a determined look on his face.

"My turn! I'm gonna knock your ball all the way to China!" He grips the cue stick with both hands, his tiny body straining with effort.

He swings the mallet with all his might, barely connecting with the ball. It wobbles a few inches before coming to a stop. Cory giggles, unfazed by his lack of success. He throws his head back and laughs, his infectious laughter echoing through the warm summer air as they chase balls and strategize their next moves.

Lunch is a simple affair, a feast of sandwiches piled high with fresh ingredients. They eat in the cool shade of a large oak tree, the heat of the day making a big meal seem unbearable. But the food is almost an afterthought. It's the easy camaraderie that truly matters, the laughter that bubbles up between them, the effortless way Chad interacts with her boys. Octavia watches him with a contented smile, his smile radiating warmth and genuine enjoyment. He fits in perfectly with her little family, a comforting thought that sends a flutter of excitement through her, a reminder that maybe, just maybe, this was exactly what she has been waiting for.

"I have an idea," Octavia declares, gathering the plates. "Who's up for some ice cream?"

Wide smiles illuminate the faces of her boys. "Yay!" Cory shouts, clapping his hands with glee.

"I want ice cream!" Ryan excitedly announces. "Can we go to Henry's?"

With full bellies and satisfied smiles, the decision is unanimous.

"Henry's?" Chad asks, a curious glint in his eyes. "I can't say I've actually ever been there."

"Oh, it's our favorite place to get ice cream," Octavia explains, her eyes twinkling. "I think you'll love it. As long as you love ice cream, of course."

He sends her a wink, "Oh you bet I do."

"They have so many different flavors to pick!" Ryan tells him, his eyes wide with excitement.

"Yeah! Like fifty flavors!" Cory announces with wide eyes and a big smile. "My favorite is the Superhero!" He says as he gestures his arms reaching into the sky, mimicking a superhero flying.

The afternoon sun glints off the windshield as they climb into Chad's truck, the air thick with the promise of adventure. Henry's Convenience Store, a local legend boasting a staggering twenty flavors of ice cream, is a mere five-minute drive away. A sense of sweet anticipation fills the air, a palpable excitement buzzing between them. For Ryan and Cory, this isn't just any ice cream run; it's an expedition, a chance to explore the ever-changing flavor landscape of Henry's, a delightful dilemma that always leaves them wide-eyed and indecisive.

Octavia chuckles as she watches them scrutinize the colorful display, their noses practically pressed against the glass as they gaze down at the enticing flavors. For Octavia, the outing holds a deeper significance; a chance for Chad to connect with her boys, a chance for them to build memories together. And as she watches him interact with them, a sense of security blooms in her chest. His interactions with the boys are gentle, respectful, and filled with a genuine warmth that makes her heart swell.

They find the perfect spot outside Henry's, a shaded table beneath a vibrant mural of ice cream cones. Chad, holding a melting cup of mint chocolate chip in his hand, looks at Octavia with a hopeful smile.

"So," he begins, his voice laced with a hint of nervousness, "how about I show you guys my place this evening?"

Octavia's heart skips a beat. An invitation for all of them to his house. It feels like a significant step forward, a deepening of their bond. She looks at her sons, their faces smeared with ice cream.

"You boys don't like animals, do you?" Chad asks. "I've got a bunch of hungry animals at home that need to be fed."

Their eyes light up with wonder. The idea of the boys spending more time with him, of exploring the space he calls home, holds a strange allure.

"That sounds great," she replies, her voice warm and genuine.

Looking back at her boys, she continues, "What do you think about going to Chad's house after we finish our ice cream?"

A silent cheer erupts from the boys, their eyes widening with excitement.

"Yeah!" Ryan says, his tongue darting out to lick a mischievous streak of melted chocolate from his cone. "Where do you live?"

Chad nods, "Not too far from here, buddy. It's about a 10-minute drive."

The drive to Chad's house is filled with a cozy silence, only broken by the comforting sound of the boy's banter in the back seat. Octavia steals glances of Chad, his profile bathed in the golden light of the summer sun mesmerizes her. When he turns to look at her, the sun lights them right up. It's unreal, really. The earlier invitation, which is now a tangible prospect, sends a thrill through her.

The wonder can be heard emanating from the backseat as they pull up to Chad's place. Before Octavia can even comment, the back door of Chad's truck flies open, revealing a scene of pure joy. Ryan and Cory, unable to contain their excitement, bolt straight for a group of fluffy animals huddled in a nearby pen, their laughter echoing through the air. Octavia and Chad follow closely behind them, a smile spreading across Octavia's face as she watches her boys discover their new adventure.

"Look, Mom! There's goats! And HORSES!" Cory shrieks, his voice a joyous melody.

Several horses graze peacefully in a nearby paddock, their coats gleaming in the afternoon sun. A coop full of chickens cluck and scratch in their enclosure, a symphony of feathery activity. But it's the cows that immediately draw Octavia's attention, and not in a good way.

"Just wait." She reaches her arm out to signal the boys to stop.

There is one cow in particular that stands out from the rest, a hulking creature with a perpetually watchful gaze, humanly almost. Its massive crescent shaped horns possess an unearthly energy that seems to transcend the animal world. It fixates on Octavia whenever she ventures near, prompting goosebumps on her skin deterring her from going too close.

"I don't want you two near this pen, or that cow." She demands. "Okay?" The last time Octavia entered its pen, it charged towards her.

She doesn't trust it at all.

"I won't." The ever cautious observer, Ryan, has no qualms with this and can be easily trusted to follow his mom's guidance. Cory, on the other hand, typically tends to need a bit of extra guidance.

"Okay, Cory?" She kneels down to his level to ensure his understanding is clear. "That cow can be dangerous, so I need you to stay away from it."

"Okay, mommy." Cory responds, likely unsure of the weight of the situation.

"Hey now, don't be dissin' the mighty bull here, he's my guardian." Chad butts in.

Octavia shoots him a confused look. She has no idea what he's talking about, how could a cow be a guardian? It's probably some weird cowboy thing. Kind of like how some people say a dog is a man's best friend. Maybe a cow is a cowboy's guardian. Either way, she still doesn't like the thing and definitely doesn't want her kids around it.

The horses, on the other hand, are a different story. Sweet and gentle, they stand patiently as Cory, the adventurer, attempts to scale the fence for a closer look. Their acceptance of his enthusiastic petting, even with his less than graceful climbing technique, warms Octavia's heart. Seeing Chad's natural connection with her boys intensifies Octavia's feelings for him. It's a powerful combination. His kindness, his acceptance, and the way he so effortlessly fits into their little family unit. It feels... right. And even though they've only known each other for a short time, the depth of their connection surprises even her. A smile tugs at her lips as she watches Chad and the boys. There is a lot to explore here, with these animals, with this man, and with the feelings that bloom within her. And it brings her joy that this is her life now.

Ryan, ever the pragmatist, is peppering Chad with questions about their names and what they eat. Octavia chuckles, a warmth spreading through her chest. Chad, ever the patient soul, kneels down to their level, answering their questions with a gentle enthusiasm that reflects his genuine smile. The next two hours fly by in a whirlwind of exploration. They learn about chickens, playful sheep, and even a grumpy but secretly sweet old goat. The boys are in their element, their laughter echoes across the farmyard.

As dusk settles, they migrate into the house, everyone pleasantly exhausted. The recent renovation has transformed the space into a breathtaking masterpiece. Dark mahogany floors gleam under the soft light, a perfect contrast to the sleek black marble countertops with their surprising yet elegant gold accents. It's a design unlike anything they've ever seen, a fusion of modern sophistication and rustic charm. A quick tour reveals two downstairs bedrooms, each painted in a calming light beige. The meticulous attention to detail speaks volumes about Chad's personality. A man who appreciates both style and functionality. As they explore, Octavia can't help but imagine the possibilities that could unfold within these walls, now that Chad has *officially* met her boys. The potential for shared meals, cozy movie nights, and laughter-filled evenings with her children dance in her mind.

Chad breaks the silent awe.

"How about some popcorn and a movie?" A delicious collaboration of popcorn and laughter is a welcome respite from the day's adventures.

"That sounds like an amazing way to end the day," she interjects with a soft smile, her gaze lingering on Chad.

"What do you say boys, want to watch a movie before we head home?" Octavia asks, her attention shifting to her sons.

"Ryan?" She pauses, looking around. "Where's your brother?"

"I don't know," Ryan replies, his brow furrowed in concern. "He was just right here."

"Cory, love?" Octavia calls out, her voice echoing through the house. "Where are you?"

"He's not still outside is he?" Chad asks, making his way to the door.

"Not unless he went back out. We all came in together," she says, a knot of worry tightens in her stomach.

"I'll take a look outside," Chad assures her, his voice firm. "You check the house, every room. Make sure he's not hiding somewhere."

With Ryan instructed to stay put, Octavia scours the main floor of the house, her heart pounding in her chest. He's nowhere to be seen. Panic starts to rise. She looks out the window and sees Chad looking near the animals, his face etched with concern. Cory loves animals, it's not far-fetched to think he would have been drawn to the pens, perhaps trying to get a closer look at the rabbits or any of the other cute fluffy animals.

The main floor is checked and cleared. Octavia heads upstairs, her heart pounding, he's got to be here somewhere. She checks the first room, her gaze sweeping across the room, searching for any sign of Cory. Nothing. As she wanders further down the hall, a low murmur of voices reaches her ears, the sound emanating from the next room.

"Cory?" she calls out, her feet thud against the floor as she rushes to the next room. The door is mostly closed, a sliver of light escaping from the gap. Carefully, she pushes it open, her gaze sweeping across the room, searching for any sign of movement.

Octavia finds him sitting alone on the floor, an old toy truck clutched in his hands.

"There you are!" she calls out, her voice a mixture of relief and exasperation. She kneels down, pulling him into a warm embrace. "Didn't you hear me calling you?"

Cory looks up at her with big brown eyes, a hint of sadness clouding his features. He slowly shakes his head.

A flicker of a flashback crosses Octavia's mind.

"Who were you talking to, love?" she asks gently, her voice soft.

He doesn't answer. His gaze fixates on the toy in his hand.

"Look at what I found." he says, his voice barely a whisper.

"Let's head back downstairs and show Ryan and Chad," Octavia suggests, her voice a mixture of curiosity and concern.

CHAPTER EIGHTEEN

A buzz of excitement fills the air. Today is the lake trip with Chad's friends, and Octavia is a mix of nerves and anticipation. She's arranged for her mom to watch Ryan and Cory at her campsite, a twenty five minute drive out of town down a dirt road. Her mom owns a gold claim and the boys love spending time there with her. With Ryan and Cory buckled in and a cooler full of picnic supplies in the back, they set off. The highway stretches out before them, promising a day of sunshine and good company.

"I love you guys so much." She says, showering them with hugs and kisses before leaving them and taking off for the day.

The car thrums with a satisfying rumble as they pull away from Octavia's mom's site. Leaving the boys behind, a wave of relief washes over her, they are always safe in her care. A nervous flutter of excitement blossoms in anticipation for the day ahead.

Chad grins at her from behind the wheel. She looks back at the boys as they drive away, until they are out of sight.

"Alright," he announces, his eyes lit up with a flash of mischief, "let's get this show on the lake!"

Before Octavia can react, his foot slams down on the accelerator. The gravel road blurs into a dusty brown streak, the truck bouncing and jostling with each uneven patch. Her heart jumps out of her chest, a primal fear battles with a perverse thrill. Octavia isn't one for reckless driving. Yet, as Chad navigates the winding road with practiced ease, a strange sense of exhilaration bubbles up in her chest. The world outside the truck is a blur of dust and scrub brush, the only constant is the firm grip she has on the door handle and the wide smile plastered across Chad's face. Part of her wants to scream, to demand him to slow down, but the burgeoning excitement holds her back. It's like being on a wild roller coaster, the fear tinged with a delicious sense of danger. They crest a hill, the vast expanse of the lake shimmering in the distance. A cheer erupts from Chad, and for a fleeting moment, Octavia could swear she's right there with him, fueled by the adrenaline rush.

They reach the paved highway and the spell breaks. The truck settles onto the smooth surface, the wild jostling replaced by a gentle hum. Octavia's breath hitches, the adrenaline leaving behind a wave of nausea. Chad, oblivious, glances over with a triumphant grin.

"Was that fun or what?" Chad yells out.

Octavia can only manage a weak smile. Her voice, when she finally speaks, is barely audible. "Wow, that was... something." Chad's grin slightly falters, a flicker of concern replacing the earlier excitement.

"You okay? I thought..."

"No," Octavia interrupts, forcing a brighter tone. "It was... exhilarating. Just, not expected."

"Oh, shoot," he says, sheepishly easing off the gas. "You could have told me to slow down if you didn't want to white-knuckle the entire drive."

Octavia shakes her head, a ghost of a smile plays on her lips.

"It's okay," unable to find any more words. Maybe a little scared, but undeniably more intrigued by the man beside her. He isn't just charming and fun, there's a wild streak beneath his easy going exterior, a spark that mirrors the thrill that still danced in her veins.

"I'm just glad you waited until the boys were not in the vehicle." She says, her voice laced with a thinly veiled warning.

"I'd never drive like that with them in the vehicle." He clenches his jaw, an offensive tone in his voice. "That's why I waited until they were dropped off."

The dusty back road stretches out behind them like a fading memory as Chad pulls into the designated meeting spot by the lake. A vibrant mix of laughter and chatter greets them as they emerge from the truck. James and Baily are sprawled out on colorful beach towels, coolers casting cool shadows on the warm sand.

Baily, the witty one with a mane of fiery red hair and face full of freckles, is the first to greet them.

"We've been waiting for you guys."

James, excited like a little puppy, speaks up. "Took ya long enough."

"Well, we had to drop the kids off," Octavia sets the cooler down, still a little shaken from the ride, slightly irritated with Chad.

"Don't set that down yet." Baily interrupts. "I hope you like boats." She states as she whisks them towards a sleek speedboat bobbing lazily at the dock.

"Oh definitely," She replies with a sleek smile. "I love being out on the water."

James, with sunkissed skin and stands as tall as Chad, takes the helm with a practiced ease. The cool spray of water kisses their faces as they skim across the glassy surface of the lake. "Have you ever water skied before, O?"

"I haven't." A nervous pit forms in the bottom of her stomach. They are going to convince her to, she's sure of it.

"Surely, someone like you would have no problem picking it up." James says with a mischievous smirk.

"Someone like me?" What does he mean by that? She's never water skied before. Sure, she's into sports and can be athletic, but how could James know any of this?

Chad clears his throat.

"Yeah, Chad told us that you're different. We know." James explains as he slows the boat.

Chad darts a quick and menacing look into James' direction.

"Know what?" A forced smile tugs at her lips, unsure of what he's getting at. "How am I different?"

Chad speaks up before James can answer. "That you're just not like anyone I've ever met. You're good at pretty much everything I've seen you do. That's all."

James shoots Chad a confused look but quickly wipes it off with a smile. "Yeah, that's all I meant." he says as he pulls out the water skis from a cubby next to Baily.

"Why don't I go first and show you the ropes? Then if you feel up for it, you give it a try? Yeah?" Chad asks Octavia, a confident smile playing on his lips as he picks up the water ski handle. It's a sleek, red bar connected to a vibrant yellow rope, ready for action.

"Yeah, for sure." She agrees, a surprising enthusiasm bubbling up despite the growing nervous anticipation in her stomach. Watching them, it really does look like fun. Besides, she thinks, it won't hurt to try.

The afternoon plays on, a perfect symphony of the warm sun beating down and the refreshing feel of the cool lake water. Chad, with effortless grace, cuts across the wake, sending plumes of spray high into the air. He weaves and turns, his movements fluid and precise, making it look incredibly easy. James and Baily follow suit, each taking their turn on the skis with an impressive display of natural athletic ability. They glide over the surface as if born to it, true pros.

Finally, it's Octavia's turn after finding the courage. They all make it look so easy. She slips her feet into the bindings, the cool water instantly chilling her ankles. With a deep breath and a nod to James at the helm, the boat lurches forward. For a moment, she struggles, her body wobbling precariously, but then something clicks. She straightens, finds her balance, and against all odds, rises smoothly out of the water. Her first run is surprisingly successful, especially for a beginner. She carves a clean line, the wind in her hair and a triumphant grin spreading across her face.

The more time Octavia spends with Chad, especially now, sharing laughter and daring attempts on the water skis with his friends, the more deeply connected she feels to him. She actually feels like a part of his world, not just an observer, and that they are creating something truly beautiful between them. It all feels so perfect, she thinks, a blissful sigh escaping her lips as her hair waves wildly in the wind on their way back to shore, the last rays of the sun painting the lake in hues of orange and gold after an exhilarating day on the water.

CHAPTER NINETEEN

Cracks, faint at first, begin to spider web across the seemingly perfect facade of Octavia's new life. Are they truly living in a sun-drenched paradise, or is it all a carefully constructed illusion? The thought, unwelcome and unsettling, occasionally snakes its way into Octavia's mind. She swats it away like a pesky fly, dismissing it as leftover baggage from past relationships that had left her wary. Trusting men comes with difficulty, a consequence of a string of failed connections. But Chad, oh, Chad's different. He has to be. His charm is undeniable, his treatment of her is nothing short of dignified. He even embraces her sons, integrating seamlessly into their family dynamic, seemingly enjoying their rambunctious energy. She's accepted by his friends. Yet, a tiny voice, barely a whisper, lingers in the back of her head. Is this too good to be true? Does such effortless perfection exist, or is there something lurking beneath the surface, waiting to be revealed? No, this relationship is perfect in every way, she always concludes, turning a blind eye to doubts that creep in.

The days hum with a comforting rhythm. Octavia and her boys love spending the mornings at Chad's helping with the animals. The clucking of hens, the enthusiastic bleating of the old resident goat, and the low rumble of the tomcat. Chad and the boys tackle the chores together, a well-oiled machine honed by practice. Ryan, the aspiring veterinarian, approaches each task with a scientific curiosity. He carefully gathers eggs, his brow furrowed in concentration as he checks for signs of fertility. Cory, on the other hand, is a spirit of pure affection. He showers the animals with pats and nonsensical chatter, his laughter echoes through the barn. Some days, they work side-by-side, a symphony of rustling hay and playful banter. Other days, the boys weave their own adventures. They might disappear into the backyard, their shouts muffled by the tall grass as they build forts or stage epic battles with sticks as swords.

Sometimes, they venture down to the neighbor's house, their laughter mingling with the sounds of other children at play. And on rainy days, the house transforms into their own personal kingdom. The playroom upstairs, with forts built, becomes a pirate ship navigating treacherous seas, or a rocket blasting off to explore distant galaxies.

Sunlight streams through the windows, casting a warm glow as Octavia sweeps the floors. The rhythmic swish of the broom is a familiar comfort, a soundtrack to her domestic routine. A routine that just kind of happened slowly and casually. But welcome, nonetheless. Music plays softly in the background. Chad's outside handling the main animal chores, a responsibility they both readily agree to. Octavia, with a touch of old-fashioned pride, revels in the homemaker role. It feels good to create a cozy haven for their new little family. Suddenly, the peaceful melody is shattered by a thunderous clatter echoing from upstairs. Tiny footsteps pound down the hallway, each thump resonating with a mischievous energy that brings a smile to Octavia's lips.

"Slow down up there, little man!" Octavia calls out with a playful lilt in her voice.

She leans the broom against the wall, grabs the dustpan and begins to gather the debris with a practiced flick of her wrist. Octavia's playful warning dissolves into a faint smile as the thundering footsteps resume their chaotic rhythm upstairs. It seems her usual method of gentle admonishment isn't working its magic today. With a sigh that holds more amusement than annoyance, she sets the dustpan down. Curiosity, tinged with a hint of apprehension, tugs at her. Perhaps a more hands-on approach is required. Straightening her back, Octavia starts towards the stairs, a determined energy swirling within her.

However, her ascent up the stairs is met with an unsettling silence. The rhythmic pounding has vanished, replaced by an unnerving quiet. Octavia's brow furrows. She checks Ryan and Cory's usual hideouts, the bedrooms, the cramped space beneath the beds, but finds nothing. A sliver of unease pricks at her. Someone, undoubtedly one of her boys, was definitely creating that ruckus just moments ago. With a determined push, she opens the third bedroom door. It's always been a bit of a catch-all space; a place to store boxes and unused furniture. Octavia was always unsure of its purpose and didn't really care to ask. Now, the question lingers unanswered: what, or who, awaits her inside?

Octavia hesitates at the threshold of the third bedroom's door. It hangs slightly ajar, a sliver of darkness peeking out like a secret waiting to be unveiled. The silence is heavy, a deafening contrast to the playful chaos of moments before.

"Hey, boys?" she calls out, her voice laced with a hint of cautious warning. "If you're in here, it's time to come out."

She doesn't step inside. A strange prickling sensation runs down her spine, a sudden urge to leave the room undisturbed. But the memory of the pounding footsteps, the certainty that one of her sons is behind the door, pushes her forward. Taking a deep breath, she reaches out a hand, her fingers hovering over the surface of the doorknob. The silence stretches, heavy and unbroken. A shiver dances up her arms. There's no playful reply, no muffled giggle. Just an unsettling emptiness that feels heavier than the absence of sound. With a frown, she pushes the door open wider, peering into the shadowed room. But the interior reveals nothing out of the ordinary. Boxes stacked, furniture shrouded in dust sheets. An unsettling calm washes over her. Where did the noise come from? Had she imagined it altogether?

Unease gnaws at her. She doesn't like the strange feeling this room evokes, a prickling sensation that urges her to retreat. Leaving the door open, she quickly heads back down the stairs, the echo of her footsteps swallowed by the silence. She puts the broom and dustpan away and grabs the mop bucket, a disquieting sense of unease lingers. The playful chaos of moments ago had morphed into an unsettling mystery, leaving her mind churning with unanswered questions. What had caused the noise? And what secret does this room hold, shrouded in darkness and silence? The warm water splashes into the mop bucket, a soothing disparity to the disquiet churning in Octavia's gut. Glancing out the window, she sees Ryan and Cory kneeling by the rabbit hutch, she notices Cory and his adorable blond hair, as he turns in concentration offering a dandelion to the twitching nose of a furry inhabitant. Relief washes over her. They've been outside the entire time.

So, the racket upstairs? Had she imagined it? Could the house be haunted? That seems as far-fetched as the idea that Chad isn't human, based on what Mateo was seemingly trying to get at. The silence in the house now feels extra heavy, amplifying the echo of her own thoughts. Shaking her head firmly, Octavia banishes the unsettling notion. It has to be a simple explanation. Maybe a loose floorboard creaking in the changing temperature, or a stray animal seeking refuge in the attic. Taking a deep breath, she dips the mop into the bucket, the rhythmic swish against the floor is a grounding presence. Yet, a sliver of unease remains, a niggling feeling that the house holds a secret, a silent echo of the unexplained sounds upstairs. This wasn't the first time she'd had this unsettling feeling, a prickling sensation that seems to emanate from the mysterious third room.

* * *

She takes a step back, admiring her handiwork. The once-dull floor is now gleaming with a wet-look shine. The house, bathed in the warm afternoon light filtering through the windows, looks immaculate. A surge of pride swells in her chest. She's transformed this space into a haven, a testament to her love for her family. Pushing aside any disquiet, Octavia grabs a basket with intention to stop at the greenhouse while outside, and makes her way out. The familiar sounds of chirping birds and the boys' laughter greets her. Chad stands by the coop, scattering feed for the chickens, his smile as warm as the sun.

As Octavia approaches, the unease begins to fade, replaced by the comforting normalcy of being with her family.

"Hey, were one of you just in the house?" She asks them.

"We were outside with the animals, mama." Cory replies. "Look, the bunny likes dandelions."

"Awe, cute, my baby boy." She reaches out and picks Cory up for a great big hug. "I love you so much."

She extends her arm to Ryan for a hug from him, too. "Love you, my boy." Cory wriggles, indicating to be let down. She lets him down and meets Chad with a kiss on his cheek, feeling too embarrassed to mention the sounds that she heard from inside the house. "Is there anything left out here for me to do, or did you fine gentlemen get it all finished up?" She asks. The fresh air and sunshine is doing wonders for dispelling the lingering unease in her gut.

Chad chuckles, repositioning his cowboy hat.

"We're pretty much done here for the day. Actually..." he trails off, his eyes twinkling with mischief, "if you guys wouldn't mind a little dust, maybe we can go for a ride?" The boys' faces erupt in a chorus of excited yelps. Their eyes widen with a brilliance that rivals the afternoon sun.

"Yes!!" Cory declares ecstatically.

"I want to!" Ryan announces with an infectious grin on his face.

They'd been dreaming about this ever since they first laid eyes on the majestic horses grazing in the pasture.

Octavia can't help but grin at their infectious enthusiasm.

"A ride sounds perfect," she declares, her voice laced with excitement. "Let's go see what adventures await us!... And," Octavia adds, a hint of practicality peeking through her excitement, "this works out well because the floors need time to dry before we head back inside anyway. By the time we're finished it will be close to dinner time."

Chad chuckles, his reassurance as warm as the afternoon sun.

"Perfect. Let's do this." He gestures towards a shed tucked away near the animal pasture, its weathered wood hinting at years of service. It wasn't renovated like the house was. "Everything we need is right in there." The excitement is evident, thick enough to taste. Since it's the boys' first horseback adventure, they decide to saddle up only the calmest, most experienced steed.

"Can I go first?" Cory, a whirlwind of impatience, practically vibrates with excitement, barely containing his demands to be first.

"Sure." Ryan looks up at his mom and replies. The elder and more patient soul understands the unspoken agreement, let Cory have the first go, and he'd likely snag a longer turn himself afterward.

Octavia, with her camera from her phone poised, captures the pure joy radiating from her sons. Ryan and Cory practically burst with it, their unspoken gratitude fills the air more potently than any words. As Cory perches proudly on the horse's back, he takes his first tentative steps around the pasture with Chad leading the way.

"Awe", Octavia begins, "I love this!" She holds up the photo for Chad to see. Ryan is up on the horse with Chad guiding it. "Can I post this?"

"You know I don't like my picture being taken." He impatiently tells her.

"Okay, but why?" Octavia demands. "You can't even see your face. Do you not want to be seen with me?" Her tone turns slightly defensive.

"No, it's not that." dropping his voice. "Now is not the time." He immediately shuts down the conversation.

Octavia doesn't know exactly what that means, but for the sake of preventing a potential argument in front of her boys, she decides to let it go, for now.

Dinnertime is fast approaching. She sends Ryan to help Chad with the saddle while she takes Cory's hand, heading towards the greenhouse. Inside the warm and moist sheltered space, the rows of vegetables thrive. Reaching for a head of lettuce, upon inspection, she realizes it's the only harvest-ready item. With Cory's eager help, they gather enough for a crisp salad. But the vibrant greenhouse reminds her of another task, watering.

"Alright, champ," she says, handing Cory a small watering can, "let's give these thirsty plants a drink."

Cory, the enthusiastic helper, beams and begins diligently watering the nearest tomato plant. Meanwhile, Octavia tackles the larger rows, a sense of satisfaction washes over her as she nurtures their little slice of green paradise. By the time they finish, the sound of laughter drifts from the house, signaling Chad and Ryan are done washing up. With a quick rinse of their own hands, Octavia and Cory join the growing chorus, ready to face the evening with full bellies and happy hearts. The sound of the bathroom door shutting sends a shiver down Octavia's spine, a stark contrast to the warmth of the afternoon sun. Chad's voice, casually calling out echoes through the house.

"Oh hey, I think I forgot my phone and wallet in the truck." He calls out. "Would you be a doll and grab it for me?"

"Sure, babe," Octavia replies, her voice a touch too bright. The truck, bathed in the golden light of the setting sun, seems to hold its breath as she approaches. Her search for the items becomes a mechanical exercise. She searches the door cubby, seats, dashboard, center console, each empty space feels like a tiny tinge of disappointment. There it is.

The phone, nestled in the center console, lights up with a flurry of notifications. A primal urge, a curiosity sharper than a knife, compels her to pick it up and look.

"Sarah?" she whispers, the name a foreign object on her tongue. A million questions swarm her mind, a dark cloud threatening to engulf the warmth of the afternoon. She forces her hand to dim the screen, the name burns into her memory. Her fingers tremble. She has to see for herself that it's nothing. She opens up the screen again to rummage through the messages.

If you say so, cowboy. Is the only message that is there. The rest of the conversation has been deleted. Pushing past the rising tide of unease, she closes the phone and continues searching for the wallet, her heart a frantic drum beating against her ribs.

A release of tension that's forming in her shoulders lightens as she finally retrieves the wallet. But the victory is short-lived. A glint of plastic catches her eye, nestled beneath the leather folds.

"What the hell?" she breaths, picking up a crumpled sleeve of condoms. The discovery isn't inherently strange. Condoms are a fact of life. But the timing and the secrecy gnaw at the comfortable certainty she's built. She and Chad have stopped using them and rely solely on other birth control contraceptives, such as the pill, after becoming exclusive, a milestone they've celebrated. Now, finding this illicit stash feels like a betrayal, a crack in the carefully constructed facade of their relationship.

A sliver of reason tries to intervene. Maybe they're old, leftovers from before their commitment. They haven't exactly cleaned the truck together before. But the negative gut feeling won't be silenced. With a silent vow, she tucks the condoms into the pocket of her jeans. Disposing of them without Chad's knowledge feels like a silent act of defiance, a tiny rebellion against the unsettling potential truth. The kitchen, once a haven of warmth and contentment, now feels sterile and cold. Octavia moves on autopilot, her earlier joy replaced by a steely resolve. Thoughts of a woman named Sarah and the discovery of the condoms seer through her mind. She chops vegetables, her mind a whirlwind of questions and accusations. The discovery in the truck has shattered the illusion of their perfect life, leaving behind a jagged mess of doubt. Maybe it is all too good to be true.

Despite the turmoil within, she prepares dinner, her movements measured and precise. A plate for Chad, a plate for Ryan, a plate for Cory, each one a silent testament to the life she's built. She even manages to pack a lunch for Chad's lunch before she heads home for the night, the act a strange mix of defiance and domesticity. She can't jump to conclusions, although her gut is telling her what she doesn't want to believe.

The house settles into an uneasy quiet as she prepares to head home for the night. Exhaustion tugs at Octavia, a heavy weight against the churning emotions in her gut. She finds Chad on the back deck, a solitary figure silhouetted against the night sky. The air, once warm and inviting, now feels heavy with unspoken words. She intends to confront him. He gestures beside him, and Octavia sinks onto the chair, the wood cool against her skin. He pours them each a drink, the clinking of glasses a jarring sound in the tense silence. Chad takes a long sip, his brow furrowed in what seems like genuine concern.

"Mmm," he finally murmurs, a low sound laced with worry. He reaches out, his hand hovering over hers for a moment before settling on her shoulder. The touch, usually a source of comfort, sends a chill through her tonight. It feels...different. Forced.

"What's wrong?" she quietly asks. The question hangs heavy with unspoken accusations.

"I don't know," he replies, his voice strained. He stands up from his chair.

"Don't know what?"

Her confusion is laced with a sliver of something sharper, suspicion. Looking up at Chad, she stands up to join him. He hesitates, a muscle in his jaw clenching and relaxing.

"What if this doesn't work out?" he finally manages, his voice soft, barely audible.

Octavia stares at him, her mind a tangled mess of emotions. What does he mean, doesn't work out? The memory of the text message along with the condoms in her pocket flash through her mind, a reminder of the unsettling revelation she now harbors. Could he be talking about his infidelity, if that is actually what's happening? Or does he have suspicions about Octavia? Here, under the cloak of night, her facade of normalcy threatens to crumble. She needs answers, and she needs them now. But a more cautious part of her knows this conversation won't be easy.

Octavia recoils slightly, needing to see his face, to decipher the truth in his eyes. Confusion is etched on her features, a contrast to the storm brewing within. His lack of an explanation offers no solace, only fueling the fire of her suspicions.

"Do you mean...between us?" she ventures, her voice barely above a whisper.

The question hangs heavy between them, a silent accusation. A slow, hesitant nod from Chad confirms her worst fears.

"Does this have anything to do with you talking to other women?" she stammers, her voice cracking with a mix of hurt and confusion. The idyllic picture of their day, the laughter echoing in the pasture, now feels like a cruel mirage.

"What are you talking about?" Chad asks, defensiveness creeping into his voice. "Where is this coming from?"

"Who are the other women you talk to?" Octavia questions, her voice trembling, despite how hard she's trying to play it cool. She knows not to jump to conclusions.

A desperate plea for reassurance, is met with a heavy silence. Chad pulls her in once again, the embrace feels more like a cage than a comfort. They sit in a tense tableau, the warmth of the night indifferent to the icy chasm that has opened between them.

"Babe," He says, finally breaking the silence. "I don't know what you're talking about, but the only people I talk to are just friends. I promise."

The unanswered questions gnaw at Octavia, a relentless chorus demanding answers. But for now, beneath the silent gaze of the evening's sky, a fragile truce is declared. The truth, a venomous serpent lurking in the shadows, would have to wait for its moment to strike. The moment won't be found in tonight's conversation. The air, thick with unspoken accusations, offers no easy answers. Chad's embrace, usually a source of comfort, feels like a question mark pressed against her skin. Octavia sinks into it, a weary truce for a battle yet to be fought.

With a sigh, Octavia leans into Chad, the gesture a desperate plea for normalcy. He responds with a tightening of his arms, a silent promise of a future both desired and dreaded.

CHAPTER TWENTY

A cold breeze makes its way through the bedroom. Octavia stirs, the remnants of a troubled sleep clings to her like a shadow to its source. The silence of the house is broken only by the rhythmic hum of the refrigerator. The night has offered no solace, only a fragile truce that threatens to shatter at the slightest touch. It's possible Chad is being honest, and perhaps the women are just friends. There really isn't any way of knowing for sure. All she really has to go off of is his word and faith. With a forced smile, she wakes the boys, their youthful energy is like a breath of fresh air. Breakfast is a hurried affair, punctuated by the clinking of spoons and the cheerful chatter of Ryan and Cory. Lunches are made and packed, a practiced routine performed on autopilot.

On her way home from dropping off the boys at daycare, everything seems different. The once comforting sights; the grazing horses, the mountains, now hold an unsettling air of mystery. The memory of the hidden condoms and Chad's fearful confession plays on a loop in her mind, a constant reminder of the fault line that has fractured their seemingly perfect facade. She flips through the radio stations, the cheerful pop music doing little to dispel the leaden weight in her gut. Each burst of melody feels like a mocking reminder of the shattered illusion of her perfect life. She forces herself to focus on the road. The music comes to life, and the opening chords of "What ifs", fills the car. Octavia feels a pang in her chest, a strange connection to the song's hopeful lyrics and the turmoil of the night before. Comforting others is her nature, and a fierce protectiveness surges for Chad despite her own churning questions.

Love, a powerful force, threatens to drown out the doubts gnawing at her. Is it enough to weather this unexpected storm? With a silent plea, she pulls over and reaches for her phone, the familiar action a small comfort. She pulls up the song and sends it to Chad in a text. It's a fragile message of hope amidst the uncertainty. The messages, a wave of conflicting emotions wash over her. Relief battles with a nagging suspicion. Perhaps the song will offer him solace, a reminder of their bond. Or maybe, it's a foolish attempt to paper over a gaping crack in their foundation. A flicker of apprehension flares within Octavia. She can't fathom what could be causing Chad's doubts. Is he projecting the doubts of his actions onto her?

After all, actions, she believes, have always spoken louder than words. The memory of home-cooked meals, shared laughter with the boys, the comfort she offers are all testaments to her unwavering love and commitment. The song, a bittersweet reminder of their bond, offers a sliver of hope. Perhaps, tonight, with open hearts and honest communication, they can navigate this unexpected turbulence and emerge stronger.

The response comes back to her, quick and sharp. Searching for any kind of reassurance she doesn't hesitate to open the message right away.

Love you. Reads the message, a hopeful bridge across the chasm that has opened between them.

Relief washes over her, chasing away the serpent of doubt as Octavia sees Chad's reply. The two words 'love you' resonate with a depth that echoes the song's sentiment. It's a balm to her anxieties, a promise that reaffirms their connection. A smile, genuine and wide, blooms on her face as she tucks her phone close. The melody is now a sweet echo of their rekindled certainty. Perhaps, she thinks, his doubts stem from the upcoming rodeo. He'll be gone for a couple of days, and the uncertainty of separation might be weighing on him.

With renewed hope, Octavia sets about the day. She has a list of chores to tackle after work, but a lightness has replaced the leaden weight in her gut. Tomorrow, while Chad prepares for the rodeo, they will spend that time together, a chance to reconnect and rebuild the bridge between them. The unanswered questions still linger, a storm brewing on the horizon, but for now, she will focus on the sunshine and the love song playing on repeat in her heart.

Since you'll be at the rodeo this weekend I figured it would be good if you walked me through all of the animal chores.

If she helps with the chores while he's away, he will see her dedication to their relationship, perhaps it will ease any doubts he might be having.

Chad replies almost instantly.

Yeah, good idea. Let's make sure nothing gets missed while I'm gone.

After work, they step outside into the refreshing evening air. On their walk towards the greenhouse, Chad points out the various tasks: refilling the chicken feeder and waterer, collecting eggs from the nesting boxes, and checking the automatic watering system for the vegetables. Octavia listens attentively, nodding occasionally, but a keen observer might have noticed a flicker of apprehension in her eyes. She already knows most of these routines, having helped Chad on countless mornings. But this time, the responsibility feels different, a weight settling on her shoulders.

"...And of course," Chad continues, his voice strains. "There's always Murphy." Chad's beloved aging goat greets them with a bleat. "Murphy only gets a cup of grain," He goes on, "otherwise he will just keep eating. Then he will get fat, which will add to more complications."

Octavia kneels down, scratching him behind the ears, a familiar comfort in the face of the growing unease. "Awe, we don't want that, do we, Murphy?"

"The best time to let him out and roam is in the morning or evening, because then it isn't too hot for him." Chad iterates, a concerned look across his face. "He should be fine, but if you notice any signs that he isn't well, then call me, and I'll let you know what to do."

"Got it." Octavia concurs as she stands up.

Just then Chad's phone chimes and he pulls it out of his pocket. A casual glance at his phone screen reveals something that sets her nerves on edge. There, nestled amongst the rodeo details, is a picture. A woman with an unfamiliar smile, a knowing smirk playing on her lipstick-filled lips, stares back at Octavia. The caption below simply reads:

Excited to share the arena with you again, Champ!

"Exciting weekend coming up, huh." Octavia notes. "Looks like your friends are excited to see you again." She says nervously, not so confident that the photo and message she just caught a glance of is nothing more than a friendly gesture.

"Always are." Chad recalls.

"She isn't the reason you haven't invited me to the rodeo with you, is it?" Octavia accuses.

"Are you crazy?" Chad demands. "She's just a friend. Besides, the rodeo is no place for the boys. They need you here with them."

Hmm.. is that some kind of excuse? Who is he to decide what's good for her boys? However, there is nothing to go off of right now, except for trust. She has no evidence, and she isn't about to start acting like the jealous girlfriend that has no proof. Her insecurities eat away at her logic but Octavia soaks the rest of the tour in, her mind a tornado of thoughts. Taking care of the animals is manageable, a familiar routine. But facing the truth about Chad's fears, the condoms, and now the image of this pretty lady, the hidden secrets that threaten to shatter their carefully constructed world.

That's a challenge she isn't sure she's ready for. Yet, with each step they take, a sliver of determination grows within her. This weekend, while Chad competes at the rodeo, she won't just be tending to the animals. She will also be tending to the fragile embers of their love, hoping to rekindle the warmth before it's consumed by the flames of doubt.

CHAPTER TWENTY ONE

Chad leaves today. He's currently in town gathering last-minute items he needs for the trip while Octavia is at home with the boys. Standing outside, she hums along to the stereo, the twangy melody a cheerful counterpoint to the rhythmic clip-clop of hooves from the horse's nearby. She keeps a distant eye on the boys as they play in the yard. Leaning against the elegant porch rail, she watches the fiery ascent of the sun, painting the old ranch style house in hues of orange and gold. A movement on the road suddenly snags her attention. A cherry red pickup truck cruises by slowly, the windows rolled down. The driver, a woman with dark red hair and a knowing smirk, locks eyes with Octavia for a beat too long. A cold sliver of unease slithers down Octavia's back. The truck lingers for a moment before disappearing into a cloud of dust. Could that be the woman from the photo? Octavia frowns, the cheerful twang now grating on her nerves. The red truck feels like a tangible red flag, a discordant note in the melody of her peaceful morning in Chad's home.

The unease in Octavia's gut intensifies as the red truck fades into the distance. She can't explain it, but the woman's stare feels like a brand. She slips her phone out of her pocket and sends a text off to Chad.

Do you know who would be driving by in a red truck? A woman with red hair.

A beat of silence follows, then a reply.

Don't worry sweetheart. Just my friend, Sarah. She needs some pointers on her horse before the rodeo.

The explanation feels hollow. Sarah? Chad hasn't mentioned her before. Although, she does recall the messages appearing on his phone screen the other day and she looks oddly like the woman who sent Chad a photo of herself yesterday. But why would she slowly drive by and not pull into the driveway?

Suddenly, the pieces click into place. The deliberate slow drive-by, the knowing smirk, the way Chad had nervously glanced at his phone during breakfast. This woman isn't just some friend. This Sarah is someone with a strong presence in Chad's life. The unease in Octavia's gut morphed into a cold dread. Could this be where his insecurities were coming in, the reason he's *worried?* Octavia wants so desperately to trust Chad. She's always believed that there isn't anything that could ruin their perfect relationship. But the carefully constructed exterior feels like it is crumbling around her. Why hasn't Chad mentioned Sarah before? Why didn't he tell her that she would be stopping by for a hand? Why did she drive away after making eye contact? And lastly, why didn't he tell her they were going to be performing in the same rodeo? Could she be the reason Chad didn't invite her to the rodeo with him? His shallow excuse for it being no place for her boys seems like a stretch.

A wave of conflicting emotions wash over Octavia. Part of her yearns to confront him, to demand answers. But another, more cautious part, urges her to wait. After all, Chad is less than hours away from leaving. Did she really want their last moments together to be consumed by chaos and doubt? With a clenched jaw, Octavia buries this red flag deep within her. She will deal with Sarah, with the truth, when Chad returns from the rodeo. For now, she will focus on the practicalities, on ensuring the smooth running of the ranch while he is gone. But the warmth of their earlier truce has vanished, replaced by chilling suspicions.

Chad's return rattles the fragile peace they'd established this morning. He strides through the door, a practiced ease in his smile.

"Hey babe," he says, his voice warm. "I'm all ready to go."

He reaches down to pick up his pre-packed duffle bag from the floor. Octavia offers a forced smile in return. She can't help but think he is not being completely honest. The day's chores had been completed on autopilot. Sarah's image, that knowing smirk, burns in her mind, a hint of the truth she craves. Chad reaches out, his arms encircling her in a warm embrace. The familiar scent of him should be a comfort, but it only heightens her agitation. Is this a genuine gesture, or a calculated move to lull her suspicions?

She leans into him, embracing a battlefield of emotions. A part of her yearns to cling to him, to believe in the love they'd built. But another, more cynical part, recoils from his touch.

"Have a good trip," she murmurs, the words laced with a hollowness that mirror the emptiness she feels inside. Is he leaving her to spend his weekend with this woman? No, that would be absurd, he's a cowboy, he's going to compete. Octavia's insecurities threaten to consume her thoughts. She needs to set her insecurities aside for now. She refuses to believe Chad would do something like that to her, especially after all they have talked about with past relationships. He knows how much it would hurt her.

Chad pulls back, a frown creasing his forehead.

"Everything alright?" The question lingers, a challenge and an opportunity.

No, everything is not alright, the words long to break free from the prison of her mind, but the time isn't right. Not yet. She won't unleash the torrent of questions swirling within her, not with him on the brink of departure.

"Just tired," she lies, forcing a smile. "Long day."

Chad seems to accept the explanation, albeit with a lingering concern in his eyes. He plants a quick kiss on her forehead, the gesture feeling more obligatory than affectionate.

"You know I have to go right? You know how much the rodeos mean to me."

"Yeah, of course." More meaning than he's letting on. That seems like a selfish thought. Of course they mean a lot to him, he's been competing for years. It's like a world away from home for him. Chad going to the rodeo is and never was the issue, it's now about what or *who* he's doing while he's away.

"I'll call you tonight," he promises, his voice laced with a hint of uncertainty that mirrors her own.

"Will you, though?" The words escape her despite how hard she fought to keep them back. She can't shake the feeling that he's going away to be with someone else.

"What do you mean?" Chad takes a step back. "Of course I will." He stares into her eyes as if he's looking for something revealing. Once again, the words in her throat are stuck. "What's really going on here?"

She looks up at him and crosses her arms. Speak dammit. How can she have so many thoughts run through her mind and have such trouble verbalizing them? Finally, she manages to squeeze out a quiet question,

"Is it Sarah?" She regrets the words as soon as they are spoken, yet a sliver of relief surges through her as she gets it off her chest.

"Is what Sarah?" He asks, "I told you she's just a friend." He pauses and looks at her for what feels like an eternity. "Is this why you're acting strange? You think that I am sleeping with someone else?"

A single tear can be seen forming in the corner of her eyes, confirmation that his accusation is accurate. She draws upon her strength to shut down any further emotion. She doesn't have the facts, is she overreacting? Should she have said anything at all? Now what is Chad going to think of her? She's so carefully constructed this perfect image of herself and of this relationship. And he's so confident and capable.

She fears that revealing her insecurities and vulnerabilities could shatter it, scaring him away for good. The logic and the gut feelings are battling, unsure if she can contain the worries any longer. How can she allow her man to walk out the door, into the arms of another woman? She needs confirmation that she is the only one for him.

"Tell me I'm the only one." She blurts out.

"How could you think otherwise?" He asks, an offensive tone in his voice. "Where would I even find the time for anyone else? We're always together, and when we're not we're on the phone or messaging."

This seems like an attempt to manipulate reality. She wouldn't be having these doubts if there weren't a reason to. Her intuition has rarely failed her in the past. Whatever it is that he's doing to try to convince her is only heightening her suspicions, escalating the ball of anger she feels deep down within.

"Just tell me!" She shouts.

Reaching out, she pushes into Chad's chest with her hands. He immediately grabs hold of her wrists. Tight, but not enough to hurt her. He lowers her hands down next to his side, with a swift motion, he inches her back against the wall with his body pressed against hers. The look in his eyes reminds her of anger mixed with compassion. She's not sure if she should be intimidated or fascinated. She struggles to move her wrists free but she can't and she's not sure if she wants to.

"Octavia," he says, looking intently into her eyes. "Look at me."

She looks into his eyes for a few seconds longer, looking for any clues to decipher whether his intentions are pure. Her breath is heavy. He leans in, perhaps assuming her stare is an invitation, and kisses her soft lips. He lets go of her wrists and picks her up. She kisses him back, hot and heavy while instinctively wrapping her legs around his waist. His hips thrust into her slow and heavy one time before letting her back down. It's so incredibly hard to be upset with him, he's so handsome and so damn charming.

"It's always been you." he whispers into her ear.

With a final, lingering look, Chad turns and walks out the door, leaving her razzled. She reaches up to feel the sensation on her lips as she steadies her breath. What the hell just happened? She went from skeptic to frazzled in seconds. He has a super power, the power to make her lust for him like she has for no other, causing her to forget everything aside from his gorgeous green eyes and very... very kissable lips.

The silence that follows his departure is deafening, a clear contradiction to the storm brewing within her. She is alone now, facing the weight of her suspicions on her own.

Doubts gnaw at the edges of her love, a relentless chorus demanding answers. Yet, amidst the uncertainty, a powerful conviction remains: their love is strong. It isn't invincible, but it's worth fighting for. *It's always been you,* replays in the depths of her mind as her mind tries to process her thoughts. This isn't blind faith that she has for Chad. It's a testament to the love they'd built, a love that has weathered challenges before. Memories flash in her mind; late-night conversations tangled in warmth and the quiet understanding that only comes with deep affection. And the passion, a striking reminder of their intense physical attraction before he walked out the door.

Octavia shifts her focus to her boys and the animals, finding solace in their familiar routine. She retreats inward. With the thoughts of the mystery girl in the red truck on her mind she continues on with her day, welcoming any attempt to distract her and move those thoughts from the forefront of her mind, to the back. He says she's the one. It isn't the clear answer she was looking for, but that interaction was enough to remind her that what they have is worth the effort.

Octavia and Chad keep in contact as usual, a sliver of relief washes over Octavia as the phone rings. Taking a deep breath, she answers with a light, teasing tone. Perhaps if she's gentle with him, she won't push him away into another's arms.

"Hey, how's the roughest grounds in the country treating you?"

The sound of Chad's chuckle, genuine and warm, fills her ear.

"Not bad," he replies. "Just finished helping set up the bucking chutes. How are things holding down on the ranch?"

They continue to chat for a few minutes, the conversation flows easily between them as if the tension had dissipated. Discussions of the weather, Ryan and Cory's latest antics, and a funny story about a runaway chicken Octavia had chased earlier that day are this evening's distractions. It's almost as if everything is back to normal, as if their latest interaction has rekindled their love. There are no deep dives into emotions, no probing questions about the day. It's a sweet, fleeting moment of connection, a fragile bridge built on shared experiences and a love that, for now, refused to be overshadowed by doubt. As the conversation nears its end, a comfortable silence settles between them.

"Alright, well," Chad says, his voice tinged with a hint of sleepiness, "I gotta get some shut-eye. Big day tomorrow."

"You win 'em, cowboy," Octavia replies, a playful edge to her voice.

"I'll try my best," he chuckles. "Miss you already."

The words echo in her mind, a sweet promise amidst the uncertainty. "Miss you too," she responds, the sentiment genuine.

"Hey," she adds. "I love you."

"I love you, too, babygirl." Chad assures her.

They end the call and the silence returns, heavier this time. Octavia knows this sweet interlude won't last. The truth, a dark cloud on the horizon, couldn't be ignored forever. But for now, she holds onto the warmth of their conversation, a tiny ember of hope flickering in the growing darkness.

* * *

The next morning as Octavia forces herself through the usual routine. Chad must be thinking about her because a text message has just arrived.

Relief washes over her when she sees his name.

I think this one is a little more your speed. Is all it says.

A flutter of butterflies swirl around in her stomach as she presses play. "Never be the Same" a song recently released, yet familiar to Octavia, tugs at something deep within. Goosebumps rise on her arms as the lyrics wash over her, each verse echoing a hidden corner of her own love story. A warmth blooms in her fingertips, a yearning for a connection both new and deeply cherished. She closes her eyes, letting the music transport her, a bittersweet symphony of recognition in the guise of discovery. There's no way he'd do anything wrong by her, this simple act of love must be proof that she is the only one for him. He really does love me, she concludes. This song had instantly eased any doubts that were still grudgingly swirling around in her mind. But then again, maybe that's his exact intention.

I love you too! Is all she writes back.

The rhythmic melody and the fact that he cares enough to send it, says it all. She tidies up after breakfast with the boys and when she opens the fridge, a piece of paper catches her attention. It's got Lilah's name on it, highlighted in shiny metallic red. Etched on the back of the card, in the same colour, is a cryptic message she doesn't quite understand. It's like some kind of odd business card. She's never seen this card before but she grabs a magnet and slips the card underneath, pressing it against the fridge.

Chad talks about Lilah once in a while. He admits they speak on occasion, but doesn't really share personal details. Lilah has a strong place in Octavia's thoughts. She knows not to ask about her but she will never forget the night they met. As she observes this card she can't help but be left in deep thought about friendships. If that's what she can call the relationship between Chad and Lilah. However, it triggers her to think about her own friendship with Ben. She hasn't seen him much since she's been seeing Chad. She figures that if Chad and his best friend, who is a woman, can uphold such a strong friendship, then she can too. It's not as if she intentionally shrugs Ben off. She just never thought to spend much time with him because she's been so consumed with Chad. The recent events, however, remind her how important it is to keep these strong friendships alive and well. And with doubts that have been swirling in her mind lately, it wouldn't hurt to bring her friends close. Perhaps they will offer some comfort as her mind struggles between her love for chad and the lingering doubts of infidelity. She reaches down to grab her phone out of her pocket. She misses Ben, so she just calls him right up. Unfortunately, there's no answer so she texts him instead.

Hey Ben, just thinking about ya, we haven't hung out in a while. Give me a shout back when you get the chance.

A sudden knock at the door startles her. It's a man that sometimes helps Chad out on the farm. He's a very large man. Octavia's only met him a couple times and has never really interacted with him much. He gives off a weird energy so she prefers to keep her distance when she can. What is he doing here now, while Chad is away? He stands there like a gentle giant, casting a large shadow across the entrance way. His overalls are shaggy, a size too small, revealing his dirty white socks around his ankles. His face round and weathered, holds a perpetual air of childlike wonder. Blue eyes, clear and startling, are outlined by bags that speak of sleep deprivation. His crooked smile reveals a space between his yellowed two front teeth. A scar, the size of a toothpick reaches from his cheek to his chin, disrupting the growth of his stubble.

He speaks little, his words come out slowly and deliberately, often accompanied by a shuffle of his oversized boots. Yet, when he does speak, his voice holds a surprising childlike warmth.

"Hey, is Chad home?" He asks with intention.

"No, he is away at the rodeo this weekend." Octavia replies, slightly hiding behind the door. How could he forget to tell his farm hand that he was going to be away all weekend?

"Oh. okay." He speaks quietly.

"Is there something you need?" Octavia asks him. "I could call him for you if you need me to."

"He was supposed to pay me and didn't." He says, slowly closing the gap between them.

"Oh," she takes a step back, "why don't I try to get a hold of him to see what's going on with that."

She closes the door completely and steps inside for privacy, uncomfortable with his invasiveness. It's likely unintentional, he doesn't seem like the brightest one on the block. She pulls her phone out of her pocket and calls Chad. There's no answer. However, she isn't surprised as he's likely busy with the rodeo, so she proceeds to text him instead.

Hey babe, your farm helper, Clyde? Is here. He says that he was supposed to get paid and hasn't yet so he stopped by to pick it up. What do you want me to tell him?

The door creaks open behind her, Clyde steps in. What is he doing? Does he not have any boundaries?

"Um," She steps forward, hoping to deter him from coming in any further. "He must be busy," She explains to him. "He didn't answer his phone and I am not sure what time he competes, so I don't know when he will get back to me."

"Okay, did he leave the check here maybe." The indigent man asks, inching closer. "I need it." This man is very large, She couldn't defend herself if she wanted to.

"I'm sorry, I haven't seen anything and I don't know anything about it. But I can let you know as soon as Chad gets back to me."

He stares at her as if there is something more she can do.

"I will tell him to call you as soon as he can." Octavia raises her hand and places it on the door.

He clearly doesn't understand social cues. She needs to be straight with him. His presence becomes increasingly uncomfortable. A buzz in her pocket offers a thread of relief. *Please let it be Chad.* It is of course, except it doesn't bring her comfort at all.

Do not let him in the house. Is all it reads.

What? He clearly knows something that she doesn't, but she trusts the warning. Not only that, her boys are in the house and she will protect them at all costs.

"It's Chad, he says that he will call you. It's time for you to go now."

"It's Chad?" Clyde asks.

"Yes, now please, go, he will call you." She says, raising her hand towards the door.

He clumsily steps out the door. What can be so bad about this guy, other than his size? Honestly he seems harmless. But she will not undermine Chad's message. Relief runs through her now that he's outside, but just as she's closing the door, an unusual movement catches her eye. Clyde turns, his gaze fixed on her. Time seems to freeze as their eyes meet. A chilling whisper escapes his lips,

"The ancient pact with Lilith prevails. They meet in the dead of night, or plain sight. The demon's wrath is inevitable. The demon is here."

In sync with his words, a startling thunder-like noise travels down the stairs. Goosebumps like she's never felt before run from the top of her head, down her back to the very tip of her toes. She slams the door shut and deadbolts it. Her heart is pounding and she breathes heavily as she tries to gain her balance against the door. She has no idea what she just witnessed. And she doesn't care to hang around to find out.

"Boys?" She calls out. They are in the living room watching a show. Hopefully the show was loud enough that they didn't hear anything. Not sure that they would comprehend any of it anyway. She composes herself the best she can, completely forgetting to text Chad back.

"We're going to go home for the weekend, okay?" *Forget about checking on the sound that came from upstairs. Yeah right!* Octavia thinks to herself. There's no way she is about to go upstairs after what had just happened. She just wants her and her boys out of there and home where she feels safe.

"How come?" Ryan asks.

"We just haven't been there much and I think it would be nice to be home for a bit. Besides, I miss Maya. I'm going to see if she wants to do something this weekend. How does that sound?"

Her home feels familiar and comfortable, and her boys seem happiest there. It feels like the smartest move and Chad isn't around anyway so there really isn't much point in hanging around his house, especially when weird shit like that is happening.

The demon is here? The pact with the Lilith? What in the actual hell is he talking about? Clearly he's delusional and has been reading way too many children's stories. Thankfully he was long gone by the time Octavia had packed her kids up and headed out the door.

She needs to get away from here and find someone normal, like Maya, to spend the day with. Maybe that will help her sort her thoughts and feel a sense of grounding. She desperately needs a change of scenery after that.

CHAPTER TWENTY TWO

The lake's surface shimmers like a turquoise invitation under the warm sun, its gentle waves glinting as if beckoning them closer. Octavia, with Maya by her side, begins unloading the beach bag. It's bursting at the seams with snacks, sunscreen, and an assortment of inflatable beach toys. This is exactly what she needs and is feeling much better already. The air is thick with the scent of pine and freshwater, a quintessential summer day in British Columbia. Laughter echoes through the air, mingling with the excited shrieks of Octavia's children as they bolt towards the water, their little feet kicking up sand as they run. Their colorful beach towels flutter behind them like capes, adding splashes of bright reds, blues, and yellows to the scene. The children's joy is infectious, drawing wide smiles from both Octavia and Maya as they watch them race to be the first to reach the cool, refreshing embrace of the lake.

"Look at them go!" Maya exclaims, her voice filled with laughter.

"They're so happy out here," Octavia agrees, her heart swelling with pride. As the kids splash into the shallow water, their playful banter is a joyful symphony, harmonizing with the gentle lapping of the waves against the shore.

"Mom, can you blow up the floaties?" Ryan calls out.

"Sure thing, my boy," she responds. "Just give me a couple of minutes, k?"

Octavia and Maya exchange a glance, their eyes twinkle with the shared happiness that comes from watching the little ones enjoy the simple pleasures of summer despite being shaken up from this morning's shenanigans. They spread out the towels on a patch of soft sand near the water's edge, setting up their own little oasis where they can relax and soak in the sun while keeping a watchful eye on the kids.

"Perfect day for a tan." Maya says stretching out on her towel.

"Right!? You have no idea how badly I need this today," Octavia replies. "Thanks for coming out with us." The normalcy of being with Maya and her boys almost clouds the worries of Chad and his potential infidelity and with what happened with Clyde... Almost. The uncertainty still lingers like a serpent in the night waiting to pounce on its prey any second. How much can she tell Maya, how much should she? What Clyde had said is bizarre and should be written off as so and forgotten. However, the eerie sound that emanated from upstairs that accompanied his cryptic warning was far too real to ignore.

They keep a watchful eye on the children, who are now fully immersed in their watery adventures, their joyful shrieks filling the air. Every so often, Octavia rises from her spot on the towel and wanders to the water's edge, dipping her toes into the refreshingly cool lake. The sensation is invigorating, a delightful contrast to the sun's heat that leaves her feeling revitalized. She lingers there for a moment, feeling the soft sand beneath her feet and letting the water lap at her ankles before returning to the comfort of her towel and the warmth of the sun.

The rhythmic lapping of the waves against the shore, occasionally interrupted by the gentle wake of a passing boat, provides a soothing soundtrack to their afternoon. The sound, combined with the murmur of distant conversations and the occasional cry of a bird, creates a peaceful, almost meditative atmosphere. As the sun climbs higher in the sky, the scent of barbecue smoke wafts over from nearby grills, mingling with the fresh, pine-scented air. The smell is a tantalizing reminder of the picnic lunch they've packed, now waiting patiently to be enjoyed.

"Do you ever question how Mateo feels about you?" Octavia asks out of nowhere, the words tumbling out awkwardly, as if she's unsure they should be spoken out loud. She feels a gnawing unease inside her, a feeling she can't quite put into words but needs to voice.

Maya, caught off guard by the question, turns her head to look at Octavia, her curiosity piqued.

"What do you mean?"

Octavia hesitates, searching for the right way to express what has been weighing on her mind.

"Like... does he ever do anything that gives you, I don't know, red flag vibes?"

Maya's brow furrows slightly as she considers the question.

"Umm, I'm not sure what you mean. I mean, I've known Mateo for a long time, and we were friends for years before we started dating. But you know that." She explains, her tone a mix of confusion and reassurance.

"Yeah," Octavia murmurs, her gaze dropping to the sand. She absently begins tracing patterns with her fingers, her thoughts far away.

Maya watches her, sensing the discomfort that Octavia isn't voicing. Aware that something is clearly bothering her.

"Is everything alright with you and Chad?" she asks gently, her concern evident.

Taking a deep breath, Octavia nods, though her voice lacked conviction.

"Oh yeah, for sure." The words feel hollow, even to her. "Sometimes I just wonder if things are too good to be true," she admits, her words somewhat unconvincing. "He treats us so well, but..."

Maya's expression softens, and she reaches out to place a reassuring hand on Octavia's arm.

"You seem to really love Chad. Almost like you're under some kind of spell, I've never seen you so in love before and I'm happy for you. But if there's anything going on, you know you can always talk to me, right?"

Octavia wipes a tear from her cheek. Maya reaches out to place her hand on Octavia's.

"Hey, it's me you're talking to." She says softly. "You know, I support you no matter what. It's how we've always been. But I worry about you with him sometimes."

"What do you mean? Why would you worry?" Octavia questions, a tinge of defensiveness in her voice.

"Do you ever wonder about what Mateo said that night we all got together?" Maya asks, her voice hushed.

"Actually, yeah, I do sometimes."

"Well, he wouldn't talk to me about it at first, but he doesn't like Chad. He thinks that there's something really off about him. I mean, you have to admit that he must be right about him starting that fire, right?"

Octavia looks at her, intently listening.

"The pit was damp from the rain, he had no paper, hardly any kindling and Mateo couldn't get the fire started. There's no way he would have been able to without some kind of help. But Chad just leans in, blows on it and suddenly it's lit? You gotta admit that's weird, right?" Maya goes on.

"Yeah, I guess I never really realized it. Maybe I wasn't paying good enough attention." She looks Maya in the eye. "Can you apologize to Mateo for me? I should have believed him right away. I know he was just looking out for me."

Octavia temporarily gets lost in thought. Chad is really warm, his kisses tingle, and sometimes burn like the first night they met when he kissed her hand. The strange noises in the house... That *weirdo* from this morning who said the demon is here and something else about Lilith. Could it all be connected? She can't help but wonder if there could be more to what he's leading on.

"Is this why you were asking about Mateo?" Maya questions.

"Huh?" Octavia flinches.

"Oh, no. I actually forgot about that." She sighs.

"I'm just starting to feel confused. He just always seems to have an explanation or an answer for everything." She says, her voice soft.

"What is it that you're feeling confused about?" Maya scrunches her eyebrows.

"I don't even know where to start, these things seem so small. Like I found condoms in his truck the other day. I didn't confront him about it because we are still kind of new. They could have been from before. And I saw his phone, it had a message from someone named Sarah who I've never heard him talk about before." She stops for a second. "It seems small but I guess they have been texting and she drove by his house yesterday and Chad says she just needed help with her horse before the rodeo or something." Octavia lets out a long sigh as she realizes how it sounds coming out of her mouth.

"See how these things just seem silly?" It seems silly but the memories that prick at her feel like a thorn she can't remove. However, the thought of Clyde is what really haunts her, but for some reason, she's having a hard time gathering the courage to share what happened this morning.

"Listen O, if your gut is telling you that something is off then it's probably right." Octavia nods again, her throat tightens with emotion. She knows Maya is right, and the words she needs to say hover on the edge of her mind, threatening to spill over. After a moment's hesitation, she takes a deep breath and decides to fully confide in her friend.

"Not only that, I've been hearing strange noises in his house and when I go to check it out, I find nothing. Okay I know this sounds silly but I think his house is haunted. There was something that happened this morning that I can't quite explain...," she begins, her voice faltering as she tries to articulate the fears she had been keeping to herself.

"Strange noises?" Maya interrupts.

"Yeah, as if something is running down the hall, or smashing things. There is a room upstairs that completely creeps me out. The day the boys met Chad, Cory was playing upstairs and it sounded like he was talking with someone. But when I went to check on him, he was by himself. I mean, I guess he could just have been playing, he does have a pretty wild imagination." Octavia pauses, trying to find the will to tell her about what happened earlier.

"You finally introduced them to Chad, eh?"

"Yeah, sorry I didn't tell you sooner. We've both been so busy, you know. And honestly, it wasn't that long ago."

"You don't worry that you don't really know each other well enough yet?" Maya interjects.

"Of course I do, it's just that the boys are the biggest part of my life, and I've been spending so much time with Chad, I just want them to experience this with me, as a family."

"It's okay you don't have to explain yourself to me. I know you better than anyone, and you are raising amazing boys. You've always done right by them. I have no doubt that if something is wrong, you will protect them like you always have."

"Yeah." She says, grateful for Maya's support.

"What were you saying about this morning? Sorry I think I cut you off."

"Oh, it's okay. I don't really even know. I think that the farm hand that works for Chad might be a skitzo or something going on about Liliths and demons." She raises her hand and mocks Clyde's warning. *"The demon is here."* she says.

"Seriously?" She questions with an unbelieving grin on her face. "Like the Lilith - Leader of the underworld Lilith? And who's the demon, Chad?" she laughs. "I get there are some weird things about him but demons? There's no such thing. Everyone knows that."

"Heh, yeah. That's stupid." Octavia chuckles in agreement, yet a spark of something new ignites within her as if it hit her like a bolt of lightning. It's far-fetched, but could that explain his abnormal warmth, the tingle when he kisses her, the fire he'd started from scratch? It's a stretch. A ridiculous one at that. It wouldn't explain the weird noises in the house.

"I know just what you need." Maya says, breaking Octavia from her revolutionary thought.

Octavia looks at her, a confused expression streaming across her face.

"A night out with your bestie of course. The perfect distraction from all this nonsense and help you gain some perspective."

CHAPTER TWENTY THREE

"I invited Ben." Maya says casually, glancing at Octavia in the mirror as they both apply their makeup.

"Ben? I should check my phone, I totally forgot I texted him earlier." Octavia's hand holds the eyeshadow brush still. " But I told Chad that this was just going to be a girl's night out." Octavia says, her voice carefully neutral, attempting to block any indication of hesitancy.

Maya sees right through her. "I didn't think you'd mind." She says with a sly side smile.

"No, of course. It's Ben. I've actually been thinking about him a lot lately anyway." She assures her, forcing a smile and continues applying her eye shadow. "He's always welcome. I just wouldn't want Chad getting the wrong idea. Especially since I just questioned him."

Maya sets down the mascara, her expression suddenly serious. "Questioned him... About what?"

"You know how I was telling you about the condoms earlier, and that woman, Sarah?" She asks.

"Of course! And right before he heads out of town?" Maya scrutinizes her with wide eyes.

A nervousness lands in the pit of Octavia's stomach. What did she just say? Of course it's all happening right before his trip, the condoms, the messages, the drive-by... it sparks suspicion considering they were deleted. Why else would he delete them if they were just friends?

"Hey," Maya snaps her fingers one time, pulling Octavia out of her trance. "You okay?"

Octavia blinks, startled. "Yeah, yeah, I'm fine. Just... thinking."

"You don't think he's cheating on you, do you?" Maya asks, her voice laced with concern. "Hey, I'm sure it's nothing. But if he is, I'll kick his ass." She shoots an intense stare at her through the mirror. "Besides, he doesn't have to know Ben is coming. And honestly, what does it really matter? You guys have been friends for ages... Way before he came along. It's not like you're doing anything wrong."

A sudden, sharp knock at the door startles them both, the sound echoes through the room.

"That must be Ben." Maya states, quickly throwing all her makeup in her bag. "Time to go have some fun, girlie."

The nightclub is unusually packed tonight. The group sticks together as they navigate their way through the pulsating crowd. Hours tick by, and they find themselves lost in the bliss of the music, dancing to the infectious beat of the DJ. This is exactly what Octavia needs. A distraction from the uncertainties of Chad, while mingling with her most beloved friends. She submits to the music as her worries wash away.

Octavia and her friends slip outside in an attempt to escape the crowded and muggy dance floor. To her surprise, it's not any less busy out on the patio.

Maya pipes up, pointing a finger. "Hey, there's Luke, let's go say hi!" She suggests, pulling Octavia along with her.

Luke is an old high school acquaintance. He was Maya's friend from back in the day, more than anything. But the obligation to follow is strong.

"Hey Luke!" Maya greets him with a friendly hug. "You, remember Ben and Octavia, right?"

"Of course, how could I forget." Luke says, reaching out for a handshake from Ben. He leans in to give Octavia a hug, but Maya interrupts him.

"Don't get too close to that one, she's taken," Maya blurts out, a mischievous glint in her eyes.

"Oh yeah? Who's the lucky guy?" Luke asks, his eyebrows raised in amusement. "Ben?"

"You probably wouldn't know him, his name's Chad. Chad Lilson."

"Chad Lilson?" Luke asks, his voice laced with curiosity. Octavia nods, a sense of pride momentarily eclipsing her doubts.

"Yeah, that's who I'm dating. Why, you know him?" Her eyes reveal a hint of confusion. What does this guy know about him and what exactly is he asking?

"Umm, so I really have to pee," Maya interrupts. "Ben, would you mind escorting a lady to the washroom?" she asks, linking arms with him.

"Of course. O, you okay?" Ben asks.

She nods.

"We'll be right back." He assures her as he's being pulled away.

The sudden shift in Luke's demeanor is intoxicating. His casual expression transforms into one of concern. "You're not honestly dating that guy, are you?" His tone is laced with disbelief.

Octavia's brow furrows in further confusion. "Yeah, why?"

Luke's voice lowers as he shares his knowledge.

"I used to work with him," he begins, his eyes fixed on Octavia, "and let me tell you, he's not a good guy." His words cast a pall over the carefree atmosphere that has previously dominated the night. The man seems uncomfortable with his revelation, his apology hanging in the air. "I'm sorry for bringing this up. I know this probably isn't what you want to hear."

Octavia meets his gaze, her expression a mask of composure.

"Don't apologize," she replies, her voice steady. She's being polite and accepting the information. "It's better to know these things. I appreciate your honesty." She pauses, considering her next words carefully.

"There are things about him that aren't normal... he's not normal." Luke continues. He raises his hand and gestures for Octavia to come in closer, he speaks but it's quiet. "Have you ever heard of 'The Legend of the Liliths Demons'?" She looks at him intensely, curious.

"Hey, we should get a photo." Maya abruptly suggests, making a grand entrance back out on the patio, breaking the tension.

Grouped together they snap a shot of the memorable evening. A touch of sadness runs through her. She wishes Chad would take photos with her, but he refuses. She doesn't have a single photo of him, or of them together.

"Octaviaaaa, let's go back inside and dance." Maya clearly had a little too much to drink.

"Just a minute, Maya. I just need to finish up this conversation." Octavia has also had a little too much to drink, but she wants to hear what this guy has to say.

Turning back to Luke, she continues the conversation.

"No? But demons and Liliths are just a myth."

"Are they though? I never would have believed it either until I met that guy. Working with him on night shifts, I saw some really weird... not just weird, but unexplainable shit. Like supernatural unexplainable." Octavia looks at him intently, she has no words, not yet. Can she trust this guy? She hardly knows him. "You'd be kidding yourself if you think you haven't been seeing some weird shit, too." He shoots her a serious look, his eyes are bloodshot, likely from the alcohol and the fact that it's nearly two a.m.

"Octavia!" She jumps, breaking her from her spell-like concentration. Maya insists that it's time to go back inside. "They are making last calls! Let's gooooo!"

A part of her remains vigilant. She knows she can't ignore her instincts completely. The incident has planted a seed of doubt, and it will take time to determine if it's a harmless weed or a growing threat. Could this man's words have any weight, or is he just crazy like Clyde? Maybe she just had too much to drink and is making it out to be something that it's not.

"I'm gonna go get another drink!" Octavia tells him, pointing to her empty glass. She's shaken up by Luke's revelation but won't allow herself to show it. Too many things are adding up and it's just too unrealistic to believe. Maybe she's the one hallucinating.

She stands in line waiting to be served, the music pulsating around her and bodies casually bumping into her. Then suddenly, what feels like a hand, slams down on her back side.

"What the hell are you doing?" she yells, spinning around to face the offender.

A tall, intoxicated looking man grins roguishly and takes a step towards her, his hand lingering on her hip.

"Back off, you creep!" she shouts, pushing him away with all her might.

Like a guardian angel, Ben appears beside her, grabbing the man by the shoulder and spinning him around. With a swift, unexpected move, Ben lands a powerful punch to the man's face, sending him reeling backwards.

Octavia throws her hands up to her face, trying to contain the laughter bubbling inside her. She jumps up, throwing her arms around Ben in a sudden, impulsive hug.

"Where's Maya?" she asks, her voice high and urgent. "Let's get out of here before he comes back with his buddies."

The cab ride home is bursting with excitement as they reminisce about tonight's wild adventure. However, the mood comes to a calm as they pull up to Maya's house, the first on the way. Without Maya, the dynamics have changed. The ride to Ben's is quiet, the air filled with gratitude and a lingering warmth from the adrenaline of the evening.

"Thanks so much for being there for me tonight," Octavia says, her voice soft with gratitude.

"Octavia," Ben begins, his voice husky, "I would do anything for you."

She looks down at her fidgeting fingers, a sudden pang of guilt hitting her like a cold wave. Ben has always been faithfully by her side, a true and unwavering friend. Doubt gnaws at her and a wave of introspection washes over her. Has she overlooked their relationship? The numerous times they could have become a couple, and didn't, all for fear of losing him. Has she been unfair to him all this time? One thing stands out above all, her profound gratitude for this amazing friend.

Nerves tremble in her stomach as they pull up to his house. The old adage, 'Speak now or forever hold our peace,' keeps replaying in her mind, a constant reminder of a decision she can make right now, tonight. Maybe it's the alcohol, she admits to herself, but she's not ready to end this night with him.

"Did... you wanna come in with me?" Ben asks, his voice soft and hesitant.

A nervous flutter forms in the pit of her stomach. They seem to be on the same wavelength. A strand of his blond hair falls in front of his mesmerizing blue eyes and she fully surrenders to his request. It's as if tonight, Chad doesn't even exist. She reaches her hand out, gently placing it in Ben's, allowing him to gently assist her out of the car. She knows she should say no, to stay in the car and catch the cab home, but she feels a magnetic pull towards him that she's unable to fight. She's fought these feelings for Ben for so long, why now, why tonight is the urge controlling her impulse? All the nights she has longed for them to be a couple but has rejected the idea time and time again for fear of ruining their friendship. For fear of potentially losing him forever if their relationship didn't work out. Maybe it's the uncertainty she feels from Chad and the mysterious Sarah that draws her closer to Ben's familiar comfort. Maybe it's the way Ben had stood up for her against that creep at the bar. There's no denying how attractive that was. Maybe it's just the alcohol. Whatever the reason, she's here now and she's not mad about it. Besides, it's not as if anything has to happen. They've been friends forever, they've spent plenty of time alone without anything sexual happening.

The inside of his house is warm and familiar, a comforting blend of lived-in comfort and masculine charm. A feeling of warmth and familiarity washes over her. Ben kicks his shoes off and heads straight to the speaker. Sweet sweet music to ease the mood. He nervously shuffles through his phone. What is he looking for? His playlist? A specific song? Or is he trying to find a distraction, anything to avoid the inevitability of tonight? A comfortable yet apprehensive nervousness washes over Octavia as she looks around the room, the music playing softly in the background. Ben sneaks up behind Octavia and wraps his arms around her waist, pulling her close. They sway to the rhythm of the music, lost in the moment. His advance takes her a little by surprise but he's been drinking too.

"I love you Octavia, I always have." Ben whispers in her ear, his breath warm against her skin. Apparently the alcohol is making him brave as well. He's never confessed his feelings to her like this before. A flutter forms in her stomach awakening a suppressed emotion.

Ben turns Octavia around to look at him, his eyes intense and focused. Shadows from the dim light dance on their faces and a breath of tense emotion can be heard emanating from Octavia's lips as she sits in anticipation awaiting whatever is to happen next. Her heart races. A grin forms on the one side of his lips as he leans in towards her. He leans in, lifting her hair as he places his hand behind her neck.

"Ben... I..." she whispers into his ear. Octavia's voice trembles, her body overwhelmed by a wave of emotion. Just then a thrill is sent from Octavia's face all the way down to her stomach where it turns into a flight of chaotic butterflies.

Relief floods through her as she grabs the back of Ben's neck. Her touch, soft as a feather before deepening as he brushes his lips against hers. This heated kiss is a spark that ignites an even deeper connection and escalates unspoken desires, as if that's even possible. Octavia reluctantly pulls away, breathlessly exhilarated. Ben grins and his eyes gleam with a newfound intensity. Without warning, he scoops her into his arms, his strength both comforting and thrilling. Unable to resist the muscles radiating from Ben's body she meets his gaze head-on. A spark of defiance flickers in her eyes, quickly extinguished by the overwhelming desire that consumes her. She wraps her arms around the warmth of his neck. Her legs instinctively wrap around his waist. She tilts her head down, closing the distance between them in a kiss that is both desperate and tender. His hands roam her back, sending shivers down her spine as their kiss deepens.

The air crackles with unspoken needs, their inhibitions melt away with each touch. Her kisses trail along his jaw and down his neck. The brisk air whispers with unsaid promises, an intoxicating mix of desire and anticipation. The strength of his hands press firmly as he holds her back, unable to pull her in any closer. Warmth invades her chest accompanied by a buzz of electricity that arcs between them. The passion that intermingles between them hits a boiling point, almost intolerable. It's a wildfire threatening to erupt, fueled by the unspoken tension and the dance of their bodies. Octavia gasps as Ben's hand slides down her back, sending a jolt of electricity through her. His touch is a brand, searing through the thin fabric of her dress. Her heart beats so quickly, mimicking the frantic dance of the fireflies outside the kitchen window.

Ben's grip tightens on her back, his touch no longer a gentle hold but possessive. His eyes, once playful, are now a storm cloud of desire, mirroring the tempest within her. His breath hitches as she leans into him, her body a map he longs to explore. A primal need burns in her core, a yearning that transcends words. But a sliver of uncertainty flickers in the corner of her mind. The question remains unanswered, lost in the urgency of the moment. Octavia, overwhelmed by a mix of fear and desire, reaches up and tangles her fingers in his hair, pulling him closer. The uncertainty of the unknown is drawing her in closer. In that silent plea, all reservations are tossed aside. The stairs leading to the master bedroom, Ben's bedroom, once a playful challenge, now seem an insurmountable obstacle. A trace of disappointment crosses Octavia's face, but is quickly replaced by a smile that holds a hint of mischief that she receives from him.

"Looks like fate," he murmurs against her lips, his voice husky with desire, "has different plans for us tonight."

Octavia's cheeks are flushed with heat, she follows his gaze as it lands down the hall. Without hesitation, their lips meet once again in a kiss that is both desperate and exhilarating. It's a collision of heat and hunger, a wildfire ignited by the unspoken emotions that had simmered between them for too long. Her back is pushed up against the wall, in the hallway, before even making it to the spare room. Ben, his presence a whirlwind of cologne and heat, looms close. He braces himself against her with his hard length, a subtle pressure that awakens every cell in her body. His arms reach up, the white t-shirt stretches taut across his broad shoulders before giving way with a soft rip. The reveal is deliberate, a glimpse of chiseled muscle and sun-kissed skin beneath. A surprised gasp escapes her lips. The dim hallway light, usually unremarkable, suddenly seems to intensify, highlighting the ripple of sculpted muscle beneath the torn fabric of Ben's shirt. A shiver trembles at the back of her neck, a delicious blend of surprise and something altogether more primal. Her breath catches in her throat.

The heat in Ben's gaze is undeniable now, mirroring the sudden warmth radiating off his body. His hands, calloused yet firm and gentle, brush against the exposed skin of her thighs. He grazes the hem of her red dress, the light fabric whispering against her skin as he nudges her forward. A sliver of crimson-red lace peeks out, a tempting contrast against her sun-kissed skin. In a smooth motion, he scoops her up, the hallway dissolves into a blur as he carries her towards the bedroom. As the bedroom door closes with a soft thud, she is enveloped in darkness, the only sound the erratic thudding of her own heart. The room takes on a new aura in the dim moon light filtering through the window. Ben lets Octavia down and as she stands before him, tossing her cute little purse onto the floor, with surprising gentleness, he helps her shed her light dress, his fingers lingering a touch too long on her bare shoulder as his eyes consume her body with one long and delicious glance. The discarded party dress lands on the floor next to her purse, a silent testament to their overwhelming desires. In the intimate space of the room, their passion is fueled by the thrill of the unexpected and the forbidden nature of their rendezvous. The night, once filled with the promise of music and dancing, has transformed into a whirlwind of uncontrollable passion, their love finding a haven in the most unexpected of places.

Octavia's phone rings, abruptly shattering the intense and intimate atmosphere with Ben, breaking them up. Both a burden and a relief. Unable to fathom what she's actually doing, she pulls away, her breath catching in her throat. She can't be doing this. Despite her connection with Ben and the undeniable pull of the moment, she's committed to Chad. The music fades into the background as she picks up her purse and scrambles for her phone and she looks at the screen. It's Chad, she refuses to answer, she needs to pull herself together. What is she doing? A text notification following the call flashes in front of her, the words making her heart skip a beat.

Got hurt at the rodeo.

A knot of dread forms in her stomach as she reads the message. Her mind races, conjuring up worst-case scenarios. With trembling fingers, she quickly types out a response.

What happened?! Are you okay? She frantically writes back, not even considering the time. The warmth of Ben's touch, the sound of the music, and even the glow of the night, all fade as she braces herself for the news that's about to follow.

Octavia looks at Ben. "Chad got hurt at the rodeo," her voice tinges with worry as she stares at her phone, anxiously awaiting another message.

CHAPTER TWENTY FOUR

Chad's house sits quietly on the street, the only sounds are the distant chatter of farm animals and her boys playing in the yard. She watches from the window as she anxiously prepares dinner. Finally, the sound of a truck pulling up the driveway grabs Octavia's attention. She feels bad about having left Ben so abruptly last night, but Chad needs her. She wanted to be home for his arrival, although unsure of when that was going to be. Thankfully her mom was kind enough to drop the boys off this morning. With Chad being hurt, and the guilt of her night with Ben, her mom helping out with the boys is one less thing for her anxious mind to be worrying about.

Her heart pounds with a mixture of relief and anxiety as she hurries out the door to greet him. But as the truck comes to a stop, she notices something that causes her to pause. Another man is driving. He's tall like Chad. Wait a minute, it's James, his good friend and long time rodeo buddy. Chad's sitting in the passenger seat. Octavia's warm smile falters slightly as she tries to mask the surge of concern that rises within her. She quickly recovers, greeting Chad with a smile that she hopes will reassure him, even as her eyes scanned him for any sign of injury. Nothing seems immediately obvious, but the fact that he didn't drive himself home only deepens her worry. As soon as Chad steps out of the truck, Octavia approaches him with a welcoming hug.

"Ugh." Chad moans as he welcomes her hug.

"I'm sorry! I didn't mean to hurt you. I've been so worried! I haven't heard anything since you said you were coming home from the hospital."

Chad's usual calm demeanor is intact, but there's a hint of weariness in his eyes. "I'm fine," he assures her, but Octavia can see that he clearly isn't fine. Without saying a word, Chad unbuttons the top three buttons from his shirt, revealing a severely bruised upper chest. The sight of it makes Octavia gasp, her hand instinctively flying to cover her mouth.

"That looks terrible," she says, her voice filled with worry. "Is it broken?"

Chad shakes his head with a wry smile, trying to downplay the injury.

"It's just a broken collarbone, Octavia. I've had worse. No need to fuss."

"Okay, what about the cast and sling?" She prods further. "Okay so my arm is also broken."

"What the hell happened? You get slammed into a gate or something?"

He nods. "It's not the first time. But trust me. I'll be fine."

Octavia isn't entirely convinced, but she doesn't want to push too hard. She knows Chad well enough to understand that he doesn't like making a big deal out of things. James, who's been unloading Chad's gear from the truck, chimes in with a reassuring grin.

"He's tougher than he looks. Trust me, he'll be alright... although, doc did say he has a concussion, any more of those and he won't be competin' again."

"Alright," she shakes her head, looking back at Chad, finally relenting, though the concern in her eyes hadn't diminished. "But promise me you'll rest and let me take care of you tonight?"

Chad nods, appreciating her concern.

"Promise." He says, giving her a reassuring smile as he pulls her close again, grateful for her care. Chad tries hard to get out of the truck without making it look like a painful charade. She notices there's more than he's letting on.

"Why are you limping?" She asks.

Chad looks at her, seems as though he's unsure whether to tell her or to lie.

"The bull jumped on my leg while I was down." Her hand flies up to her mouth once again. "It's just bruised, nothing broken." He assures her.

"Do you need crutches?" She asks, feeling completely helpless.

"Kinda hard to use crutches with a broken collarbone, babe." Right, of course it is.

Once inside, Octavia can't help but glance towards Chad, her mind still racing with worry. She just hopes that whatever he's downplaying really is as minor as he claims. "I'm sorry this happened to you," Octavia says, her voice filled with genuine concern as she hands him a glass of water and some ice.

"All part of the game, sweetheart." Chad replies with a shrug, his tone casual. "Ya win some, and ya lose some."

Octavia leans in and gives him a light peck on the cheek. "I missed you while you were away." A flashback of Clyde enters her mind being back at his house. Now is not the time to bring this up. Surely the guy is just mentally deranged. Probably why he didn't want him in the house. And Ben, so much has happened over the weekend. Does she tell him? Does she bury the secret deep in hopes it won't be found out? No, she can't do that, especially after she had just questioned him about another woman. She's no better. She could blame it on the alcohol, and that very well could have been why she was willing to go the extra mile. Part of her desperately wants to believe that as she has always been a loyal person. But another part of her can't deny the desire she felt for Ben last night, the desire she's felt for him all these years that she's chosen to bury deep down never to be acted upon.

However, she snaps out of it, Chad is hurt and suddenly those events don't seem as important right now. Her concern is with Chad and if he will be alright after getting another concussion.

Chad's expression softens as he looks at her, his eyes reflecting warmth. "I missed you, babe," he says, his voice tender.

Octavia smiles, feeling a bit of the tension ease, despite the gnawing guilt in the pit of her stomach.

"You guys must be hungry," she says, noticing the time.

"Heh, yeah, a little," Chad admits, patting his stomach with a grin. "Have you even eaten since you were admitted?" She turns to James, including him in the conversation.

"Have you ever tried hospital food? I don't think it really classifies." Chad says.

"Would you like something to eat too, James?" She asks.

"I would love that, I'm starving. Thank you," James, his loyal rodeo companion, responds eagerly, his rugged exterior giving way to a genuine smile.

Octavia serves the food that she prepared earlier while she was anxiously awaiting Chad's arrival. The kids have already eaten and are just outside with the animals seemingly unaware of his arrival. That or they are just preoccupied with the animals and don't really care at the moment. Chad takes his stetson off and sets it aside, uncomfortably attempting to position himself on the couch. The meal is simple but hearty, perfect after a long day. They dig in and the atmosphere in the room grows more relaxed, the earlier tension fades away. After a few minutes, Octavia looks towards James.

"Are you going to need a ride home?" She asks.

"No, ma'am," He replies with his characteristic charm, his response short and to the point. "Baily's on her way."

"Well, thank you for driving Chad home," She says, her gratitude evident. "Did you have to leave early too, or were you finished up for the weekend?"

"I'd just offered to bring him home." James says confidently, his voice carrying a note of pride.

"Awe, well it's really appreciated." Octavia says, even though she isn't quite sure that it actually answered her question.

"My pleasure," James nods, "We've been rodeo partners for years, I'm not about to abandon him now." His gaze drifts toward the window. The sound of a car pulling into the driveway draws everyone's attention. "That would be my ride. Thank you for dinner."

As the door closes behind him, Octavia turns to Chad.

"You really should take it easy for the rest of the night," she suggests. Chad smiles, pulling her close.

"Don't worry, I'm not going anywhere," he assures her, his voice filled with affection. For now, at least, they could enjoy the quiet comfort of being together again. Octavia meets Chad with a kiss. Her embrace enveloping him in the scent of summer wildflowers. Her kiss, quick but fervent, conveys both her worry for his wounds and the joy of his safe return.

"I'm glad you're home," She says, her voice soft and genuine as she looks into Chad's eyes.

"Me too, babygirl." His reply is soft and his gaze is tender as he attempts to stand up from the couch.

"Easy there, cowboy," Octavia says with a gentle laugh, guiding him back down onto the couch. She quickly grabs a pillow and places it under his head to support it, her movements filled with care. Chad manages a smile, though it's tinged with a hint of pain.

"Just a bruise," he mutters. "Victories ain't always pretty."

"Victory?" Octavia echoes, her curiosity piqued.

"There's something in the truck I need you to go grab," Chad says, wincing slightly as he tries to reposition himself on the couch. Octavia looks at him with a mix of surprise and concern.

"Okay?" she responds, unsure of what to expect.

"You'll see when you get out there," Chad assures her, his voice carrying a hint of excitement despite his discomfort. "It's on the passenger side in the back, in the saddlebag."

Octavia raises an eyebrow, intrigued.

"Alright, I'll be right back," she says, giving him a reassuring smile before heading outside.

"Maybe when you get back you could run a shower for me. I'd be forever grateful, babydoll." Chad suggests.

Octavia grabs the keys from the coffee table where James left them. Cory, always curious, sees her walking towards the truck from the yard and follows her, likely eager to see what his mom will find. She opens the passenger door and begins rummaging through the saddlebag, expecting to find one of the usual trophies Chad often brings home from rodeos. Sure enough, near the top of the bag, a trophy. It's solid and familiar, a testament to Chad's hard-earned win. But as she lifts the trophy out, her fingers brush against something unexpected, something soft. It's barely noticeable, but it's there and it's purple – an unusual colour for his rodeo attire. She feels the smooth texture between her fingers as it slips from the folds of the bag. Curious, she carefully pulls it out, her breath catching as the item reveals itself. Lavender silk, delicate and shimmering under the soft glow of the porch light, tumbles into view. It's a nightgown, its fabric flowing like liquid in her hands. Octavia stares at it, momentarily stunned, before a secret smile begins to bloom across her face.

It isn't just a celebration of a rodeo victory that Chad has in mind tonight. He's planned something more, something intimate and special. The realization sends a warm flutter through Octavia's chest, and her earlier worries about Chad's injury are momentarily eclipsed by a wave of anticipation and affection. When would he even have had the time to pick this up, and how long has he been planning this for? Could he have picked it up before he left? Maybe that's why he needed to run to town.

Cory, who digs through the truck, notices the trophy right away.

"Did Chad win again?" he asks, his young voice filled with awe.

Octavia quickly tucks the nightgown back into the saddlebag, her smile grows as she looks down at her son.

"He sure did, sweetie," she replies, picking up the trophy for him to see.

The realization of Chad's plan dawns on her and a flicker of amusement dance in her eyes, tempered by her concern for his injury. She tucks the nightgown securely under her arm, the trophy in her hand, and returns up the porch and back inside. Her steps grow lighter with each movement, her mood buoyed by the surprise. Chad has made himself comfortable on the couch, looking like he's on the verge of falling asleep. Cory trails closely behind her, absorbed in the tape measure he's found in the truck, stretching and retracting it with fascination.

"Got it," Octavia says with a playful smile, holding the nightgown up just out of reach. "Looks like celebrating victory might have to wait until your body heals, cowboy. How about we focus on some pain relief first?" She lifts the trophy, teasing him with it.

"You're all the pain relief I need, baby." Chad groans good-naturedly, his expression a mix of relief and affection. He reaches up with his good arm and grabs the nightgown, pulling Octavia close. He kisses her intimately, his touch warm and reassuring. Octavia's smile grows as she kisses him back, feeling a deep sense of contentment. This is her heaven, the moments of intimacy and love that makes everything feel right.

"Ewww." Cory says, with an adorable disgusted look on his face.

They both chuckle.

"Mmm, okay," She says, pulling away reluctantly. "I love you, but you need to heal. And I need to get these kids to bed soon. We will stay here tonight to keep an eye on you."

Chad lets out another light groan, but his smile is now one of genuine relief and affection.

"Alright, alright. You win," he concedes, his voice carrying a hint of desire. "But the nightgown isn't going anywhere, dollface."

She laughs softly, her heart full.

"I wouldn't want it to," she says, gently touching his face. "Now let's get you showered and comfortable. Then we will figure out how we're going to take care of you. After all, a victory's worth celebrating properly."

Octavia settles on the couch next to Chad, Cory and Ryan close by admiring yet another trophy Chad had brought home. Her boys close by, the playful banter with Chad, the tenderness, and the promise of a special evening ahead are more than enough to put her mind at ease. For now.

* * *

With Chad in the shower, Octavia turns her attention to her children.

"What do you have there, buddy?"

Cory is completely absorbed in playing with a tape measure.

"I found it in Chad's truck." He looks at her with his big brown eyes.

"You guys sure do make toys out of the funniest things." She says. "But for now it's time to put it away while we get ready for bed, okay my boy, we're gonna have a sleepover here tonight."

Despite her concerns about the sharp edges and the potential for accidents, Octavia can't bring herself to take the tool away from him. His innocent curiosity and the joy it brings him are too precious to interrupt. She watches as Cory's eyes light up each time he pulls the tape out and lets it snap back into the roll, his movements a dance of exploration and wonder. Ryan, slightly more subdued, has less enthusiasm for Cory's new 'toy'.

Despite the chaos and disruption this weekend has brought, one thing still lingers in Octavia's thoughts. The noise that drifted from upstairs when that creepy farm hand was speaking. Could something have fallen over? Could there have been a trapped animal? Too embarrassed to run it by Chad she takes the investigation into her own hands. It's time, as much as she doesn't want to, she needs to check out the source of the sound if she can continue to be in that house with a clear conscience. She assists Chad out of the shower, helps him get dressed, and gathers her boys. It's their turn to clean up and prepare for bed. While the boys bathe, she takes it upon herself to check around upstairs. She's not going to ask Chad to do it, not in his condition, not now. The boys' rooms are clear, as is the master. There is no sign that anything had been disturbed. But she already expected that. It wasn't those rooms that she suspected in the first place. She steels her nerves as she slowly paces towards the third bedroom, her heart beats a little bit faster. It almost feels like the room itself is alive, holding its breath as she inches closer.

She presses her hand against the door, slowly pushing it open. It's dark, the only light is the brightness from the hallway gleaming into the room. Hesitantly, she reaches up to flick the switch, illuminating the room. She looks around expecting to see something out of place, something broken.

"Mom!" Octavia jumps. Ryan calls from downstairs. "I'm done!" That was quick. He probably didn't even wash his hair.

"Okay hunny, I'll be down to help in a minute."

With one last look around the room, she doesn't see anything out of the ordinary, just a plain old storage room. It was probably a rat that had knocked something over. She closes the door, just in case, and heads back down to her boys.

As the evening wears on, Octavia's thoughts drift between caring for her children and the anticipation of a quiet, romantic moment with Chad. She's determined to make the most of the night, blending her responsibilities as a mother with the intimate plans Chad hinted at. The contrast between Cory's playful innocence and the tender moments with Chad only deepen her appreciation for the little joys in life. With Ryan's favorite bedtime story read and the familiar routine completed, Octavia finally manages to get her children settled into bed. The boys drift into a state of contentment cuddled up next to each other in the guest room. The room is filled with the gentle, rhythmic sound of their breathing as they fall into a deep, peaceful sleep.

Octavia quietly tiptoes out of their room, her heart full from the simple pleasure of tucking them in. As she closes the door softly behind her, she lets out a contented sigh, ready to shift her focus back to Chad and the evening they have ahead. The house is now calm and tranquil, the perfect setting for the night's more intimate moments with her man. Octavia makes her way back into the living room, only to find Chad fast asleep on the couch. Seriously. She debates whether to wake him and help him up to bed or let him stay there for the night. After grabbing herself a glass of water, she settles into a chair, her gaze fixed on Chad as she ponders her decision, she looks at the nightgown and back at Chad. He's fidgeting with the lining of his sweats, that seems like an invitation to wake him. With a playful energy, she picks up the nightgown, rushes to the bathroom, and puts it on.

"Hey babe," she pulls her hair to the side and whispers in Chad's ear, "I kind of have the hots for a rodeo champion right now."

He stirs, slowly opening his eyes. That grabbed his attention.

"I think it's important that we celebrate, don't ya think?" She rubs her hand along the side of his face.

Chad reaches his hand up to place it on Octavia's leg and feels the nightgown against her curves as his hand follows its way up to her waist. A spark ignites in his gaze,

"Oh I definitely think so." He attempts to reposition himself. "Ugh." He winces in pain.

"Hey, you just lay there, let *me* show *you* how a real champion wins."

She says, kissing his neck, right underneath his ear. She skips his bruised chest and places her hand on his length, rubbing with a soft caress until it's hard. That didn't take long. With care, she reaches around the rim of his pants, shimmying them downwards.

"This is how you get diamonds, babygirl." He says as he places his hand gently on her head.

"Shhh" she purrs.

CHAPTER TWENTY FIVE

Octavia stirs, realizing that she'd fallen asleep next to Chad on the couch. The last thing she remembers is the show they were going to watch together. The credits are playing so she must have been asleep for at least an hour. A familiar sound reaches her ears, one she has been hearing all evening. The distinct click and whirr of the tape measure being played with. It pulls her back from the edge of slumber, and worries that Cory might be awake.

She sits up, trying to gauge the sound's proximity and intensity. After a solid minute of listening, the sound persists, making it clear that Cory is indeed awake. Octavia knows she won't be able to rest fully knowing one of her children is up, especially if it means there could be potential mischief or danger. With a resigned sigh, she pushes Chad's hand aside and quietly gets out of bed to follow the sound of the tape measure. The house is quiet, she moves carefully to avoid waking anyone else. She creeps across the hall, her mind filled with a mix of concern and maternal instinct. With the long summer days providing just enough light, Octavia quietly makes her way into the room where the boys sleep. To her relief, both Cory and Ryan are sound asleep, their small bodies nestled comfortably in their bed. The tape measure is still tucked close to Cory, just as he had left it. How could she hear the tape measure mere seconds ago when the boys are sound asleep? She picks up the tool and places it up on the shelf and climbs into bed with the boys, a maternal instinct.

Once again, Octavia is jolted awake by a sudden but subtle crash. She sits up abruptly, her heart pounding. Her eyes dart to the corner of the room where she sees a small shadow darting out. Horror grips her. She looks over to see her boys sound asleep beside her. She isn't going to let this slip away this time. This can't just be another night terror, it feels like much more, it feels and looks incredibly real. Too real to deny. She jumps out of bed and makes her way to the living room, back to Chad. She's determined to find an answer for this, for all the strange noises that have been plaguing this house.

"Chad," She urges him with a soft voice, as to not risk waking the boys. "Chad," she whispers, nudging him on the arm, careful not to hurt him.

"Hmm," he groans.

"Chad," she whispers, her voice urgent, "There's something in the house."

"You're safe here, Octavia." he murmurs.

"No, there's something small running around the house. It was in the boys' room." She desperately pleads.

"Don't worry," he groans. "The imps are harmless little buggers." He grumbles, scratching his chest.

"What? What's an imp?" She asks, her voice rising slightly, fear prickling at the back of her neck.

He mumbles incoherently, still half-asleep.

"Chad, wake up!" She demands, shaking him gently, careful not to hurt him.

Well, if Chad isn't going to wake up then she'll have to take things into her own hands. She has boys to protect and whatever this *imp* is, she is going to find out. A distinct patter of footsteps, tiny feet race down the hallway. A chill invades her insides. It's a sound she knows all too well. A sound that's become familiar in this house. Octavia has always believed there's *something* off about Chad's house. Either way, it's a haunting undercurrent that seems to linger in the shadows. She strains her ears, listening intently. She looks over at Chad who's fast asleep. The footsteps grow louder, then fade away as abruptly as they had begun. Chad stirs beside, mumbling something in his sleep. She reaches out and squeezes his hand, hoping to ground herself.

This house has a history that she knows nothing about. There's a room untouched by the recent renovations that feels eerie, haunted perhaps. She often wonders about it, about the stories it might hold. But the question always remains unspoken, buried deep within her. She isn't scared, not exactly. These occurrences are like cryptic messages, hinting at a hidden truth. Yet, the fear of what she might find is a constant companion. A jolt of adrenaline propels Octavia upwards. The sound, those unmistakable footsteps, vanish completely. Her heart pounds. She walks quietly upstairs from room to room. It's dark, aside from the soft glow of the moon filtering through the curtains. She creeps from one room to another, the house feels empty, yet something lingers in the silence.

She moves through the house listening intently with her senses on high alert. The upstairs room, the one that holds an air of mystery, calls to her. With a deep breath, she opens the door. Dust motes dance in the moonlight streaming through the window, illuminating the room's emptiness. There are no signs of any disturbance, no overturned furniture, no unexplained objects. Could the noises be a figment of her imagination? Is this place actually haunted, perhaps by a child spirit? Is an Imp a ghost? Or is she going crazy? Disappointment and relief wash over her as she slowly makes her way out of the chilled room. Something suddenly catches her eye, a peculiar object standing out amidst the dusty chaos.

A black book, adorned with vibrant red patterns, beckons from a shelf. Curiosity piques, it's almost as if it's calling out to her. She slowly reaches for it.

"Babe." Chad startles her from behind, she jumps. "What are you doing in here?" He demands.

"I... heard something." She attempts to steady her breath, trying hard not to look at the book that whispers.

"You have no business being in here." he says, his voice low and commanding. He reaches his arm out and ushers her out of the room with a pained limp.

"Chad, I heard something." She insists, pulling back slightly. "I tried to wake you up."

"It's been a long night, we need to get some sleep," he says, his hand lingering on her arm.

She stops dead in her tracks, forcing her will against his.

"What's an imp?" She blurts out.

"Huh?" Chad questions, rubbing his eyes.

"Imp," she repeats. "You said it in your sleep."

Chad shakes his head.

"Octavia, if I was asleep then I was probably dreaming." He pauses and looks at her right in the face. "Now, I'm in pain and extremely tired, can we please just go back to sleep?"

She takes one last look at the ominous book. They walk out and he closes the door behind them. She crawls in with her boys, despite having only a sliver of the bed. They are her main source of comfort and maternal instinct gravitates towards them. However, sleep eludes her. She tries to focus on other things but her mind is always drawn back to that room, the unexplained noises, the eerie atmosphere and that mysterious book. She needs to get her hands on it, should it hold answers to everything she seeks. But she can't right now, not while Chad is around.

CHAPTER TWENTY SIX

The following week is a whirlwind of nurture and chaos. Between making time to write, caring for her boys, getting them to and from daycare, caring for Chad, and taking on much of his responsibilities on the farm, she's definitely feeling the overwhelm settle in, though she won't admit it. She keeps assuring Chad that they don't need to hire help, besides, she doesn't want *Clyde* back any time soon. Or ever. He's assured her through conversations throughout the week that he won't be back, that he's gone for good. But that's not good enough. She still gets chills thinking about him. She doesn't really even want to be at the house with all the unexplained events happening, it just gives her the chills. But she's there for Chad, she loves him and he needs her. If there was any danger, she's sure Chad would protect her and the boys from it. But no harm has even threatened them, so what has she got to be so worried about?

The man at the bar, Luke, pops into her mind. She shakes her head at his revelation. If Chad was a demon then she would have seen something bad happen by now. Sure, weird things have happened, but nothing that extreme. That's just pure craziness. Maybe all the people in this town are a little cray cray. Must be something in the water.

She's scrolling on her phone when an awaited text message comes in.

Hey O, I'll be heading out of town soon and wondering if you want to get together before I go? Maybe get some people together and camp for a couple nights.

A message from Ben. She hasn't spoken to him since that night. Not really. She'd be lying if she said she wasn't avoiding him and what had happened between them. Besides, she hasn't even told Chad about it yet. She plans to. She has to, she has to get it off her chest. It's not fair to Chad to hide what had happened, even if she does suspect that he cheated on her first.

However, a night away from this creepy house and time with her most beloved friends sounds pretty tempting right about now. And she does feel bad the way she left Ben when Chad got hurt. The thought of going sparks a surge of excitement in Octavia but once again she buries them deep down. But wait, out of town? Where could he possibly be going, and how hasn't she heard of this until now?

The trip is made even more appealing by the addition of more friends. Maybe it will take the tension away from Ben. She knows she has to confront him. But how? She can't allow something like that to happen again. It's not fair to herself, Chad, or Ben. She just about gave into her desires with Ben, but her heart belongs with Chad. Maya for sure, must come. Wait, Ali mentioned she would be in town for an appointment, and that Josh would be staying home with the kids. Maybe she'll make a trip of it. Octavia can see her boys already, running wild, building forts from sticks and splashing in the shallows. The idea brings a warm smile to her face, envisioning the pure joy that the children would undoubtedly experience.

Count us in... Octavia begins to type, but as much as she longs for the trip, a familiar worry begins to creep in. Chad. The thought of leaving him behind, especially after his recent injury, makes her hesitate. Despite his reassurances that he's fine, she can't shake the concern gnawing at her. She's torn.

The internal tug-of-war between her desire for a carefree getaway and her instinct to stay close to Chad causes a moment of pause. She knows how much she needs this break, how much they all do. Octavia sighs, the weight of her conflicting emotions heavy in her chest. She knows she needs to talk to Chad about it, to see how he feels. Maybe he will encourage her to go, or maybe he needs her to stay. Either way, the decision doesn't feel like hers alone to make. With his injuries and a somewhat grumpy demeanor he's limited with what he can do. While the initial concern had been soothed by painkillers and promises of nurturing, she can't ignore the pang of guilt that twists in her gut. Here she is, contemplating a weekend getaway, while Chad is stuck at home to rest and heal.

Chad insists she go.

"Relax, have fun," he says, his voice tinged with good-natured teasing. "Just promise not to burn down any forests."

No, that's not good enough. Who's going to cook for him or help him get dressed? He *needs* her..

Sorry, as much as I want to, I don't think we can make it this time, Chad needs help at home.

And sends it with a mix of regret and lingering worry. With that she begins tidying, starting with the laundry.

Laundry has been piling up. It's washed and dried, but she's got a mountain to fold that she hasn't been able to get to yet. Folding a worn flannel shirt that belongs to Chad, a memory of the injury floods back, this is the shirt he was wearing when he arrived home. She raises the shirt, folds it in half and presses it against her chest to straighten and fold down. In doing so, her fingers brush against a lump where the pocket lives. Intrigued, she unfolds the shirt, her smile fading as she pulls out a square package. Condoms. A short sleeve of condoms. Not again. One time seems like an innocent mistake, perhaps a pack from the past. But a second time, and the fact it's tucked into the shirt he wore home is too coincidental. Her breath catches in her throat. Her heart skips a beat and her blood runs hot as the small colourful package hits the floor. It lies there, an unwelcome intrusion in the heat of the moment. The sight of the condoms feels like a punch to the gut. The air, once filled with the fresh scent of laundry and anticipation, now feels heavy with more uninvited uncertainty.

She stands frozen, her mind racing. Questions flood in. Why are they there? She and Chad haven't used them in a while, relying instead on other forms of birth control. Had Chad put them there recently? And if so, why? Was the nightgown even meant for her, or did she misread it entirely? Is there a connection? Is there something she doesn't know, or is it a simple oversight? Her thoughts spiral as she tries to make sense of it all. She wants to believe it's nothing, maybe just an old pack that had been forgotten in the rush of their busy lives. But the doubt gnaws at her refusing to be silenced. The excitement for the camping trip, the warmth of Chad's reassurances, all of it seems to dim in the shadow of the uncertainty she's grappling with.

Octavia bends down and picks up the sleeve, her fingers slightly trembling. She examines it with a mixture of curiosity and apprehension. The expiration date hadn't passed. This is the second time she's found condoms, once before his trip, and now that he's back. It's time to confront him. The last thing she wants is to jump to conclusions, but the discovery has thrown her off balance.

The camping trip, once a source of joy and anticipation, now feels like a clean escape. But can she even trust Chad while she's away? Would going away be an open invitation for him to make use of them? Will Chad have an explanation that would put her at ease, like he always seems to have, or would this discovery lead to a conversation she isn't prepared to have? The thought of confronting him makes her stomach churn, but she also knows she can't leave without addressing it. It isn't just about the camping trip anymore. It's about the trust between them, something far more important.

With the sleeve of condoms in one hand and the flannel shirt in the other, Octavia makes her way upstairs. She needs to clear the air before anything else, especially before camping, before any more doubts take root. But how will Chad react? The uncertainty pricks at her as she braces herself for the conversation that's about to unfold. She finds Chad settled on the couch, a grimace playing on his face as he tries to reposition himself.

"Hey," she begins, her voice betraying a hint of nervousness. "I found something interesting in your rodeo shirt." She holds it up, watching his reaction carefully.

Chad's brow arches in confusion.

"Interesting? What is it?"

Octavia places the package on the coffee table in front of him. His eyes widen a fraction, then narrows as he looks back up.

"Those?" He scoffs, feigning surprise. "I have no idea how they got there. Must be from a long time ago. That shirt's been through a lot, rodeo dust and all."

His explanation feels hollow, lacking conviction. Octavia's gaze holds his, searching for a strand of truth. The weight of her unspoken question hangs heavy in the room.

She studies his face, searching for a flicker of anything that betrays his words. His explanation, though lacking in detail, isn't entirely unbelievable. Rodeos are chaotic events, and the shirt has definitely seen its fair share of spills. Maybe she's letting her newfound feelings cloud her judgment. But she feels in her gut that it's just a shallow excuse, a mask to hide what's really going on between him and Sarah, or whoever else he might be sleeping with while he's away at the rodeos.

"Maybe," she concedes, taking the package back.

Relief swims across his face, a fleeting emotion she can't quite decipher. She's not going to let it slide so easily this time. He may have gotten off easy last time, but this is the second time she's found condoms. His charm isn't going to get him out of it this time.

"I need a better answer than that," she demands.

"Well, I'm sorry babe, I don't know what to tell you. I don't know why they are there." The words are as hollow as his excuse. He can't even come up with something clever? If he's not willing to be upfront about the condoms or where they came from then she doesn't feel as though she owes him an explanation about Ben either.

"It's your shirt. How could you not know?" She raises her voice. "Did you need them while you were at the rodeo? Do you just go there to party and sleep around?" She finally accuses.

"What? No! I haven't worn that shirt in a while." He snaps back.

"Except that you wore it this time. You were wearing it when you got home. How could you not notice that in your pocket, it just makes no sense!" She looks towards the ground, takes a deep breath in, looks back up at him and finishes the conversation. "I think that we need some time apart. I need to process everything. I'm going camping with Maya and you'll have to figure out a way to take care of yourself. Maybe your bimbo's from the rodeo can help. Maybe *Sarah* can help."

"C'mon, don't do this." He pleads.

Octavia turns to leave, too angry to shed a tear, she can't shake the unease that lingers in her gut. Her hands are shaking and her body vibrates. Chad's explanation, though possibly plausible, has done little to quell the nagging doubt that's taken root. The tension between her desire to trust him and the unsettling discovery leaves her feeling conflicted. Is she overthinking something insignificant? Or is Maya right and she should trust her gut feeling?

Back in the laundry room, she wastes no time shooting out impromptu texts to her friends about joining them on this getaway. She leaves his clothes and begins to pack her own. She tries to refocus on the task at hand, but her thoughts keep drifting back to the brief exchange. Until he's ready to come clean, she has no desire to be at home with him.

She's taking her boys home and they leave in the morning.

"Octavia."

"Chad, what are you doing up and walking around again? You need to be resting." She asks, her tone a mix of anger and concern.

"How do I rest when I know that you're so upset? Besides, I'm not fragile, I can't just lay around all the time, *healing*."

"Well, suit yourself." She shakes her head. "If you're able to get up and argue with me then surely you can help out with a few things around the house."

"Who's arguing?" He blurts out. "I just want to talk."

"Okay, well I don't. Not right now." She places one foot in front of the other in an attempt to leave the laundry room, to leave Chad and his deceitfulness behind. She doesn't know if she's more mad at him or more mad at herself for hiding the truth about Ben. What good could come of it if she tells him now? She needs to figure out what's going on first. She needs to talk to Ben and they will realize it was just a mistake. A mistake they can move on from and be friends like they've always been.

"Just stop, would ya?" He places his arm up on the wall, blocking her exit. She has no choice but to stop, pushing her way through would likely be painful for him. She's upset but she would never intentionally hurt anyone. "I love you and I would never do anything to ruin what we have. You have to believe me."

She pauses.

"Sure, but I need time to process this. I'm going to take the boys camping for the weekend. We can talk when I get back."

CHAPTER TWENTY SEVEN

Ben and Maya await at the designated spot, a hidden cove nestled amongst towering trees offers both shade and seclusion. With Maya already here, it doesn't leave much room for her to have a private chat with Ben without creating suspicion from anyone else. Although she's relieved her friends are here so that she doesn't have to face the awkward conversation that she and Ben should have, right away.

This gorgeous place is not known to many. Octavia has brought Chad here a couple of times, it makes for a great hang out spot for the day. The boys, united by their boundless energy and love of exploration, waste no time exploring. They build forts out of fallen branches, declare war on unsuspecting bugs, and chase each other through the dappled sunlight filtering through the leaves. Soon Ali shows up. It's a beautiful feeling, when friends can forge their spontaneous plans and make it work.

The evening fire is when the real magic usually happens. Friends bond over conversation, catch up, open up and be vulnerable with one another. With the boys already in bed for the night, Octavia and her friends are huddled up next to the warm blaze. Stories and laughter, a cherished sentiment, are shared amongst them as the night deepens.

"What exactly happened to Chad anyway?" Ali asks.

"Ugh, I really don't want to talk about him right now," Octavia says, leaning back in her chair. Her words feel like a betrayal to him, but likely deserved. And to talk about Chad in front of Ben after how close they got almost feels like a betrayal to Ben. "But I guess he got bucked off a bull into a gate and stomped on." she finishes, trying to keep it short and simple.

Ali looks at her, Octavia looks back, and they both burst out in a fit of laughter.

Octavia composes herself and sighs, "It's been a chaotic week taking care of him, the boys, the animals, and also trying to juggle work. This right here, with you guys, is all I need right now. I'm so glad we're doing this."

"Well, we're glad you came out. I know you need this," Maya says sympathetically. "You made the right call." This group, they are the symbol of true friendship, they not only offer a reminder of the strength found in true friendship, they're a source of comfort and guidance as she navigates the uncertain path ahead.

With the night nearing an end, Maya and Ali have already found their way into their tents, leaving Octavia and Ben to their own devices. Of course Ben is the last one to retire, yet, Octavia doesn't seem to mind. She's been missing his company. He's a familiar face, a welcome presence amongst the turmoil she's experiencing within. Now that it's just the two of them, it's the perfect time to connect.

Finally, Ben breaks the silence between them.

"You seem a little distracted." He observes, his voice gentle.

Octavia hesitates, then nods. "I am," she admits, her voice barely a whisper. "There's just so much going on right now."

"Seems like it, and clearly with more than just us." He offers a sympathetic smile as he points out the obvious. "Want to talk about it?"

Octavia pauses as if her heart has just stopped. That night with Ben has been on the back of her mind but has been overruled by Chad's accident and everyday responsibilities. She takes a deep breath, her mind racing. She's been avoiding this conversation as much as she can, burying her doubts and uncertainties beneath a facade of normalcy. But now, with Ben sitting across from her, offering a safe space to share her thoughts, she feels a surge of courage to spill the worries she's been clinging onto for so long.

"I'm sorry Ben, I don't mean to ignore you. It's just Chad," she begins, her voice barely audible.

"Of course it is." Ben snarks.

Octavia looks at him, her eyes hardening. "Hey, that's not fair. I know you don't like him, but we're dating."

"You're right, I'm sorry." He says, shaking his head and running a hand through his hair, clearly unhappy with the whole situation.

"You will always have a special place in my heart and that will never change." She looks him in the eyes and confesses. "But I am committed to him and it's not right what we did. It's not fair to anyone."

Ben sits in silence, perhaps processing her words.

Octavia sighs.

"I'm so sorry. I just don't know what to do." She finally breaks.

"What do you mean? About what?"

"Chad," she admits quietly, knowing full well Ben doesn't want to talk about him but she needs to get it off her chest, she needs to spill her guts.

"It's just that we've been great together, but there are things... complications." She continues, "Perhaps I shouldn't be talking to you about this but, at the same time, I can't help but wonder if you could offer some perspective."

Ben listens intently, his expression a mixture of concern and understanding. Ben has always been there for her, and perhaps she's taking advantage of that, but not intentionally. Ben is a good friend and nothing can change that. As Octavia pours out her heart, sharing her doubts about the condoms, Chad's distant behavior, and the growing sense of uncertainty, she feels a weight lifting off her shoulders.

"Sometimes I feel absolutely sure that he loves me. But other times, I can't help but feel that I am just some pawn in some game." She admits.

Ben finally offers his perspective, his words a gentle balm to her troubled soul. He reminds her of the importance of trust, the need for open communication, and the strength she possesses to navigate through the complexities of her heart. As much as he doesn't care for Chad, he cares for Octavia, and this isn't the first time she's come to him with boyfriend problems.

"Octavia, I'm sorry that you're going through this. It's so hard for me to watch you struggle. You deserve only the best, and anyone who can't see that… frankly, doesn't deserve you." Ben reaches out and grabs her hand. It's not warm like Chad's, a sensation that causes her to miss his touch, but it's still comforting, it's Ben. "No matter what Octavia, I am here for you. I always have been, and I always will be."

He's right, he has always been there for her, since they were kids. How has she not seen this before? A newfound realization has sparked more hidden and dormant feelings. How could she have been so blind? This man, who's handsome, loyal, respectful, and all around an amazing human being, has been there from the beginning. He would never leave her, he's proven it time and time again. How would dating be any different than friendship? Has she made a massive mistake by keeping Ben on the sidelines all this time, when she could have been calling him her man instead? She's sitting here with doubts about Chad and his probable betrayal when Ben is the most loyal person she's ever known.

His gaze lingers, Octavia lifts her hand and places it on the side of Ben's face. He must be interpreting this as an invitation, he leans in meeting his lips with Octavia's. She screams in her mind as she struggles between these two men she loves, yet she doesn't pull away. Rather she embraces his touch, a touch that feels like home. It's almost as if they are picking up where they left off a week and half ago. This camping trip, which has taken an unexpected turn towards introspection, also ignites a flame that's been eager to break free.

Early in the morning, the sound of a vehicle nearby wakes Octavia from a peaceful sleep. A shaft of sunlight peeks through the trees, dappling Octavia's face as she emerges from her tent. The cool morning air carries the familiar scent of pine needles and woodsmoke. As she stretches, a yawn escapes her lips and a wave of surprise washes over her. She blinks, unsure if she's still dreaming. Chad's presence in the quiet, early morning forest seems surreal, especially given how she left things before the trip. Her heart skips a beat as she takes in the sight of him, leaning casually against a tree, his sling a clear reminder of his injury. His face is etched with exhaustion, but a genuine smile crinkles the corners of his eyes.

"Morning, beautiful," he rasps, his voice slightly hoarse.

"Chad?" she finally manages, her voice a mix of surprise and disbelief. "What are you doing here?" The surprise on her face mirrors Ali's, who's just emerged from her tent, bleary-eyed but curious.

He smiles, a warm, familiar smile that makes her heart ache with a mixture of emotions. "I couldn't let my favorite girl have all the fun," he teases, pushing himself off the tree and limping over to her, his voice tinged with humor. "Besides, I missed you."

Octavia shakes her head, a small laugh escaping her. "You're crazy, you know that? You're supposed to be resting, not driving out here in the middle of nowhere."

"Resting is overrated," Chad replies, his tone light but his eyes searching hers. "I wanted to be here with you. Maybe... to clear the air a bit, too."

A warmth blooms in Octavia's chest. Despite the unresolved questions swirling in her mind, the sight of him brought a wave of relief. Yet, a flicker of concern remains. "But you're injured," she says, her voice laced with worry.

Chad chuckles. "Doctor said fresh air wouldn't hurt."

"Come on," she says softly, taking his hand. "Let's sit down for a bit." He drove all the way out to see her, that has to account for something, right? Although it doesn't make matters better, he still deserves to be heard. They walk over to a fallen log to sit down, the cool bark rough against her palms. The forest is still and quiet, with only the distant sound of birds greeting the dawn. Octavia takes a deep breath, trying to steady her thoughts. "You didn't have to come all the way out here, Chad," she says, her voice gentle but firm. "I'm not ready to talk about things yet."

"I wanted to see you, Octavia," Chad said, his voice sincere. "I know we didn't really finish our conversation before you left. And I didn't want you to spend the whole weekend worrying or wondering. I know how you can get into your head sometimes."

Octavia nods, feeling a lump in her throat. "I appreciate that, Chad. But I have to be honest with you... The condoms I found, they threw me off. I want to trust you, but..."

"I get it," Chad interrupts, his tone earnest. "And I'm not going to sit here and give you some half-baked excuse. The truth is, I don't know how they ended up in that shirt, but I do know that I haven't been with anyone else. You're the only one I want, Octavia. I don't know how else to show you that, that's why I am here."

She searches his eyes, looking for any sign of deception, but all she sees is sincerity. Still, a part of her couldn't completely let go of her doubts. "I want to believe you," she says softly. "I really do."

Chad reaches out and takes her hands in his, his touch warm and reassuring. "Then let's work through this together. I don't want anything to come between us, especially something like this. We've been through too much to let doubt ruin what we have."

Octavia feels her resolve soften. "Okay," she whispers, squeezing his hands. Chad's arrival throws a wrench into the introspective mood Octavia's grappling with. "Well, there's something else we need to talk about, too."

The boys emerge from the tent, ecstatic to see Chad and immediately bombard him, just as she was about to confess her kiss with Ben, not just the first, but the second from last night as well.

"Does your leg still hurt?" Ryan asks.

"When did you get here?" Cory questions.

Octavia watches their interaction with a smile, a familiar tug of warmth pulling at her heart. The boys love him, how could she not try to make this work. They look up to him. In all honesty, he could very well be telling the truth. But the thought of betrayal crosses her mind. Last night, with Ben. A pang of regret sears through her mind as she watches Chad interact with her boys. What has she done? And Ben? How will he feel seeing Chad here? It's a good thing her boys came out and interrupted the conversation because this is not the time nor the place. Not in front of everyone, not like this.

The boys eventually find a new interest and off they go.

"As much as I appreciate that you came here to see me, to work things out. I think it's best if you go." Octavia says to Chad with a heavy heart. "I'm just not ready yet." She struggles internally with her love for Chad and her newfound realization with Ben. She's always loved Ben, there's no question. But lately, something has been transforming within her.

"Uh, alright." Chad says, a tinge of offense in his voice.

"It's not you." She says.

"Yeah, the 'it's not you, it's me' bit. I get it." He grabs his crutch and winces as he stands up.

"I'm sorry." She affirms. The guilt she's struggling with is real, but she's not wrong. She needed space and Chad isn't respecting that. As bad as she feels sending him away, she knows it's the right thing to do.

Ben must have been woken by the commotion. He emerges from his tent. Chad looks over at him.

"I thought this was a girls trip." Chad states, a glare in his eye.

"He's my friend, too." Octavia defends herself. Avoiding the fact that she kissed him just last night. A part of her feels guilty as hell, but another part doesn't regret it at all.

"Yeah, you're right. I'm sorry. I should probably get back home anyway," he says, a hint of regret in his voice. "I shouldn't have even come out here. I just really needed to come see you and clear the air." A pang of disappointment shoots through Octavia, she wants him to stay but at the same time, she's got a lot she needs to process and work through on her own.

Octavia reaches out, a hand hovering over his arm for a moment before retracting, unsure of what her next move should be.

"Yeah, I suppose you're right. Thank you for coming out to see me, though. For working to make things right between us."

As she takes his hand, a jolt of electricity shoots up her arm. She loves this man so deeply. The physical connection, coupled with his unexpected presence, intensifies the complexity of her emotions. Just as she watches Chad drive away, a sense of emptiness settles over her.

"What's he doing here?" Ben asks suspiciously, startling Octavia. "Did he actually come all this way just to check up on you?"

"That's not fair, Ben." She replies, her voice tinged with defensiveness.

"What do you mean? How long was he even out here for? What was the purpose?" His questions rain down.

Octavia grabs hold of his arm, leading him away from where the boys are playing. "He came out here to ease my mind."

"To ease yours... or his?" He says. Maybe Ben has a point. Maybe he did come all this way to check on her. But why? To see who she was with, if it was really her friends? What would cause him to think she'd be with anyone else? His own guilt perhaps. That just seems far fetched, though. It's possible that he did come all this way to ease her mind. In her mind, that's the most logical possibility. He's making the effort in this relationship, and so, she must as well. After-all she loves him, she's still drawn to him like a moth to a light.

"There's no way you could understand this, Ben," she says. "But I'm gonna have to work things out with him." Her tone is apologetic, her heart is sinking.

"So last night? Last week?" Ben questions, brows arched, there's a worry in his voice as if he knows where this is leading.

"You mean so much to me. You've always been there for me, and I will always have a deep love and appreciation for you. But, I'm sorry, I have to see this through with him. When we get home, I will have to go back to him."

CHAPTER TWENTY EIGHT

Octavia finds herself gazing at Chad. He's sprawled out beside her, a comfortable sigh escaping his lips. The camping trip was short but it did help her gain some perspective. She knows she loves this man and has to do what she can to make it work. If she gives up now, what does that say about her? She loves Ben too, though. But what's worked for them has always been friendship and maybe she was right to keep it as just that, a friendship. With a newfound resolve about her lovelife, other pressing matters cling to her thoughts.

"Are we ever going to talk about the strange things that happen around here?" She asks, her voice patient. "Not even just around here but between us, too?"

"What do you mean?" He asks, his eyes darting towards her.

"I can't keep pretending like there's nothing weird going on. I have a duty to protect my kids and I can't hold my tongue any longer. There are weird things going on and I know there is a lot that you're not telling me. Like, why are you so abnormally warm, why do your kisses sometimes feel like they burn, can you explain all the weird noises in the house? And if I'm being completely honest, my friends don't really like you, you scare them." She pauses and takes in a deep breath. "That night my friends were over, did you light that fire out of nothing?"

Chad listens intently before he speaks.

"Octavia, you're right. I guess that I kind of assumed that there was a certain level of understanding that you already had. But the more I got to know you, the more I realized you don't actually know anything."

She scoffs. "Well, that's kind of rude."

"That's not what I mean."

"So why didn't you tell me? Why don't you tell me now!" She demands, her voice rising with each word. "I don't know how long I can keep doing this. I have my kids I need to think about."

"I would never let anything happen to you or the boys. Ever." He says, placing his hand on hers, his gaze unwavering.

"How can I be sure of that when you won't open up to me?" She asks, her voice trembling slightly.

"Uhh, yeah. You're right." he says, rubbing his hand through his hair.

"And... How do you do this?" She questions, her voice filled with a mixture of annoyance and fascination.

"Do what?" He asks with a side grin, reaching his hand up and placing it on the back of the couch.

"I don't know," she admits. "You place your hand on me, or wrap your arms around me and suddenly I feel so calm, like at peace."

"Oh you know, it's just a gift. Or... some might call it a curse." He says with a playfulness in his eyes.

With a snap of his finger, a lone candle positioned in the middle of the coffee table lights up. Octavia glances at it for a split second as if that was normal and turns her attention back to Chad. Just as quickly she looks back at the candle as it just registered.

"Wh–" She stutters. "How?... You?" Is all she can manage. This goes beyond anything that she knows to be real.

"Please don't freak out." His voice gentle, his eyes searching hers.

How could she, he's got some kind of calming tranquility spell on her or something. How the hell does he do that? . She obviously knew that weird things were happening but Luke from the bar was right, this is some weird supernatural shit.

"I know that you will probably hear things about me. Maybe you already have, but a lot of those things aren't true. I need to show you for myself." He begins, his voice serious.

"Hear things?" She asks, as if she doesn't know.

"I'm showing you now, a secret that only you are special enough to know. I am not like others in this world, just like you. And I know your head is probably spinning with questions, just know that I am here for you. I would never do anything to hurt you."

Octavia isn't understanding anything that's happening right now. The warnings from her friends, how could they see things and she missed it? Was she that blinded by love that she subconsciously refused to see, or believe it? Was she so blinded by her desire for him, for a normal life, that she just looked past it?

He takes a long pause."You know the stories, the myths... the *children's books,*" He emphasizes, "they're basically all true."

"Well, I don't know what stories you're referring to–" She says in an attempt to phish more information from him.

"Of course you do." He says, his eyes gleaming in the soft light of the living room. "The stories you would have grown up with." He pauses, a chilling smile playing on his lips. "Demons? Imps?... They exist."

Of course she knows the stories, everyone does, classic tales that go back to the beginning of time: ifrits, demons, liliths. Imps is a new one for her though. She's sure there's stories out there, just none she's ever heard or read. It's definitely on her list of things to look up though.

He interrupts her train of thought, "Okay, let me rephrase that. The creatures in the stories exist. But I can assure you that those stories are all hyped up. A lot of them are exaggerated folklore. Truth to them, nonetheless." His eyes hold an intensity that both frightens and intrigues her.

"What exactly is it that you're telling me?" She speaks gently, fear creeping into her eyes. "That you're a... demon or something?" She can hardly believe the words that just came out of her mouth. She had suspected, but it just seemed so far-fetched. Yet here they are, Chad showing off his supernatural abilities. The puzzle is all being pieced together. A puzzle she never thought would have even existed. A puzzle she shrugged off her shoulders because of the complete absurdity of it. But Chad, he stands before her shattering her idea of what reality really is.

Without a word, he just stares into her eyes, a thoughtful expression settling on his face. He tilts his head slightly, acknowledging the truth of her statement.

"I've wanted to tell you, I've tried, but the time was never right. But you have to trust me." He pleads. "I'm nothing like how they are portrayed in the stories. You must know this... I've been so good to you."

"So, M... Mateo was right?" She asks, gazing into his eyes. "You started that fire from nothing?"

"Mateo? Don't be ridiculous," he hisses, his voice a low growl. He leans in, invading her space, his eyes burning with an unsettling intensity. "Don't you worry about him."

"But he's my friend!"

He raises a hand, his fingers brush against her chin, tilting her head back.

"Promise me, Octavia," he demands, his voice dropping to a dangerous purr. "This stays between us. My life depends on it."

"Bu–" she begins, fear creeping into her voice.

"No." He cuts her off, his grip tightening slightly. "Tell me you understand?"

For a split second, his eyes glaze over, a fleeting crimson red reflecting the dying light of the setting sun. The change is so sudden, so unnatural, that Octavia gasps, her breath catching in her throat.

A knock at the door shatters the tension. Chad's gaze remains fixed on her, his eyes burning with an intensity that makes her shiver. Her eyes widen in fear, and she nods slowly, a silent agreement.

Octavia takes a deep breath, composing herself, before answering the door.

The knocking continues.

"James? What are you doing here?" She asks, her voice a little too loud.

"Just came to check in on Chad. Haven't seen or heard from him all week." He tells her, his gaze lingers behind her as he invites himself in.

"Alright, well we were…" She trails off, watching him kick his boots off. "just in the middle of something."

There's an uncomfortable silence between them. The ticking of the clock, the soft hum of the refrigerator, and the distant sound of traffic creates an annoying backdrop to their quiet company.

"It's alright, Octavia." Chad says, much too casually.

She frowns. "Fine I guess I'll go then."

"Please stay, I'll explain everything, just please stay."

"Why?" She demands "I need answers Chad! I don't want my boys around this, I don't even know what's going on!"

"Look, the boys are at your moms tonight." He pleads, an urgency in his voice. "Who knows when we will get another chance. Please, whatever you do… don't leave."

His plea is too sincere to ignore. A million questions ravage through her mind, unable to escape the confines of her own thoughts due to James' untimely presence. She decides to stay. He has never harmed her in any way. She owes it to him to stay.

* * *

As the sun descends casting the backyard in a golden hue, James decides to extend his stay. They take it outside and retreat to their usual hangout, the firepit. Octavia settles back into the living room, a soft glow emanating from the kitchen, she finds herself drawn to the window. The backyard is bathed in a warm, inviting glow, a new group of people had just shown up and were huddled around the fire pit, their silhouettes dancing in the flickering light. She has no desire to be out there tonight. Who, of all Chad's friends, knows about this? None of them? All of them? Are any of them demons too? If Chad is a demon, then why is he good to Octavia, why hasn't he tried to hurt her? There has never been anything good said about demons. Everyone knows they are inherently evil. So what's his deal?

The sunset, typically a source of warmth and tranquility, suddenly feels like an unwelcome intrusion. Octavia, completely unaware that other guests would be showing up, feels a jolt of unease. Who are they and why are they here? With the growing disquiet, she makes her way outside to confront Chad.

"Hey, I didn't know that you were having people over." She remarks, a hint of annoyance in her voice.

"Oh yeah, it just kind of happened." He shrugs, his casual demeanor is doing little to ease her discomfort.

"You just dropped a bomb on me, asked me to stay, and now you're completely ignoring me, socializing with them like it's nothing." She says, a tremble in her voice. A wave of hurt and confusion washes over her. "I'm going inside and going to bed. And I expect you to be in soon."

"Yeah babygirl, I won't be long." Chad assures her, inattentively.

Chad's laughter, deep and resonant, fills the night air. It's a sound she's grown accustomed to, a comfort in the chaos of her life. Yet, as the hours pass, a sense of unease begins to creep in. The late hour, the growing intensity of their laughter, and a subtle change in the dynamic, grow the anger and disappointment within her.

Around 11 pm, Octavia finds herself drawn back to the window. The group is still gathered around the fire, their bodies huddled close together. A pang of jealousy shoots through her as she watches Chad, sitting close to another woman, hearing him laugh while his face is illuminated by the dancing flames. Tonight, this feels different, tinged with a sense of possessiveness she hasn't experienced before. Did he actually tell her that he's a demon? That could explain a lot of the weirdness that happens around here. A secret that he's shared with only her, as far as she knows. The seriousness of the interaction they had earlier tells her that he doesn't tell just anyone. So, Octavia has to be special to him. She has to be.

The clock ticks past midnight and the group's laughter begins to take on a different tone, a raucous energy that clashes with the quietude of the night. Octavia feels a sense of intrusion in a world she isn't meant to be a part of. She's so disheartened that he would drop this bomb, then have people over and completely ignore her. However, perhaps that's not such a bad thing, she really needs to process all this new information. She doesn't know whether to be relieved he shared his secret or to be scared of him.

Octavia lies in the embrace of Chad's bed, and she begins to doze off. Then, it happens, a sharp, unexpected crash echoes through the house, jolting her wide awake. A surge of adrenaline courses through her veins. Fear, sharp and immediate, claws its way up her throat. With a silent prayer, she swings her legs over the side of the bed and paddles barefoot across the room. She glances outside the bedroom window to see Chad and his friends still sitting next to the fire pit. The house is shrouded in darkness, the only light spilling in from the moonlit window. Her heart pounds in her ears as she cautiously makes her way through the house. The source of the noise seems to have originated from another upstairs bedroom. With each step, her grip tightens on the hem of her nightgown, a makeshift shield against the unknown.

Reaching each room in the house, she fumbles for the light switch. The rooms burst into illumination, revealing a scene of undisturbed tranquility. The furniture is in place, no obvious signs of disturbance. The house creaks and groans, settling for the night. She knows enough now that it couldn't have been just anything. An imp, most likely. The fear that has gripped her heart refuses to dissipate. The third room, the one Octavia has been avoiding since moving in, sends shivers down her spine. Every noise of the house seems to amplify her unease, and she can't shake the feeling that the noise has come from this very room. Yet, despite the unsettling sounds, the house is eerily silent, no one is here, just her.

Ignoring Chad's warning, she stands at the doorway, her heart pounding in her chest. The room remains cloaked in shadow, its contents hidden from view. With a deep breath, she hesitates for a moment before slowly pushing the door open. The hinges creak loudly, echoing in the quiet house, a chill runs through her as she peers inside. The room seems to hold its breath, and the darkness within only deepens her apprehension. The book that once stood out, the one that likely possesses the answers she seeks, is not where it once was. With short shallow breaths Octavia scours the room, looking for the book that once whispered out to her. It's nowhere to be found.

Just as she goes to exit the room a quick flash of a shadow startles her, it's small, like she had seen the other day. An imp! It has to be! Her breathing becomes heavier as she's about to come face to face with something that could alter her very idea of reality. She's frozen with fear but she so desperately wants to know what an imp actually is. After-all, Chad did mention that they are harmless. She bends down towards the source of the movement, trying to gather a better look.

Suddenly, the front door of the house closes and startles Octavia. She'd already been warned not to be in this room and after what Chad revealed earlier in the day, she isn't about to test her boundaries with him. She quickly closes the door, her heart racing. She makes her way back to the bedroom with hurried steps. Each creak of the floorboards seems to echo louder in the silence, amplifying her growing anxiety. Once safely inside her room, she locks the door behind her and leans against it, trying to calm her pounding heart. The eerie silence of the house presses in on her, and the unsettling feeling lingers despite the safety of her own room. She looks around, trying to shake off the unease.

She throws some clothes on, the image of the small, mysterious shadow replays in her mind. She glances back at the clock, the night stretches before her, a silent battle between logic and fear. But the echo of that crash lingers, a haunting reminder of the inexplicable.

Downstairs Chad is shuffling around. She composes herself and heads downstairs to confront him about being out so late, especially since they have so much to talk about. Why is he gathering his things? Where is he going? Octavia becomes increasingly uncomfortable with this whole situation.

"Why do you need that?" Octavia asks, her voice strained.

He hesitates, then pulls out a board game from beneath a pile of magazines. "It's just a game." He explains, a defensive edge to his voice.

"A game where people get naked." Octavia, becoming increasingly irritated, states. There are other issues that are clearly more urgent but she can't help the sudden rush of jealousy that is consuming her.

"What's the big deal?" Chad questions as he continues to reach for the game.

"What do you mean, what's the big deal?" Octavia can feel her blood boiling, anger replacing her recent fear. "It's a game where you get naked, other women will be there and your girlfriend, me, will not be. Not only that, I thought we had some unfinished business. You owe me some answers! This might not be a big deal to you, because you have been living this life. But this is all new to me and I am being far more than patient with you about it. But I need some answers, I need you!" She stops and stares at him. "Chad, do you remember when we agreed to commit to each other? Did that mean nothing to you at all?"

A few of Chad's friends walk into the living room, mid argument. Octavia tries to hide her discontent. Chad must have already mentioned this game with the group, Octavia assumes, since he's so intent on grabbing it. Octavia sits down on the couch, along with a couple of the others.

One of the other gentlemen, a tall man with a friendly smile, notices the tension in the air. "Everything okay?" he asks Octavia, his voice laced with concern. A wave of frustration washes over her.

She tries to ignore the growing unease, but it's becoming increasingly difficult to maintain a facade of normalcy.

"I just don't feel comfortable with this," she blurts out, her voice rising slightly. "Chad leaving like this, after everyone's been drinking."

The room falls silent, the weight of her words hanging heavy in the air. Chad, who's been listening intently, looks surprised and hurt.

"It's just a game," he defends, his voice rising in pitch. "We're not going to do anything crazy."

Octavia shakes her head, her anger growing. What about any of this does he not understand? Is he not even listening to her?

"It's not about the game," she retorts. "It's about trust and respect. I don't want you to leave me here alone, and you take off, hurt, and especially when you've been drinking."

The tension in the room is palpable, the atmosphere houses a cold silence. Octavia feels a surge of regret, wishing she could take back her words. But the fear and anger she feels are too strong to ignore. She deserves his presence, especially after what he had just revealed to her.

A heavy silence settles over the room as the argument reaches its climax. Octavia's heart pounds in her chest, a mixture of anger and fear coursing through her veins. Chad, his face flushes with a mix of surprise, stares at her in disbelief. After what feels like an eternity, Chad stands up, his movements stiff and deliberate. He picks the game up and places it back on the shelf. Without a word, he turns and limps out of the house, his friends trailing behind him like a pack of wolves. She watches them go, another wave of anger washing over her. She grabs her keys and her bag and storms out the front door, slamming it behind her. Without a second glance at Chad, she gets into her vehicle and roars out the driveway, leaving him in the dust.

CHAPTER TWENTY NINE

"What in the actual hell, Chad?!" Octavia's voice cracks, panic rises in her chest. "It's five o'clock in the morning!" She had finally just fallen asleep after getting home. It took a while for her to calm down. And after a mere hour of sleep Chad calls and wakes her up. It's infuriating.

"There's been an accident." He says, his voice low and strained.

"Okay? What kind of accident?" Octavia's nurturing side kicks in, overriding her anger as she struggles to pry open her eyes, but they sting. "Is it serious? Is everyone alright?" she groans.

"No, I, I don't think so... I don't know. I need to go find James." Chad seems to be struggling with the situation, trying to make sense of it himself.

"You can't go, you've been drinking." She manages to croak out.

"I'm fine." He replies irritably. "They took off not long after you did and I have to go. I don't have a choice."

She knows there is no stopping him. A pang of guilt settles in her stomach. Maybe leaving them was the wrong decision.

"Let me know as soon as you hear anything." Octavia says with a lingering tone.

The room seems to shrink. In a flash, Octavia feels guilty about being so upset with Chad. A potentially horrifying scenario painted in stark reality. Minutes stretch into an eternity. The silence of the house is broken only by the tick of the clock. Octavia lies in her bed, wide awake, overtired, her worry manifests in restless energy. She cares about Baily and James, despite their unwelcome visit. She continuously looks up at the time, willing the hands to move faster, each tick a tiny hammer blow against her already frayed nerves.

Finally, after what feels like a lifetime, the phone in her hand vibrates, the ringtone a jarring intrusion on the oppressive silence. Her heart lurches in her chest, a mixture of hope and terror warring within her. With trembling fingers, she answers the call.

"Chad?" she chokes out.

"Octavia," his voice sputters with raw emotion. "I can't find him. I can't find James." The words loom large in her mind, a chilling confirmation of her worst fears.

"What do you mean?" she whispers, the air suddenly too thin to breathe. Where could he have disappeared to? The thought is too much to bear.

"Can I come over?" Chad asks with raw emotion.

"Okay." She says, confused and worried. She knows there's no stopping him, Chad will do what Chad does. Octavia struggles to find the right words. "What do you mean you can't find him? Where could he have gone?"

"I'll be there in a little bit." His voice crackles with helplessness.

The call ends, leaving a hollow echo in its wake. Octavia lays there, the phone clutched tightly in her hand. Octavia sees headlights gleaming into the room as Chad pulls into the driveway. Making her way into the living room, she waits nervously for him to enter the house.

"The road's a mess." Chad gasps, stumbling into the house, his face pale. "They haven't been able to get to the car yet. But there's no sign of James anywhere."

A choked sob escapes him, a raw vulnerability that sends a surprising jolt through her. Octavia's breath catches in her throat. James, the life of the party just hours ago, might be gone. The weight of the situation settles on her like a physical blow.

"I looked everywhere," he began, his eyes wide and filled with a desperate fear. "But I..." he trails off, his words lost in a strangled sound. "There's branches and debris all over the road. He fought. I know he did but I don't know if it got him."

"The ambulance?" she asks. "I don't know what you mean, who got him?"

He lets out a soft sob.

"It's okay, Chad," she interjects gently.

"And the water was just too high." He lets out a shaky breath, his shoulders slumped. "I swam and I looked everywhere and..." He chokes out, his voice raw with a mixture of fear and frustration.

"Come here." She whispers, holding her arms out, the gesture a silent invitation to draw him in for comfort. Her heart is racing. She's caught between the guilt of racing off, and the overwhelming need to be a source of strength for Chad as he navigates this terrifying unknown. He stumbles towards her, burying his face in her chest, his body trembling.

"Thank you, Octavia. I don't know what I'd do without you right now." He whispers. She holds him close, wrapping her arms around him. "If it wasn't for you, that could be me out there."

He looks at her, desperation in his eyes.

"I need to go see Baily," Chad declares, his voice urgent. "I have to check on her. The paramedics were loading her up when I got there... But I didn't..." He grips the banister, his knuckles white. "I need to find out what happened, I need to find James."

"Hey," She says softly, her gaze unwavering. "Hey, it's okay. Go."

Octavia wishes that there was more she could do. The minutes stretch into an agonizing eternity, and hours crawl by. Each tick of the clock feels like a hammer blow against her already frayed nerves. But she won't give into despair. She has to be strong, for Chad, for Baily, and for the sliver of hope that still lingers within her. James has to be found. Despite her worry, she's dreadfully tired. Her eyes fall heavy before her phone abruptly goes off, she quickly answers.

"Octavia?" Chad rasps into the phone, his voice thick with emotion.

"Chad? What's going on, is Baily alright?" Her voice, laced with concern, breaks through the receiver.

"I'm not sure yet, she's with the nurses now." He takes a deep breath, trying to find the words. "But James," he begins, his voice tight. "There's still no word." A choked sob escapes him, a raw vulnerability laid bare, he has no reliable information. Silence stretches on the other end of the line, then a soft sigh.

"Oh, Chad," Octavia quietly speaks, her voice thick with sympathy. "I'm so sorry."

"I'll probably be here all day. I'll call you the minute I know anything." he goes on, his voice regaining a semblance of control. "Umm, Octavia, there isn't anything you can do so try to get some sleep. I'm so sorry for everything."

"Chad–," she says before he interrupts.

"I'll call you when I know anything."

"Okay," her voice steady despite the tremor she feels. "Stay strong, Chad." With a shaky breath, they end the call. For a demon, Chad sure has human elements.

Perched on the edge of the bed with phone clutched tightly in her hand, she stares out the window wondering if each passerby was Chad. Sleep eludes her, but she's already accepted the fact that there won't be any. She lays in bed too concerned to sleep. The events of the last twenty four hours replay on repeat in her mind, trying to process it all. Chad has promised he'll call as soon as he hears any news. A gnawing worry, a disquiet she can't quite place, begins to twist in her gut. She can't help but wonder if James is alright. She doesn't really know anything at this point and the worry is becoming a lot to bear.

Sleep finally consumes her.

* * *

Nearing the afternoon, the phone vibrates making her jump. Relief floods her momentarily, but then she sees it's not Chad's number. It's an unknown caller. Disappointment pricks at her. With a sigh, she answers, forcing a cheerful lilt into her voice.

"Hello?" The voice on the other end was familiar, rugged and warm. Of course it's Chad.

"Hey babe, sorry I didn't call earlier," he says apologetically. "My phone died." There's a calm in his voice that wasn't there earlier.

A wave of relief washes over her, battling with the lingering worry that has settled in her gut.

"That's alright," she manages, forcing a smile into her voice. "I was just worried when I didn't hear from you." There's a beat of silence on the other end. "Is everyone okay?" she asks, her voice betraying concern.

"Baily's okay, just a few bumps and bruises."

"Oh good." Octavia interrupts.

"But James…" He stutters.

"James?" The name sends a jerk through her. "What about James?"

"They found him," Chad says, his voice tight.

Relief washes over her, warm and welcome.

"Oh Chad, thank goodness!" she exclaims, the worry lines on her forehead smooth out. "I was so anxious."

"Yeah, me too," Chad admits. "The cops and the rescue team eventually found him, but he doesn't have his phone on him. He needs to stay in the hospital another night because they pulled him out of the water and need to keep him for observation."

A pang of sympathy shoots through Octavia. "Oh no. I'm so sorry!"

"It's not your fault, Octavia." Chad attempts to console her despite his own turmoil. "They say he's likely going to be alright," he goes on, his voice still tinged with worry. "It's not life-threatening. It would take a lot more than a bit of water to take James down. But the doctors are just doing their job."

Relief washes over her, a wave cresting and then gently receding. "Oh thank goodness," she breathes, the tension draining from her shoulders.

"Listen, Baily's with a friend and they will be keeping James overnight, so I am going to head home here soon."

Concern remains in Octavia's voice. "Does he need someone to stay with him at the hospital?"

"Nah, the doctor said he'll be fine for the night," Chad reassures her. "He's got a roommate, some old guy who keeps telling stories about skydiving in his twenties." He pauses, "Besides, I need to be home with you."

Octavia chuckles, a welcome sound in the tense evening. "Sounds like a character. Alright, well I'll see you soon."

"Definitely," Chad promises. "Um, are the kids there?"

"No, I asked my mom to hang on to them a little longer. She wants to take them camping anyway. Then she will drop them off at their summer camp." A sudden thud hits the bottom of her stomach – she wants to see her boys before they go to camp, but with everything that's going on right now, it just doesn't seem like the best course of action to have them around. Not until she really figures out what's going on.

"Alright. See you soon, babe."

He hangs up, Octavia lets out a long breath she hadn't realized she was holding. Relief mingles with worry for James, but at least everyone seems to be okay. Curled up on the couch, every creak of the building sounds like Chad's truck pulling in.

Finally, the telltale rumble of the engine announces his arrival. Moments later, Chad bursts through the door, a tired but relieved smile etched on his face. Octavia hurries to his side and he holds her tight, the familiar scent of him grounding her after a chaotic evening. They disentangle, and Chad's gaze softens as he looks at her. Despite the worry etched on her face, there's a quiet strength in her eyes.

"Octavia, I'm in so much pain. Lay with me."

"You have a new sling on?"

"Yeah, he had to reposition my collarbone, I didn't even realize I put it out until I got to the hospital."

After a very long and eventful night with little to no sleep, they are too tired to get into anything that had happened since yesterday. There's too much to talk about and they are running on fumes. They lie in bed and are finally able to succumb to some rest.

The sounds of a low muffle wakes Octavia from her deep sleep, She lays there groggy, trying to make out the sound coming from beside her. Why isn't Chad sleeping, and who is he talking to? Hospital, Baily, Nightstalker? She must be dreaming, with the lack of sleep and the traumatizing events with James and Baily, she has to be imagining things. She shuffles, turning towards Chad, still half asleep.

"Who are you talking to?" She can barely make him out with her eyes still closed. "Shhh, go back to sleep." He says, and gently rubs her forehead.

CHAPTER THIRTY

Octavia stands in line at the store, despite being stuck between parental responsibilities and her mind completely consumed with a desperate search for answers about Chad's world, she plays it cool. Chad recently revealed that he's not human. It's a lot to process and for whatever reason, he clearly wasn't in the mood to continue the conversation. He could have sent his friend away, he could have sent them all away. Part of her feels like it was all a ploy to avoid it all together. With her phone in her hand, and fixated on the screen, she types in key phrases like 'demon,' 'imp' and 'nightstalker'. The world around her fades into the background as she scrolls through endless results, trying to make sense of the bizarre and terrifying changes happening in her world and to her body. She's so absorbed that she barely notices the people moving around her. Suddenly, a voice cuts through her concentration.

"You're not going to find what you're looking for on there." An unfamiliar voice speaks quietly.

Startled, Octavia looks up to see a young woman standing beside her.

"Excuse me." She says, lowering her phone.

The stranger has pale skin and short black hair, her dark, goth-inspired attire gives her an air of mystery. A teenager perhaps. Octavia's surprised, not only because the woman had spoken to her out of nowhere but because she seems to know exactly what she's searching for. The idea that anyone can see what she's doing on her phone, let alone comment on it so directly, sends a jolt of shock through her. How could this stranger know what she's looking for? The woman's words echo in her mind, leaving her both intrigued and unnerved.

Octavia is unsure how to respond, her thoughts racing. Is this a coincidence, or does this mysterious woman know something? Before Octavia could find her voice, the woman offers her a knowing smile, as if she has glimpsed a part of Octavia's hidden world, and then turns away, leaving Octavia with more questions than ever. The encounter has shaken her, but it also sparks a glimmer of hope. Perhaps she's closer to the truth than she realizes. With the idea of the strange woman lingering in the back of her mind, Octavia retreats back into her fortress of solitude, shielding herself from the world's noise.

You're not going to find what you're looking for in there. Octavia replays this in her mind over and over again, trying to decipher what it means. Who was that strange woman and how did she know what I was searching for?

If she can't find it on the internet, where can she find it? She racks her already overwhelmed mind. She can't ask his friends, he has no family. She doesn't want to drag her friends in further than they already are, she can't risk anyone's safety until she has some answers about what's really going on. The book in Chad's house comes to mind. But how could she access it without Chad knowing? It feels like an impossible puzzle with no solution. There has to be another way.

The afternoon offers no solace as questions continue to ring vigorously through her mind. She stares at the computer, the glow of the screen reflecting in her wide, troubled eyes, too distracted to work. Website after website offers no real consolidation, only a frustrating sea of unanswered questions. A knock at the door startles her. She isn't expecting anyone, not today while she's *supposed* to be working. She slowly rises from her chair, placing one foot in front of the other as she creeps towards the door, her heart pounds against her chest. She hopes whoever is outside doesn't hear or see that she's home. The thought of company right now is enough to churn her stomach. She peeks through the peephole in the door and she scans the deck. Relief washes over her when she sees no one there.

She cautiously opens the door, her eyes darting around suspiciously. Something at her feet snags her attention. A cylinder-shaped package, wrapped in plain brown paper, lies abandoned on the welcome mat. She picks it up, the paper rough beneath her fingers, and closes the door with a soft click, locking it securely behind her. Curiosity, a dangerous and alluring temptress, quickly overcomes her. She carefully unwraps the package, her fingers tracing the rough texture of the brown paper. Inside, nestled amongst soft tissue paper, lives a scroll, its edges laced with shimmering gold. She unravels the elegant scroll and her heart sinks. It's blank.

With overwhelming frustration, Octavia breaks down, tears streaming down her face. She falls to her knees, the blank scroll clenched in her grasp. The confusion she bears is unlike anything she has ever experienced before, a suffocating weight settling over her. A single tear lands on the scroll, and suddenly, a shimmer of gold begins to dance across the blank surface. Octavia gasps, her breath catching in her throat. The gold shimmers and swirls, slowly revealing a message etched in an elegant script.

Beware the one who wields the fire. A beguiling entity, warm to the touch. With saliva of acid which carries a curse it defies all boundaries of morality. This darkness knows no love.

Octavia, who's more confused now than ever, wipes a stray tear from her cheek as she tries to decipher what the message could possibly mean. The message fades, the shimmering gold retracting back into the parchment, leaving behind only a faint, ghostly outline of the words.

Who could possibly have left this? The girl from the grocery store? Who else could know she's searching for answers. And what exactly does it mean? Chad? He can start a fire from nothing and is so abnormally warm. Demons are known to be entities of darkness, to possess pure evil. And saliva of acid? That could be why his kisses irritate her skin, but wouldn't they sear? But Chad loves her... right? He has to, he's proven it time and time again. And she loves him despite what others might think of him. He's not evil. They just don't know and understand the *real* him like she does. Whoever is trying to break them up is making a mistake. Her love for him is a force stronger than any whisper of doubt, stronger than any chilling warning. She will fight for him, for their love, no matter what. Just as he has done for her.

CHAPTER THIRTY ONE

The clock ticks closer to midnight. Octavia prepares to retire for the night in her own bed, in her own home. Just as she's about to surrender to sleep, her phone rings, jolting her awake. It's Chad. His voice, usually filled with warmth and reassurance, now carries an undercurrent of distress.

"Octavia, please come out and be with me," he pleads. "I've gotten myself into a bit of trouble, and I need you."

Despite how tired she is, without hesitation she accepts Chad's request. His vulnerability, laid bare in his plea, triggers a protective instinct within her. The thought of him facing trouble alone is unbearable. She will be there for him, no matter what, just as he has been for her. These weekends are really beginning to take their toll on her. She wanted the excitement, she was hungry for it. But not in a million years did she think it would be a continuous rollercoaster of late nights and unexplainable events with a demon.

The night is still fairly young when Octavia pulls up to James's house. The familiar glow from the porch light is the only illumination in the quiet suburban street. A knot of apprehension tightens in her stomach as she steps out of the car. The chill in the air did little to dispel the icy sensation that creeps into her heart. Her mind races with possibilities, each more unsettling than the last. Has Chad gotten into an accident? Was he involved in a confrontation? Or is it something more personal, something he's too ashamed to disclose over the phone? The uncertainty is a heavy weight on her shoulders.

As she approaches the front door, her hand hovers over the doorbell, hesitant to disturb the peace. A deep breath steadies her resolve, and she presses the button. The sound of footsteps echo through the house before the door swings open, revealing Baily's tired face. Octavia's heart pounds in her chest as she stands on the porch, the cool night air doing little to calm her rising anxiety.

"Can I help you?" Baily's abruptness and the late hour only serve to heighten her unease.

"I am so sorry, Chad called me to come over, and I'm not sure where they are." Octavia says.

"They are in the shop." Baily points into their direction and immediately closes the door. With a slight nod, Octavia turns and heads towards the shop. What's her problem? Maybe Baily's just tired and irritated, but that seems out of character, even for her.

The walk to the shop feels like an eternity. The night is silent, except for the distant chirp of crickets. Each step brings her closer to the unknown, and with it, a growing sense of dread. It's a dark walk to the shop, except for the glow emanating from the cracks of the shop. She pushes the door and it creaks open. The familiar scent of sawdust and old wood fill her nostrils. The interior of the shop is a world away from the cozy domesticity of James' home. It's a cavernous space filled with the raw energy of creation. A large boat dominates one corner of the shop, the same one that was used to take Octavia and Chad on their recent lake adventure. An old truck, covered in a layer of dust, stands sentinel near the entrance, its weathered exterior hinting at countless miles traveled. Tools of every shape and size are scattered around, each one a potential weapon in the hands of a desperate man. Octavia's eyes dart around the room, taking in the scene. This isn't the place she imagined finding Chad. Despite the industrial nature of the space, there's a comforting familiarity to it. The worn wooden workbench, the tools hanging neatly on the walls, and the soft glow of the lights create a sense of warmth and security, a place that reminds her of her late father. It's a space where things are made, where problems are solved, and where, Octavia hopes, solutions could be found. A flicker of determination ignites within her. She needs to focus on the present, to assess the situation calmly. Her gaze shifts to Chad, slumped in the chair. His stillness is unnerving.

Octavia's attention shifts to James, seeking answers. His face, etched with concern, offers little comfort. A wave of nausea washes over her.

"Alcohol and magic mushrooms are a dangerous combination." James concludes. Octavia's heart pounds in her chest as she realizes the gravity of the situation.

"Magic mushrooms?" She manages to croak out "mixed with alcohol? What were you guys thinking?" James nods, his face a mask of regret.

"I mean, it's just mushrooms. It's not like this is our first time. I don't know what's going on. We just wanted to celebrate his birthday."

His birthday? She questions herself. She doesn't want James to think that Chad wouldn't share such an important event with her. Which he hasn't, and she doesn't know why. For now, it's best she keeps it to herself.

Her mind continues to race. She's heard stories about the unpredictable effects of magic mushrooms, especially when combined with alcohol. This sounds like a recipe for disaster. She moves slowly towards Chad, her fingers numb. She kneels beside him, the cold cement of the floor seeping into her knees. Reaching out, she gently shakes his shoulder. "Chad, wake up," she says softly, her voice filled with concern. She looks back at James, "how much did you guys take?" She asks.

James shrugs his shoulders as he hands her a bottle of water, a silent gesture of support. She takes a deep breath and splashes some water on

Chad's face. His eyelids flutter and he groans softly. "How long has he been like this?" she demands. Chad's eyelids flutter open slowly, his gaze focuses on Octavia.

A weak smile spreads across his face. "Octavia," he mumbles, his voice thick with sleep... and something else? She offers him the water bottle, and he takes a small sip, his hand trembling slightly. When he lowers the bottle, his eyes meet hers. "I knew you'd come," he says, his voice filled with a strange intensity. "I love you so much, Octavia." Octavia's heart skips a beat. His words are unexpected, and the intensity in his eyes is unsettling. She doesn't know how to respond. Is this the effect of the magic mushrooms, or is this coming from the heart?

Her heart swells with a mix of emotions. Relief, love, and concern wash over her. Chad's declaration is unexpected, yet it feels nice. She's always felt a deep connection with him, and despite any differences they might have had, his words confirm what her heart already knows.

"I love you too, Chad," she replies, her voice soft and gentle. A moment passes between them, filled with a raw vulnerability. Then, her concern resurfaced. "But what happened? Why did you do this to yourself?"

Chad's response is simple, almost childlike. "I don't know, Octavia," he mumbles, his eyes avoiding hers. "I wasn't sure if I'd lost James, and I needed to be with him tonight."

"You're right," she says to Chad before turning her attention to James. "You know, you and Baily are really lucky to come out of that wreck mostly unharmed, like you did." She knows there has to be more to his excuse though. It just doesn't feel complete. Especially since he didn't tell her it's his birthday! She knew it had to be coming up, but the one time she asked when it was, he changed the subject, leaving her no clue.

"We were pretty stupid that night, we knew better than to be out in the dark." James says, "When it comes to nightstalkers, you have to be smart."

There's that word again, *nightstalkers*.

"What the hell, James!" Chad calls out, using every last bit of energy he has.

"What?" He defensively shrugs. "I thought you told her!"

"Told me what?" Octavia asks.

"You know I'm not even supposed to *be* with her. Why don't you mind your own damn business for once, James." Chad slurs his snarl before leaning over, burying his head into his knees.

Octavia feels a surge of frustration and concern mixed with annoyance that he would take drugs in the first place, and now they are out here arguing about something ridiculous that she also has no idea about. Chad has been keeping secrets. This clearly isn't the time or the place to confront him about everything, not while he's barely conscious, but she will get to the bottom of it, somehow.

"Okay, I don't know what you two are going on about," she says, trying to keep her voice calm. "But let's just chill. We can talk about this later, when you're not high... or drunk." The moments tick by slowly. Octavia finds herself in an unexpected role: caretaker for the night. She monitors Chad and James closely, making sure they stay hydrated and out of trouble.

Chad drifts in and out of sleep, his mind still clouded by the effects of the drugs and alcohol. James seems lost in his own thoughts. The silence in the shop is punctuated only by the occasional snore from Chad or the ticking of the clock.

"Maybe I should get Chad home." Octavia suggests. "He needs to get to bed."

James looks at Octavia with a newfound respect. "I want to thank you for sticking by Chad," he begins, his voice heavy with sincerity. "It's times like these you really see who someone's true friends are." Suddenly, Chad's wide awake and brimming with energy.

In a flash, he's on his feet, a newfound energy propels him around the shop. His eyes scan the room with a curious intensity, taking in every detail. With an impulsive surge, he makes a beeline for the boat, his hand reaching up to the gunwales to hoist himself aboard, failing his first attempt.

"Chad, what the hell are you doing? You're never going to heal climbing around like that." She feels like such a mother to him sometimes.

Once up there, he begins to explore, testing the vessel's balance with his shifting weight. "Whoa, okay. So you're feeling much better, great." Octavia observes with a sarcastic tone.

"Whoo! I feel amazing, babe." He says, bringing a smile to her face. Chad's energy is contagious. The night continues in a blur of fun and joy.

Octavia can't help but laugh at his silly antics. "Just be careful, you don't want to hurt yourself more than you already are." She reminds him, her nurturing side always taking precedence.

"Ah that old thing," he rubs his collarbone, "ain't got nothing on me," he replies. "Besides, it's my birthday, let me let loose a bit."

"Your birthday?" She questions. "Now you want to tell me it's your birthday?"

"Ah well, I think we're in the clear now!" He shouts.

Clear? Clear from what? He clearly needs to lay off the drugs, he isn't making any sense.

The first light of dawn begins to seep through the shop windows and Octavia feels a wave of exhaustion wash over her. Her eyelids are heavy, and her body aches from the prolonged wakefulness. Yet, she can't abandon Chad and James. They need her, even if they don't realize it.

"Where can I go to the washroom, James?" She stands up and asks.

"Oh, you'll have to go behind the shop so we don't wake Baily." He replies.

Yeah, wouldn't want that.

"Okay." She says and makes her way outside.

Just as she sits back down with the two men, a sudden noise startles her. She turns to see Chad sitting up abruptly, his eyes wide with panic. He bolts upright, his irises brighten with a shade of crimson red, terror fills his face. Sweat beads on his forehead as he scans the room frantically.

"It's happening!" He shouts, his voice hoarse and filled with fear. His body tenses. James sits straight up, quickly opening his eyes to the sight of Chad's panicked state. Octavia's heart pounds frantically in her chest as she realizes something is terribly wrong.

A cold dread washes over her as she scrambles to her feet. Her mind races, trying to process what's happening. She looks to James for answers, but his face is as pale as a ghost. The humming sound grows in the room, a low, insistent drone that vibrates through her bones. Octavia's mind is clouded and confused of what could possibly be happening. Could this be related to the dark secrets that she knows Chad harbors? Or is it a terrifyingly delayed reaction to the magic mushrooms? Did they spike her water as some kind of sick joke? The possibilities are terrifying. Her eyes widen as she looks at Chad, his eyes filled with a primal fear that she's never seen before. She longs to protect them, but she has no idea what they are facing.

"I've been trying so hard to be good for you, Octavia." Chad's voice trembles as he lets out a soft sob. "You have to believe me." Octavia's blood runs cold. The dark secrets Chad has hinted at, or shared, in the past, the ones he was trying to protect Octavia from since the beginning, take on a terrifying new meaning. This isn't a drug-induced panic attack; it's something far more sinister.

His eyes, once filled with fear, now hold a dark, primal intensity. The realization hits her like a ton of bricks; the man she loves, the one she had grown to cherish, is a creature of darkness. And now, is that darkness consuming him?

"Chad, I don't know what to do!" She hollers. "I don't know what's happening."

Tears form in her eyes. The humming grows louder, and a cold draft sweeps through the room, despite the closed windows. A chill runs up her spine and the hairs on her arm stick straight up. She feels a surge of adrenaline, her body preparing for a fight she doesn't understand. She looks at James, his face a mask of terror must know they are in over their heads. Chad's eyes, once filled with panic, now hold a strange, inhumane glow. Octavia's world shatters around her. This is the truth she's feared, but never fully understood. Yet, here it is, raw and terrifying.

She's always sensed a darkness lurking within Chad, a shadow side he desperately tried to conceal. He's warned her about it but she chose to love him anyway. Her love was enough to change him, to help him become a better man, she's sure of it. But nothing could have prepared her for the terrifying reality unfolding before her. The man she loves, admires, and cares for is a monster, a spawn of hell trapped in human skin. Yet, despite the horror, a profound sense of protectiveness washes over her. Her heart pounds in her chest as she faces the unknown. She's terrified, but her love for Chad is stronger. She will help him, no matter the cost. She was warned about this and she accepted the risks. She can't turn her back on him now. Not when he needs her most. The Chad she knows, the one behind the mask, the one who yearns for redemption, is there, he longing for her, begging for her to save him. And in this moment, her love for him deepens. Love, a stubborn and illogical force, compels her to stand by him, a fierce determination to help him, to fight whatever force is consuming him. She steps closer, her voice steady despite the terror that gnaws at her.

"Chad," she says, her voice filled with a mixture of love and authority, "I'm here. We'll get through this together." She stands her ground despite not knowing what's happening. But what she does know is that this is her Chad. Her love. And if she can save him from whatever is happening to him then she will do whatever it takes.

Driven by Octavia's initiative, James rushes to Chad's side, only to be met with a scorching touch that sends him reeling. Helplessly, he's relegated to the sidelines, a prisoner of inaction. The veins under Chad's skin begin to bulge. From head to toe, they turn a bright red. The flames of hell are mirrored in his pupils. Octavia's voice, filled with desperation, echoes through the quiet room. She wants to back away, she wants to run. But she pushes through her deep fear.

"I'm here, Chad," she pleads, her words laced with tears. "I love you. Please, stay with me." She plea's, choking back a heavy sob, as she holds tightly onto his hands.

Chad's eyes, wide with terror, lock onto Octavia. Fear, raw and palpable, consumes his gaze as he battles an unseen force within. His face contorted in agony, a silent plea for help etched into his features. Chad's body stiffens, his wide eyes glazing over as if he's looking through Octavia and into a distant, terrifying abyss.

"Look at me, don't look away! I'm here and I'm not going anywhere!"

She refuses to abandon him. Fear gnaws at her, but she stands firm, her arms wrapped tightly around his convulsing body. Her voice, a steady anchor in the storm, fills the room.

"Chad, it's me. You're safe. Fight it, Chad. Fight it!" Her words are like a lifeline, a desperate plea for his consciousness to return.

Eventually, with a Herculean effort, Chad's body stills, his violent tremors subside. His eyes, slowly flutter open, meet hers, they are filled with confusion and exhaustion. But they are green, as they once were. Chad's breath comes in ragged gasps as he struggles to regain control. His eyes, filled with a haunting vulnerability, search Octavia's face. A cold sweat breaks out on his forehead, and his hands clench into fists. The fear that consumed him lingers in the air, a tangible tension between them. Without warning, he reaches out for her, his arms trembling as he pulls her into a tight embrace. Tears, hot and uncontrolled, stream down his face, a vast difference to the terrifying ordeal they had just endured. Octavia holds him gently, her arms wrapping around him protectively, offering solace in the aftermath of the storm. She holds him close, her tears stream down her face but her arms are a comforting shield against the world. Her voice, soft and reassuring, soothes him as he weeps.

Meanwhile, James stands frozen in the corner of the room. His eyes dart between Chad and Octavia, wide with shock and disbelief. Octavia's voice, gentle and firm, cut through the heavy silence.

"It's okay, James," she says, her gaze shifting to him. "It's Chad. The same Chad you've always known."

Her words are a lifeline, an attempt to ground James in reality, to reassure him that despite the terrifying ordeal, the friend he knows still exists somewhere within the chaos they just witnessed. She's not so sure she believes it herself. Is it Chad? Or is he being consumed by his darkness? Is he changing? Did he change? And could it still be the Chad she knows? There's no way to know for sure until she finds some answers. Chad raises his knees and sits up.

"Hey, take it easy... your..." Chad stands up with ease. "Not hurt," she whispers to herself. How is that even possible?

She keeps the thought to herself. He's warned her of danger, she's beginning to feel what he might have meant by it. Now isn't the time to prod and ask questions, she needs to play it smart.

"What the hell just happened?" James' mind reels. "That wasn't real." he says, shaking his head, staring at Chad and Octavia. Did he truly see what he thought he did, or was this a grotesque, vivid trip induced by the mushrooms he'd consumed earlier?

"What the hell?" Panic seems to be settling in. The line between fantasy and reality blur, leaving him stranded in a limbo of fear and confusion.

"You know just as well as I do what happened, James." Chad blurts out.

"But they never told us it would be like that... Seriously." James shakes his head.

"And what exactly were you expecting?" Chad says. Octavia's eyes are following them, not a clue what they are talking about. Do they know what happened? Do they know what all this is about? They expected it?

"Well, did it work?" James asks. Chad shoots a terrifying look into James' direction.

Did what work? Octavia questions.. What are they talking about?

CHAPTER THIRTY TWO

A fragile calm settles over the room. The light of dawn peeks through the windows. Octavia holds Chad, her touch a steady anchor in the storm that passes through. Her eyes, filled with a mixture of exhaustion and resilience, never leave his face. Chad still trembles slightly. James stands by, a silent observer of their unique connection. The first rays of sunlight seep through the cracks of the doors. The world outside is beginning a new day, filled with promise and renewal, while inside the room, they are still grappling with the remnants of a terrifying night. The rising sun offers a glimmer of hope, a promise of a new beginning. But for now, as the first light touches their faces, they exist in a suspended moment, caught between the darkness of what was and the uncertain light of what's to come.

"James, you need to get some rest," Chad says. "Go inside, get some sleep. We will finish the conversation later."

Octavia and Chad escort James to his house, their concern obvious. As they approach the front door, it swings open, revealing Baily, her expression a mix of irritation and sleepiness.

"Are you guys seriously still up?" she asks, her voice laced with disbelief.

Octavia, the brave caretaker, pipes in, "this guy needs to get some serious rest. They had a major trip with those mushrooms. Take it easy on him," she adds, her tone softens as she takes in James's pale, drawn appearance.

Baily scoffs, clearly unhappy about how the night unfolded. If only she was there and saw what the rest of them did, she might have a different tone.

Octavia and Chad exchange a weary glance before heading to Octavia's car.

"I'll drive." Octavia insists.

There's no question about allowing Chad to drive in his current state. As they pull away from James's house, the first rays of sunlight paint the sky with soft hues reflecting off the scattered clouds. The night's ordeal leaves them both exhausted, their minds racing with the events that unfolded. With each passing moment, the reality of what they had experienced begins to sink in deeper. The fear, the horror, and the confusion are still raw, a heavy weight on their shoulders. The whole drive, neither speaks, their silence a shared acknowledgement of the profound impact the night has had on them.

The sound of Chad's driveway rumbles beneath them, although the familiar sight of his home offers little comfort. Inside, they move through the motions of getting ready for bed, their bodies exhausted but her minds far from sleep. Curled up in Chad's bed, Octavia feels a tempest of emotions. Fear gnaws at her, a constant, icy presence. The night's horrors shattered her sense of security, leaving her uncertain about what the future holds. Yet, intertwined with the fear was an overwhelming surge of love and joy for Chad. His vulnerability, his strength in the face of terror, has deepened her connection to him in ways she can't imagine possible. Her love, enough to combat evil, keeps her grounded enough to stick around. To seek answers. She's undeniably drawn to him, her heart pounds a relentless rhythm in her chest. The fear that consumed her earlier is gradually replaced by a profound sense of connection. In the quiet of the night, with only the soft glow of the sunrise filtering through the window, she feels a vulnerability she hasn't experienced in a long time. And yet, it's in this vulnerability that she finds a strange kind of peace. And somehow, she's not afraid.

Octavia's mind scrambles as she lay beside Chad. The pieces of a puzzle she didn't realize she was assembling are slowly falling into place. The abnormal warmth of his skin that often comforts Octavia when she feels chilled. The unexplainable sounds emanating from Chad's house that she's dismissed as random occurrences now seem connected to the secretive mischief that Chad, in some way, engages in. And then there was the chilling warning he'd given her at the beginning of their relationship, a statement that had once seemed out of place but now feels like cryptic foreshadowing. A cold dread creeps into her heart as she realizes the terrifying implications of what she's beginning to understand. Octavia's heart pounds as a cold dread washes over her. The love and connection she feels for Chad is undeniable, but a primal instinct for self-preservation kicks in. This isn't just about her. She thinks of her children, their innocent faces flashing before her eyes. How could she put them at risk?

The man she loves, the gentle, caring Chad she knows, is at odds with a terrifying darkness. And has been for who knows how long? Her mind races, trying to reconcile the two. How could he be both? She saw the darkness within him, a force so raw and primal it chilled her to the bone. She'd also seen his fear as well. And yet, he's also been a loving, supportive partner and a wonderful step father figure to her children. Doubt pokes at her. Can she trust her instincts? Or is she overreacting, allowing fear to consume her?

"Chad?" She cautiously prods, she needs answers.

"Hmm," He grunts, his voice barely audible. He's barely awake. He pulls her in, wrapping his arms around her.

Exhaustion finally overtakes her racing mind. The familiar warmth of Chad's body, a comforting anchor amidst the storm of her thoughts, lull her into a state of uneasy slumber. As sleep claims her, the terrifying images of the night begin to fade.

* * *

Chad and Octavia spend the day in bed trying to catch up on some much needed sleep. The boys are still at summer camp under the watchful (and safe) eye of the camp leaders. The evening sun tries to beam through the curtains. Octavia stirs, her sleep disturbed by a recurring nightmare. The terrifying events of the night before replay in her mind, the fear and confusion still linger. She turns to find Chad sleeping peacefully beside her, his face relaxed and serene. A pang of guilt washes over her. How could she be so suspicious of the man she loves? The fear that consumes her must be irrational, a product of a mind grappling with the unknown. She reaches out and gently strokes his hair, feeling a surge of love and protectiveness. How could there be any darkness in him, he just looks so innocent lying there sleeping.

Octavia can't shake the memory of James's failed attempt to touch Chad. The invisible force that had repelled him was conspicuous to her own experience. While she felt a powerful energy emanating from Chad, it wasn't hostile. Instead, it was a force she met with her own, a cool counterpoint to his intense heat. The realization intrigues her. However, with a deep breath, she focuses on the present moment, determined to continue on with hope and optimism. Chad begins to stir, his eyelids slowly flutter open. He stretches, a contented sigh escaping his lips as he becomes a little more awake.

"Hey, baby girl." Chad says with a groggy voice.

"Hey you, it's nice to see you're back to your normal self." She replies.

A look of joy mixed with confusion crosses Chad's features.

"Normal hey."

"Well, you know what I mean." She says with a smile. Chad rolls over, his bare skin next to Octavia's feels like home. Warmth radiates from her chest as she places her cool hands on his shoulders. Chad stops and looks her in the eyes.

"Thank you for being there for me, like you said you would." Chad expresses his gratitude for Octavia's unwavering support, his voice filled with genuine appreciation.

"This world," She pauses. "There's so much more to it, isn't there?"

"Like you'd never imagine." He says.

"Okay, so what's a nightstalker? And please don't give me some half-baked answer, not after what we've been through together."

"Octavia..." Chad begins, his voice grave. "There are entities out there, hunters, who prey on those like me. They don't comprehend our significance, our value. Their sole purpose is to find us and eliminate us. I don't know how they discovered us here, but they did, and they almost claimed my best friend."

"The accident?" She whispers, her gaze fixed on his, searching for answers.

Chad nods solemnly.

"So, James?"

"Baily too." He confirms.

Silence stretches for what feels like an eternity as Octavia processes the newfound information.

She approaches Chad delicately with her questions, he's finally answering them but she doesn't want to push it. Her voice is soft as the questions roll out.

"Chad, why was James forced back when he tried to touch you, but I wasn't?"

Chad's expression turns thoughtful, a hint of confusion in his eyes.

"I don't know how you don't know this, Octavia. You're different."

He replies and lets out a sigh as he sits up. "With humans, it's almost repulsive to touch them. But with you it's different.

"Humans?" She asks.

"Huh?" Chad looks at her with a confused look on his face.

"You said humans." She reiterates.

"Oh, people," reassuring her, that's what he meant.

"Well, I mean sometimes it burns, like when you kiss me, that can't be denied," Octavia admits, her brow furrowed in concentration. "I thought I was just having an allergic reaction, but it's not, is it?" She takes a deep breath as she hesitates to ask another question. "You really are a demon... aren't you?" She asks, her voice filled with intrigue and a mixture of concern. She's still in disbelief that she's actually saying these words.

"But, James isn't human."

"Look at me, Octavia. I'm me, I'm good. I fought for you, you fought for me." Chad continues, his voice low and contemplative, almost begging. "There's a pull between us, something deeper than attraction." He pauses. "James is my best friend, and has been for ages. But I don't have that same connection with him, like I do you."

"Wha..." She pauses, looking for the right words. "What did James mean when he asked 'did it work'?"

He pauses, "umm." Chad's quiet voice lingers. "If you weren't there with me that night, I don't know what would have happened. This is going to sound super cheesy, so don't laugh, and I could be wrong, but I believe that it is our love that saved me."

A surge of warmth and understanding pulsates through her. He didn't really answer her question fully, perhaps he doesn't really know, but does he need to? She accepts his answer. And besides, he's right... right? She leans into him, her hand finding his, offering comfort and support.

"Maybe," she replies softly, "Maybe this is all something we are meant to discover together." Octavia, and her calm, cool, and reassuring demeanor, is a counterpoint to the internal turmoil, and the burning feat, that Chad grapples with. Her presence seems to offer him a sense of peace and stability. Underlying fear threatens to creep up after all that's happened, but for now she needs to be cautious and smart. She won't show any sign of weakness, not after what she just witnessed. She will keep any fear and doubts tucked away for as long as she needs to. Her love for him is pure and real, there's no denying that. But the fact is as evident as the elephant in the room. He is a demon. And all that she's ever learned about them is that they are bad, inherently evil. For now, she will tell him anything she thinks he needs to hear as she navigates the gateway into this new world.

Exhausted, they fall back into a deep sleep.

CHAPTER THIRTY THREE

"It's Maya's birthday this weekend." She stops for a few seconds. "I know we haven't really been able to talk much about it lately but we made plans to go to Vancouver for a couple days. And I'm going to take the boys camping for one last night before I go." Octavia's smile falters slightly at Chad's sudden change in demeanor. A flicker of concern passed through her eyes as she senses his underlying worry. "Chad?" she asks softly, reaching out to take his hand. She waits patiently for him to continue, her gaze filled with understanding and reassurance.

He hesitates, his grip tightening around Octavia's hand. He takes a deep breath, his eyes search her face for any sign of fear or discomfort.

"I just... I don't want you to be scared," he confesses. "After everything that happened. Is that why you're leaving?"

Octavia squeezes his hand reassuringly, her expression gentle.

"Chad, I told you," she begins, her voice soft but firm, "I'm not afraid." That's not entirely true, she's definitely shaken up by the whole experience. She needs space, room to process her own thoughts, on her own without being under Chad's influence. Besides, her boys are coming back to town and she doesn't want them around him right now. She believes that he's trying to be good, he has never done anything to hurt any of them, but she needs to figure out what's really going on before bringing her boys around this mess.

"Why do you love someone like me?" He says in an accusatory tone. "You saw what happened that night. What if that happens again and I can't control it?"

"I'm not scared, but I need some time away, the boys will be back from summer camp and I want to have one last camping trip with them before school starts up again." She rationalizes, it's the perfect excuse. "It will be a good opportunity for them to see Ali's kids because they won't get another chance until next spring. Besides, don't you think it will be nice to get a bit of a break. I mean, you don't need my help anymore, now that you're... mysteriously healed."

"Octavia, I'm not–"

"Like the other demons, I know. It's just something I need to do. And I need you to respect it, okay? It has nothing to do with us. I love you." She assures him, hardly convinced with her own words. Chad is so charming and so convincing she doesn't know what to believe. She can't think straight when she's around him, she needs to get away.

A glimmer of hope is revealed through his eyes. "Okay, so is it *just* going to be you and the boys this time?"

Octavia shoots a piercing glare into his direction. "What is that supposed to mean?"

"Oh, I don't know. You haven't talked to Ben much since the last time you went camping with your friends." He says, his perception correct. "I can't help but wonder if something had gone on between you two." There's no way she would ever drag Ben into his crosshairs. Not with what she's just learned about who he is; what he really is.

"Ben is just a friend. Please leave him out of this." She remarks.

"Oh, I touched a nerve." He throws his hands into the air apologetically. "Sorry."

"You know, I'm not stupid Octavia." He says, reaching out for her hand and sliding it into his. "I know that there's more between you and Ben. I see the way you look at each other. Nothing gets past me, so I think it would just be best if you were honest right now." He pauses. "I mean, knowing what you know now, we wouldn't want to take any unnecessary risks, would we?"

Is that a threat? Chills wriggle their way under her skin. She wanted to come clean about Ben, but couldn't and now he says he knows something. It could just be a ploy to try to get her to admit it. But she can't risk it. Not now, not knowing what Chad is and what he could potentially be capable of. And what about him and Sarah? She dare not bring that up. Maybe they can count it even and let it go for good. She pulls herself together and refuses to show any kind of weakness. She straightens up, forcing the fear out of her body. She won't be giving in to his scare tactic, if that's what he's doing. She can't be sure.

"No, Ben won't be there. It will just be me, Ali, and all the boys. I need some one on one quality time with them. I feel like I haven't gotten a lot of it this summer." The urge to prove that to him is overwhelming, she can't help but blurt out "feel free to check in on me, if you must."

Octavia heads upstairs to grab one last item from Chad's room before heading out to meet Ali.

Chad's downstairs and she finds herself drawn to the upstairs room once more. Now is her chance to grab that book. With a deep breath, she quickly enters the room before Chad ever suspects she's in there. It's as if the room holds its breath, waiting for her. She walks slowly, examining every corner, every shadow. Underneath a drape it lies. She reaches out to grab it but the book bites back with a ferocious burn, skimming the tips of her fingers. She drops it and runs out of the room.

Disappointment washes over her. Perhaps she is going crazy. Maybe it's time to let go of the mystery, to focus on the present. But a small voice inside her insists that there's way more to this story, a truth hidden just beyond the surface. She leaves the room and glances back once more. It seems to watch her, holding its secrets close.

* * *

The weekend comes around quickly. The couple days Octavia spent camping with her boys is exactly what she needed. She misses them so much when they are away. And now, the trip to Vancouver that Maya and Octavia had planned is well under way. The getaway is a perfect prelude to their impending separation: Chad, off to a rodeo adventure, and Octavia, embarking on a girls' getaway with Maya. With childcare secured, Octavia feels a wave of relief wash over her. Her mom, her rock-solid supporter, has graciously agreed to watch the kids, once again, a gesture that fills Octavia with immense gratitude. It's more than just having someone to care for her children; it's a testament to the unwavering bond they share.

Anticipation mingles with excitement, the prospect of spending quality time with Maya and her friend Mimi is intoxicating. She needs to get away, to clear her head, and to celebrate her closest friend. It's a perfect storm of gratitude, friendship, and freedom, and Octavia can't wait to embrace it fully. Octavia's heart flutters as she prepares for bed. Her house is quiet; her children are safely tucked in at her mom's. Tomorrow, the adventure with Maya and Mimi will begin.

Just as she's about to surrender to sleep, her phone buzzes, interrupting the tranquil moment. A text message. Her fingers hover over the screen, a mix of curiosity and dread coursing through her.

Mateo broke up with me. He fucking broke up me. It's Maya. Octavia can't believe what she's reading. Mateo?? What?! Her thoughts shatter in that moment. The excitement for the upcoming trip evaporates in an instant. Her mind races, trying to process the shocking revelation. Mateo, her friend's partner, has betrayed her. The betrayal is a dagger to the heart, but her loyalty to Maya is unwavering.

Are you serious?!?! WTF, what happened? When did this happen?

A barrage of questions flood her mind and her texts, each one more painful than the last. Her protective instincts kick in.

What do you need me to do, do you need me to hurt him? Cuz for you, I will!

The words pour out, a raw expression of her anger and loyalty. She's ready to be Maya's rock, her shield against the storm that's about to engulf her friend's life. Octavia's hands tremble as she waits for a response. Minutes feel like hours as she stares at her phone, her mind racing with possibilities. Did she overreact? Is Maya okay? A million questions swirl in her head. She sits straight up, staring at her phone waiting for an answer. Sleep is now the furthest thing from her mind.

I just need a cigarette.

Octavia's heart sinks as she reads Maya's terse reply. Without a second thought, she swings her legs over the bed. There's no time to waste. Her best friend is hurting, and she needs to be there for her.

Octavia's heart aches as she types out the simple, yet powerful words, *I'm on my way.*

There's no need for explanation, no need for promises. Maya knows what that means. It's a silent pact of unwavering support. Ignoring the fact that she's still in her pajamas, Octavia rushes to her car. The cool night air hits her face as she pulls out of the driveway. Her mind is a hurricane of emotions, but one thing is clear: she will do anything to comfort Maya. She gets in her car and drives to the store to buy Maya a pack of cigarettes.

Pulling up to Maya's house, her breath hitches. The familiar glow of her friend's home feels different tonight. As she steps inside, the absence of Mateo is clear. It doesn't matter. Her focus is solely on Maya. She's here, and that's all that matters. Octavia hands Maya the pack of cigarettes, they walk back outside and light one up as they take a seat on Maya's front porch. They don't smoke often, it's more of an occasional habit they've been trying to kick. There are not a lot of words spoken. They sit there silently in each other's comfort for at least an hour. Octavia asks but questions go unanswered. Maya isn't in the mood to talk, she's barely processing what's happening or why Mateo would dump her like this. It makes no sense. Her company is all she needs.

Eventually, Mateo pulls into the driveway and Octavia's blood begins to boil. Her fists clench, and she prepares to unleash her fury. Just as she's about to open her mouth, Maya's subtle gesture stops her. It's a silent plea, a silent command. Respecting her friend's wishes, Octavia takes a deep breath and forces herself to remain silent. The rage simmers within her, but for Maya, she will hold her tongue. Octavia's heart aches as she watches Maya's stoic figure. She wants nothing more than to shield her friend from the pain. Maya's silent strength is both admirable and heartbreaking.

"Did you know he was coming back?" Octavia asks.

"No."

"Do you want me to stay?" she offers, her voice soft.

Maya shakes her head, her eyes filled with a determination that both frightens and inspires Octavia. "No, it's okay. We have some things to talk about. And I'm pretty sure you aren't going to want to hear what he has to say."

Octavia nods, her throat tight. "Alright, text me right away if you need anything."

She turns to leave, her gaze lingering on Mateo, glaring for a moment before she forces herself to look away. The anger simmers beneath the surface, but she will keep it contained, for Maya.

"I told you about him and you chose to stay anyway." Mateo snarls.

"What did you just say?" Octavia asks.

"Mateo leave her alone!" Maya shouts. "Octavia, just go!"

Her mind races the whole drive home, she's shaken up. What does her being with Chad have anything to do with him and Maya? The planned weekend getaway seems like a distant dream. Yet, a part of her clings to the hope that a change of scenery might be just what Maya needs. After all, sometimes, escaping reality, even for a short while, can provide the clarity and strength to face it head-on.

* * *

The morning feels like it came much too quick. Octavia stands on Maya's doorstep, her excitement from the previous day replaced by a heavy sense of dread. The bags, packed with anticipation, now seem like unnecessary burdens. The moment Maya appears, her words are a cold shower to Octavia's enthusiasm.

"I don't want to go anymore," Maya says, her voice nearly inaudible. The words hang heavy between them, carrying the weight of a world collapsing. Octavia's heart sinks. This isn't supposed to happen. They had been planning this all week. Disappointment washes over her, but more importantly, concern for her friend's well-being takes precedence.

Octavia's voice holds a mixture of disbelief and concern. Her gaze hardens as she looks at Maya, her frustration evident.

"Are you sure about this? This could be a great distraction away from *him*." She presses, her voice low and firm. The thought of canceling the trip is a bitter pill to swallow, but Maya's well-being is her priority. She glances at the door, anticipating Mimi's arrival any moment.

Maya's voice holds a tone of finality. "I don't really want to talk about it right now." Her sadness and anger visible, a storm brews within her.

A familiar black Volkswagen Golf pulls into the driveway. Mimi lives in Vancouver and is only up for a visit. It's the perfect opportunity to grab a ride down with her and fly back.

"Mimi's here," Octavia says. Her arrival is a beacon of support in the midst of the brewing chaos. Octavia's heart pounds, unsure of what to do next. The carefully laid plans are crumbling, and the weight of the situation is heavy on her shoulders.

"Heeey, yo!" Mimi yells as she gets out of her car.

She's pretty excited to be here and to go on this trip as well. Especially since she doesn't have to drive all the way back home by herself. And she's also very much looking forward to celebrating her best friend's birthday. Mimi's cheerful greeting is a vast difference to the somber mood inside the house. Her infectious energy is momentarily dampened as she senses the underlying tension. As she steps closer, her enthusiasm wanes.

"Okay, what's going on?" she demands, her intuition picking up on the unspoken words.

"She's not ready to talk about it, but I don't think she wants to go anymore," Octavia explains, her voice filled with disappointment.

Mimi's eyebrows furrow as she looks at Maya, confusion evident in her eyes. "Talk about what?" she asks, her voice laced with concern. Nothing gets past Mimi.

Maya takes a deep breath, her voice trembling slightly. "Please don't freak out, but Mateo broke up with me." The words fill the air with thick tension.

Mimi's face contorts into a mixture of anger and disbelief. "Oh no he didn't, where is he?!" she demands, her voice rising.

"He's not here." Maya says with a sigh of relief, because she knows Mimi will let all hell break loose on him.

"He better not be." Mimi's understandably infuriated. She's always had Maya's back, ever since grad school. Even though her approach is a little more aggressive than Octavia's, Maya is and always has been appreciative of her. It's her personality that attracted her to Maya in the first place.

Octavia's heart lifts slightly at the prospect of salvaging the trip. She turns to Maya, her eyes fill with hope. "So, what are we going to do then?" she asks, her voice laced with uncertainty.

Mimi's determination is unwavering. "No, you're still coming with us, doll," she declares, her tone leaving no room for argument. She isn't about to let some guy ruin their eagerly-awaited trip.

Octavia's voice holds a gentle firmness as she speaks. "I think this will still be really good for us. We're here to support you and I think it will be a good distraction from all this and will give you some space away from Mateo." Her words are infused with genuine care and concern.

Mimi, ever the optimist, chimes in with her signature enthusiasm,

"Yeah, O is right." She gives Maya a reassuring smile. "Let's get your stuff together and be on our way." Her words are a beacon of hope in the midst of the storm.

Maya nods, her eyes fill with a mixture of sadness and determination. Maya already had her stuff packed and ready to go yesterday, before she found out about Mateo. So it isn't that much of a reach for her to get ready.

"Okay, well I guess we already had this planned, so let's just go." Maya says, feeling obligated. She grabs her suitcase and throws it into the back of the car. It feels surreal, like she's sleepwalking through a nightmare. But deep down, she knows her friends are right. This could be a much-needed escape, a chance to breathe and regroup.

"I know how hard this is for you right now, and you are so strong. We are here for you and we are going to make this weekend amazing and try to take this guy off your mind." Octavia says, empathizing with Maya.

Octavia and Mimi both give Maya a hug before they load up and begin the drive to Vancouver. With heavy hearts, the three friends pile into the car. The once-anticipated road trip now feels like a somber journey into a forced trip. However, quite possibly a distraction that Maya needs, a distraction they both need.

The drive to Vancouver is a rollercoaster of emotions. One moment they're singing at the top of their lungs, the next, delving deep into conversations about heartbreak and relationships. Laughter and tears intertwined, creating a tapestry of experiences that strengthen their bond. Eight hours can feel like a long time in a vehicle with others, but they make the most of it. Nearing the end of the drive, Octavia's head lolls to the side as sleep begins to claim her. The rhythmic hum of the car, combined with the emotional rollercoaster of the day, create a perfect storm for slumber. She glances at Maya and Mimi, their faces etched with a mix of sadness and determination. A pang of sympathy shot through her. She knows this trip is a lifeline, a chance for Maya to escape the chaos of her life and begin to heal and a chance to grieve, if she needs to. As her eyelids grow heavy, Octavia thinks about the weekend ahead. Vancouver, a city of dreams and possibilities, awaits them. Maybe, just maybe, this weekend will be the beginning of a new chapter for Maya. With a final, comforting glance at her friends, Octavia drifts off to sleep.

The car finally rolls to a stop, the city lights of Vancouver fill Octavia with a familiar warmth. Vancouver's neon lights blink a welcome as the three friends arrive at Mimi's place. She stretches, her muscles stiff from the long drive. Maybe even a little car sick. Despite the exhaustion, a sense of anticipation fills her. This city, with its promise of new experiences and endless possibilities, offers a much-needed escape. Maya and Mimi are already out of the car, their spirits seemingly lifted by the change of scenery. Octavia follows. She knows this weekend might be a challenge, but she's determined to be a constant source of support for her friend. Octavia can't shake the feeling that this trip is more than just a vacation. It's a journey of healing, friendship, and rediscovery. They unload their belongings and are ready to take on the evening.

"Where to first?" Octavia asks, still a little groggy.

"The liquor store, of course," Mimi says, a grin plastered across her face.

Armed with a shopping list of spirits and mixers, they embark on a quest to curate the perfect pre-game. This was a well-established ritual for Octavia and her friends; a blend of creativity and camaraderie as they concoct their signature drinks. Mimi's apartment becomes their temporary headquarters. They transform into their night-out versions of themselves, the apartment is filled with laughter, music, and the clinking of glasses. They experiment with flavors, sharing sips and offering critiques. The process is as much about bonding as it is preparing for the night ahead.

Octavia's face pales as she clutches her stomach.

"I am not feeling so good," she manages to say, her voice wavering.

A wave of nausea washes over her, and an unfamiliar tingling sensation spreads through her body. She's never felt like this before, the sudden onset of discomfort alarming her.

"I think my body is rejecting this alcohol." Octavia says as her discomfort grows with each sip. Octavia remembers having negative reactions to alcohol in the past. Her body is sending clear signals that something is wrong. But the desire to fit in and support Maya is a powerful counterforce. She forces down her first drink.

"What do you have there?" Octavia asks Maya. "Maybe yours will be better than whatever that was that I made." She takes a sip. "Yeah, I'm going to make one of these."

She mixes herself another drink. She forces herself to drink slowly, her mind battling between physical distress and the need for social cohesion. The tingling sensation intensifies, but she pushes through it, her determination to enjoy the night unwavering.

Maya and Mimi are both enjoying their drinks, and it finally seems as though Maya is at peace. Octavia isn't about to ruin that for her. As hard as it is to drink, Octavia tries. She sips very slowly on her second cup. That's the best she can do to keep the vibe going. Maya and Mimi, oblivious to her internal turmoil, are in high spirits. Their laughter and excitement fill the small apartment, creating a vibrant atmosphere. Octavia smiles, trying to match their energy, but the effort is draining.

They take a skytrain to the town center where they plan to hit up the night clubs. Once they make it to their stop, they hop off and walk the remaining blocks.

"You guys, I need to stop. I have bad heartburn." Octavia says, holding her cup up. "Can someone please take this, I can't drink it anymore."

Disguised in a to-go cup, Mimi takes Octavia's drink. "Happy to," she says. "Won't let this go to waste." She says with a smile on her face.

"Okay we can go." Octavia says. The heartburn intensifies as they walk, each step a painful reminder of her discomfort. Octavia's face contorts in silent agony.

Maya looks over at Octavia.

"Are you okay?" She asks, her voice laced with concern.

"I think I'm going to be sick," she mutters under her breath.

The prospect of a night out is fading fast, replaced by a desperate search for relief. Octavia never gets heartburn. She can't fathom why she's getting it now. It must have been the drink. As they walk towards the club Octavia notices a burger king. As they pass by, a glimmer of hope ignites within her. Maybe, just maybe, a simple burger could soothe her burning ache.

"Let's stop here," Octavia suggests, her hand drifting to her chest. "I think something to eat might help." She stops abruptly, her friends turning to look at her with confusion.

"Alright, let's stop Mimi." Maya says. "We could probably use a washroom break. And I'm kind of hungry, too."

"I'll be right back," Octavia says, her voice barely a whisper as she hurries to the washroom.

They are surprised to realize how late it's getting. In their excitement for the evening, they completely forgot about dinner. A pang of hunger joins the growing discomfort in Octavia's stomach. They find a seat to occupy for only a few minutes so they can have a quick bite before heading to the club.

"That feels so much better." Octavia says finishing up her burger. The warm food soothes her system, and the gentle distraction helps her to relax.

Octavia pauses, "I don't get why I would have heartburn," she muses aloud. "The only time I've ever had heartburn was when I was pregnant."

The words roll off her lips and a cold shiver circles through her. A sudden, inexplicable dread settles in the pit of her stomach. Her heart pounds in her ears.

"Could you imagine?" Says Maya.

But then, just as quickly as the thought had come, the fear dissipates.

"Nah, it can't be," she dismisses, forcing a laugh. "We took precautions. It's probably just from that strong drink I had earlier."

Relief washes over her as she takes another bite of her food, relieving her heartburn. They finish their meal in relative silence, the lingering tension from Octavia's brief moment of panic gradually fades into the background. She forces a smile as they hop from one club to the next. After all, this is a trip she's been anticipating, a celebration of her friend's birthday. She can't possibly be a party pooper, so she dances and laughs, putting on a convincing show of enthusiasm. But beneath the facade, a growing weariness creeps in. All she wants is to curl up in bed and sleep. The irony isn't lost on her; she usually loves nights out with her friends. Watching Maya, Octavia feels a wave of content. Her friend seems genuinely carefree, her laughter ringing out in the crowded clubs. It's clear that the night's distractions have offered a much-needed respite from the pain Mateo has recently inflicted upon her. Finally, before dawn approaches, they stumble back to Mimi's place, exhausted but exhilarated. They collapse onto the couches, their bodies aching but their spirits surprisingly lifted. With few words spoken they all quickly and quietly drift to sleep.

CHAPTER THIRTY FOUR

Octavia wakes with a start. A glance at her phone confirms her suspicion: it's barely dawn. With very little sleep, she gently extricates herself from her tangled blanket, and slips out of the apartment, eager for some solitude. The morning air is a balm to her weary soul. A soft, golden light paints the sky, casting shadows over the city. The gentle warmth of the sun on her skin is a comforting embrace. The symphony of birdsong fills the particularly warm air. It's a moment of pure, uncomplicated peace, a respite from the chaos of the night before.

Octavia buys a coffee and a pastry from the local bakery, the warmth of the food a comforting contrast to the gnawing uncertainty in her stomach. As she takes a bite, her mind races. The heartburn, a persistent and unwelcome guest, refuses to be ignored. It's a nagging doubt, stuck in her mind like chewed gum on the underside of a table. She knows she's being irrational. The odds are overwhelmingly in her favor. But the thought of spending the weekend partying, only to discover she's pregnant, is a risk she won't take. She heads over to the local pharmacy. With a mixture of dread and determination, she places a pregnancy test into her basket. A negative result will be a weight lifted from her shoulders, allowing her to fully enjoy the weekend with her friends. She savors the last few moments of tranquility, the morning sun casts a warm glow on her face. There's a peacefulness to the quiet that's almost addictive. She heads back to Mimi's apartment, the weight of the unopened pregnancy test grows heavier with each step. Finding Maya and Mimi still lost in dreamland, Octavia opts for the couch and her phone.

Good morning, my love. A text to Chad is a familiar comfort, an easy way to start the day. After-all she does truly love him, despite everything that's happened. And in this moment, she misses him and his warm embrace.

He's already up, the early morning rodeo schedule demanding it. *How was your night out?* He asks.

Good, we had a lot of fun.

They exchange casual morning greetings, the conversation flowing easily. No mention of the pregnancy test. For now, it's just a quiet moment between lovers, a brief respite before the day truly begins. Unable to face the uncertainty alone, Octavia postpones the test until everyone is awake. She craves companionship for whatever the test reveals. A negative result would be the best-case scenario. A positive result would be a game-changer. She can't fathom how her life would shift, but she tries to remain optimistic about the possibilities. It wouldn't necessarily be a bad thing. It would just be different, and unexpected. She'd have to make some changes, like anyone expecting a baby into their lives. She already has two children from a tumultuous relationship. Adding another baby, especially with Chad, creates a complex scenario. Her kids' reactions and the impact on her relationship with Chad are unknowns that fill her with dread.

She tries to push the worrying aside. How might this affect her relationship with Chad and how would her children feel about having another sibling? Would this complicate their lives? Octavia tries not to think about it too much because she's sure it's going to be negative. Although she and Chad have chatted about growing their family in the past, they, in no way, intend for this to happen so soon.

Maya and Mimi stir as they start waking up. Octavia waits about half hour before compelling them to take part in her pregnancy test shenanigans. She goes into the bathroom with the test and pees on the stick. Time seems to crawl as she waits for the results. After what feels like an eternity, but is really only thirty seconds, Octavia picks up the stick to take a look. It hits her like a ton of bricks. Her muscles go weak, and she falls to her knees.

Positive. The test stares back at her, mocking her. How could this be? Minutes later, she finally composes herself. Octavia, stunned by the pregnancy test result, shares the news with Maya and Mimi, who are equally shocked.

"This can't be right," she insists.

"I bought the cheapest test. I should've gotten a better brand." She's in complete denial of the results.

"Well let me check." Mimi exclaims. "I have a test somewhere, it might be expired but take it anyway and see what it says." Yep, upon looking at the date, it's expired for sure. But Octavia doesn't care, she wants some kind of reassurance that the 'cheap' test is wrong. So Octavia took the expired test.

Positive.

Octavia feels like she can no longer deny the results of the tests. After all, both tests are telling her the same thing. The same thing her body has been telling her since last night. This is so unexpected for Octavia. Overwhelmed by a whirlwind of emotions, so many feelings rush through her mind and body. Surprisingly, beneath the initial shock, a wave of joy and excitement finds its way to the surface. Octavia's distant dream is becoming a reality. They're going to be a nuclear family. It's happening now, whether anyone is willing or ready. "I need to call Chad." She tells the others. The joy surrounding her newfound pregnancy surprises her. She's so sure that he's going to be just as stoked as is. Octavia makes her way out to the deck of Mimi's apartment for some privacy. As she sits in the sun with a relaxing posture on the lawn chair, she dials his phone number. Her nerves are racked.

"Hey, babe." Octavia addresses him.

"Hey gorgeous." Chad's always been a smooth talker, it makes Octavia feel like a queen.

"I've got something to tell you." Octavia says, feeling both nervous and excited. They skip the small talk.

"What is it?" Chad asks confidently, as if it's going to be news about their night or something.

"You know how we had talked about maybe growing the family one day and having a baby together?" She asks.

"Yeah?" he says slowly, slightly confused.

"Well," Octavia hesitates. "It's happening sooner than we thought." Octavia takes a deep breath. "I'm pregnant." she says while instantaneously sending him a photo of the tests through text message.

"How could you be pregnant?" Chad questions instantly, with no break in his voice. "We will talk about this when you get home." He says in a firm and unpleasant tone.

Octavia feels mortified. What did he just say? She feels as if her heart sank right into her stomach.

"Okay," is all she could think of to say before she says goodbye and hangs up the phone.

Maybe he's just in shock, attempting to justify his heartless response. This is not the reaction she expects, based on their history and their previous conversations. But Octavia realizes, in this moment, that Chad might not feel the same way that she does. Her heart feels heavy. Unsure of what to think, Octavia walks back into the house. Maya and Mimi both look at her in suspense. Octavia silently walks over to the couch, buckles down and just begins to cry, unable to hold it in. Maya and Mimi sit down beside her. Maya gives Octavia a hug from the side.

"He sounded upset and I don't think he believes me." Octavia cries, leaning into Maya.

CHAPTER THIRTY FIVE

The weight of the world seems to rest on Maya's shoulders, her smile a fragile mask hiding the turmoil inside. She's always leaned on Octavia, her steadfast anchor in the chaos of life. But now, even Octavia is navigating her own storm. Their weekend plans, once a burst of neon lights and thumping music, have taken an unexpected turn.

"We don't have to go clubbing again tonight, O." Maya suggests with sympathy in her words. "Maybe we can just go to the movies, or just do something chill." It's an acknowledgment of the heaviness they both carried, a mutual agreement to seek comfort in each other's presence rather than the fleeting distraction of a dance floor.

"I just feel so bad," Octavia explains. "This is supposed to be a weekend dedicated to you, and I feel like I am derailing it."

"Hey, we're together." Mimi butts in. "It's not really important what we do, right Maya?"

"Yeah she's right," Maya confirms.

"Hey, have you guys ever been to an escape room?" Mimi pipes up with enthusiasm, attempting to lighten the overall mood of the room.

Escape rooms, with their promise of adrenaline-fueled fun, offer a different kind of escape, one that seems fitting for their current state of mind. They throw themselves into the puzzles, using the challenges as a temporary respite from their own struggles. But even as they work through the intricate clues and race against the clock, their thoughts often drift back to the storms they're battling. In the silence between their laughter and high-fives, the weight of their realities pressed in. Yet, in the shared experience of trying to solve the impossible, there's a quiet understanding that neither is truly alone. They don't need to speak of the burdens they bear; their companionship is enough to remind them that, no matter how tough the puzzle, they can face it together. As they stumble upon a solution, their relief is palpable, but the quiet despair in their eyes betrays the truth: this isn't just about escaping a room. It's about escaping their own thoughts, their own lives, even if only for a moment. The subsequent rooms blur together in a mix of codes, riddles, and physical challenges. Together, they're a formidable team, their minds working in sync as they piece together the puzzles. By the end of the day, they've conquered every room, their bodies worn out but their minds still churning. They celebrate their victories with forced enthusiasm that echoes hollowly in the otherwise quiet room.

The night settles in and they finally let themselves relax, the exhaustion of the day masks the deeper unease that still simmers beneath the surface. The escape rooms have done their job, providing a temporary reprieve from reality. The cool night air offers little relief to the storm brewing inside Octavia. She sits on the deck, the city lights spread out before her like a sea of distant stars, but their twinkling feels cold and indifferent. She calls Chad to talk, to check in and to pick up where they left off. Her nerves are heightened and her stomach is in a flutter. But a sliver of hope she hangs on to. This is Chad, her Chad. They will work it all out, she's sure of it. He just needs some time to process the new information.

"Hey," she says quietly, unsure of where this conversation will lead.

"Hey," he replies. No evidence of any kind of sentiment in his voice.

"Can we talk about this?" Octavia asks. "I can't get it off my mind. I can't wait until I get home. I need to know how you feel about this."

"Octavia," he begins. "I don't know how this could have even happened. Aren't you on birth control?"

"Well yeah, but we both know that's not one hundred percent guaranteed." She replies. "I thought that you might be happy about this. You're not happy at all?" She asks, her voice breaks.

"Uh, how do I say this?" Chad pauses. "I'm just going to say it."

"Say what?" She urges.

"I think we should terminate." He says without any more hesitation.

"What did you just say?" Octavia asks, unsure of what she just heard.

"I don't want to have a baby with you." He says adamantly.

The phone pressed against her ear is a lifeline she now wants to sever. Chad's voice, usually a source of comfort, has turned cold, his words laced with an undertone that feels like a punch to her gut. His suggestion hangs between them like a toxic cloud. Termination. The word echoes in her mind, each syllable striking her like a physical blow. She hoped, perhaps naively, that Chad would stand beside her, that he would embrace this unexpected turn in their lives with her, like she has done for him. But his words shattered that fragile hope, leaving her feeling exposed and alone. A lump forms in her throat, cold and hard. She suddenly feels dizzy, she can't hear anything around her. Tears threaten to spill over, but she swallows them down, refusing to let them fall. Not here, not now. The night is too quiet, too still, and she feels as if the whole world is listening, waiting to see her break.

"Chad..." Her voice cracked, barely audible, almost lost in the night.

She struggles to keep the tremor out of her tone, to hold on to some semblance of control. But she can't do this, not with him on the other end of the line, not while she's still trying to understand the depth of what he had just said.

"I need to go," she finally manages, the words tumbling out in a rush.

Without waiting for a response, she ends the call, the click of the disconnect button rings in her ears. The phone slips from her hand, landing with a soft thud on the cool wooden deck. She sits there, staring out at the city, her mind numb, her heart heavy. The future she dared to imagine has just crumbled to dust, leaving her adrift in a sea of uncertainty. The night presses in around her, the silence overwhelming, she can't move, can't think. All she can do is sit there, the phone lying forgotten beside her, as the tears she's been holding back finally spill over, tracing cold paths down her cheeks. Octavia's world, once a vivid tapestry woven with vibrant colors and endless possibilities, has become a bleak, monochrome canvas of despair. The call with Chad was the spark igniting a wildfire that's consuming her from within.

The pain is not just emotional; it's visceral, searing through her with a ferocity that leaves her breathless. She looks down at her chest, where her heart once beat with unbridled love, and feels an unbearable ache, a devastating change that has taken root deep within her. It isn't just an emotional wound; it's a physical manifestation of her anguish. Her skin, once a flawless canvas of sun-kissed perfection, is now marred by jagged fissures with her heart the starting point. These lightning-like cracks are not just figments of her imagination; they're real, stark white scars etched into her flesh. Each one represents a fragment of her broken heart, a piece of her soul that has been shattered by the cruel reality she's now forced to confront. The pain is a living, breathing entity, a relentless force that's carved its way outward, leaving her body as fractured as her spirit. With every breath, the fissures deepen, the cracks widen as the agony within her grows. It's a grotesque beauty, a twisted reminder of the love she cherishes. She runs her fingers gingerly over the jagged lines, feeling the surrealness of the scars beneath her fingertips. The sensation is a cruel reminder of her suffering, a tangible proof that the love she's fought so hard to protect is now lost.

The weight of it all is overwhelming, suffocating. The air around her feels thick and heavy, pressing down on her as she struggles to breathe through the anguish. And yet, even in the midst of her despair, there's a perverse beauty in the pain. The cracks in her skin, the physical manifestation of her broken heart, are a testament to the depth of her love, a love so profound that it's left its mark on her very being. But it's also a reminder of her vulnerability, of the fragility of her heart when faced with the harshness of reality.

As she sits there, staring at the scars that now adorn her body, she feels a deep, unrelenting sorrow wash over her. The world around her has changed irrevocably, and she's left to pick up the pieces of a life that no longer resembles the one she once knew. Her confusion deepens as she has no idea what's happening to her. It creates much anxiety in addition to the pain and sorrow. But even as she grapples with the pain, she knows that these scars, these fissures in her skin, will forever be a part of her story. A story of love, loss, and the indelible marks they leave behind. Octavia's world shatters into a million jagged fragments, each piece cutting deeper into her soul. The suggestion, so casually tossed into the night air, is a cosmic slap that reverberates through her entire being.

This is not a conversation she's ever anticipated, not in a million years. She envisioned their future painted in soft pastels and shared dreams, a growing family, a life built on love and mutual understanding. But Chad's words are like a violent hurricane, tearing through that idyllic landscape, leaving behind nothing but devastation. Anger and sadness surge through her, hot and overwhelming, mingling with a disbelief so profound it leaves her breathless. How could he, of all people, suggest such a thing? They've talked about this, haven't they? About wanting children, about building a life together that's as much theirs as it is the children's. He really is a demon. It's pure evil to do this to someone, and so damn coldly.

The weight of his suggestion bears down on her with crushing intensity, the magnitude of the decision looming like a dark cloud, heavy and suffocating. Fear gnaws at her, a deep, primal fear that threatens to consume her entirely. What does this mean for them? For their future?

The foundation she thought they were building together now seems fragile, as if it could crumble beneath the slightest pressure. The love she thought was steadfast suddenly feels uncertain, as if it's teetering on the edge of an abyss.

Tears, hot and relentless, break free, tracing burning paths down her cheeks as she pulls her shirt back over her chest. The weight of the moment is suffocating, an overwhelming tide of confusion and heartache that threaten to pull her under. She sits there for what feels like an eternity, the stillness of the night pressing in on her, broken only by the soft rustling of leaves in the breeze, and the hum of the city. Her mind is a chaotic commotion, a storm of emotions battling for dominance as she tries to make sense of it all. Suddenly Chad seems like a stranger, his suggestion a brutal wake-up call to a reality she never wanted to face. Was this the side of him that he tried to warn her about? Of all the possibilities of danger that he had spoken, this was something that had not crossed her mind at all considering he shared so much love for her. This isn't the man she had fallen in love with, the one who had spoken so tenderly of building a life together, of having children and growing old side by side. The man she has trusted with her heart has revealed a side of himself that's foreign and terrifying. A cold dread settles in the pit of her stomach as she tries to process the implications of his words.

Octavia finally composes herself, wiping her tears, and makes her way back inside.

"Hey Mimi, would you happen to have a hoodie I could wear? I didn't pack one." Octavia asks. The room seems way too quiet.

"Yeah of course, I'll grab you one." She says, her voice soft. She heads to her bedroom.

"Are you okay?" Maya asks Octavia.

"I will be. I am pretty drained though, is it okay if I just lay down?" She replies.

Seconds later Mimi comes out with a nice big hoodie that Octavia can drown herself in.

"Oh thank god that you like oversized hoodies as much as I do." Octavia says to Mimi, "Thank you."

She throws the hoodie on and lays on the couch facing away from her friends. Octavia retreats into herself, a silent fortress built around the turmoil within. She's acutely aware of the shift in their dynamic and the unspoken tension. Maya, her constant, is there, but even her presence can't penetrate the walls Octavia has erected. Her thoughts loom large in her mind, overshadowing everything else. And though she's surrounded by friends, she feels more isolated than ever before. As the night wears on, exhaustion finally claims her. Her eyelids become too heavy to fight open. As she drifts off to sleep, the image of Chad's words, cold and indifferent, haunt her dreams.

The morning rolls around much too soon. For the first few seconds of being awake Octavia feels joy. However, that's short lived when she fully awakens and remembers the scars on her chest, the manifestation of the heartbreak of Chad's betrayal. She looks around, surprised to see everyone else already awake. How late did she sleep?

"Hey, I have a great idea." Mimi says, the group slowly stirring. "Why don't we go to a smash room today. There's clearly a lot of feelings going around that could use some release."

A smash room, a place where they could channel their frustrations into physical destruction is a radical idea, but one that holds the promise of much-needed emotional purge.

"Let's do it." Maya doesn't hesitate to answer.

They enter the smash room and are greeted by a scene of organized chaos: piles of discarded glass and broken furniture await their intervention. The air is thick with the clamor of shattered objects and the charge energy of their collective anger. They look around and smile at each other.

"Yeah, I'm into it." Maya says as she picks up a bat, a sense of liberation is beginning to take root.

Octavia picks up a hammer, each swing is a cathartic release, the shattering glass and splintered wood mirroring their inner turmoil. Shouts of rage mixed with bursts of laughter, creating a jarring yet exhilarating symphony of sound. The physical act of destruction became a metaphor for their emotional upheaval, each crash a temporary escape from the weight of their problems. Amidst the wreckage, they find unexpected solace. The act of breaking things together fosters a unique camaraderie, a shared understanding of their individual struggles. The physical destruction of the room seems to echo their inner battles, and in this shared experience, the burdens they carry feel momentarily lighter.

"Well, we should go and get packed up, our plane leaves in a couple hours." Octavia says, looking at the time on her phone. "I really needed this release, thank you guys for being so great." The weekend had been a whirlwind of emotions, a roller coaster they hadn't signed up for.

Maya looks at Octavia, her eyes filled with a mixture of concern and admiration.

"I'm so glad we had this weekend together," she says softly. "We needed it."

Octavia nods, a small smile playing on her lips.

"Me too," she replies. "We've been through a lot."

They hug, the embrace is a silent acknowledgement of their shared experiences. As they pull away, they exchange a knowing look. This weekend has changed them both, and while the road ahead is uncertain, they face it with a renewed sense of strength and solidarity. Octavia's heart aches with a familiar pang. As she stands in Mimi's living room, the weight of the weekend pressing down on her, her thoughts drift to Ben. His steady presence and his unwavering support have always been a comforting anchor in her life. Now, more than ever, she craves his strength.

The sharp sting of Chad's rejection has left a gaping wound in her heart. She shares laughter, tears, and anger with Maya, finding solace in their shared experiences. But there's a depth of vulnerability she can't quite expose, a part of herself that only Ben might understand. As she chats with Maya and Mimi, the familiar ache in her chest deepens. She knows she needs to reach out to Ben. His support is always like a lifeline, a beacon of hope in the stormy sea of her emotions. Ben's absence has been a nagging thought in Octavia's mind throughout the ordeal. More accurately, throughout her entire relationship with Chad. She misses his steady support and comforting familiarity. Is it a twist of fate, then, that he's spending the same weekend at a camp just an hour away. Octavia's mind races and her heart pounds. The idea of seeing Ben, of feeling his comforting presence, is a siren song pulling at her. She shares her thoughts with Maya and Mimi, their shared misery a fertile ground for impulsive decisions.

"I could really use Ben right now," she admits, her voice trembling slightly. "He's only an hour away." Octavia sends him an impulsive text message. *Hey Ben, thinking about you. How is camp life treating you?*

Maya and Mimi exchange a knowing glance.

"If you need to see him, you should," Maya says softly. "We're here for you, no matter what, we will go with you, make a day of it and we can change our flights to tomorrow."

Octavia hesitates. The thought of burdening Ben with her problems is daunting. She knows he'll be there for her, but part of her also wants to protect him from the emotional turmoil she's experiencing. Besides, they are so far away from Chad, he won't know. Ben is her friend, she made up her mind to keep it that way. She's not going to give up a life-long friendship because of jealousy. If he can have friends that are girls, then she can have friends that are guys. Not only that, she really doesn't care right now. Ben is like home to her and after what Chad had just said, she doesn't care what he thinks.

"I don't know," she finally admits. "I also don't want to drag him into this mess."

Ben replies almost immediately. His text is short and sweet, as always, but it carries the weight of his unwavering support.

Hey! I just got back home today! How are you? Missing you! Octavia's heart skips a beat. Always loyal, always present and always welcoming. However, the realization hits Octavia like a tidal wave. Ben, her steady rock, is so close yet worlds away. The idea of reaching out to him, of seeking his comfort and support, is both tempting and terrifying. Octavia forces a smile, she won't allow her selfishness to drag him into this mess.

She replies to Ben with lighthearted banter about her day, deflecting the deeper emotions swirling within her.

It's so nice to hear from you! Been missing you, too. I didn't know you were home! I'll be back later today. For now, she needs to focus on getting home, confronting Chad, and most importantly, reuniting with her precious boys. With a heavy heart, she packs her bags and prepares for the flight.

Is everything alright? One last text from Ben pops in.

She'll respond later. The internal struggle to run to him for support, and distance him from her drama is all too real.

At the airport, Octavia watches as the car carrying her two friends disappear into the distance, a lump forming in her throat. Maya has chosen to spend an extra day with Mimi, she doesn't know when she will see her next and wants to make the most of the trip with her, so Octavia travels alone.

The airport, once a place of anticipation and excitement, now feels like a desolate expanse. The weight of the past few days, filled with both joy and turmoil, settles heavily upon her. As she checks in for her flight, her mind races. The weekend was a rollercoaster of emotions that had left her feeling raw and exposed. She's leaving Vancouver with a heart full of conflicting feelings. Maya, Ben, Chad, there's so much she is forced to navigate. As the plane ascends, Vancouver transforms into a miniature model, its vibrant colors gradually fade into shades of blue and gray. Octavia thinks about the weekend, replaying the events of the past few days, a mosaic of experiences that have reshaped her entire perspective.

The weight of Chad's betrayal lingers, a heavy cloud casting a shadow over the brighter memories. She wonders if she will ever be able to fully recover from the pain he's inflicted. A single tear traces its path down her cheek, a silent tribute to the complexities of life. As the plane soars higher, carrying her away from Vancouver and towards an uncertain future, Octavia realizes that this journey is far from over. A dark aura of anxiety gathers within her. She's newly pregnant, a secret she carries like a fragile treasure. She clutches to her carry-on, the soft fabric offering a small sense of comfort. The prospect of facing Chad, of navigating this new chapter in their relationship, fills her with a mix of dread and anticipation. She spent the weekend building a wall of resilience, but as the plane ascends, that wall begins to crumble. Vulnerability washes over her. She's a stranger in her own life, a woman teetering on the brink of a new reality. As the city of Vancouver shrinks into a distant memory, she's left alone with her thoughts, a captive audience to the storm brewing within her.

CHAPTER THIRTY SIX

I'll be there to pick you up from the airport like we originally planned. The message she read from Chad before she got onto the plane rings in her mind. She doesn't want to see him at all when she gets home. The man she thought she knew has become a stranger overnight, and the idea of facing him now fills her with dread. But she knows she has no choice. This is a confrontation that can't be avoided, a reality she has to confront head-on, no matter how much it tears her apart inside. As the plane begins its descent, her heart pounds in her chest. The city skyline, which once symbolized home and comfort, now seems ominous and overwhelming. The familiar landmarks she used to find solace in only heightens her anxiety. Chad's unexpected request to meet her at the airport has set off a storm of conflicting emotions within her. She isn't ready to see him, but she knows that avoiding him wouldn't make the situation go away. However, part of her aches to see him, to fall into his arms and convince herself that maybe, just maybe, he's changed his mind. Maybe he's realized the gravity of what he suggested, and they can find a way forward together. But another part of her, the part that's wounded so deeply by his callousness, urges her to be wary. Trusting him now feels like walking on a knife's edge, and she doesn't know if her heart can withstand another break.

Octavia looks out the window, hoping to distract herself from the rising tide of anxiety. The city below, with its endless grid of lights and pulsing energy, seems both vast and indifferent. Each light represents a life, a story, but in this moment, she feels insignificant and incredibly vulnerable, as though her own story is unraveling before her eyes. When the plane touches down, a surge of adrenaline shoots through her. The wheels hitting the tarmac feels like the tolling of a bell, marking the inevitable moment she's been dreading. With a deep breath, she forces herself to stand, gathering her belongings with hands that tremble ever so slightly. As she steps off the plane and into the terminal, the bustling crowd around her seems to fade into the background. Her focus is solely on the confrontation awaiting her. She squares her shoulders, bracing herself for what's to come, knowing that no matter how painful the encounter might be, she has to face it. She has to face him. Her stomach churns as she spots Chad waiting for her in the arrivals area. The man standing there, with his familiar face and reassuring posture, should be a source of comfort. But now, all she can see is the tension etched in his features, a subtle sign that things are far from normal between them. With each step closer, a mix of dread and resignation weighs her down, making her feet feel like lead.

"Hey," she whispers, her voice barely rising above the hum of the busy terminal.

Chad's eyes lock onto hers, scanning her face as if searching for answers or reassurance. There's a flicker of concern in his gaze as he notes the weariness in her expression.

"You look tired," he says softly, his tone tinged with a concern that feels out of place after their last conversation.

Octavia's heart clenches as confusion takes hold. The man in front of her is a paradox, exuding an attentive care that contrasts sharply with the cold indifference she felt from him just yesterday. He's dressed impeccably, every detail in place, as if he's prepared meticulously for this meeting. His hand reaches out to her, a gesture that once would have brought her comfort, accompanied by a smile that seems almost too perfect. It's disorienting, like seeing two different men occupying the same body. The Chad who suggested something so unthinkable, who had made her question everything about their future, seems like a ghost from a bad dream. But this man, this charming, thoughtful Chad, is the one she fell in love with, the one who swept her off her feet with his effortless charm and kindness.

Her mind struggles to reconcile the two versions of him. The man standing before her is the Chad she had always known, the one who made her feel safe and cherished. Yet, she can't shake the memory of his earlier coldness, the harsh reality of the words he spoke. The duality of his nature leaves her feeling unsteady, unsure of which version of him is real and which is an illusion. As she stands there, staring into the eyes of the man she loves, Octavia realizes that the path ahead is uncertain. She has no idea which Chad will emerge in the coming days, the one who previously supported her dreams, or the one who has nearly shattered them. But she knows one thing for sure, she has to find out, no matter how much it hurts. She nods, unable to muster the strength to respond verbally. The weight of the past few days, coupled with the uncertainty that clouded her future, has drained her completely. Her energy is sapped, and though she knows the conversation ahead is inevitable, the mere thought of it fills her with dread.

She can't help but reflect on the fact that Chad is as involved in this pregnancy just as much as she is. He has played a role in creating this life, and she believes, deep down, that he needs to be part of the process going forward. She's always been considerate of others' feelings, it's ingrained in who she is. Even when faced with difficult situations, she approaches them with a sense of responsibility, ensuring that she doesn't shy away from the hard conversations that life demands. So, with her heart pounding and her thoughts racing, Octavia prepares to step into the unknown, ready to confront the man she thought she knew and to seek the answers that will define their future.

"We need to talk," she begins. The words feel heavy on her tongue, each syllable laden with the weight of everything they haven't said to each other. She steals a glance at Chad, whose expression remains a mask of indifference. She knows it's a façade, a carefully constructed wall to shield himself from the storm that's undoubtedly brewing within.

"I know this isn't easy," she continues, her voice gaining a bit more strength as she speaks. "But we need to figure this out together."

The words hang heavy with unspoken implications and the tension of what lies ahead. Octavia takes a step closer, her eyes locking onto Chad's, silently urging him to engage, to show something, anything that can make her believe this is still a partnership, that they are still a team. But deep down, disbelief gnaws at her. She can't shake the feeling that Chad's initial reaction to the pregnancy was shockingly cold, almost callous. It's as if he hadn't given it any real thought, like his mind had been made up from the moment she told him. It feels as though he has a clear vision of what his future looked like, and she isn't a part of it. Octavia feels a pang of sadness as she realizes how quickly things have deteriorated between them, how the man she once saw as her partner in everything now seems like a stranger.

"Before you say anything," Chad begins. "Let's head to the truck."

When they get into his truck, Octavia is greeted with a surprise, a bouquet of flowers waiting on the passenger seat. She hesitates for a moment before picking them up, her gaze immediately drawn to a small note nestled among the blooms. The peculiar illustration of a man inside a doghouse catches her eye, and curiosity tugs at her as she unfolds the note, her heart pounding in her chest. The message is simple, yet laden with emotion:

Hi Beautiful, I know these flowers don't make what I said better. I just want to say I'm sorry. I wish it was all handled differently. I love you, and I hope you can forgive me and talk later. I missed you, and Zipper did too. I hope you come home when you're ready.

Octavia's stomach sinks as she reads the note. The gesture is unexpected. A wave of confusion washes over her once again, leaving her feeling unsteady. Is this a genuine attempt at reconciliation, a sincere expression of regret and love? Or is it just a carefully orchestrated performance, an effort to smooth things over without addressing the deeper issues that now lay between them? The conflicting emotions surge within her, anger, hurt, hope, and doubt, all vying for dominance. She wants to believe in the sincerity of the note, to take comfort in the idea that Chad is truly sorry and wants to make things right. But the memory of his earlier words, the casual cruelty of his suggestion, still linger, casting a shadow over the moment.

Lost in her own thoughts, Octavia says nothing about the flowers or the note. Chad starts the truck and pulls away from the airport, an awkward silence rests between them. Octavia stares out the window, the flowers resting in her lap. The city lights blur into streaks of color as they drive, a fitting backdrop to the turmoil in her mind. She clutches the note tightly, as if it holds the answers to the questions swirling inside her. The road ahead is uncertain, and the path to forgiveness, if it was even possible, seems fraught with obstacles.

As they pull up to her house, the silence between them is palpable. The familiar surroundings seem to amplify the tension, casting a long shadow over the evening. Octavia hesitates before getting out of the car, her mind a whirlwind of conflicting emotions. She turns to Chad, her eyes searching his face for any clue to his true intentions.

"Thank you for the flowers," she says softly, unsure what else there is to say right now. It's all so much to process.

"I mean it." Chad acknowledges, his tone serious.

Octavia doesn't know how to interact with him anymore. He wants her to come home, but only if she terminates. To wrap her mind around that feels too overwhelming. She feels like she doesn't even know who he is. The energy between them is calm, yet estranged. She glances at

Chad, his expression a mask of indifference, and a pang of sadness shoots through her. She longs for him to say something, anything that she wants to hear. But he's not going to, is he? She's convinced there is nothing she can say to change this man's mind.

"Octavia," he spouts before she gets out. Maybe this is it, maybe this is where he will tell her what she needs to hear.

Octavia doesn't say anything. She feels hurt, her eyes reflect her pain, her skin, pale. The apology from Chad, though heartfelt, doesn't erase the pain or the lingering doubt gnawing at her. His words, like the flowers, are small gestures that do little to mend the deeper rift between them. She feels torn, her heart oscillating between the anger and hurt that has been building and the small, fragile hope that maybe things could be different. Chad's face turns a shade of crimson. He opens his mouth to speak, but no words come out. The silence that follows is deafening. She turns away from him, once again feeling rejected and unimportant. Octavia isn't here to pretend that they don't have issues to work out. This pregnancy is creating a toxic environment. She feels a pang of anger. The realization that Chad is deliberately avoiding the crucial conversation about their future feels too real. It's suddenly sinking in, hitting her like a ton of bricks.

"If you can't talk to me about the pregnancy then there isn't anything left to talk about." She turns and slides out of the truck. But before she closes the door, he shouts.

"Would you just stop!"

The hairs on the back of her neck rise in an instant. What is it that he wants? He won't talk and yet doesn't want her to leave. The sudden shift from calm and passive took a quick turn to aggressive almost. She stands there in disbelief that he raised his voice at her. He's never talked to her like this before.

"Look at me! You want to talk? Fine, let's talk!" His tone is not angry, but it's not pleasant. She slowly turns to meet his gaze. She studies his face and is reminded of the Chad she once fell in love with, the Chad she can't imagine living without.

"How did this even happen?" He asks, his tone is accusatory but a little more relaxed. "We were careful, weren't we? You said you were on birth control."

"I was. Clearly it didn't work. I don't know how it happened." She says in a defensive tone.

It's almost as if he's blaming her.

"Why are you so upset anyway? You said that you'd have kids with me. Was that just a lie to keep me happy?" she asks.

No answer. But he looks at her as if she just hit the nail on the head.

"This just keeps getting better. Not only are we pregnant, but now I find out..." She pauses, her eyes narrow as the truth is confirmed about wanting to grow a family. "Was *all* of it just a big lie?"

It was all so real though. Well, to her anyway. If that's the case for him, how could he fake his way through that relationship for so long? None of it is making any sense.

"Not all of it was a lie." He says, it almost sounds like there may be a hint of sincerity in his voice. "I just don't want you to have that baby."

"But why?" She begs for an answer. "I love you! And I think you love me! We can figure this out, we can make it work! After everything we've been through together, and your *secret*... How could you?"

A mix of sadness and anger bubbles to the surface. Chad's pause stretches into an uncomfortable silence. His words, once filled with desperation, now seem to hang in the air, heavy with unspoken implications. Octavia can feel the weight of their decision hanging between them, a silent battle for their future. If he demands this termination, she can no longer see a future with him.

"I can't have kids though. It goes against who I am." Chad explains in a low toned, accusatory voice. Octavia's world seems to tilt on its axis. The revelation that Chad couldn't have children is a shock that reverberates through her being. It's a cruel twist of fate, a painful irony that mirrors the challenges they are already facing. He told her he wanted kids, and they had discussed this.

"What do you mean you *can't* have kids?" she asks, her voice firm yet laced with confusion. The question hangs heavy with disbelief. Octavia's voice echoes with a mix of hurt and anger. "What are you accusing me of? You're the love of my life. The only person I've been with!"

Her words laden with tension, a chilling difference to the fragile hope she clung to just moments ago.

"This is your child, whether you like it or not."

She slams the door, throws the flowers on the ground and stomps her way into her house, fumbling for her keys as she chokes back her tears with every bit of strength she's got left. Her mind races, she wants nothing more than for Chad to reach out and tell her that it will all be okay, that they will work through this together. That he doesn't mean what he's saying. That it's all because he's just scared. But he says nothing. The truck sits idle in the driveway. She's right, there is nothing she can say to change his mind. Once inside, she closes the door and loses every last bit of strength she had to hold it together. She hears the truck pull out of her driveway. Her knees buckle and hot tears stream down her face as she sobs. Her heart breaks once again, the pain almost unbearable. Has she just lost who she thought was the love of her life?

Can you please come be with me? Her eyes are bloodshot from the tears and she couldn't get a word out if she wanted to, but through her blurred vision and vulnerable state of mind, she manages to get a quick text out to Ben before throwing down her phone.

CHAPTER THIRTY SEVEN

Octavia leans against the cool porcelain of the bathroom sink, she splashes water on her face, desperately trying to compose herself. She doesn't want Ben to see her like this. She dries her hands, her reflection a pale ghost in the mirror. A quick peek down her shirt reveals the cracks are still present. Will they ever go away? Though barely audible, she hears the familiar rumble of a truck pulling into the driveway. One last, critical glance in the mirror, a quick tug on her hair, and she answers the door for Ben.

"Chad? What are you doing back here?" Octavia's voice is tight, a mixture of confusion and simmering anger.

He holds up a brown paper bag. "A peace offering. It's dinnertime, and I figured you haven't eaten." He gestures towards the bag. "Veggie burger. I remember you don't eat meat. And these, the roses you threw on the ground earlier."

"What do you mean, a peace offering?" Octavia accuses him, her voice trembling with a mixture of anger and disbelief. "You've already made your decision. You don't want me. You don't want this baby. You made that abundantly clear." Her heart hammers against her ribs, threatening to burst.

Chad steps back, his hands raised in a placating gesture. "Please, can I come in? There are things you need to know. Things that might...

might help you understand." Regret, genuine and raw, lace his voice. "I'm truly sorry for everything. For the pain I've caused you."

Octavia feels her head shaking, she's always had a hard time saying no to his mesmerizing green eyes. Deep down inside, she still longs for him. She wants so badly for him to tell her that they will have this baby together, that they will be a happy family.

"Then make it quick," she says, backing away from the door and sinking onto the couch. "Honestly, I don't even know what to say to you right now. So I hope this is worth it." Her gaze follows him as he carefully places the food and the flowers on the coffee table, a strange mixture of apprehension and trepidation courses through her.

"Do you want any?" He asks, pointing at the food.

"I'm not hungry right now." She replies, her voice flat. "I think we should just get to the point." She's not looking for small talk or to make up. She needs clear, honest answers as to why he's putting her through all of this. He takes a seat beside her and she inches back.

He throws his hands in the air, "okay." And takes a deep breath. "If that baby is mine..."

"What do you mean *if* it's yours? Of course it's yours." She interrupts, scowling at him.

"Right, I don't want you to have that baby." He spits out, his words tumble like an unwanted confession.

"I already know that! Can you get to the point?" Frustration bubbling over, she stands up.

"Why can't we terminate it and maybe try again in the future, when we are more prepared and know what we're getting into. Maybe when we know what we are dealing with?" His voice lacks sincerity. She watches him closely, searching his face for any sign of genuine emotion, but finds only a cold, calculating mask. His words, however, leave her reeling, more confused than ever.

"I don't know what you mean! How is it fair to trade one life for another? Terminate now and what?… Try again later? That just doesn't make any sense to me." Her anger flares. "If you want me to terminate this pregnancy, then it's over between us. So what's it going to be?"

"Octavia! You don't understand!" He roars. "What if it turns out to be like me? Then what?"

She recoils. "I think it's time for you to go." She says, her voice trembling. She's heard enough of his excuses for the rejection.

He grabs her arm, his grip surprisingly strong. "Listen to me, you can't have that baby!" He demands.

"What are you doing?" She cries, her eyes wide with fear and surprise, "let go of me!" She pulls away and he releases his grip "Get out!" She commands.

Just then, a familiar voice echoes from the doorway.

"Octavia?"

Relief washes over her, momentarily. "Ben?" she breathes, a flicker of hope igniting in her eyes. But then the relief suddenly retreats when she remembers how Chad feels about him.

"Get away from her!" Ben yells, surging forward and positioning himself in between them offering protection for Octavia. Clearly he senses immediate danger, and as always, he will do anything for her.

"This is none of your business. Back off!" Chad bellows back.

"You made it my business the moment you laid a hand on her," Ben growls, his voice a low, menacing rumble. He takes a step closer to Chad, his stance unwavering, gesturing towards the door with a chillingly calm hand.

"I believe she said that it's time for you to go." He announces, his voice steady despite the tremor running through him. She's never seen Ben like this before, a fierce protector. A newfound appreciation for his strength, his unwavering loyalty, blooms within her. She had always known he was there for her, but this… this was on a whole different level.

"You can't have that baby, Octavia, you don't know what it'll do to you. It could kill you!" Chad shouts.

"Baby?" Ben's voice is a low growl, his gaze darting back to Octavia, concern etched on his face. "What did you do to her?" He surges forward, pinning Chad against the wall with a force that sends a nervous shock through Octavia's body.

"What did I do to her? Why are you even here?" Chad spits, struggling against Ben's grip. "Get off of me!" He shoves Ben with surprising force, sending him stumbling backwards.

"Chad, we're done! I don't want to be with you anymore! It's over!" Octavia declares, her voice trembling with a mix of fear and heartbreak. "Please, just leave!" She pleads, her eyes wide with desperation.

"And leave you here with him?" Chad sneers, pushing Ben roughly aside. "How do I know it's not his baby?"

Fury explodes in Ben. He punches Chad hard in the face, the sound echoing through the room. He grabs Chad by the scruff of his shirt and shoves him out the door with brutal force. "You don't get to talk to her like that!" He growls.

"Ben! Stop it!" Octavia cries.

Chad staggers back, clutching his jaw, his eyes blazing with a dangerous, unnatural crimson. The sudden shift, the way his eyes seem to ignite, sends a jolt of fear through Ben.

"What the hell?" He mutters, his eyes widening in alarm. He instinctively takes a step back, but Chad lunges forward, grabbing him by the front of his shirt with a strength that belied his previous weakness. He hoists Ben off the ground, his crimson eyes boring into Ben's, a chilling, predatory gleam in their depths.

Octavia, witnessing this terrifying transformation, gasps and stumbles out of the doorway, fear gripping her heart.

"Chad! Leave him alone!" She screams, her voice raw with terror.

He lets out a humorless chuckle, the sound chilling in its intensity. His gaze, now a terrifying crimson, flickers back to her.

"You want me to leave your lover boy alone?"

Just when Chad isn't paying attention, Ben seizes the opportunity. He grabs Chad's shirt and headbutts him with surprising force. Octavia gasps, her hands flying to her mouth in shock. This isn't Ben. This… this isn't the man she knows. In all the years she's known him, she's never seen him act with such aggression. It's utterly out of character.

Suddenly, Chad's face contorts with a chilling fury. He raises his fist, a bone-jarring punch that connects with Ben's jaw. The world tilts violently for Ben as he stumbles backwards, losing his balance. He tumbles down the stairs, each step a jarring blow, the world exploding into a kaleidoscope of pain and disorientation.

Octavia watches in horror, her heart pounding in her chest. She never wanted any of this.

"Stop! Leave him alone!" Octavia yells, her voice raw with terror. Chad doesn't respond. He walks up to Ben, leans over, and unleashes a barrage of punches, each one connecting with sickening force. "Chad, please stop!" she cries, hot, relentless tears streaming down her face. She feels utterly helpless, trapped and paralyzed by fear.

Ben, his face a mask of pain and blood trickling from his mouth, manages to spit out a few words, his voice a hoarse whisper.

"You will never be good enough for her," Ben growls and spits blood out of his mouth.

A chilling grin, predatory and cruel, spreads across Chad's face, the crimson in his eyes intensifying. He pulls his leg back, the muscles in his leg bulging, and delivers two vicious kicks to Ben's stomach.

Chad steps back, surveying the damage with a cruel satisfaction. He takes a deep breath, gauging the distance, before exploding forward with a powerful, calculated kick that slams into Ben's face.

"Chad! Stop, you're going to kill him!" Octavia cries, scrambling towards him. She grabs his arm, her fingers digging into his skin, trying to pull him away from Ben. He ignores her, shrugging her off with brutal force. Octavia stumbles back, landing hard on the ground, having the breath knocked out of her.

Octavia scrambles to her feet, her eyes wide with horror. She notices that Chad is about to spit. She remembers the scroll, the warning. She doesn't quite know exactly what it means, she can only speculate and she's going to take it seriously.

"No!" she screams, rushing towards Ben and throwing herself over his body, shielding him from the impending attack. Chad's saliva, a viscous, acidic substance, would be far more dangerous than any punch or kick.

"Get out of here... Now!" Octavia screams. He stares at her for what feels like an eternity, his crimson eyes burning into her. "Go!" she cries, her voice cracking.

He stops, a chilling silence hanging in the air.

Then, with a disgusted sneer, he snarls, "It didn't have to be this way. This... is on you."

And with that, he slams his foot on the gas, the tires screeching as he speeds off. Octavia doesn't take her eyes off him until his truck disappears down the street.

"Ben?... Ben?" she pleads, reaching out, her hands trembling. She gently places her fingers on his face, searching for any sign of life, any reassuring movement. "Ben, talk to me!"

Her cold hands graze the side of his face, the skin clammy and cool. He's unconscious. Panic claws at her. She fumbles for her phone, her fingers clumsy with fear, and dials 911. As the sterile voice of the operator echoes in her ears, she collapses beside Ben, tears streaming down her face, the weight of betrayal and guilt crashing down upon her.

Follow Octavia's journey and find out what happens with Ben in book two of the Mystique series: ~*Mystique: A World Unknown*~ Also, enjoy this exclusive excerpt about Octavia's potential fate as her new world becomes unraveled.

"Lilah?" Octavia stammers. "wh- what are you doing here?"

"Darling, I'm here to finish what Chad had so utterly failed to do!" Lilah's voice vibrates with contained fury. "That spineless whelp actually *cared* for you! Pathetic!" Her voice drops to a dangerous quiet as she paces back and forth, her heels clicking sharp against the floor. "He forgot what you are. What you represent. He forgot his purpose. I, however, have not. That ridiculous... protection you've enjoyed... it's been a... frustrating obstacle." She stops and looks straight into Octavia's eyes. "But no more." A cruel smile spreads across Lilah's face. "I believe I've found a way around it." Her eyes gleam with malicious triumph. "A tiny flaw, a minuscule oversight... but it's just enough to finally silence that irritating little spell and unleash what Chad was too weak to deliver." She raises her hand, and a swirling vortex of obsidian energy crackles in her palm.

Octavia's breath hitches in her throat. Her eyes, wide with terror, are fixed on the swirling darkness. A cold dread grips her heart and her fingers tremble.

"Prepare yourself, Octavia. Your borrowed time has come to an end."

THANK YOU FOR READING

I truly hope you enjoyed reading *Mystique.* This is a story that I hold close to my heart and I am so happy that you took the time to read it.

If you enjoyed this story, please consider recommending it to others. It is one of the best ways to support an indie author, like myself. Please leave a review on amazon and goodreads, I am eternally grateful for all the support I receive from my readers.

ACKNOWLEDGMENTS

A huge heartfelt thank you to my sons, Bryson and Hero,
The lights of my life, my daily motivation,
The unwavering belief they have in me is surreal.
And for their patience while I spent endless hours on this project.
To my mom, Elaine,
For a lifetime of unconditional love and support.
And for always being there for me no matter what,
Any time during the day or night.
To my dearest friend, Laura,
One of my biggest cheerleaders,
The invaluable encouragement has been a source of strength
since day one.
To my editor, Kate Norman,
Who's helped me transform my book into something
So much better than what it was.
To the team at She Rises Studios,
For the guidance, support, additional editing, cover design, and
finishing touches.

ABOUT THE AUTHOR

Born and raised in British Columbia, Kaila is a dedicated single mother raising her two wonderful sons. As a family of three, they love to explore the outdoors; hiking, walking, biking, camping, spending the day at a lake, and skiing in the winter. British Columbia offers a vast array of forestry, bodies of water, and mountains, making outdoor activities easily accessible all year round. When their free time isn't spent outdoors, they like to play board games, video games, chill with a good binge-worthy T.V. show, or chat about the worlds Kaila creates in her mind that eventually end up on paper.

While she's earned certificates and diplomas in different fields, writing has always been her true passion. After gaining valuable experience working with children in a school setting, Kaila finally decided to pursue her lifelong dream of becoming an author. She's already begun working on new fantastical stories, eager to continue the captivating story she's started. Finding solace and expression in her words, Kaila has a knack for crafting engaging narratives. Not only does she love writing poems, and creating fictional worlds, she's also passionate about personal growth and sharing what she's learned with her community in hopes to inspire anyone who needs it. Her debut novel series, *Mystique,* and the several anthologies she's participating in, is a testament to her talent and dedication. Book two of the series is well under way; keep an eye out for its release set for early 2026!

Balancing her responsibilities with her writing career hasn't always been easy. Finding time to write and navigating the publishing world, while raising her family, requires dedication and perseverance. Kaila is grateful for the unwavering support and belief she receives from her family, friends, and supporters alike.

To stay up to date with her work, and sign up for exclusive offers, please visit her website by scanning the QR code below or visit <u>www.kailanike.com</u>.